LUCK

"Barfoot (. . . humorous and br . . . **DATE DUE** . . . nugly within the narrative are num . . . f, the making of art, the uses (and misuses) of beauty, w. . . . .le of chance looping through them all." —*Kirkus Reviews* (starred review)

"Brilliantly conceived, masterfully realized . . . Barfoot alternates among the three women's points of view with comic but never trivializing adroitness, and expertly spins their backstories and recent lives together. . . . The real fireworks are in the minute explorations of this closed set of unorthodox relationships. . . . Coming upon this novel is a fine piece of luck indeed." —*Publishers Weekly* (starred review)

"Sharp and surprising but always responsible, no tricks for tricks' sake; so satisfying, with its shifting and puzzles. So much fiction turns out to be diversion, in spite of fancy claims, and doesn't really look at anything. Well—this does."—Alice Munro

"Like . . . *Six Feet Under* and *Desperate Housewives, Luck* is a sustained, sardonic satire on mortality." —Amanda Craig, *The Independent*

"Barfoot has been compared to Carol Shields and *Luck*, her tenth novel, will not disappoint. From the start her comic talent is clear, while her eye for 'the miracle of life's sudden perfections' confirms her as a writer of considerable power. Luck is one of her best yet." —*Daily Mail*

"[Barfoot] beautifully captures the irreverent and banal details of coping with death and funeral-arranging, as well as the huge pain of physical absence." —*Good Housekeeping* (UK)

"Her novels read like Margaret Drabble rewritten by Patricia Highsmith and are hugely entertaining." —*The Times* (London)

Also by Joan Barfoot

Luck

JOAN BARFOOT

CARROLL & GRAF PUBLISHERS

NEW YORK

LUCK

Carroll & Graf Publishers
An Imprint of Avalon Publishing Group Inc.
245 West 17th Street
11th Floor
New York, NY 10011

AVALON
publishing group incorporated

First Carroll & Graf edition 2006

Library of Congress Cataloging-in-Publication Data is available.

ISBN-13: 978-0-78671-646-3
ISBN-10: 0-7867-1646-0

9 8 7 6 5 4 3 2 1

Printed in the United States of America
Distributed by Publishers Group West

THE FIRST DAY

One

There is good luck, and there is bad luck, and then there's the ambiguous sort of luck that's a lot of this and some of the other. For instance:

When Philip Lawrence, already recipient of a reasonably gratifying life, has the misfortune to die, he is just forty-six, which in some other part of the world or some other century would be a grand old age, but is terribly young in this place and time. On the other hand it is his good luck to die quietly in his bed, apparently in his sleep, a remarkably mild and merciful, even enviable, ending. So when Philip Lawrence drifts in the embrace of good luck and bad out of life in the course of an August night, while the air conditioning wafts its comfort indoors, while outside, grass shrivels, flowers wilt, trees droop, animals pant for moisture and air, when the moon is bright but the curtains are drawn and the big old house is mainly silent except for the sounds big old houses make to themselves in the night, there is no particular need to feel sorry for him. Surely if he has suffered at all, it can have been only briefly.

A different matter entirely for the living.

Not at all enviable or awash in good fortune is whoever wakens beside him and stretches, running the planned events of the day muzzily through the mind, reorienting slowly to the deliciously ordinary or the warmly anticipated, and finds herself on the pillow next to, on the same mattress as, the inert, the cooling, the truly departed. An unambiguously nasty moment for that person, turning to speak, turning to touch. This is no way for a day to begin; nor, really, for anything else to begin, but like it or not there is death lurking, life's great big vanishing question mark. Might as well see what's to be made of it. Buck up and face it since, one way and another, everyone must.

Today death is rolling into the lives of Nora, Sophie and Beth, and it won't be long before the entertaining question will arise: which of the three draws the cosmic short straw, who wakens amiably beside Philip Lawrence and is hurtled, unprepared, into horror and shock? What does she do? How does she tell the others—oh, many questions to spark the tongues of the villagers; those villagers, Nora has lately come to feel, who might in another country, another century, have gathered up torches to carry to the house on the hill, intending to punish, and with any luck burn.

But Nora's imagination is in morbid overdrive anyway, since she is, in fact, the one who draws the short straw. It's Nora who feels consciousness creeping back an hour or so after the dawn. Who is cooled by air conditioning, not by death. Who rolls onto her back and stretches her legs and curls her plump arms over her head, feeling the exhilarating blood warming her arteries and her veins. Who begins ticking off in her mind the anticipated events of the day ahead, and who finally turns to Philip, her husband (and wouldn't the villagers be disappointed to know it's Nora respectably beside him at this unrespectable moment?), and sees him smiling a strange, drawn, pale smile.

A rictus, as it turns out. Nora does not understand this right away. Most people don't absorb new information quite that swiftly. She thinks he is having a dream. Even a pleasant dream, considering the strange smile.

There's much to be done, though, no time to waste waiting for dreams, however pleasant, to run their generally unmemorable course; and so she says, softly but cheerfully, intending to give an optimistic bounce to the start of the day, "Philip, wake up, time to get going." Their plans are to drive to the city a couple of hours away and meet up with Max for lunch and a discussion of a show of her work within the next year or so. Max, who owns a gallery and has represented her for almost two decades, only a few days longer than she's known Philip, wants to set tentative dates. He has also mentioned he would like to see fresh directions, as she would herself, but these things take time to begin revealing themselves, and then to sink in. So: lunch at a fine and far-away restaurant with Philip and Max, an intense but also languorous conversation with two good men on various interesting subjects—what could be a happier prospect?

Not to mention that this could be one of those exciting days in which new directions come clearer.

As it will be.

"Come on, let's go, we've got lovely big plans." Philip, an exuberant man, tends to respond to exuberance, if also, less openly and appealingly, to certain kinds of mute need. Whatever his preferences, Nora can only use the devices and charms she has. It is too late to figure out new ones.

Later than she could have imagined. Philip is not merely resisting her, content in his dream. She realizes this as her hand grips his arm, intending to shake him, although gently, beginning the day as it should be begun if it is to continue as it ought to continue. His arm is curiously unmalleable. It will not be easily shaken. It implies an absence that has not been implied before.

Nora screams. She leaps up.

She immediately regrets, not the leaping—who would not leap?—but the scream. It calls attention, it calls the others, she has lost the moment that was just hers. Drawn by the highly unusual sound of Nora screaming, Beth dashes into the bedroom doorway from one direction, her thin cotton nightie awry, and from the other direction comes Sophie still in the process of struggling into her robe, one arm caught and the material flying. Sophie sleeps naked, which it would please the villagers to know, but which does not please Nora, already thoroughly distressed and in no mood for a vision of Sophie's large, bounding breasts, her fleshy hips, that clutch of invasive red pubic hair, particularly tasteless and bold in the circumstance.

Also, what if Philip weren't dead, what sort of state would this be to arrive in?

"What? What?" Beth has the slight voice of a girl, insufficient to many occasions, absurd and offensive in this one. Sophie's tone, her "What is it, what's wrong?" is also inappropriate. Too hearty, too ready to take action: to defend or to diagnose and then repair.

No defence possible. No repairs to be done. Diagnosis too late.

"He's dead," Nora says, her own voice, not quite under control, still surprised.

Well, what a mixture of voices then, a choral chaos—what is to be done? Make coffee, make tea, close the bedroom door, not in that order. Shut out the sight of Philip, dead and smiling his dreaming rictus smile, shut out his easy overnight departure, shut out the tightening of his limbs, shut out the chill.

Call his doctor. Call an ambulance. Why? Never mind, it's what's done. No one thinks to get dressed, except for Sophie pulling her peacock-bright robe properly around her large bounding breasts, her fleshy hips, her invasive red pubic hair; and so Beth is still in her cotton nightie, Nora still in her white panties and Philip's blue pyjama top, all three of them in disarray when the ambulance screams up, its mechanical wail a reproach, making Nora's already-lost scream insufficiently shocked, inadequately shocking, for the occasion.

Philip's doctor, Ted Marlowe, pulls up in his Jetta. Here comes a police car as well, although without sirens or lights.

A man and a woman in matching dark blue rush from the ambulance up the bricked walkway, and up the four steps, and across the hardwood-floored porch to the massive front door, already opened by Nora. Between them they are wielding a stretcher of black rubber, black plastic and something like chrome. "Up there," and Nora gestures to the staircase. "Second door on the right." Her thighs, revealed to the daylight, are not what they once were. Neither are Sophie's, or even Beth's, but theirs are concealed.

Ted Marlowe touches Nora's hand before proceeding upstairs. The cop follows. It seems necessary for the three women to wait silently at the bottom of the shiny wide staircase, listening to the mutters and shufflings, awkward movements above. Beth grasps the newel post of the banister in a pose perhaps suggestive of frailty. Sophie and Nora are sturdier, although otherwise different. There is a version of Philip's death that some unpleasant villagers, having speculated and ruminated, perhaps with helpful hints from the ambulance attendants, Ted Marlowe, the cop, will prefer to believe, and that being so, it will become mythic, a vibrant tale large in its lurid sins and shameless combinations, its dark secrets all the darker for being played out in the deepest hours of night.

This is the story of Philip's death those interested villagers will whisper, adding from one lip to the next various delightfully repeatable frissons: that Beth was riding him, riding him hard, while Sophie's luxuriant breasts fell onto his lips and Nora's sharp tongue roamed his flesh. And Philip exploded. Blew up all over them. To their shame, to their pleasure, to their just desserts.

There is nothing the three women can do about this, no quiet quibbles by those who know better, least of all them. The ambulance attendants, struggling down the stairs balancing the stretcher with its bagged burden, do not meet their eyes. The woman attendant says, "Excuse me," so that Nora steps out of the way, taking her closer to Sophie, but that's it. The women have nothing to say either. They're busy staring at the bulky black zippered bag riding on the black and chrome stretcher, trying to understand that inside it is, suddenly, Philip. That he is just—gone. *Heavens,* is what Beth is thinking. *Sweet Jesus, no,* are the words in Sophie's head. Nora has had an instant longer to redirect her perspectives, and so as that household emperor, that domestic paladin Philip is borne out the door, down the steps, down the walk, and is slid, not without jostling, into the back of the ambulance, and is driven slowly downhill towards disapproving or sorrowful or envying myth, Nora is thinking, *Now what?* Not unsentimentally, not at all without grief and grave shock, but nevertheless: now what?

Two

How disappointingly undramatic the actual facts of Philip Lawrence's last wakeful hours are. There was no great abandon. No one was naked or even especially active. The four of them gathered around the Philip-built coffee table in the living room, where they played two peaceable games of Scrabble. Nora and Sophie shared a bottle of wine, Beth had one of her teas, Philip a couple of after-dinner bottles of beer. Philip won one game, Sophie the other, and Nora rang up third place both times. As usual Beth had the lowest scores—she doesn't seem to know many words—but she never appears to mind losing, at Scrabble anyway. Then Nora and Philip went off to bed, an early night in advance of today's busy schedule. "Wake me up in good time," Philip said. Sadly unimpressive last words.

"I will. Goodnight." Those, too. Nora likes to sleep on her side. She turned away while he adjusted his pillow, making himself comfortable to sleep, as he generally did, on his back. Presumably Sophie and Beth headed off shortly, one this way, one that, to their own rooms, and the house fell silent, until Nora woke up and leaped up and screamed.

How untitillating. Nevertheless, "I'm scared," says Beth.

But Beth too often trades on delicacy, which over time and in close quarters creates a hardening of response. "Oh, for goodness' sake, why?" Sophie snaps, and the hostility diverts them slightly from bewilderment, from loss, from the fact of Philip being gone, not out to clear his head or his temper with a brisk march down the road, not off fishing by the riverbank for a few hours, not out for a drink "away from all you *women*," as he put it on days he was refusing to recognize the sum of his blessings, but—gone.

How can this be?

"Well, because, all that," Beth says, waving a languid arm. "Everybody out there. Everything."

"Don't be sillier than you have to be, Beth. This is no time to be stupid."

Beth has a point, though. If lurid tales amuse one faction of the local populace, there's also that opposing, dangerous, lightning-strike extremity to take into account.

Is it fair to cast those villagers, as these days Nora does, as drooling, gap-toothed, hunched, lopsided, moronic? As in *Frankenstein* (the movie, that is, the zesty, wild-haired original), with destruction on their lips, bloodlust in their hearts, torches and pitchforks in their upraised hands?

No. And yes.

This is not Frankenstein country. Nor for that matter is it an inbred backwoods, although no doubt it contains its representative share of sins of that sort. This is not even a village, but an unamazing town of merchants, retired farmers and shopkeepers, young families. It even has a few minor industries. Its public institutions include an elementary and a high school, a hospital and a very old, stone, public library. Besides stone, the town's primary building materials are brick and wood, here and there covered by more efficient and recent aluminum or vinyl siding. There are lawns and gardens and trees, and for the most part streets go directly from one edge of town to another. It is a simple matter to keep going on one of those roads all the way to the very large city a couple of hundred kilometres away for a night or a weekend, a trip to the theatre, the museum, a decent hotel. Some people do this often. Nora and Philip were planning to go there this very day.

Nor is the house itself foreboding. It's on more of a knoll than an actual hill, for one thing, and not in the isolated country but only on the outskirts of town. It has no turrets or dungeons or even secret panels to secret rooms. True, it is large, and more than a century old, and set apart from its nearest neighbours by hedges and fences and a gate and a small acreage of lawn gone more to seed and weed than when Nora and Philip moved in; but nothing about its sprawled brick two-storeyness, its gingerbreaded front porch, its farmhouse-style rectangular windows, its small cement iron-railed back stoop, and far across the backyard its unattractively utilitarian, steel-clad workshop-that-once-was-a-small-barn, suggests evil afoot.

And evil is not afoot, never has been. Ask Sophie, for one, what evil looks like, and her answer will have nothing to do with this house or even this town.

I'm scared? Beth doesn't get out enough. Or at all, really. Nora either. Only Sophie and Philip have stayed in close touch with the town, Sophie because she is paid to deal with the outside world, Philip because, maddeningly, he insisted on actually liking the place.

At least it's diverting of Sophie and Beth to have squared off in a small quarrel. It's also irritating. Their voices grate on exposed, wired nerves. "Please, both of you," Nora snaps. "Have some respect," although respect is not quite what is required. And, "This doesn't help," although she understands that it does. And, "We have to calm down, there are things to be done," although there aren't, really. Not right away. Basically Philip, and problems and tasks associated with Philip, are in others' competent, professional hands. What is left for Nora, Beth and Sophie to do right this second? Wail, mourn, grieve, rend their garments and howl?

They are not, any of them, wailing, rending, howling sorts of women. "Okay," Sophie says, turning from Beth, annoyance suddenly vanished—such an actor she is, maybe a hoaxter. "Maybe we ought to get dressed."

But if Beth removes her light cotton nightie, with what does she suitably replace it today? Sophie's garish robe is clearly inappropriate, but then what? Nora's white panties have only been worn overnight, but Philip's pale blue pyjama top—she is going about barely covered by something that belongs to a dead man! An amazing, stupendous, unbeliev-able notion: Philip is dead! Not possible.

At least get his pyjama top off.

Upstairs there are smudges on the hardwood floor of Philip and Nora's bedroom, and the sheets are tossed about. It is suddenly an unbearable room. Nora focuses on the closet, the drawers, finding something to put on, flinging her nightclothes aside. When she and Sophie and Beth arrive back in the kitchen, they find they have each, without con-sulting, gone traditional: all three in black blouses, black pants, a trio of crows. They will roast outdoors on this hot August day, though indoors they're fine. The air conditioning hums as if nothing has happened, immune as all machinery to human event, and a very good thing that is, since otherwise how could they brew up more coffee, how could Beth, who shuns coffee as poisonous in the long haul, boil the water for the elaborate preparations of another of her elaborate teas?

"This is for strength," she says, offering to share the dense, crimson results. "And compassion."

"Interesting combination," Nora says dryly. "Quite particular."

"Thanks, Beth, but no," Sophie says. "It smells good, though."

This is just habit. It's the way they have fallen into protecting Beth from each other, even though they both tend to assume, on no great evidence, that Beth herself is oblivious. They suppose her more or less immunized against irritation and insult, maybe by her teas but more likely because staring into mirrors, and staring into herself as reflected in Nora's most tempest-inducing work, must have rendered her dull-witted. Smooth and unreachable as the figure on canvas, in glass. Baffled by her own skin.

It's a good thing Beth is beautiful, and in a particular way that is useful. Otherwise, what is the point of her?

Sophie has plenty of points. Or as Philip said to Nora not long ago, "I don't know how we managed without her." Whereas of Beth he never got beyond what he said in the first place, which was, "I don't know what you see in her." Now these three women of different sizes, shapes, ages, gifts and purposes, but all dressed similarly in black, take their usual places at the kitchen table. The empty chair is large, the silence astounding. Finally Sophie sighs. "Should we get those sheets changed, Nora? We could, if you want. We could even start sorting his things while we're at it."

This is the kind of sharp gift for absorbing details and spitting them out that makes Sophie such an excellent assistant, but—how shockingly tactless and precipitous, any notion of launching into closets and drawers, going through Philip's underwear, his jewellery, his shirts, sweaters and pants, discarding some, saving the rest for keepsakes or for the poor. A brutal use of these first few hours without him. Nora frowns hard. Sometimes Sophie's history manifests itself in strange ways; like an old wallpaper pattern under paint, it shows through in certain lights.

Still, considering what Nora slept through last night between those white cotton sheets, it would be pushing whatever governs these matters, assuming anything does— maybe good luck, maybe bad—to lie between them again. She nods. "I wouldn't mind turning the mattress as well. In a while."

"Oh, please don't talk this way," Beth cries. Well, she would.

"We should try to eat, then," Sophie suggests. As she would. Sophie is tall, and also no sylph, having grown increasingly roly-poly, from a tidy size twelve to a blooming sixteen, in her four years in this house. "I thought I'd let myself go and see how far I got," she has told them. She got this far: to this table, with this full body, on this harried, startled morning. "I'll make toast."

More and more toast, slice after slice, wholewheat and heavy and lavish with butter—even Beth chews and swallows and reaches for more until soon a whole loaf has, like Philip, vanished. Crumbs lie scattered over three black laps and the pine tabletop and the blue-tiled floor at their feet, and still they are hungry. People don't stock groceries with such ravenous emergencies in mind, so when their collective desires shift to the sweet they do not have on hand the chocolate ice cream, vanilla cakes, muffins flecked with raisins, cookies stuffed with jam, also butter tarts, also cinnamon rolls, that they crave. Even Beth lusts after sugar despite considering sugar, like coffee, ruinous.

Better to eat than to think. Or to feel. Not uncommon in the event of any great shock.

Did caffeine, sugar, other bad habits cause Philip to die? That strong, big-shouldered, *physical* man, was he tipped over by one weakness too many? He didn't have many bad habits really.

Sophie shivers, and abruptly she is leaning over, throwing up on the blue-tiled kitchen floor, no time to bolt for the bathroom. Just as swiftly Beth, of all people, is on her feet, narrow hands holding back Sophie's brilliant red hair. "I've got you, it's all right, let go, it's all right, I've got you." None of this takes long. In only a couple of minutes Sophie is shaking her bent head out from under Beth's hand and sitting up straight again.

"I'm sorry. I'm okay now. I'll clean up."

Beth says, "You stay still, I'll take care of it." And she does, with paper towels and warm water. Another highly unlikely event.

"Are you so very upset, then?" Nora asks Sophie.

"Too much toast."

"I see."

This time the silence that follows is broken by Beth. "We could," she ventures, "have some kind of ceremony."

"That's called a funeral," Sophie replies, tartness already recovered—how quick she is! "If you want ceremony, it's already kind of built into the system."

"It's a nice thought, Beth, I'm sure," Nora adds. "We'll have to do something. I can't quite think what." Or where. In this horrible town, open to its horrible people, a place, nevertheless, that Philip said was lodged in his bones—what is her current duty to him and his bones?

He was born here. Then his parents, leaving behind their own histories, including their respective mothers and fathers, moved off in search of more promising and ambitious prospects, but he came back every summer for romping holidays with four doting grandparents. As he described it, he was familiar on a daily basis with the bakery that sold hand-made cream puffs. He fished with one grandfather and that grandfather's buddies and played cribbage with his paternal grandmother who was, he said, short and unathletic but "a killer at cards." His other, more sinewy grandmother threw baseballs for him to hit, and his other grandfather, a man of few words but many skills, helped him build a go-kart for himself and spice racks for his grandmothers, and watched him produce his first carving which was, Philip said, in theory a duck.

Hard to suppose those summers were so entirely idyllic, or even that there were very many of them, just a few childhood seasons, but although he grew up and away, and one by one his grandparents died, he retained an unshakeable sense of the basic kindliness of the place, of the careless affection of its residents, of the rare and splendid combination of freedom and cosseting of those summers. And so fifteen years ago he returned, a grown man with his second and more interesting wife, like a boomerang, a homing pigeon, one of those things that turn back to where they began.

He even remembered this house. "It was like a castle," he told Nora the first time they toured it. "A combination of creepy and mysterious and glamorous. I don't know who lived here then, but I remember being impressed. A little scared of it, too."

And where were his parents during those summers? "Actually, I have very little idea. I suppose they worked. And they took holidays, just not here. Here was mine. I lived for those summers." Even in recent hateful faces, he recognized familiar features and with familiarity, basic harmlessness.

When they moved here, besides being generally in a cheerfully whither-thou-goest frame of mind, Nora saw for herself the town's excellent prospects, and its charms, and believed that tucked away here she might work without distraction and with a graver concentration than was previously possible. In practical terms, she saw it as a place where, still young and starting again, they could live fairly well compared with the exorbitant city, and where they would be far from any further eruptions and fomentations from Philip's first wife. Moreover, she thought it unlikely either she or Philip could get into much trouble here.

Now look how much trouble he's got himself into.

An artist should be able to perceive what is not obvious, so it's embarrassing, really, that when they first drove here together, and saw this big red brick house for sale, and not only spent some hours examining it, inspecting it, rapping on its walls, climbing into its attics, ducking through its cavernous basement, but also strolling randomly around the streets noting the tidiness, the orderliness of homes, the care obviously expended on the many gardens, the inviting cosiness of the shops, and their variety—well, it's something of a professional shortcoming that she felt no tremors, foresaw no darker impulses.

Or: there were no darker impulses until Nora herself made it otherwise. That was more or less Philip's view.

By the time they moved here, the house, while firm in its foundations, was abandoned and ramshackle and required a

good deal of repair: their first big project together, if they
didn't count as a big project extricating Philip from his original wife. They sanded and painted, stripped wood and
cleaned it, ripped out walls and built new ones in new
arrangements, tore apart the small barn at the back and
reshaped it into a workshop for Philip, designed and added a
glassy second-storey addition to be Nora's studio. Plumbers
came and went; so did electricians, and building inspectors.

People carried casseroles and cakes to the door, and said
how glad they were to see the old house coming to life. They
advised on the subjects of fertilizers and soils and brought lists
of service clubs and activities: Rotary, bowling, churches,
needlepoint. "Shit," Philip said, "service clubs, I don't think so."

Nora, though, already feeling free and rampant and overflowing with affection, or love, or something, and new to
neighbourliness, was further warmed by this array of open
hearts. Once she and Philip were more or less settled, furniture arranged, spaces divided between them and small habits
and daily customs en route to formation, she set out to work,
in fact, on a very bright, vivid painting, narrow but long, of
open hearts on a slab. Veins were detailed, arteries large. The
hearts were lush. Given their hearts' desires, they would leap
joyfully from butcher's tray into somebody's, anybody's arms,
willing to beat ecstatically in any embrace.

She wondered, even, if the piece was sentimental, over the
top, positively gushing, but apparently not. The local butcher,
delivering beef to their freezer, took a particular dislike to it;
as if he, a man who dismembered raw flesh with his cleavers
and hands, had been rendered by her painting into a sly subject of fun.

Thus the first aggravation, the first dent; leading, not irrev-
ocably in Philip's opinion, to the inflammations and extremes

of the past year or so; the ones that completed the transformation of an unremarkable town into an outpost of Philistines, a colony of the demented, a haven for trolls and bad witches.

"Double, double, toil and trouble," Nora says now. Beth looks puzzled, but Sophie lets out one of her belly laughs.

"Fuck 'em," says Philip—said Philip—heading into the night. Besides having a presence large enough to give pause to insult, he could in depths of ale, lager, Scotch be viewed in the after-dark eyes of men as quite the lad. Sufficiently capacious for life with three women; sufficiently brave. "And you know," he told Nora, "you're exaggerating. Even if you weren't, being friendly reduces the chances of real harm being done."

Depends what you consider real harm.

And where was his loyalty?

Where is his loyalty now, leaving like this?

Now it is into that town that Philip's lucky and unlucky body has descended: in that town's ambulance, followed by a cruiser and Ted Marlowe's Jetta, to its hospital, and into the hands of its pathologist, to the ministrations of its undertaker and funeral home, to the rejoicings of its florist and to the depradations of its curious. Nora takes a deep breath, and another, and discovers these deep breaths are suppressed, withheld sobs—how long since she turned her head on the pillow and reached out and began learning that everything, everything will be different?

Not long. What does she mourn? What will she come to mourn? Because these are sometimes different things.

"So," Sophie says, her voice tight, but practical as ever, "what do you think, should we plan a service for here?"

"I don't know." Nora shakes her head sharply.

"What? You don't want to?"

"It's not that. It's just, I can't believe this is possible. That it's true."

"Oh!" Beth cries, so that Nora and Sophie turn. What exactly caused that sharp yelp of, what, grief?

Nora ought to be grateful for Sophie's offer, she *is* grateful, but she is also Philip's wife. Was. Was wife, is widow, new definitions and tenses that will become clear and automatic in time but certainly not yet, not today. It should, anyway, be Nora's role to act on funereal matters.

She and Philip fell so easily into letting Sophie take over tedious or bothersome chores.

Also having first Sophie, then Beth, move here meant Nora and Philip had less time to themselves than they used to. Then too, the time they did have, they may not have used entirely wisely. Or so it seems to Nora right now. It couldn't have felt that way at the time; *the time* being anything up to last night.

As with, probably, having children: the more people involved, the more distracted, diffuse, a household becomes.

Not one of the three women at this kitchen table is a mother. Perhaps that's why they don't automatically fall into embraces and other solacing gestures they might have known how to make if they had children. Or perhaps that's not why. For the most part everyone has learned, with greater and lesser degrees of effort, and with greater and lesser degrees of sincerity, to suit each other's purposes, fit into each other's hollower spaces, but they have not been quite this harshly tested before.

Also that was with Philip alive, when they were four. Death changes everything. Suddenly Nora is a forty-three-year-old widow. Suddenly Sophie, ten years younger, only has one employer. Suddenly Beth, four years younger still, and already surplus to requirements, is further exposed within this smaller, disrupted group.

Each is bound, too, to have different perspectives on Philip himself. Even physically Sophie met him nearly eye to eye, while Beth was chin-height, while Nora's head dipped nicely into his chest, comforting and obscuring. Also, Sophie and Beth have only known his middle age, a more limited point of view than Nora's. Sophie thinks of him with B-words like *bulky, brawny, boisterous;* plus several non-B words. Beth, coming from a world of thin female beauty, found him, more negatively, too loud and too looming. Neither of them knew the man who did odd jobs around town when he and Nora first moved here because they needed the money and he was not too proud to build a deck here, paint a porch there. "It's all work," he said, "it's all cash." They did not know the man who made the bold decision to earn his own living, minimal in the early days, then rather splendid, designing and building sofas and loveseats, chairs and mantels and buffets and tables which, being unique and individual and very expensive, put his work in demand among those who could choose to afford it. "Snob appeal," he laughed, although he was serious about the work itself.

As with Nora's paintings, his market was not in this town. Here, people evidently do not care for her work, and could not afford his.

All three women jump when the phone rings—if death waits for no man, not even a relatively young one like Philip Lawrence, neither do its demands. When Sophie, who answers, hands the receiver to Nora, she says, "It's the hospital," and for an instant every heart shifts. Could they have been wrong, might Philip, with some clever medical handiwork, have come alive? Just for a second, an eyelash of time, they each hear fast heavy feet on the stairs, they hear Philip's voice. He would head first for the coffee pot. Then he would look at them in their various poses and say, "What's up for the day, then? Not much, I guess, if you're all still hanging around." He wouldn't mean this unkindly. It would just be a remark. Among the many things already missing is the deep, anchoring tone of the male voice adding heft and timbre to the higher-pitched choir.

"Hello?" Nora asks cautiously—what if, what if?

It's a young-sounding voice, a man's, an employee, he says, of the hospital's morgue. So that's that.

"I'm sorry to trouble you," he says, and maybe he is. "But there's a question with regard to your arrangements."

"Arrangements?"

"I mean who to release the body to when the time comes. We've already determined it was too late for organ donation, but it'll probably be ready by mid-afternoon or so, unless there's something unforeseen, which I need to advise you is always possible. So do you know yet where it'll be going?"

What is he, a student, a trainee? "I see," Nora says. *It*, says this voice. Not *Philip Lawrence*, or *Mr. Lawrence*, or even *your husband*, but *it*. "Well, I'm afraid we're not quite as efficient as you people. Would you be able to hold on to him a little longer if necessary, or is there a risk of losing his place in your fridge?"

Most unpleasant; the townspeople, guilty or otherwise, do bring out the worst in her. The young man's voice drops to a matching unfriendliness. "Not at all. At your convenience. It's merely a courtesy to advise when the autopsy should be completed and the body available for release."

Autopsy. Nora puts down the phone. There will be no fast heavy feet on the stairs. Her head wants to rest its new great weight on the table. "It must have been a heart attack, don't you think?" Sophie says. "Or a stroke, I suppose. It's strange. He seemed so healthy, didn't he? Robust."

Indeed. Nora regards Sophie, contemplating the possible extent of Philip's health and robustness. "Where there is smoke," she asks, "is there fire?"

"What?"

"Never mind."

"Okay, so listen, I should start calling around. It sounds as if we need to get moving." She's right, of course, but what a bully Sophie can be. Too much time, maybe, spent striding among the desolate, picking and choosing, doling out and withholding, every life on the edge, not excluding her own. She is useful on many grounds, not least when it comes to cutting through crap, but still, Nora sometimes thinks, *Poor refugees. On top of massacres, starvation, deprivation—Sophie.*

Three

Aside from her bedroom—they each have their own bedroom—Sophie's only private space in this house is her little office, a room off the front hall that would originally have been a coat-and-hat-and-boots room for earlier, more sociable occupants and their guests. Now it contains desk, chair, phone, computer, shelves, filing cabinet.

Everything in it has a sharp connection to Phil. Among other things he refinished this old oak desk and its matching chair with the curving arms and spindles and upright back that he found at an auction. When Sophie arrived four years ago, there was space to spare when she sat in the lap of this chair. Now her hips touch each side, she damn near fills it up.

At the moment she also feels stuck to it, glued in place. "You'll find things much simpler and quieter here," Nora said when she and Phil hired Sophie. Simpler, anyway. For the most part.

It's perfectly simple to reach for the phone book and look up funeral homes. One small, manageable task at a time. A little too simple are the rules of engagement Nora has set out in such brittle fashion she might still have been talking to the man from the morgue: "No visitation. Closed casket. Day after tomorrow if that's at all possible. And cremation."

In which case, what's the point?

"Make sure the funeral home understands about visitation especially. I won't have these people staring at him."

Sophie and Nora are both divided and bound by their local disasters. Common experiences, some known, some not, make them comrades, but adversaries as well. Never mind that Sophie offered to do this, if she's going to organize funeral arrangements, Nora might have given her a say in what exactly she's organizing. "Are you sure? Cremation, that's kind of a big decision."

"No, it's what he would want. Burn whatever doesn't get used, which I gather is everything—that's what he'd say. If nothing else, he didn't like waste." That's true. He built a huge wood-and-plastic-framed composter at the very far end of the yard, and got mad if he found eggshells or coffee grounds in the trash. There he is, hollering, "Okay, who threw orange peels in the garbage?" There are his stomping footsteps, there's the back door slamming behind him as he pounds out with his handful of peelings.

Here is the silence of that voice not yelling, those footprints failing to flatten the grass.

Funny to discuss his funeral and yet be startled to remember he's dead. Not funny-funny, of course; funny-strange.

"Day after tomorrow, that might be hard." For the funeral home, Sophie meant, to make whole what was presently being dismembered. Also an unseemly hurry to have Phil disposed of. That kind of hard, too.

"Maybe. But it's what I'd prefer."

"What about people from out of town? It's awfully short notice." Not a mob of mourners, necessarily, but Phil was a gregarious person, with friends and acquaintances here and elsewhere. Here they'd be people he drank with and guys he played poker with every week or went fishing with now and again. Elsewhere he had clients, suppliers, all sorts of people attached to him professionally who grew attached personally.

"They can change their plans on the fly. Or have a memorial in their own good time, if they want."

"But won't no visitation seem odd?"

"It's a little late to worry about what's considered odd around here, don't you think? Anyway, I have no intention of standing around for people to gawk at."

"Even his friends?"

"They're not mine."

And whose fault was that, and what did it have to do with Phil?

Another funny thing: this felt as close as Sophie and Nora have come to an actual quarrel. They were more amiable with the living Phil than the dead one, it seems. But it's early hours yet. There's a lot to absorb. Phil is dead. As Nora said: how can this be?

There is only one funeral home, called Anderson and Sons, in the phone book. Having the local death monopoly must make for brisk business—what if they can't fit Phil in at short notice? Although Sophie supposes it's basically a business built on short notice. Has she met Andersons? Might an Anderson, or an Anderson son, be the proper owner of one of those bags of shit left on the doorstep not so long ago; could an Anderson tyke have been among those scrawling rude words on the fence in the dead of night?

She knows what Nora means: some known and all unknown locals are suspect. It's not a nice feeling.

The voice that answers the phone identifies itself as
Hendrik Anderson, whether father or son he doesn't say. The
name is vaguely Scandinavian, and becomes more so when
Sophie tells him what they have in mind—what Nora has in
mind. The voice takes on what she hears as a northern
European formality, not accented but cool, as if it comes
from a glacial place where sunlight is rare and barely warming. "It's . . . unusual," this Hendrik Anderson, this undertaker, funeral director, mortician, whatever the hell he's
called, says. "An unusual combination of requests."
Presumably he means it's rare and, judging from his tone,
unrespectable for mourners to desire speed and virtual
anonymity in the treatment of loved ones, followed by swift
transformation of flesh into ash.

"But you can do it?"

"Oh yes, if I get the body today there should be no problem." Perhaps he thinks it doesn't matter, since she's an
employee, not family, if he refers to Phil as *the body*. "But
sudden death at a fairly young age, you see, there may be
questions and, if so, delays." He might not intend accusation,
maybe he's simply inept. Still, he's right, who knows, the
theory will go, if one of the three witchy women in the house
on the hill is a killer? Which of them might draw the short
straw in that sort of tale?

"All I know is that the person who phoned from the hospital suggested they'd likely be finished by mid-afternoon."

"Then that's promising. I can take care of confirming that
and, of course, the transportation here from the hospital. You
probably know, though, that there's bureaucracy involved in
even the simplest death. Not," Hendrik Anderson hurries on,
"that any death is simple, I didn't mean that." This blunder
makes him more human, or less northern. It humbles him,

and warms him up. Still, you'd think undertakers would know precisely what they mean at all times before they open their mouths, their opportunities for misspeaking being as capacious as they must be. "Beyond the, uh, physical requirements, there are legal ones. Considerable paperwork, plus quite a number of other details we handle." He sounds as if details are onerous, as if details are not really blessed, life-saving occupation.

Never mind. The point he is slowly making turns out to be that even in its most pared-down, fast form, the process will cost a shocking amount. Thousands! Not that it'll be Sophie's money, but the waste—Phil would surely have been appalled. Sophie is horrified. Living bodies in the place she once struggled were not treated with the hovering luxury with which Phil's dead one will be.

Because of Phil's very high standards for what he created and built, each piece was unique, and because he didn't take commissions from just anyone, the furniture he made was highly prized. Therefore very expensive. In the economics in which Hendrik Anderson is busy educating Sophie, three of Phil's funerals might add up to one of Phil's sofas. That makes better sense.

"Then I'll leave it with you," she says, and, "I'll be in touch," he says, and when they hang up, she folds her arms on the desk and puts her head down. There's no place to run. She can't go home because this is her home, at least for now; although realistically not for long. She can't see Nora sticking around without Phil, and even if she did, why would she need or want Sophie?

Sophie has come a long way in her four years here, but whether it's far enough to avoid falling back into virtue's ghastly embrace is as suddenly uncertain as everything else.

The whole point of moving here to be Phil and Nora's resident practical person was to build fortress walls against suffering, but here comes suffering anyway.

Now what?

Oh, shit. Max. Poor old guy, waiting for Nora and Phil to show up for lunch.

When Sophie gets through to the restaurant, she is told Max arrived for his reservation, waited an hour and left. That's too bad. Maybe he tried calling. Sophie was on the line with Hendrik Anderson for, she guesses, a fairly long time. Time is odd today, not quite calculable. All stretched out, but in tiny, sharp, individual moments. She tries him at home. "Ah, Sophie," he says, annoyance in his voice but also relief. Then his voice darkens. "What's wrong, what has happened? Something has happened?"

She hasn't had to say the words before. This makes a difference, it makes her voice crack. "It's Phil. I'm sorry to give you bad news, but Phil died in the night."

She hears a sharp breath, then courtly old Max's first words are, "You're kidding."

Kidding? No, she doesn't think so. Who would kid about such a thing?

"I'm sorry, Sophie, forgive me, that was a terrible thing to say. Was it an accident? How is Nora?"

"No, not an accident. Something else, overnight, in his sleep. Nora's okay, she's just not up to talking to anyone yet. But we're really sorry about leaving you to wait in the restaurant. There's been a lot of confusion."

"He hadn't been ill?"

"Not as far as anyone knew. Including him."

"What a dreadful shock. Dreadful. Should I come, or wait to hear from Nora herself?"

"I don't know." Sophie hears her voice quiver. "I don't know what anybody should do. The service will probably be the day after tomorrow—can you come for that, do you think?"

"Of course I can. And you tell Nora that anything she needs me for, I will do."

Ah, yes. Nora the widow. "Thanks, Max, I will."

Working her way through a brief list of other people who need to be told, Sophie learns that Max is not the only one to whose lips "You're kidding" leaps. She phones one of Phil's poker pals, a drinking buddy, a couple of suppliers and most intimate customers and several of his designer friends, establishing a telephone tree in which each person will call others within these various circles, and is disconcerted by how often that's the first response. "No," she says over and over, increasingly coldly, "I'm not kidding."

Once past that they do better. They're ashamed. Like Max, they say, "That was stupid, I'm sorry," and, "Oh no, that's terrible," and, "What a shock," and, "What happened?" and, of course, "How is Nora?" It's interesting that no one says, "This must be hard on you, Sophie, having to make this kind of call. Are you all right?"

She is all right. Only tired of repeating the same words, and making clear she is not kidding even one little bit. She is a thirty-three-year-old woman with two political economics degrees and an unfortunate habit of screeching her way up out of nightmares, sometimes waking the household. She has been for four years a bookkeeper, errand-runner, clean-up person for two people who decided to afford such a person. She has kept track of their sales and commissions, their incomes and outgoings, work for any drudge with a gift for arithmetic. She has picked up upholstery and sometimes lumber for Phil, cadmium this and violet that for Nora, along with brushes and glues and needles of various purpose and size. All low-level, obedient grunt work not very open to error, and not requiring personal judgment either, since in the actual selection of paints, fabrics and threads, or of wood of particular grains, Nora and Phil made sure they chose for themselves.

Sophie has also handled most of their correspondence, generally businesslike but for a time often obscene or threatening. Plus she has picked bags of shit off the doorstep.

She sends ten per cent of her small wage to that overseas aid agency whose most successful volunteer she was not.

That's about it.

Phil is dead? The more often she's had to say those words, the more remote they've become from the fact: Phil is dead. No kidding.

Too many bodies entirely, wherever she goes.

It may have been an awful mistake, beginning the relearning of skin.

Flesh is weak; sometimes surprisingly and suddenly so.

Compared with Beth, Sophie is enormous; compared with Nora merely billowy, pillowy, zaftig. That's how Phil described her: *zaftig*, he said, burrowing his face between her bountiful breasts—*bountiful*, he called them—and kneading her belly, her thighs, with his strong long-fingered hands.

She had her nightmare—those withering arms, those sharp fingers—and woke herself up crying out. As she sometimes does, she crept downstairs from her tangled bed and, because it was a warm night, early summer, just a couple of months ago although it seems like for ever, poured a glass of red wine, that reliable sedative, and went outside to the front porch and its weatherbeaten old wicker sofa. In other skies elsewhere, millions more stars are visible than here. In the earth's revolutions, the moon looks down on a terrible, glorious array of human activity: babies, loved and unloved, being born; middle-of-the-night acts of solace or cruelty being performed; kind words and vicious ones being spoken. In some places there would be laughter. The screen door squeaked open and there was Phil, in bare feet and green terry bathrobe, carrying his own reliable sedative, a six-pack of beer. Sitting, he adjusted the robe so it covered his thighs but left his calves and feet visible. "Okay if I join you?"

"Of course. I'm sorry. I woke you up, didn't I?"

"Probably. Something did. But it's okay. It's a good night for not sleeping, don't you think?" He seemed to mean the stars, the peacefulness of three o'clock in the morning, the crickets, the night-scent of the nicotiana planted by the steps of the porch, the comfort of company.

Then after a while he said, "I've watched you for a long time, Sophie."

Had she watched him? He was not unattractive. He was energetic, and male, and a bulwark against external difficulties and threats; hard not to wonder if he'd be a bulwark against internal ones also.

But wonder only. No touch.

"I've watched you for a long time," he said, with no stalking, absolutely no obsession implied. "You're very beautiful. Full of light."

Really?

"A man could dream of burying himself in you, did you know that?" She shook her head. He turned and kissed her as if there were no question about doing so. When she'd almost stopped trembling, he picked up the tattered plaid blanket kept folded at the end of the sofa and took her hand and pulled her to her feet and led her off the porch, around the house, across the backyard, past his workshop, to the property's last outpost of yard, and spread the blanket and dropped onto it and drew her down and proceeded to surround and cover her with his larger bones and fuller flesh. He was patient and very slow. Her own full flesh kept leaping away, but he touched and touched until his skin finally began to feel indistinguishable from her own, no longer electrically separate.

This was more magical than he could have dreamed.

He took her hands two months ago and laid her down and wrapped himself around her and pushed them slowly off together on a smooth, swift, downhill run—but not so often. They had to take care. If Nora knew—well, Nora is passionate when it comes to unforgiveness and vengeance, that's clear enough from her attitude to this town. Anyway, even if nothing worse happened, if anyone found out, the private charm of the thing would be ruined. So when Phil said, "Shhh" or "Not today" or "Half an hour?," Sophie heeded.

He claimed to enjoy the geography of Sophie's now-lavish flesh. Then again, since he also mistook her for someone who gives little thought to herself, it's hard to know how clearly he saw her. She did not correct him. "It's one reason I love you," he said, and neither of them enquired why a gift for selflessness on her part would encourage love on his. Or for that matter, what form of love he intended. Their specific perspective on love anyway was for the most part horizontal.

He could say all he wanted that he'd finally abandoned himself to opportunity and long desire, but there would have been other factors, personal to just him, or to him and Nora, hard to say. Just as there were factors personal to just Sophie. Anyway, there is something to be said for knowing a good deal about reduced expectations. Phil was wary that Sophie might have what he supposed to be higher hopes. "You should know, I can't see leaving Nora. I've been through that," because indeed he had left one wife in favour of Nora, years ago when they were young. "I don't think I want to go through it again."

"That's fine," Sophie said. "Fair enough."

When Nora said, *Where there's smoke*, what did she mean? Wouldn't revelations at this point be ironic? At best, ironic?

People have died before overnight in Sophie's experience, but mostly their hands were reaching out to receive, they were ebbing, demanding, panicking hands. Phil's hands were enthusiastic and generous. In how he perfectly fitted together pieces of wood from his own designs, in the way he undid what he saw as mistakes and started again, in the way a particular wood of particular grain had to be chosen and shaped to become a particular sideboard or sofa or chair—that was exactly the minute way he understood Sophie's body. To watch him run his hands over potential upholstery, regarding texture and colour with a view to how it suited a specific design, to see him so engaged he said he could hear how one fabric would sound when it encountered another, that was the same care he took with Sophie's tentative skin. Even boisterous, he was paying attention. His hands spoke of delight that was infinite.

So she felt.

She must have been quite a challenge, a woman to whom touch was acidic, but Phil's rough, hammering, carving, nailing, precise hands were scrupulous. She supposes with Nora as well, and for all she knows, over the years maybe others. Not Beth, of course. "No, I can't imagine going to bed with her," he told Sophie, laughing. "It'd be like making love to a garden rake." Which meant, actually, that he could imagine it, just not in a pleasing way, not the way he could burrow deep into Sophie and come out gasping.

At least he did not die in Nora's arms, only in the same bed. Enough that Nora's the widow, that she possessed the bed from which he could slip away at dead of night. It would have been an awful mess if he'd died in Sophie's arms, which is the sort of thing that does sometimes happen. Of course, if he'd been with Sophie, he would not have been sleeping, he would have been active, alert to the very last second. With Sophie, he didn't sleep. The opportunity did not arise.

Imagine the sensation, the appearance, of a man tremoring overhead, growing rigid and remote, imagine feeling him, watching him, die in your hands—Sophie has never had people die in her hands in such a stupendously personal way.

Real flesh covers real people. There is such a thing as real smell, and real touch. Nora, who illustrates flesh, is a step removed from all that, and her model Beth must be at least two steps from any skin but her own. But Sophie, Sophie grew careless, or was forgetful, or hungry, and now look what's happened.

Soon Phil will be not solid or sheltering or precise but in a state to flow through her fingers, be tossed about by a breeze. People take on new forms periodically. Sophie has. Now it's his more radical turn.

There might be sympathy, if also a tinge of contempt, for a well-intentioned woman shattered by far-away sorrows as seen on TV, but there'd be none for a snake-hearted woman sneaking through hallways, skulking across the backyard, taking advantage of silent moments, now left holding a bag of huge secrets. A secret is only good if at least two people are keeping it. Poor Sophie, mourning hers, grieving for skin—but no, no sympathy for that either. It's a tough, judgmental world. She supposes the rock in her throat is what she deserves.

She straightens. This won't do. Phil's death is only one of many, many, many scattered over the earth today. That god's-eye perspective ought to be comforting: what's the loss of one man, however clever his hands, measured against the world's huge, genuine tragedies? But how offended Phil would be by the notion that the weight of his life comes up short in comparison. And he'd be right. Either every death counts, or no death does. Which religion calls despair the most terrible sin? Doesn't matter. Even at this moment, Sophie knows the difference between grief and despair. Grief is running into Phil's room this morning and learning from Nora's scream, her distraught, pointing finger, that he has died overnight. Despair is . . . something else.

And then there's mere shock. It was exceedingly harsh and abrupt to suggest sorting through Phil's closets and drawers, and Sophie's sorry about that. But then, it was an excessive moment.

She's doing the best she can, honestly.

"It's a completely different thing," Phil said, and Sophie believed him. "It's totally separate." Nora was with him for almost seventeen years which is, yes, a lot more, and different, than a couple of months. Seventeen years, fifteen of them in this house, is day after day and night after night of custom and habit, not to mention hostility, not to mention inspiration, not to mention consolation. It's many views, encounters, moods, words and tones.

But, "I love you," he said to Sophie.

Now, whatever he promised Nora, whatever he told Sophie, he has upped and left both of them, hasn't he? He has slipped away as if he were one of those unmanly men who say they're going out for a beer and never return. Widowhood can take several forms, not all of them open or righteous or kind. Nora can be one sort, Sophie another—one more thing that will have to be fine in its way, fair enough.

Four

$\mathcal{A}$ steady diet of mortality and morbidity and grief and bewilderment is not to everyone's taste, so it's a good thing, a happy break, to find that Beth is a whole different story.

Indeed, Beth is floating, Beth is lighter than air, Beth is helium-hearted as she rises upstairs, grasping the banister to hold herself down, weighting her feet to unsteady floor. She is about to make her bed and darken her room so that Nora can rest because, with Sophie off making funeral arrangements, Nora turned to Beth in the kitchen and asked, "Would you mind if I borrowed your room for a while? I'd like to lie down, but I can't face my own."

"Of course you can." Beth leaned forward and touched Nora's hand. "You can have anything. Just give me a minute to change my clothes and close the curtains. Maybe you'll be able to sleep."

"Maybe I will."

Philip is neither here nor there, really. Beth did not feel joy in his presence and does not feel grief in his absence. If she is guilty of anything regarding Philip, alive or dead, it is merely

of a relatively minor ill-will. But that scream this morning—
Beth leaped from her own bed. To the rescue! Turned out
Philip was not hurting Nora, at least not in any predictable
way, but then, he never hurt Nora in predictable ways. He
failed to protect, though. He did not scrupulously defend, his
loyalties were divided; whereas Nora warrants a gladiator, a
knight with full armour, sharp sword.

Opportunity presents itself.

Is Beth drunk? No, but something much like that.

The air in the house is light, too, like Beth, like April, not
deep-summer August. Except for a lingering tinge of crisp
toast—and whatever possessed her to eat so much bread, so
much anything?—the atmosphere is pure, rarefied, intoxicat-
ing. Oh, Beth could skip to the top of the stairs, she could
slide down the banister, she could skitter through every
room, a jolly gaunt mouse on tip-tapping toes.

It's the absence of bass voice, heavy feet and sheer bulk
that already lightens the house. Philip would have stomped
around and banged doors if he'd pictured disappearing like
this. What Beth glimpsed in his newly grey face this morning
was nothing: like clay before it's been cast into something
useful or beautiful. Or like Beth's own face some early mornings before she has prepared herself properly. A little too
naked and raw is what she means, an encompassing vacancy.
Beth could nearly feel sorry for him, but not quite. He was
Philip after all, that leech, that appendage, that anchor now
lopped from its attachment to Nora, unweighting her, leaving
her free to fly upwards, helium-hearted herself.

Not yet, of course. Patience, patience. Everyone's still in
the process of adjusting to a day no one expected, Beth does
realize that. Nora is not away having a long lunch with Philip
and Max. Sophie is not doing the laundry, or washing the

kitchen floor (which now, with all the toast crumbs, needs at least a good sweeping), or paying bills, although she is spending a lot of time on the phone. Beth is not curled up in the living room with her new, lavish gift to herself, a huge, heavy, illustrated encyclopedia of herbs and roots and certain flowers and their various combinations in compresses and teas. There's always something new to learn, no matter how long and intensively a person studies a subject; and also knowledge itself evolves and expands. It's very complex. Has anyone noticed that fevers and chills, colds and aches, don't last long in this household, and that none of the women has had cramps in the nearly two years since Beth arrived? It's ages since Beth herself has had a period at all, with or without cramps.

If she'd known, she might even have saved Philip last night, if he'd asked, if she'd cared to.

Instead, right from its start, this day went off its predictable course. No wonder that in the tension of the moment, Sophie threw up. Sophie's brilliant red hair is gloriously full of itself, every unruly strand with its own buoyant texture, good to touch, good to hold—of course Beth was happy to hold it and help. It's useful that Sophie, recovered, is organizing the funeral, since Nora seems disinclined to and Beth would not know where to begin. Everyone has their own purposes. For her part, Beth will know how to bring Nora tea, and wine, and how to stroke her hair and embrace her shoulders and draw her head into the long space of Beth's throat. Nora, with her neat dark cap of hair, her quick little plump body with its quick little plump limbs, will be glad for Beth's angles, the sharp weaponry of her bones.

Oh, Beth has some high, wild hopes today.

She has spent enough time, several hours, in black. Much is silently spoken by shape, colour and style, and obviously she's not going to change into colours of jubilation, no bright yellows or reds or even purples or greens. The gossamery, pewtery dress that dips at the neckline and floats to mid-calf will be appropriate but not entirely grim. It will be respectful but not actively mournful. Another great thing about the language of shapes, colours and styles is that it can mislead, even lie.

There are subtleties to beauty. Mysteries, too. Also worries. Beth is nearly thirty, and takes care to cream and massage her skin upwards, and not to smile or frown too hard or too often. She keeps herself thin. She concocts her strange flaky teas. She is aware—how could she not be?—that Sophie and even Nora prefer to suppose she notices little beyond her own beauty, but they ought to know better. Anyone with her knowledge of complicated combinations of teas can't be any more dense than a pharmacist or a chemist.

Still, beauty suits her. For the most part, it allows for smooth sailing.

Beth's room is the smallest of the three bedrooms. She likes it to be as spare as herself, and to that end painted it a flat startling white when she arrived. Her bed is white-painted metal. Her dresser, however, and its matching chair are tulip-yellow, and so are the frames around the mirror above it and the full-length one attached to the closet door. That's about all the furniture there's space for. There are gauzy white curtains at the window, but also dark blue drapes to draw over them. Beth likes the effect, which seems to her to contain a whole day, the white and yellow of daytime, the blue darkness of night. She hopes Nora, too, will find it restorative.

This is a special occasion. Well, obviously; but ordinarily in this house, people's rooms are their own private spaces.

Ordinarily Beth can sit at her dresser and stare into that yellow-framed mirror for as long as she wants, massaging her skin or scouting for changes. Tiny lines. Small witherings. She will look like her mother, her future is more or less prefigured in old photographs, or would be if Beth kept any old photographs here. By the time Beth was born, a latecomer to her parents' lives, her mother was no longer a beauty, but pictures showed, among many other things, a filmy child dancing around a living room; a glamorous bathing-suited teenager, one hand on slim hip, at a beach; a young woman solemnly posed for high-school graduation, blonde hair, fluffy as Beth's, framing unsmiling features that were open, or empty, at any rate inviting to any interpretation at all.

Beth has her father's slightly wonky left eye, though, with its pupil aiming marginally rightwards. The thing about beauty not everyone realizes is, it mustn't be flawless. There are other qualities involved, among them the kind of imperfections that cause people to look more closely, and more kindly as well, than they would look at perfection. That's what Beth's mother said, and it seemed mainly true.

There was the wedding album—all that white! When it comes to clothes, white would not be her mother's—or Beth's for that matter—most flattering colour; also the colour, it appeared, of regret. "I married too young," Beth's mother said. "I didn't wait to see what other opportunities might arise." She suffered as a result a vast and prevailing disappointment with not only Beth's father and his limited career maintaining and repairing big trucks, highway rigs, and his habit of shooting live things from the sky in his free time, but with the splendours that might have been her own but were not, due to being cut short, perhaps by love, perhaps something else.

"Beauty is a gift," said her mother as she drove Beth to one or another distant competition or pageant. "It would be a sin not to use it. I wasted mine, to my eternal regret, and I don't want that to happen to you." Naturally she didn't mean either *sin* or *eternal* in any theological way.

Beauty is strange. It's strange because it simply is. It's not earned or achieved, and it's not exactly an ambition, it's an outcome of genes and good fortune, and even so, it's also what you are: beautiful. Beth feels sorry for people like Sophie, who looks as if she used to at least be attractive, but has let herself go, such a waste of an amazing gift, why would anyone do that? Whereas starting with beautiful-baby contests of infancy, and right through the trophies and tiaras and sashes of adolescence, Beth was trained up in loveliness. She knows its tricks. Her father was a hunter; at least, he was a hunter two weeks a year. One of the ways Beth thinks of her body and face resembles her father's view of his duck blind: as camouflage. Soft, flying things may fall dead around her as well.

In a childhood and adolescence of stiff competition, Beth's talent, since a nod to some sort of skill was required, was singing. She took lessons, cultivating a feathery sound reflecting her feathery hair and her feathery body. Her usual speech, on the occasions she had to make one, had to do with ambitions to teach music to the world's children because music was basic to life and could even save lives. It didn't matter what she meant, which was, really, nothing at all. It wasn't her speech anyway, but her mother's.

"You need to be careful with people," Beth's mother told her. "A lot of them will be jealous you've accomplished so much." Looking into mirrors here, mirrors there, hundreds and thousands of mirrors of all shapes, sizes and purposes,

Beth was utterly familiar with the details of her own beauty. She agreed to its advantages. A person works with what she's got and what, if she's lucky, she loves. One will bend hard over complicated algorithms, logorithms, equations, solving her own mathematical passions along with those of the universe; another with a powerful affection for animals grows up to be a veterinarian, even though medical care of animals won't necessarily turn out to be an easy or straightforward expression of that affection. Beth is no different. She makes what she can of what she was born with. She has never exactly discerned *accomplishment* in that but, like her speech about taking music to the world's children, it was her mother's word, not her own.

Beauty is in the eye of the beholder? No, it's not. There are preferences, there are standards, and over the very long historic and geographic haul, those standards shift in reasonably democratic ways. In some centuries and continents the fatter the better, rolling flesh signifying prosperity, success, worldly triumph. Or the dramatically marked may be considered more beautiful than those with plain skin. Light is more lovely than dark, or vice versa. Beauty is in all these ways the face and flavour of its place and time, so what luck for Beth to be a child, girl, young woman of her place and time, blessed with long, straight, adaptable legs, slender hips, little waist and gracefully unobtrusive breasts, flexible spine, a throat that's long and white and vulnerable. Her jawbones are firm but not so squared that they imply unpleasant stubbornness, and her cheekbones flare out like winged sculptures. Her brown eyes, the regular one and the slightly wonky one, have unusually large, arresting pupils, and her hair is contrastingly blonde, fluffed as an angel's. Her skin is pale and unblemished.

These are the components of Beth's beauty, but there's something else, too, which she can't quite discern for herself but which other people must be able to see; some additional aspect, some glow or compulsion that radiates her—or has radiated her—out of the ordinary world of beautiful girls into a land of tiaras, ribbons and trophies. "The sky's the limit," her mother said. The prizes piled up, they grew to fill an entire wall-sized, glass-fronted living-room display case. Beth's shrine.

Childhood is whatever a child is presented with: love, tenderness, disinterest, adoration, abuse, that's what life is and how is a child to know any different? A child's reality is narrow and small and by and large grateful. "Where's your family now?" Nora asked, making getting-to-know-you conversation not long after Beth came here to live.

"Gone," Beth said, so severely Nora didn't ask more.

Half the point of secrets is to avoid trouble.

The other half is something else.

Now along come yet more surprises and changes. Death is grim and can have undreamed-of consequences—remember poor Nora's strained, white face!—but it has other aspects as well. Once the immediate crisis is over and the sharp event, and Philip himself, begin shifting back where they belong, into memory, there will have to be hope and fresh prospects. Beth feels quite confident—helium-hearted, twinkle-toed—about that.

Nora taps on the door. "Can I come in?" Of course she can.

Once inside, Nora begins removing her own black clothes, stripping to underwear. Beth notes the small puddle of belly-flesh, the touch of thigh-rippling. After so many hours spent attentively arranging and rendering Beth's narrow and flexible limbs, Nora must be totally familiar with the ebbs and minor flows of Beth's body, but Nora's is unknown. Beth is unconcerned with flaws—she expects anyone but herself to have something unattractive about them—but she is curious. She also wonders what, exactly, Philip meant to Nora, what range of qualities he offered that Nora will miss. She does know that what sounds angry or tired isn't always truly angry or tired, and what sounds gentle or happy isn't necessarily either. People can be sly and mysterious that way.

Nora is turning towards Beth's plain little white-painted bed. Now is the moment. Or *a* moment. Beth steps sideways, intercepts, moves to fold her long, thin arms around the new widow. Slowly, slowly, she rocks the two of them back and forth, back and forth, rhythmically, comfortingly. Oh, this is nice. In Nora's hair she detects a slight staleness; a hint of Philip left behind in the night?

Too soon, Nora pulls away. She pats Beth's hand, she crawls under Beth's sheet, she lets Beth lean down to tuck her in and kiss her forehead. Beth would stroke and stroke Nora's forehead, the way she did Sophie's hair, but Nora curls away, into herself. Her eyes close, her breathing slows, and Beth finally leaves. It's all right. Endings are not necessarily what they seem. Beginnings take time.

Back downstairs in the kitchen they keep a little green plastic portable radio on the middle one of the three small pine shelves beside the window over the sink. The bottom shelf holds a round blue pottery dish for inconvenient jewellery such as bracelets, watches—wedding rings in the case of Nora and until last night Philip—and the top one displays Nora's uselessly tiny, family-heirloom set of silvery salt-and-peppers. The radio on the middle shelf is rarely turned on except when they're cooking or washing up, but Nora's asleep, Sophie's off organizing Philip-related events, and

Beth is, for once, restless with silence, or a little too happy for peace.

Her pageant speech wasn't wrong. Music does save; or at least it reflects. Not necessarily "Yesterday" which is what's playing on the oldies station she listens to. "Yesterday" is just ironic, in the circumstances. It's followed, though, by a bouncy old Neil Diamond tune about a Kentucky woman, and Beth closes her eyes and sways slightly. She has never been to Kentucky but has met girls from there, and has a recollection of long white dresses and long white teeth and voices with soft vowels and hard tones.

She has met girls from all over the place and, except for the soft vowels, they are in memory mostly like the Kentucky ones, all long white dresses and teeth, and sharp smiles, and cool scrutiny behind warm eyes like gas fireplaces, not the real thing. In that world of women, behind-the-scenes voices were pitched high with hostility and ambition; conflicting scents of nail polishes and hairsprays and perfumes, perspiration and desire, were probably what sometimes gave Beth and her mother bad headaches. "Don't ever forget," her mother warned, "those girls are your competitors, not your friends. Don't trust anyone. But always smile, and be as pleasant and nice as you can." Not, she meant, to be an actual smiling nice person, but because "meanness shows up in the face, even if it's not right away. You can see that already in some of the girls." That was true. A sort of over-the-hill, lost-opportunity narrowness grew in some faces.

Beth's mother intended to capture opportunities just the way Beth captured titles and prizes. Beth's mother spoke of fashion house runways, of international competitions, even of movies in a gloriously approaching future. What luck for Beth to possess not only beauty but a mother who could dream up couturier runways, magazine covers, travels in Europe. "You have the features," she said, running fingers over Beth's cheeks. "These are magazine-cover bones. You have a fortune in your face, we can go anywhere, you can accomplish anything we decide on." *Accomplish?* The word jarred, began to sound like something vaguely hard and opposing.

That was a long time ago. Soon Beth will be thirty. Sometimes she can nearly feel her blood close to the thin surface of her skin, heating and bubbling. The first time she sat with Nora in this kitchen hearing Nora's visions and plans she felt that, and now she feels it again. Because there will be new visions and plans, made necessary, if contrary to his desires, by Philip.

And what were Philip's desires? Not Beth, and not death. Oh, that's funny, that rhyme, she is clever sometimes.

She has a suspicion, however, that his desires did include Sophie. She has noticed his eyes following Sophie now and then with a particular light, and recently there's been a straightening, some sharp alteration in Sophie when Philip came into a room. Sophie is efficient but she is not trustworthy. It is Beth's belief that Sophie has witnessed such atrocious brutalities that her soul is toughened against more ordinary sins.

There's some of that in herself, too.

Nora was a godsend. These sorts of miracles seem random, but also intentional. They can't really be both, can they?

At an art show opening, Beth noticed a short dark-haired woman in black trousers and a pale blue, loose blouse, staring and staring at her. Which was fine. It's more or less Beth's one great *accomplishment*, what she was trained for: being noticed. The show was a sculptor's for whom Beth had done a little modelling with results, she was interested and pleased to see, that were reasonably unidentifiable. There was a good crowd, lots of perfumes and glittering eyelids, bald heads and beards, different shades and complexions and voices. Eventually Beth felt Nora, whom she did not know then to be Nora, angling more directly towards her. "Hello, excuse me, you've maybe noticed me watching you, but—are you a model, by any chance? Or"—that quick, now-familiar, lilting uptilt of Nora's lips—"would you ever consider being one?" Beth pointed towards a looping, arced bronze the height of a man's hand. She was at the time modelling, yes, not only for this particular sculptor but for trade shows and catalogues, for minor fashion shows, for minor art schools. She offered bendability as well as beauty, her body amenable to being twisted and flexed in many shapes and directions. She could hold difficult poses. Nora nodded and smiled and Beth saw they did not need many words.

Nora said she was a painter who incorporated other materials into her work. She said she had roughly in mind a series in which, it had struck her from across the small crowded gallery, Beth might feature perfectly. Oh, and she introduced Philip. "My husband."

He was a large man who looked as if he might do large things. "Are you an artist as well?" Beth asked politely.

"No chance." It was the first time Beth heard that barrelling laugh. She had no idea what he'd found funny.

That laugh of his—it was too large in the confines of this house. It wilfully, deliberately, drowned out smaller voices.

Not any more.

The music on the radio stops, news begins. People are injuring each other in several horrible ways in several parts of the world, which is unpleasant. Beth is turning the thing off just as Sophie arrives in the kitchen looking sad and ferocious, both. "God damn it, Beth, music? Do you think that's respectful?"

Respectful of what, death? Philip? Oh, but maybe of Nora. "You're right, I'm sorry, I wasn't thinking."

Without fury the air, the power, go right out of Sophie, and she's left just looking sad. That's interesting. Even her hair looks subdued and her eyes are shadowy. Shock affects anyone close, and just how close was Sophie to Philip? She has already thrown up. Beth steps forward, places her thin fingers on Sophie's arm. "Can I get you something? Come on, come sit down." Sophie flinches, but Beth tightens her grip, pulls Sophie to her chair at the table. She pats Sophie's hair, not stroking and soothing the way she did with Nora, or when Sophie was heaving on to the floor. "I'll make tea."

It takes a few minutes, but "This is for comfort and courage," she says, placing a cup in Sophie's hands. "It's bitter, but if you drink it down fast, you'll feel better." People trust Beth on this subject at least. Sophie sips, she makes a moue of distaste, but then she does drink it right down. "Are you very sad about Philip, then?" Beth dares to ask. "Are you grieving, are you distraught?"

Those are big words. Sophie sits up straight and looks a lot more alert. Which is good. With her wits about her, Sophie can resume her duties and chores, and Beth can concentrate on being helium-hearted and hopeful. It's amazing how a person can be jolted awake by a scream, that sound of awful distress, and a few hours later be aware of so many unforeseen and quite joyous prospects. Life is full of surprises. Beth's mother used to say that, although generally on unfair, unhappy occasions, such as when Beth came in second or third runner-up.

"No," Sophie says slowly. "Just tired. A lot of people to talk to."

Beth wonders how long Nora will sleep.

Nora's an expert in things that aren't visible. Which must be why, despite Sophie's bright springing-up hair and abundance of flesh, Nora has never done a painting of her. It must be why she found Beth instead: because Beth's power is untouched and private, all under the skin, not out on the bold, uninteresting surface like Sophie's. What Nora works with are the ways light can hit skin, textures can be molded and formed, bones can be reshaped. Which shows that even though Nora may not always know what's going on right under her nose, she must be good at discerning the grave depths and mysteries lying beneath. And that must be what makes her an artist, and why she chose Beth: because she knows things about Beth; even though in particular ways, and this is a good thing, she really knows very little at all.

Five

nora was faking with Beth, she is not sleeping. Among the many, many things on her mind is, what the hell was Beth's lingering, swaying embrace about, not to mention that excessive stroking of Nora's forehead? Some misplaced and transferred passion for Philip? There was something . . . lascivious about it, unnerving, and quite soon unpleasant.

Also surprisingly bold. Beth wafts about all skin and bones in her long floaty dresses, her only discernible interest her boring curative teas, so quiet and malleable that even Nora, who has spent many hours bending her this way and that, has to agree with Sophie that Beth's still waters run more stagnant than deep. Life does not thrive in her depths, nor flourish at her shores.

So that was weird.

Of course, sexual responses to death are not uncommon. However clumsy, they are at least defiant, insistent gestures of life, and in fact Philip's arms holding Nora after her mother died led slowly, then furiously, to just about the most rampageously lusty night of their lives, a wildly free and fervent display of thrusting tongues and threshing limbs and powerful assertions of one sort or another.

But still.

Wondering about Beth's embrace is a small matter, though. What's large, what's heart-cracking, is Philip as Nora saw him smiling strangely beside her this morning at that cool point between existence and non-existence, still Philip but grown disengaged and remote; and, no middle life between the last and the first, his earliest face, young and broken wide open, grinning and full of interest, in Nora.

If she'd known that last night would be the end of his voice, anger, heat, tenderness, skin—if she'd known, what then? She would have said many more words, and different ones, she would have touched and stroked him, kept him awake rollicking and remembering right through the night. Like Scheherazade, she could have fended off bad ends with stubbornly wakeful tales and vivid, entertaining delights. People forget to do that. She did—him, too, she supposes—and then it's too late. Now, no more rages and laughter, no more words and embraces, no more Philip rearing over and around her, no more of his fleshy flesh, no more shuddering and groaning and sighs. He used to say, back when they were working to fix up this house, "Come on, take a break, let's go play in the shower." She used to say, "Want to go find a forest to fuck in?" And sometimes they would. Now—never again? Her head spins so hard she feels drunk and sick and has to open her eyes. Even if urgencies grow less urgent in time, even if for the most part they are allowed to drift off towards some vaguely imagined, energetically passionate night in the future, they're not supposed to drift right over the horizon, off the edge of the earth.

Philip's body, perfectly alive and luxurious yesterday, is being mutilated today.

Nora is absolutely sure of her instructions to Sophie: damned if those villagers, townspeople, should be able to observe him in the perfect vulnerability of his death. Philip wouldn't have minded—he might even have enjoyed the attention—but Nora minds, and that's what counts now.

That's interesting: that it's only what she wants that counts. Interesting, and unspeakably lonely.

Here's a large aspect of grief: something finished, but in unfinished form, as if they were on the phone and Philip abruptly and for no good reason hung up. Half the conversation of her life is suddenly gone. From now on there will be silence at the far end of each sentence. Nora's regretful body thrusts hard beneath Beth's sheet—now, now she would pitch herself at him. She is alarmed to hear herself whimper. There is no one but her to hear that sound either.

Is it true he died in his sleep? Or did he waken in panic and pain, trying to flail but failing, desperate to be rescued, unable to waken her beside him, sleeping as she was, as she would have thought, like the dead? He would have been furious, and vastly injured, that in the moment he most needed her, Nora left him to die on his own in the dark.

Or perhaps he just buggered off. Not so different from, say, her father whistling out of the house and into the more expansive world of, according to Nora's mother, whiskey and the arms of stray women. Can death be a similar whim? It's not impossible to see Philip, a man given to impulse, choosing on the spur of the moment just to amble into eternity. Maybe he looked at her sleeping soundly beside him, and shrugged, and took off. There was no particular evidence he might be inclined towards that, but her mother always said she foresaw nothing either.

Whatever happened, sleep must be more perilous than Nora could have dreamed, containing far more dangers than even those terrible nightmares of Sophie's that make her cry out, waking everyone. Too bad that didn't happen last night. Philip might have been saved. Instead, at some accidental point in the darkness, life turned right over. Fucking Philip, how could he?

Shock, physically electric, shoots straight through Nora's body, giving fierce, surging notice that every part of her, top to toe, is affected by this. Every part hurts. Were there signs, did he mention last night that he didn't feel well, was not as sharp as he might be? No, she'd have heard him and asked questions. Beth would have got up from the Scrabble game and made him one of her teas.

Maybe he felt perfectly fine and just fell into bed, fell asleep, then found himself tumbling much further. Maybe there was no flailing, no panic, no rage or injury. No intent either. Accident, happenstance only.

Something happens, or fails to, a moment is gained here, lost there, and the result can be anything: joy, desire, inspiration, tragedy, pleasure, loss. Her first grinning Philip was happenstance also, the endpoint of an earlier randomness which was itself an outcome of triumph.

Also, wherever she looks there's a thoroughly lodged, intricate twining between Philip and work, and what happens to that now? Work is what Nora does. What she does saves; saves her, if nobody else. She would even have said, maybe, right up till this morning, that work would be worth any sacrifice; but she would never have meant this one.

At least it isn't as if Philip's death is connected in some sacrificial way to her work.

Or—who knows? Awful second thought—maybe it is.

All she has ever meant by sacrifice is choice really, the weighing of one thing against another. It's not so hard to sacrifice—choose—if desires are clear, and what have Nora's desires been but Philip and her freedom to work, in that order or not, nothing very dramatic or drastic?

Even poverty, one choice and sacrifice, was not only relative but a circumstance of relative youth. When Nora was twenty-five she was still very poor, as well as distinctly unknown. She was living, barely, above a sandwich and variety store in a cramped apartment where she slept, ate, and experimented with attaching fabrics to canvas, bedecking painted figures with beads and embroideries. She was interested in the relationship of colours and textures, as well as figures and shapes, as well as certain ideas, but no one lives on colours and textures and shapes and ideas. She was beginning to suffer rat-gnawings of desperation, not only financial. Not everyone appreciated what she was trying to do. Her only public mention to that point was in a newspaper review that called her contributions to an artist-run show "vivid and intriguing, but ideologically idiosyncratic."

Well, thanks.

That was right about when Max and Lily arrived from France via England and opened their gallery. Coming from Europe spoke, she hopefully supposed, of either sophistication or of up-to-the-minute, on-the-edge taste. New eyes, anyway. Worth a shot. Nora walked in with a selection of slides and two of her actual works, then waited anxiously through a two-month silence that some days felt like a good sign, other days not. This was her life, didn't they know that? Or care? Should she call them? Should she walk downstairs and ask for a job in the sandwich and variety shop, preferably a night shift so she could continue to work upstairs in daylight but also continue to eat? She jumped each time the phone rang. The time was coming, not that far off, when she wouldn't be able to pay for the phone.

At last, Max called. In his flat, slightly accented voice, he said just, "Come in. Lily and I will discuss your work with you."

In those days the gallery had one very large room, one lesser one and an office. There were canvases on the floors of each space, but facing the walls, about to go up or already down. Max leaned back in his chair, hands folded over a belly that was capacious even then, and tiny, silvery Lily leaned forward in hers, hands at palms-up rest on her desk. "Welcome," she said. "Tell us about your work," Max said.

What about it, exactly? They'd had two months to see for themselves. Still, Nora made her little speech, glancing towards Max but letting her eyes rest on Lily, about definitions of art and of craft and her desire to apply both. Because, she said, "I tend to think distinctions between them are basically arbitrary. As far as I can see at the moment, a stitch is as critical as a brushstroke. So differences are more a matter of who gets to decide what is art, not what art actually is." Did that sound dogmatic? As if her real interests were merely political? "I like to make possibilities larger. I want expansion. Some kind of whole-heartedness."

"The images," Max said. "We notice they are primarily domestic. That is your interest, is it?"

"Well no, not really. Partly, but not entirely. Mainly they're what's in front of me to work with." But what would elegant, portly Max, or Lily in her tailored royal-purple silk blouse, know of tiny dark kitchens and pieces of cantaloupe like slices of sun?

"I see," Max said austerely. Then, "We do think you have promise." Deadly word, *promise*. So that was that.

Till Lily smiled, and turned her hands over, flat down on the desk, a silent gesture with the effect of a gavel. "And so we would like an invitation to your studio to make selections

and discuss dates for your first show with us. Perhaps not one
all on your own at this point but, as Max says, your work has
good promise"—not exactly what he'd said, but perhaps what
he'd meant, surely his own wife could interpret him accurately—"and we would like to see you well launched and
properly nurtured." Nora felt herself flush, then nearly
launched herself across their desks to embrace them; Lily, at
least. Max was still scary. A show, even if not one all her own,
and talk of nurture implying a long term, and safety—no
wonder she practically danced off down the street.

And no wonder she wished she'd told someone about
being summoned by Lily and Max. She hadn't, for fear of creating an occasion for mournful, intolerable pity, but now she
had an occasion for celebration and no one at hand. She spun
happily into a coffee shop a few doors from the gallery,
clutching her news to herself—and whose familiar face was
that at a window table, glancing up?

"Lynn?"

"Nora?"

Lynn, yes. Long-lost and, to be honest, mainly forgotten
high-school acquaintance. Still, how cheerful, running into
anyone known. "Want to join me?" asked Lynn. "I'm just taking a break between classes."

She was still in university, nearly finished a graduate
degree in French literature. From high school Nora remembered a skinny girl with the slumpy sort of shoulders that
went with being embarrassed by height. She played basketball. What else? Didn't matter. Now she was slender rather
than skinny, willowy rather than slumped. She'd been married for almost two years, and she and her husband had
recently acquired a downtown rowhouse. "Oh my God, the
mortgage, we're petrified. But I'll be teaching soon, and I'll do

that at least till we have kids, so we figure we'll be okay." She asked what Nora was doing. "That's great," she said, sadly failing, in Nora's view, to grasp the splendour of Nora's news.

Still, a sense of occasion and a benign sort of nostalgia caused them to make an appointment for lunch. Nora would meet Lynn at her recently acquired home. "You can meet Philip," Lynn said, "before we go out."

Happenstance, accident, random cause and effect.

Three days later Nora pressed the doorbell of a tiny white-stuccoed house attached in each direction up and down the block to other tiny white-stuccoed houses, and found herself facing a lean, grinning, nude man.

It is not necessarily the case that a man will be at his best undraped; some camouflage of chubby portion or dangly bit may be wise, at least for first impressions, but not with Philip. He stood in the doorway fully formed, golden and lithe. Nora stepped back briefly; then, irritated at being so transparently startled, stepped forward again. She did not fall into the trap, either, of looking only into his grey-tinged blue eyes, but allowed her gaze to roam, coolly taking in the square-planted feet, the calves and thighs curling with a moderate crop of dark hair—nothing actually furry or unfortunately bear-like, she noted—long arms, a hand still braced on the door, chest and stomach muscularly but not aggressively outlined, and of course his penis, pinky-purple and wavering, evidently undecided about whether to remain at rest or to rise to an occasion it could, it seemed, already sense.

"I'm here for Lynn," she said.

"You must be Nora. I'm Philip."

Lynn's husband. Not for long.

Lynn, walking fast, click-click on little heels into the front hall, was fully dressed in forest-green linen trousers, matching blouse, golden bracelets. "Philip!" she cried. "Good God," and turning to Nora she said, "Honestly, I just never know what he's going to do next," and there was a pride in her tone, a self-satisfaction that rendered Nora unsympathetic.

Nora and Lynn went off for their lunch; nothing monumentally life-altering happened as immediately as that. But something did happen and obviously they then failed to pursue their old loose, unnecessary acquaintanceship. They were all young. Domestic shufflings, while awkward, weren't necessarily excruciating. Everyone involved still had plenty of future, no need to resent whole wasted decades. Naturally a certain array of emotions required display, there was the usual script to follow of injuries suffered, delight achieved. Lynn's role, for instance, was to be bitter. "Betrayed," she cried dramatically, and repeatedly, to many, many people, "by my husband *and* my friend." As if Nora had been her only friend, as Philip was her only husband. As if Nora had really been her friend at all.

Philip said it was Nora's assessing regard on the doorstep that first intrigued and appealed to him. "No flinching or blushing." Later he was drawn by "your brightness, and that drive and desire you have. Also your tits." As for answering the door naked, he said, "Well, you know what we'd been doing. Probably because I was trying to make Lynn run late. Or wanted her to stay home—one of those power-plays you won't fall for. And maybe to embarrass her. And to test her old pal. And then there's the fact I can just be kind of a pig." His smile was winsome, designed to contradict his own words; or, if Nora failed to grasp that much, intended to humbly seek praise for his frankness.

The mark, one of the marks, of the stray: the conscious adorability, the obsequious, vulnerable, soft-belly exposure.

Beth was a stray; Sophie too, in her way. Was Philip as well? Surely not.

He was large and beautiful and bold. Nora was small and optimistic and brutal. He said that when he married Lynn almost two years before he opened that door, "It didn't quite feel right, but I didn't know why. Now I do.' And what can, or should, stand in the face of right feeling? Certainly not wrong feeling. So, goodbye Philip-and-Lynn.

Now, goodbye Philip.

Quite the abandoner he has been.

Is this swift transformation to rage normal when somebody dies? Because Nora is suddenly furious.

It has been her conviction that once over her own admittedly fierce hump of rage and betrayal, Lynn's life went just fine. She remarried, an evidently compatible and clever man who does something financial. He has been more agreeable than Philip on the subject of children—it was contentious, Philip said, that he was firmly opposed while Lynn was so keen she spoke of babies as if they were already formed up inside her, hammering to get out. The sort of thing, it seemed to Nora, that should be discussed before marrying, although hardly her place to say so. Now Lynn has two triumphantly out-of-the-womb, into-the-world children who must be getting into their teens. She also not only has several degrees but teaches something or other to do with languages at university.

Sensibly, Nora asked Philip before they married, "Do you think it's mutant that I seriously do not care to have kids? Can you foresee changing your mind? Because I can't see changing mine."

"No," he said, "and no. Thank God," and got himself a vasectomy. In so many matters, large and small, they were— well, *soulmates* would be excessive, and Nora opposes excess in most of its forms, but at least they were in general and on large issues highly compatible.

That particular choice was an easy one, although not everyone believes that. Why would they want children? They cared for what they each did, and for each other. Other people might rattle on about what a unique form of love children inspire, no doubt true, but there are other unique forms of love, and other constellations for purposeful lives. It was also noticeable that in the lives of others, children were rarely unmixed blessings. They were a good deal more than love, they were often enough heartbreak and wrong turns and decades of fretfulness, not only triumph. "We live as we choose," Philip used to tell people, which could sound selfish but as he also said, "What's wrong with that?" He meant they were smart enough to live according to their own natures, mutant or not.

"So we're selfish *and* smug," they could, and did, laugh.

Lynn was so young when Philip vanished on her, she had no end of fresh chances for her quite different desires. Nora's hard heart was right; but now here's a thought: is it proper to advise a first wife of her secondhand, out-of-date semi-widowhood?

Imagine, she and Lynn might discover sisterhood over Philip's dead body. Reminisce. Contrast and compare. Lynn might also have tips on how to move on after Philip; because at the moment, Nora can't make out a future. Life goes on? Yes, she supposes it has to, but how?

She puts a hand on her chest. Of course her heart is still thumping away in there all to itself. Selfish things, hearts. Focused entirely on their own survival.

What if Max and Lily hadn't given Nora reason to celebrate? What if Nora hadn't run into Lynn in that coffee shop, what if, in the mild spirit of mutual benevolence, they hadn't made lunch plans, what if she hadn't knocked on Lynn's door? Here he is, that young man, with that young man's grin, full of mischief—fucking Philip, how dare he? Nora's hand slams back into the bare white wall behind her, hurting her fist. The house feels bursting with one pent-up thing and another—pain and grief and bewilderment coalescing and transforming to fury, sizzling and ripping its way through rooms, hearts and limbs, cracking off doorframes and walls, crashing into windows, ricocheting all around, a great storm erupting—fucking Philip, absolutely.

There must be thousands upon thousands of ameliorating, tender scenes of sweetness and thoughtfulness, of generosity and kindness. Nora's just momentarily unplugged from most of her history. She can see perfectly well that beautiful young man at the door, and she can see perfectly well the quite different, middle-aged, marble-ized man on the pillow beside her this morning. What she can't make out are the Philips in between, the progression that gradually and unmomentously transformed the first into the last.

Change is grief, grief is rage. Is that true?

And on the subject of change, grief and rage, what about Sophie, was there anything to that, given Sophie's plush and available presence? As Nora's mother said, a man who will break one promise will have little problem with two, and she was, in her small way, an expert. Nora has nothing like proof, only little pricklings sometimes, like last night as they played Scrabble and she saw Sophie and Philip glance at each other when Beth, typically simple-minded, threw down the word "lay." Surely adults would not be exchanging looks over a dumb word like *lay*, too juvenile and unworthy, but still, sometimes recently there's been something like a faint perfume in the air of a room containing both Sophie and Philip.

Why would it matter?

To stoke fury. To ward off more sorrow. To blame Philip further.

Given time and the right moment, Nora might have tackled Philip flat out. It's been strangely more difficult to enquire of Sophie if she's had designs, and moreover hands, on Nora's husband. Having endured what she has, Sophie might consider Philip fair compensation. Perhaps there are also large price tags for Nora's indulgences, and those rewards and costs may include the bodies, if not necessarily the lost hearts, of husbands. Now who will ever know what happened to Philip's heart, besides that it's very likely what blew up on him overnight. Over and over, again and again, moment after moment and hour after hour as Nora lies in Beth's bed, there's his first face, here's his last one. What comes between?

On the day they'd planned, they would have been driving home by now from their lovely long lunch in the city with Max. Sophie would be considering dinner, Beth would be lounging about doing whatever it is she does when her limbs and expressions aren't being turned in various useful directions. Once together around the table they would talk about each other's days, Nora's and Philip's in particular, since theirs would have been more interesting than the others'. Later they might watch TV or read, chatting now and then about what they were watching or reading, or about other subjects altogether. Maybe they'd have a bottle or two of wine, or a couple of beers, or a glass or two of Scotch, except for Beth, who doesn't drink. The evening would pass pleasantly anyway. Finally they would go to bed, just like last night, taking for granted they would all be waking up in the morning.

Instead, Nora is finally rising out of Beth's bed and putting on her black pants and black blouse again, decking herself in the colour of mourning. She is middle-aged, she sees in Beth's mirror, and she is pale.

Downstairs, where the other two are in the kitchen, Beth at the table, Sophie standing at the counter nearby, Nora resumes her own place in her own chair. There's the fourth place. "I keep," she says, "expecting him to walk through the door." Kicking his boots off. Stretching, calling hello.

Sophie nods. "Yes. It's very odd."

If he did come through the door, wouldn't Nora leap to embrace him! Everything could change back and be forgotten if he would just come through that door.

First, though, she would give him raging, blistering hell for giving her such a scare. She might even take a swing at his jaw, or at one of his big impervious arms. "I could kill him for this," she says aloud, "I could just kill him."

How startled Sophie and Beth look when Nora starts laughing. Then finds she can't stop. Philip would have got it, he'd have laughed, but now Nora, forced by his absence into laughing, and for that matter crying, for two, has to do it all now, all by herself. She can imagine no end to the bleakness of this sudden division of two into one, but here she is, with Sophie and Beth and a big empty place at the table, and apparently it really doesn't matter what she can imagine, or not.

Six

And so winds to a close the first day of Philip Lawrence's permanent absence from earth. Whatever full-throttle rumbustiousness and confusions his life may have contained, and whatever enviable peacefulness accompanied his overnight passing, he has certainly disrupted the day, he has captured everybody's attention.

A precarious kind of attention, however. Nora is fixated on two particular visions of him, and one of those is from just this morning. Sophie has kept herself busy, busy, busy, and otherwise seems mainly concerned with the loss of his skin, not much of substance. While Beth's gaze is stuck on the sudden main chance. Is it normal to veer like this from furious at one extreme to dazzled at the other? And surely it can scarcely be typical, the absence of sad, lively, sentimental or vivid exchanges of tales and anecdotes about things Philip did, words he said, revealing bits of who he may have been—everything that ought to enter effortlessly and even insistently into conversations among the bereaved.

There are stages in these matters. Other people may not be quite so quick off the mark with, *What does this mean to me? What have I lost? What happens now?* but they get there, too. The order of things may not mean much.

Dinner is salad and omelettes filled with tiny leftover pieces of ham. Sophie has torn, chopped, ripped, cracked and sliced to put this together. "I've called everyone I could think of," she tells Nora. "And they'll all tell other people. So I hope everybody who should know finds out."

"Thanks, Sophie. That must have been hard."

"Yes, it was."

"At least there's no family to deal with." Nora means parents, sisters, brothers, whose weight of grief might overwhelm her small arrangements. No parents, no children—no wonder she and Philip eventually added more voices to their little duet of a household.

"No. That's a good thing." Sophie, too, knows of his older brother who died when Phil was fifteen, speeding with five buddies on his twentieth birthday in his birthday gift, a new car; and about his parents, who died of separate kinds of cancer in their forties—a family custom, it seems, to wear out, or disappear, in that settled decade. "So you see," Phil said, tracing Sophie's nipples and smiling as if this were perfectly fine, "I'm alone in the world."

Well, not entirely. There was Nora.

"Did you get hold of Max okay?"

"Yes. I guess he waited at the restaurant for an hour or so, then went home. That's where I reached him."

"Poor old guy, going out in this heat and then having to wait. I wish I'd remembered in time."

"I don't believe he's concerned. Anyway, he knew it wasn't on purpose, he'd figured out something was wrong. He said he'll be here for the service, of course. Sooner if you'd like him to come."

Would Nora like that? Not yet, not really. As long as it's just the three of them, there's something slightly normal and ordinary to hang on to; as if everything is still a mistake, or a dream, and capable of being undone. "Good omelette," she says. Is it hard-hearted to be hungry again? She and Sophie both are, although as usual Beth only picks at her food.

Sophie and Nora wander to the living room when they've finished, while Beth stays behind to make tea. She'll make something soothing tonight. Tomorrow's soon enough to try a peppier brew, maybe one promoting desire.

In the living room, as in the kitchen, as everywhere, Philip's usual places leap out for their silence and emptiness. Nora huddles in her corner of the sofa, opposite what would be his corner, within easy reach. His *zaftig* Sophie settles into her usual wing chair, her flesh loosened by weariness, not temptation. When Beth enters, she hands around china cups, since proper teas, in her view, require proper china. People used to read tea leaves. Maybe they still do. Looking down into hers, Nora wonders what shapes and arrangements of leaves in a cup signify which future events or, more to the point now, what the meanings of past ones might be. "Do you think," she asks Sophie, "I ought to call Lynn?"

"What? Who's Lynn?"

"You know—his first wife. She ought to be interested, even if it's only in an academic sort of way. She is an academic now, as a matter of fact. For all I know, she might care."

"Oh, right, you knew her, you were friends."

"Hardly friends. I knew her a little in high school, that's about it. Philip had some odd ideas after the dust settled, though, and before we moved here. He said they wouldn't have been married if they hadn't cared for each other, and since she and I had known each other as well, he couldn't see any good reason why we couldn't smooth everything over by hanging out together sometimes. As if switching partners was only a sidestep, like a dance. He had the hardest time getting it through his head that never mind how bitter Lynn was, or that we weren't proper friends in the first place, it would have been *tasteless* to socialize with someone whose husband I was happily sleeping with. Well, ex-husband by then. Can you imagine?"

Sophie cannot meet Nora's eyes. "So what do you think?" and Sophie's heart pauses until Nora adds, "Should I call her?"

"I don't know. Maybe. You'd know better than I would." Although it's true Sophie is curious about his first wife, the only wife he was actually willing to leave.

"I suppose. I'll think about it tomorrow. Probably even a short marriage should be acknowledged, if she wants it to be."

Beth watches, she listens, she yawns although her day's been far more exhilarating than distressing. The yawn is contagious. "I wonder, Beth," Nora says, "if I could ask another big favour."

"Of course." Beth steps forward, reaching down to take Nora's hand from the arm of the sofa into her own. "What can I do?"

After a moment Nora carefully removes her hand, places it around her teacup, intending to avoid offence but wanting to be free of those unnerving fingers. "I don't want to sleep in that room tonight." She can't say *our room* now, or *my room* yet, so *that room* it must be. "I don't actually want anyone sleeping there tonight. So could I borrow your bed again? It'd put you on the sofa, I'm afraid, but would that be all right?"

"Anything. Anything you want, you just have to ask." More or less, Beth has said that before. She will say it as often as she needs to, until it sinks in. "I don't mind the sofa at all."

It's a full sixteen busy hours since Nora let loose that scream. Each of them, even Beth, sees that going to bed will acknowledge the day's events in a most final way; that turning lights out will be a more true farewell to Philip than anything has been so far.

Two of them are slow to give up, they move reluctantly.

Beth gathers an armful of sheets and a pillow and makes up the sofa for herself. Sophie and Nora take turns in the bathroom upstairs, then each closes a bedroom door behind her, click and click. What is left behind, in the silence and darkness?

For this house Philip made the pine kitchen table and the four pine kitchen chairs. He built his and Nora's bed, empty tonight. He did not make the old wicker sofa out on the porch from which he raised Sophie a couple of months ago, on the remarkable night of one of her nightmares, but when he led her through the late spring dark warmth around the house to the private patch of grass out back, that was his workshop shielding them from view.

That big renovated former barn was one of the selling points when he and Nora were looking at properties here. Its long, high walls are stacked with many shapes and sizes and varieties of wood. Its many shelves hold fat patterned bolts of upholstery. There are tidy rows and containers of tools and glues and screws and decorator nails. There is a wide work-table, and a smaller one, both of them jumbled with projects doomed now to go uncompleted. There are baskets of scrap wood and scrap fabric which Nora customarily loots for materials useful to her. Sawdust floats in the air and is settled and lodged in cracks in the floor. There's a mixture of smells: dust, wood, sharp chemicals. When anyone called him an artist or, as Beth did, asked if he was like Nora an artist, he laughed. "I design," he would say, "and I build. I just love

wood." So he did. Wood took shape in his hands in more gov-
ernable and perhaps more beautiful and certainly less
ambiguous ways than, say, any women were likely to.

Eventually the women sleep, the new widow first, not
because she is heartless or untroubled, more because after
this strangest of days, trying to realize and disorientingly failing to realize, of trying and mainly failing to absorb a tidal
wave, a tsunami of new ideas, new definitions, new words,
dead being one, *widow* another, *alone* the big one—after all
that, and despite having had the afternoon to herself, she is
just bone-deep worn out.

Sophie lies awake longer. In her darkened room with the
window overlooking the backyard and the workshop, she is
aching, physically hurting, frankly, for skin. This is maybe a
more acute pain than if she hadn't lost touch in the first
place. In the end she curves herself around a pillow, partly for
comfort—touch—and partly so no one will hear her weeping
her way, at last, into sleep.

Downstairs, Beth is awake longest. The living-room sofa is
wide but has gotten quite lumpy—Philip was planning to
rebuild it as soon as he had time between customers' orders,
so they're stuck with it now. She tosses and shifts, trying to
find a position in which barely upholstered bones don't clash
with springs. She is both less exhausted and less comfortable
than the other two, and so sleeps less thoroughly. Despite her
new upspringing of spirits, she is wakened several times in the
night by unhappy images, she's aware they are sorrowful
although they're gone as soon as she opens her eyes. Each
time this happens, hope and optimism feel more and more
squeezed, shoved about by a bullying sort of distress, and
around four in the morning, that vulnerable hour, she, too, has
a brief spell of weeping, although cannot think why.

And so Philip's absence begins making its differences: to air, weight, volume, and the rotations and constellations of individual left-behind souls. Pull out one of several props and see what tumbles down. Or see what rearranges itself, compensating for unexpected imbalances—these things, like life or death in the night, can go either way.

THE SECOND DAY

Seven

ora wakens early in a strange narrow white bed in a strange narrow white room. Philip is not beside her. Oh. She leaps up, much the way she did yesterday morning, although without the scream. She has slept in her underwear. Now she puts on yesterday's disreputable black clothes. This won't do, not for the whole day, but it'll have to for now.

Having slept and wakened and leaped, she is at a loss for where to turn next. She is, it appears, sadly inexperienced with events that cannot be controlled or undone. She has had a pretty smooth skate to this point—even death has previously come as a blessing as well as an occasion for sorrow, since when her mother finally took her last shallow breath, who could regret the end, any end, to her suffering? Who, also, could be surprised? This, though—this is a dive into the deep end of helplessness; or rather a merciless shove off a very high diving board.

Philip is dead!

Still, the quality of shock shifts on the second day after so unexpected and untimely a death. Brain cells zapped closed on the first day start popping open again, beginning the necessary, chaotic work of absorbing severe injury, adapting to fresh facts, seeking new alignments and compensating adjustments. In this hit-and-miss effort, survivors become more of what they already are. Extremes bubble up in silent or noisy lament. Lurking weirdnesses step out of the shrubbery.

Out in the upstairs hallway, going quietly into the bathroom (it's so early the sun's barely up, let the others sleep), then down the wide staircase, Nora can feel Philip everywhere. Not everywhere in the sense of expecting to find him in the bathroom, or in the kitchen brewing their first shared pot of coffee, or slamming cupboard doors or rooting through the fridge or wandering about in his socks asking where his workboots or waders have disappeared to; but as if he has spread out and dispersed, becoming a scattered, benign but still assessing presence in the universe.

His absence is also everywhere, and so she continues to be startled that he is *not* in the bathroom, or downstairs making their coffee. The kitchen is, in fact, deathly quiet. She sits at the table, mug in hand, looking around as if she's never been here before. The oak counters and cupboards, the pine table and chairs, the blue tiles on the floor, all those shiny appliances, the toaster, the coffee-maker, the food processor, the kettle, where did they come from? It's as if she has taken bold advantage of someone else's home to step inside and brew up this coffee and sit at this table. Look at the dawn light, the smooth shapes and bright surfaces, the way the space has its own swooping rhythm from window to countertop, up to doorway, down to table, touching the floor and swinging upwards again. Can it be that she has been regularly going in and out of this room for years? Has touched, hundreds and thousands of times, each of these surfaces?

And Philip did, too?

There is something hard inside her that bitter coffee does not dissolve. What do other widows do on the second day?

They go shopping for funeral outfits, or get their hair done, or sleep under sedation, or helplessly weep. Or they are responsible for comforting children. Nora has all the black clothes she needs, her hair is fine, she is not sleepy, she is beyond tears at the moment. She has no children to comfort, or anyone else. She doesn't even have funeral arrangements to attend to. Sophie takes care of details. They hired her, thanks more to Philip's income than Nora's, to be keeper of the household, a resident practical person in a situation intended to be of mutual benefit. She was a cousin of friends in the city who described her, with sympathy and fascinated relish, as a woman rendered distraught and unstable by a mysteriously inflexible desire for virtue that had recently been overwhelmed by experience; a smart and competent person who needed a quiet place and clear, simple tasks of no moral weight whatsoever until she recovered.

Has Sophie recovered?

She was supposed to leave Philip and Nora free for what they supposed to be their more urgent and happy pursuits, and to do so unobtrusively, which for the most part she has; so quiet, at least in the earliest months, that they could be startled to come upon her padding about just when they might have forgotten her. To be sure, there are the shrieking nightmares occasionally startling them awake in the night, but basically she has been, and done, what she was supposed to be and do. Or as Philip kept saying, "Isn't it great to be free just to work?" Of course. Nora nodded.

But now Philip has abandoned all his urgent and happy pursuits; leaving Nora with what? Sophie takes care of the details, and Nora's own pursuits make no sense at the moment. It's beyond her what material, which stitch, colour, shape, shade or texture could possibly depict the weight of being so much at a loss. It would have to be something extraordinary she has never yet seen in her palettes or threads or baskets of scraps.

Her fingers drum on the table, she stands to look out the window, she paces, she sits down at the table again. Something needs doing, but what?

Upstairs, Sophie is still in bed, but awake. She heard Nora go in and out of the bathroom, was alert to her quiet footsteps slipping downstairs. She's damned if she's going to worry about whether there's enough coffee. She has wakened from her dreams with an idea. This is different, obviously, from waking up wondering if this is a day Phil will make a small gesture, or they'll have one of those glances, or something will happen that unexpectedly leaves them alone together for an hour or so, but her intentions do nevertheless involve Phil's skin, and his hands.

Has it been only a day?

Unlike Nora, Sophie does not feel him scattered and dispersed, either everywhere or nowhere. In her mind's eye he is focused and precisely observing, her specifically. Never mind where he's looking down from, which isn't a place exactly, more like he's a camera mounted above her, the way he himself could be mounted above her. Only the past couple of months, and not so often. There could have been a lot more times if he—they—hadn't felt the need to be exceedingly careful. Beth, for instance, has to be clubbed like a seal before she notices most things, but if she did get a clue, she would either go running to Nora or more likely blurt something out accidentally. Phil said, "Watch out, she has too much time on her hands." One of these days someone—Nora—would have had to tell Beth her time here was up.

Who'd have guessed Phil would be the first gone from the house?

Sophie doesn't want him, mounted overhead, to see her behaving poorly. She also hopes he didn't see her throwing up on the kitchen floor yesterday. She knows how offputting it can be, seeing someone throw up. He's so close she could nearly reach up and touch him, she could nearly draw him down to her. The volume and flagrancy of her rolling, pale, freckled flesh is less evident and intrusive when she's on her back like this. Gravity is useful. It was nice when he revelled in her, it was good, him diving in.

"I miss you," she whispers upwards. She feels him pleased to know that, although *miss* isn't quite right. "I'm doing my best," she tells him, "I'm not letting you down"—how relieved he should be to know that even now she has little inclination towards havoc.

Interesting, though, the capacity for havoc. There'd be nothing he could do about it, no improving words or good lies he could say, no moves he could make to protect himself. She imagines reputation is important to the dead, although on second thought perhaps not, perhaps they don't care a bit. In her experience people dying in awesome number are too busy perishing to indicate particular expectations—why would it be different for someone who dies in awesome semi-solitude?

It's also her experience, though, that people may well want to leave messages. Martha Nkume, for one, thoroughly blasted by catastrophe, watching over her wrecked daughter, holding her dying son, that crumpled, pot-bellied child who might have been six months old or three years—Martha understood endings, and her bones clasped Sophie's wrist. "My children, say them be care." Sophie took this to mean, "Tell them to be careful," or "Tell them to take care of each other," but in any case neither message was deliverable: she had no idea where Martha Nkume's other children might be, or whether they were in any state to hear messages from their mother or anyone else.

What if Martha and her Mary and her Matthew and all her other children, whoever and wherever they were, what if all the suffering multitudes are gathered around Phil, a great crowd of the tormented looking down on Sophie also? Reaching down?

Oh no. That gets her up wide-eyed on her feet.

She can be nothing to them. They have other people, in different places, to hover over and watch. More people than there are stars should be out there haunting and being haunted: slaughtering armies, kidnappers of children, torturers of men, rapists of women, bombers of villages, how do they sleep, how do they rest for the multitudes of the dead gazing down, touching their nightmares with cold muddy bones?

Nora begs ill-will and baits mobs with no notion of how easily cataclysms can be aroused, far beyond shit on the doorstep and awful words on the fence. Nora thinks she can do anything, she imagines she's free, she *presumes* that her desires will have no terminal ends.

Well, she knows better now. Now she has something terminal on her hands.

Sophie's own hands fly up—such vengefulness, such meanness, where does that come from? And with Phil watching.

With luck his capacities are confined to surfaces, not what lies beneath. Sophie stretches her naked body, she moves her hands to her breasts, raising them upwards towards him; she lets them fall, passes hands over her thighs, digs in her fingertips, hard. Was he handsome? Not really. His eyebrows were too thick, his nose a little broad, and his eyes were growing smaller within an increasing middle-aged fleshiness. What he had were energy and the kind of size that is beneficent and feels almost safe. And gifted hands. In her own hands her skin feels excessive. It is too rampant, it is soft. Not quite repulsive, but she has made more of herself than she ever intended.

However thoroughly and ravenously she set out to grow this plush armament, it never has fended off the terrible thinness of limbs, the luminous reproach of eyes in the night. Neither did it fend off Phil, who said, "I'm happy there's so *much* of you, Sophie," and touched her here and there; here, too.

The abrupt beginning of pleasure and the abrupt end of pleasure—can it really be true? People often exaggerate when somebody dies, making the dead person, or themselves, either too large or too small. Still, it is nearly the case that throughout this whole summer Sophie has been aware of Phil each waking moment, and some sleeping moments, causing her to step more quickly, watch more sharply. For weeks she has been thrillingly alive. Sophie moans, and the sound snaps her back. She knows better than to conjure hovering spirits. Anyway, she has plans. *Reduced expectations.* The best she can do.

Beth hears Sophie moving about overhead, and thinks she heard the coffee-maker cha-lunking in the kitchen a few minutes ago. So the others are up. But Beth, who yesterday was so light-hearted and hopeful, is severely and thuddingly earthbound this morning.

This occurred overnight, its cause a mystery except for the sofa being so uncomfortable it disrupted her sleep. Then too, dreams, even vanished dreams, have waking effects. Her body is stiff and she has aches that are unfamiliar. She is, oh God, nearly thirty. There are all sorts of pains and debilitations ahead, along with losses of skin tone and other aspects of beauty. What happens to someone like her as she gets older? Philip is dead. This can happen, it has happened to him. Without the most enormous care, there may come a time when Beth will not be widely admired or scrutinized or painted or praised—and then beyond that, she will still have to die?

Now, finally, and not before time, death comes shockingly home to her; now that it applies specifically and surprisingly to herself. Although if the time comes, still unimaginably off in the future, when she is not widely admired, scrutinized and praised, death may just be a blessing. Aging is terrible, involving shrinkages, crumplings, witherings, losses, invisibilities. Beth shivers. She neither cares nor envisions where Philip is at the moment, if anywhere. Time is short. Despite August, she is cold. She pushes herself upright as slowly as a creaky old woman.

The mirror over the sideboard tells her: it's all right. Today she is still beautiful.

She finds Nora and Sophie both in the kitchen, Nora at the table in yesterday's clothes, Sophie standing, wrapped in yesterday's peacock robe under which, judging from thigh-glimpses and nipple-outlines, she is naked as usual. Nora looks up with, it seems to Beth, a welcoming face. "Beth!" she says. "Thank you. I feel bad you had to sleep on the sofa but I sure appreciated your bed. Did you sleep all right?"

"Perfectly. Thanks. I'm glad it helped."

Beth might remember that Nora is years and years older than her, which is hopeful. Except Nora is rounder, and her skin is different, and since she has different purposes, she also probably won't mourn too much when her more obvious appeals disappear. She doesn't look all that great this morning, but over the long haul she will hold up better than someone who has experienced real beauty and all that it means.

Look at the empty chair at the table. Philip's absence opens a huge space. There's hope right there.

One person's disaster is bound to be someone else's triumph, that's just how things are, isn't it? Say you win a beauty pageant, or a modelling job, or release from a hospital: your victory depends on loss for some other people and there's no way around it, so you might as well appreciate the success and build on the victory. Beth must put her best foot forward. Her mother used to say that, encouraging her to *put your best foot forward* on every occasion. Beth's feet are narrow and long, their tendons prominent. As feet go, they look graceful. She extends her legs and regards her bare feet. She would be hard pressed to pick one as the best.

"What do we have to do today?" Nora asks. She is speaking, naturally, to Sophie, with that *we* she uses as if she had any intention of sharing the chores. Still, Sophie's employment here, such as it is, must be coming undone, drifting loose, an attachment no more secure than a scarf tied in a bow with something pulling, none too gently, on one end.

"I have no idea. I suppose we'll be hearing from the funeral home. The guy there said there'll be forms to fill out, that sort of thing. If he doesn't call by noon, I'll drop in when I'm out shopping."

"You're going shopping?"

"Just to pick up a few things. Milk. Bread for sure. If there's anything you want, just make a list."

Because otherwise, it has occurred to Sophie, how to account for leaving the house? Which she has every intention of doing. One step at a time, that's the trick to surviving practically everything. Partly because things not dealt with build up until they're past any controllable point, and never mind wars, civil and otherwise—even in a household, and even in a tragic emergency, this applies.

Already some things are beyond doing: speaking proper last words, for one. That's one terrible undone thing.

"How about you, Beth," Nora asks, "do you have plans?"

Yes, but nothing to speak about yet, so she is relieved when the phone rings. Sophie answers, and says, "Yes," and then, "Fine. I'm sure we can manage that. Of course. Thank you," and when she hangs up, she tells Nora, "Everything's going smoothly. That was the funeral home guy asking if we can get clothes to him in the next hour or so."

"Smoothly?"

"You know—whatever they had to do to realize it was natural causes so things could get moving."

"So they've decided for sure none of us caused Philip's death." Nora still cannot quite say *die* or *dead* out loud. *Philip's death* is softer, and moreover makes it sound as if his death belongs only to him, and is therefore only his business, not anyone else's, not even hers. "Too bad nobody was that interested in checking out whoever was leaving shit on the doorstep, but of course that was just cheery children's idea of fun. Not like a coven casting spells on the man of the house." Beth is surprised to see Sophie and Nora shoot bitter little grins at each other. Sometimes Beth can almost see jaggedy slices in the air between Nora and Sophie, then all of a sudden they're grinning—how much does she miss just because of not happening to look at exactly the right moment? At least it'll be easier without Philip's signals, confusing and multi-directional; only two people to watch now. The hard part is figuring out what a word or a tone or an expression means. Which seems to keep changing anyway.

Nora, running a beat behind, frowns suddenly. "Wait a minute, clothes? For closed casket and cremation?" Yesterday morning Philip left the house inside a heavy black zippered bag, presumably still wearing the blue pyjama bottoms of which Nora had been wearing the top. So pathetic, so help-less—he would hate that.

No, Nora is not going to cry. Neither is Sophie, who shrugs. "It's easier to do it than argue with the guy. Let's just pick something." Nora wants *we?* Sophie'll give her *we*. Although not on the actual errand. "I can take them down to him, no problem."

"Oh, God. I don't know. He only had two suits and they're years old, they probably don't even fit any more." Philip has been bulking up, Nora means. He has begun—had begun—the middle-aged thickening and settling process. He found this upsetting. "Shit," he complained, standing naked, hands on hips, in front of the full-length bedroom mirrors, "I'm not putting on a whole lot of weight and I'm not doing anything different, so what's going on?" His elegant shape, which once narrowed from broad chest to tight, slender hips, was turning blockish and solid.

"Gravity," Nora had said from her perspective of bed. "Normal change." What she found most interesting was that his penis seemed to be receding in the process; becoming some-thing tender and fragile nestled in flesh, no longer a bold dec-laration. "One of these days I probably won't have a waist any more. Same sort of thing." She was only pointing out that they both had accommodations to make. She was suggesting that in making those accommodations, they were most safe, as well as most free, with each other. It was slightly disheartening, having to take the trouble to say this out loud. "We'll be a pair," she added, reinforcing the message and indeed, as best she could, spelling it out. In case he was in any danger of forgetting.

"I can pick something, if you'd like," Sophie offers. "We need underwear, too, I gather, and socks. But no shoes." No shoes. That's entirely too vivid. That gives them all pause, even Beth.

"No!" That was loud. Nora is up on her feet. "I'll do it." Sophie invading Philip's underwear drawer? Nora thinks not. "I'll be down in a few minutes," and she is off, out of the room, up the stairs—to be halted by something like a hand raised against her at her own bedroom door.

She knows the room beyond this door like the back of her hand. Better. It's their house, so she and Philip have naturally had the largest of the three bedrooms. Since the arrivals of first Sophie, then Beth, it's also been the only room that contains no outside tastes, no bits and pieces contributed, or left lying about, by the others. Neither does it contain any of Nora's work, which was both her choice and Philip's, although for different reasons. She wanted sanctuary, one place where work needn't exist, except theoretically and in her mind's eye. He said, "I'd like a peaceful room, nothing jarring," which ruled out her work and other bright things.

So they wound up with a bedroom of cool blues and pale greys and ivory whites and various old shiny grained woods. Philip made the wide, deep bed himself, from maple rubbed and stained dark and, after so many years, marked and scratched here and there from one jostling and another. They bought a broad oak bureau, four drawers for each of them, and the blanket box from an ancient neighbour auctioning household possessions. Philip refinished them both. "Texture," he said. "Grain. Very sexy, textures and grains."

The mirrors before which they examined themselves and each other were also the sliding doors to their wall-to-wall closet, reflecting the two original, rectangular farmhouse windows, more or less doubling the size of the room and the view, too, with the grey draperies opened. The draperies have been closed for a day now. It'll be dark in there. To Nora, halted out in the hallway, the room feels forbidding. Or forbidden. Which is crazy. She slams her hand into the door and once through, takes a deep breath. The air is stale: from being closed in, or from some deathly residue?

There was yesterday morning, the view, the touch, from the next pillow on that Philip-built bed over there. There are also infinite, uncountable moments of flinging arms, tangled limbs, random or purposeful encounters of shoulders, calves, hips and hands—years of this, night after night after night. Words and silences both, in their two particular voices.

Never again? No. This cannot have happened.

In the equal knowledge that it is not only possible but true, a separate cool part of Nora opens Philip's side of the closet and selects a pair of tan cotton pants, a slim brown leather belt. What he might have worn yesterday, if they'd driven off on the day they had planned. A crisp blue cotton shirt he might have worked in, did work in. No tie. A lightweight navy-blue sports coat. He would look, oh, *full* in these clothes. A large man leaning back in his chair at the end of a long restaurant lunch with Nora and Max, the three of them comfortable and familiar, stimulated and cheerful. She sees that restaurant scene as clearly as if it had been their real yesterday.

There is something to be said for touching his things. Perhaps that's what Sophie really intended, suggesting they sort through his possessions: that this is as close as anyone can come any more. But throw out the contents of his closet and drawers, give them away, find them new homes and new bodies? Sophie goes too far there. With her arms around Philip's empty tan pants and blue shirt, the clothes that will burn with him, Nora lets herself sag onto the bed. Jumps straight back up. This bed, no!

Philip's boxers are piled and jumbled in the top bureau drawer. She picks a pale blue pair with a frivolous pattern of sailboats. "Climb aboard, matey," Philip cried the first time he wore them, his thighs emerging like a couple of tree trunks, his hands on his hips as he stood at the foot of the bed, his head rolling back as he laughed; that joyous, absent roar.

Navy socks to match the sports jacket, she supposes, not black. And no shoes. Poor Philip, with nowhere to go; a tenderfoot, in only his socks. Tiptoeing through hell, his infinite punishment for sneaking off in the night.

She tastes something acidic as, embracing Philip's last outfit, she leaves the bedroom, closing the door sharply behind her. At the bottom of the stairs Sophie waits, now in beige pants and pale yellow blouse, evidently not in mourning today, hair blazing red and arms outstretched: ready as ever to receive and accept Nora's burdens.

Eight

Anyone, even a taxi, even Beth for heaven's sake, could deliver Phil's clothes to Hendrik Anderson, but it's Sophie who marches off with the little blue gym bag and a letter signed by Nora, witnessed by Beth, authorizing Sophie to handle arrangements.

Or, as she imagines, do battle.

Sophie pictures Hendrik Anderson as a man roughly her own age, neither tentative nor settled yet into deep immovable years. In her mind he has short hair and wears a dark pinstriped suit and discreet, well-shined shoes; his shape is narrow, elongated, slightly stooped. This impression comes partly from stereotype, but also from his voice on the phone, which sounds as if it's been strained and stretched for a long, thin, sombre distance.

It sounds priggish, too, and disapproving. Not that Sophie herself likes Nora's plans for Phil's swift disposal, but who is an undertaker, basically, but a service person, no different from the plumber who periodically cleans tree roots out of the drains, paid for his skills and equipment, not for nagging commentary on the damage large trees can do. Sophie got

Nora and Phil to switch plumbers last year for that very reason.

One does not so lightly switch undertakers. One can go forth, though, with clear and unbending intentions. Sophie plans to rely on his decorum, their equivalency of age and authority, her careful outfitting in clothes that do not signal deep mourning and her own bright magnitude.

Or if necessary her absolute intention not to be thwarted.

Is her plan a good or a bad one? One good thing about it is that she does not actually care—that's how far she has managed to travel in four years, just by staying still and quiet.

The small, black-lettered sign outside says simply, ANDERSON AND SONS, and scarcely needs to say more. Lawns with two precise and dignified front beds of geraniums and impatiens, the high dark-rimmed windows, the size and sprawl of the red-bricked building itself with its hovering side portico for sheltering people and very large cars, combine to announce that this is what it is.

Somewhere inside this terrible building is Phil.

Also he keeps pace overhead, keeping watch, urging her on.

The ornate, wide, wooden front doors are heavy—however do the frail or the elderly manage them?—then inside comes the sudden silence of a different world all its own: of chilled and dimly unnatural light, of dark woods and ivory wallpaper with faint ferny-green tracings, of dark red, worn carpet runner underfoot, of—she can't say what exactly, but something like reverence.

Can she do this?

Just watch her.

A discreet buzzer has sounded with the opening and closing of the door. Now here's the surprise: from a doorway along to the right bounds a blond open-faced man in blue jeans and smudged baseball-team T-shirt, hand outstretched like a pudgy salesman, and fifty if he's a day. Not remotely who she's looking for. "Hello, I'm Hendrik Anderson," he says, and the voice confirms this is so. "Pardon the outfit. I was trying to catch up with my garden."

Is that obsessive—digging one way or another in one sort of soil, potential soil, or another? What's that under his fingernails?

He's shorter than Sophie. Men often are, she is used to casting eyes downwards over a view of foreheads and scalps, as their eyes are cast upwards. She prefers not having to do this. She does not care to *loom*. And with men who are taller than she, there's a nice sense of being protected, even if protection is unsought. Or untrue. Look at Phil.

To look at Phil is why Sophie is here.

"I am sorry," says this chubby, blue-eyed, professional observer of grief, "for your loss. It must be a shock. And for the widow. An unhappy business but, as I've said, I'm here to make it easier, at least in the most practical ways." This sounds less unctuous face to face than it did over the phone. "Anything I can do."

She thrusts the gym bag and Nora's note into his hands. Sink or swim. "There *is* something you can do, as a matter of fact. I want to see him."

He steps back. Looks at his watch. "If you come back late this afternoon, that should be possible. If you've decided to hold a visitation after all, I expect we could be prepared by then."

"No. I mean now."

His mouth loops into a downturn of distress. "I beg your pardon? Do you mean you want to *see* him now? Oh, but I'm afraid, no, he isn't prepared, not by any means. In a few hours, but now, no." This must be a hard line of work. Although he chose it, and why would a person decide to make a living moulding cold stony flesh? In times and places of disease and starvation and violent hatred, there are acknowledgements of griefs, yes, but not so much in the way of elaborately manufactured arrangement of feature and limb. There are brief, desperate, profound obeisances to mortality and that's it. Less than that, even, in times and places of slaughter. This man is lucky, whether he knows it or not. Probably not. People don't.

"Now," Sophie repeats. She thinks if he were as adamant as he sounds, or as adamant as she is, his mouth would not look distressed.

"I'm so sorry, but he's not even in an area open to the public." As if that is the most compelling argument he can make. Do mourners, or just people with secrets, never make odd demands? Do they, for instance, not sometimes express a desire to regard the dead as they are, not as they could be once made false and presentable?

On the other hand, if his profession is death, it must also be life. The lives, specifically, of the bereaved, most of whom likely do require protection from the most raw and bare aspects of their bereavements.

Which has nothing to do with Sophie.

Still, she is disarmed by appearance: that he is not what she expected. This Hendrik Anderson could belong to any glad-handing service club in the town—and is there a code of ethics for people who run funeral homes, to do with the privacies and indiscretions of mourners? Otherwise how irresistible to whisper tales of not only the non-wife's unusual role in arranging proceedings and delivering clothes, but also of the same non-wife's tasteless and unnatural insistence on viewing the unprepared body. Even if he only told a couple of people, word would spread like Ebola, mutating freakishly along the way. That's how things work here.

Well, anywhere, really. And does Sophie care? Not much. If she needs to, she will barge through the place, banging into one room after another in undignified, inflammatory search of Phil, with a flustered Hendrik Anderson skittering along at her heels. Of course, she would prefer not to do that. "Please," she says. "I realize it's unusual but honestly, dead bodies don't shock me." Well, he'll wonder and speculate about *that*, won't he? "I won't be upset, and I won't tell a soul. It's a great favour, I know, but please. Trust me."

Trust her? Why on earth would he? She touches his arm. She intends to look, not begging exactly, but plaintive and sad and also respectably in control of herself. A woman seeking one small morsel of help which only he can deliver. "Really," he says, "you don't know the state of things at the moment." He frowns, but it's hard for a man peering upwards to appear forbidding to Sophie. "I'm sorry to put it so bluntly but it's not nice, a body that's been examined but hasn't yet been prepared."

No doubt. "I can imagine," she says, although she can't, quite. "I know," although she does not. "I can take that into account."

"After, frankly, you understand, an autopsy?" He's spelling it out and watching her closely, as if he supposes it possible to read fortitude or ghoulishness or cheap curiosity in expressions and eyes. Or he's challenging her; and it's true, the word *autopsy* is daunting.

"I'm very sure." She makes her eyes large. "I understand your concerns, but please believe me, I will manage perfectly well, and you'd be doing such a good deed." Her hand tightens slightly on his arm. These impure, necessary tricks—what others does she still have? Phil didn't need tricks, only lies.

She can see a shift occurring, there's a small loosening of muscle in the arm she is touching, a clearing of eyes, a relaxation of mouth. Hendrik Anderson sighs. "Well, it's against every rule, and I think extremely unwise, but . . . I am aware that you have experience in some of the harsher aspects of death." She should have known—people do hear the histories, however garbled, of other people in this town. "And I understand how things left up in the air can be the worst part of death, in a way, in the long run." What does he imagine has been *left up in the air*? Never mind. At least he's familiar with the debris that bobs along behind death, its sharp bits sticking up into the living, refusing to sink. He sighs again, lifts his hands, lets them fall. "Follow me, then."

Caught up in her ardent intentions, she lost track of actual meanings. This has happened to her before. Now she hears *autopsy* again, and is frightened. Phil will not be Phil. There's that difference again between knowing abstractly and realizing. Next will come seeing.

She is different now, though. For one thing, she is no longer addicted to virtue, obsessed about the goodness of each tiny act—at least she hopes she has broken out of that trap, with thanks to Phil for the large last step in the process. It's the powerful kind of thing that starts young and sneaks up, though, and who knows how thoroughly it's been threshed and ploughed under? It may have only been biding its time for a vulnerable moment.

How does this happen, how much is nature, how much nurture? Eventually, what does it matter?

A childish aversion to pain begins with picking stranded snails from sidewalks and lifting toads from the paths of lawnmowers. How eccentrically sweet, and hardly unusual: there is potential for pain, and one can act to prevent it, what could be more straightforward?

A child's logic is blunt and untwisted.

The tendency then blooms at the dinner table as youthful ears take gravely to heart stories brought home by parents who are, as it happens, partners in a legal firm specializing in immigration and refugee law. Their conversations add wraiths to the table in the form of mysterious hard-working men with false papers, women tortured in ways so unspeakable they can only be specified by grim tone, not detail, and blank-eyed, or sad-eyed, scary children—all needing rescue, all needing Sophie's mother or father to speak for them against the disbelief of immigration officials and refugee boards holding tight to the view that people must contrive these stories for shady purposes, that such lives could not be entirely true because if they were, what sort of world was this and what sort of person could bear not only being alive in it but making these life-and-death judgments?

Sometimes, too, the stories were not true; a fact that caused its own troubles.

How are parents to know which random gesture or unconsidered comment or fierce interest of their own can knock a child silly? How were Sophie's to know she was locking like a laser on to their dinnertime conversations while her eyes skipped right over their many indulgences: big house, large lawns, fresh flowers, real china, genuine crystal glasses? How were they to know that rather than the moderately well-behaved and respectably kind-hearted person they intended, they were raising a zealot?

"We're so lucky," her mother said, and Sophie certainly saw this was true. Her father was uninjured, her mother untortured, she herself had personally witnessed no particular sorrows, and also possessed everything she could want. Whereas misfortunes great and small were on display at the refugee centres and multicultural agencies patrolled by her parents, sometimes with Sophie in tow. How brightly those places were lit by fluorescence, how clean they were despite chipped paint and bare floors, how bustling with very busy people counselling, organizing language classes and medical treatment, filling out forms. In contrast how worn out the clients, even other kids, often looked; as if the strength and courage they'd used to get to those brightly lit places now had to stay focused on simply stopping them falling down onto those floors.

What a lesson in good luck and bad luck: Sophie's good, theirs bad; although in the future, with the help of all their good helpers, their luck would possibly be good also. Meanwhile—meanwhile, what? Meanwhile she might—more of the inexorable logic of the child—ease, even fend off, misfortune with sacrifice.

Which meant a deeply desired and most fashionable doll went, within a week of her seventh birthday, to a baffled child at the refugee centre, who received it from Sophie's reluctant, determined hands as warily as if its blonde curls might be explosive. Clothes, too, even favoured outfits— especially favoured outfits—off they went to donation boxes at the cultural centre. Just because among the many luxuries of Sophie's family was the very real one that they had enough to give away. And that some form, however small and hard, of balancing things out might prevent a reversal, an upside-downing of events that could put her in their place, and so she gave and gave, more and more frantically: clothes, toys, games, pity. What insanity! Did nobody notice?

"You're an awfully good kid," said her father. "We're really proud of you." He and her mother must have considered her blissfully untroublesome, a miracle of good fortune.

Sophie's secret was in the guilty, momentary hesitation, the persistent, sly sentence in the back of her head: *But I like that, I want it, I don't want to give it away,* diluting, if not actually nullifying, her intentions. Selfishness was bad. She could never quite catch up to genuine generosity, the kind that appeared spontaneously and flowed without resistance like honey.

In high school she joined and eventually ran the club that organized food and clothing drives for the poor of the city. So much macaroni and peanut butter! She herself took cans of asparagus tips from her parents' shelves, and added bags of expensive, weighty, nutritionally balanced breakfast cereals. Why should the poor have to eat dreary or unhealthy, sugary foods? Equally, why did she deserve them more than anyone else? Not that she would go without; her parents simply bought more. Was that cheating?

She was red-haired and lissome and clever and kind— how could she not be popular, well liked? So she set out contrary-wise to cultivate outcasts, befriending not so much those who were eccentric but the dull or unpleasant. Often enough they were outcasts for a reason; bad hygiene, say, or stupidity. They could make dull company and Sophie was depressed, if not discouraged, for most of her high-school years. And, too, that sardonic, unkind voice in the back of her head kept piping up, silently complaining, *For heaven's sake, take a shower! Wash your hair! Read a book!*

When she took her huge, confused, compulsive heart to university, it was to study political economics. In place of the step-by-step, case-by-case benevolences of her parents, and for that matter herself, she had a new, easier, more sweeping aim: to help repair the world's economies, and therefore its politics, and thus its problems of violence, poverty, hatred and suffering; possibly poor hygiene and stupidity also.

Another mad goal.

Not such a lonely one, though, but one miraculously shared—what were the odds?—by slim and fervent, dark-haired and electric Nick, who also wanted to turn the world over.

Of course they found each other.

Nick said, raising his head from between Sophie's thighs—another happy revelation, oh, yes!—that it was just her sort of marginal do-gooding and patronizing, prideful sacrifice of overflowing possessions that "lets war and suffering go on and on. People like you just put on bandages, you won't rip them off. You don't do anything about real wounds, all you do is cover them up." He could be awfully eloquent in that unlikely position, he was frequently, if intermittently, at his speech-making, rabble-rousing best down there.

"I do not," she protested. He had no idea; how could she explain herself to him, much less prove herself? "I do so want to help."

"Exactly," he replied, satisfied.

As was she.

"Talk's cheap," he said when they were upright. Her sofa was as worn as any newcomer refugee's, her secondhand Arborite-topped kitchen table as pathetically servile. They ate beans on toast and drank cheap red wine and were gratified by these tinges of volunteer poverty. Too, there was sometimes an element of tender self-regard in their love-making. At least there was when it wasn't accusatory or challenging. "It's arrogant to dip in and out of people's lives giving a little nod here and there to what they need once they're here. How about taking a look at origins, how about helping them get the power to change their own lives in their own countries in their own ways?"

What if she didn't like *their own ways?* What if *their own ways* happened to be vicious and brutal?

Never mind.

They went on, she and Nick, to postgraduate work since as he said, they would need unassailable credentials for their revolutionary future. That further long period of study felt like time bought, or maybe stolen, but of course the day had to come when he put his hands on her shoulders, his head tilted back slightly so he could look her in the eyes, and said, "Okay, what do you think about this?"

His proposal sounded brilliant. She was suitably thrilled.

"We'll sign up for two years. We'll get a good look at the real thing, we'll do on-the-ground, flat-out, stay-alive stuff while we see for ourselves and make contacts and get an idea how basic systems need to be fixed. It's just a couple of years, for a grounding. Then we can start our real work."

Our real work. They would come home not only improved and more purposeful human beings but bound and twisted together as thoroughly as ancient tree roots.

So romantic. Young love's young dream. Although they were no longer quite so young.

Sophie had to shade some facts and tell a few outright lies to get through the aid agency's interviews, tests and training sessions, since doing good was evidently considered the most dangerously unstable motivation, with fomenting revolution or even storing up economic and political ammunition for future crusades scarcely more highly regarded. Sophie said, "I have experience with refugees because of my parents' work, so I would not be surprised. It will be an adventure, and a kind of experiment, and a test of myself, and a learning experience." Evidently that was the right sort of responsible goal for a practical, low-demand, energetic, good-willed but not crazy young person.

When she and Nick got their assignment, it came with pages and pages of background, advice, photographs, accounts by their predecessors and a video, all of it thrilling, unreal, unimaginable. They were going to a refugee camp in a central African country at the time much in the news due to massive brutalities. "We'll get you out if things take a turn for the worse," agency managers told them. "Conditions are bad enough now, but if you can hack it, we need all the hands we can get on the ground."

Even at the time Sophie wondered if *hack* wasn't an unfortunate slip of the tongue; much less *hands on the ground*.

Now her parents took notice of how far virtuous impulses—compulsions—may travel, *now* they were worried. "We wish you wouldn't," they said. "We really do wish you'd think it over."

"I have thought it over." And over and over. "We'll be fine." More than fine. Fiery, passionately burning-eyed Nick, clear-eyed, hard-working, brave, adventurous Sophie, two years far away, sacrificing wonderfully to good purposes—what, in every possible way, could be better?

Three weeks before they were to leave, Nick once again put his hands on her shoulders and cast his eyes upwards. "I'm sorry, Soph, but it turns out I can't go after all."

What?

He was taking instead ill-paid but highly principled work—who knew he was looking for work?—with a relatively radical environmental organization. He would be involved in saving trees, lakes, oceans, the air people breathed; although, having left her gasping, he didn't seem to care much about the air Sophie might be breathing. "When you think about it," he said, "the environment's at the root of every kind of exploitation there is, people using other people to get the most for themselves and ruining it all while they're at it."

Speaking of ruining, "What about us?"

"I see it as a pincer movement." How happy he looked, how enthusiastic and far worse, relieved. "We'll be tackling the issues from two directions instead of just one. Like a battle. A revolution. Which it is."

Oh. Okay.

She could have backed out, of course she could have, but then what? If she did, would she not spend the rest of her life smelling blood on her hands? So off she went, clueless, and by the time she came home she barely remembered Nick and exactly how he'd been so compelling, and certainly did not care if he'd spent those two years underwater testing the purity of the oceans or perched in a tree fending off greedy loggers. Just the thought of buttocks, penis, that clever tongue, those fierce eyes—his or anyone's—made her skin feel shot through with needles.

Men and their bits and pieces, their occasional grave allures, their evidently permanent vanishings—what an expert she ought to be, and therefore detached and accepting. Instead, here she is, following an undertaker through a funeral home on her way to view the body of her ex-employer, ex-lover, her diploma in bad behaviour arduously achieved.

Autopsy: another sort of comparative luxury, really. Look at it that way.

There will be the difference today, too, between a singular man and torn humans en masse. The acres of boggy tents when Sophie rolled by truck into the camp, that was—well, it was a *vista* to start with. Almost scenic. The orientation officer back in the capital city, hours and miles distant, had advised, "You'll probably feel overwhelmed at first sight. Take care not to get swamped." He meant that these were people blown out of their homes by rampaging militias, thugs and mobs see-sawing through their lives until they gave up, or were forced out, and fled. They were starved, they were wounded, they were the lucky survivors. Some were guilty. "There's relatively few able-bodied men, but there can be problems." Getting aid past them, he meant.

There was other corruption as well. Heartlessness; he did not mention heartlessness.

Smells hit first, wiping out *vista*. Newspapers, TV, training films, websites, orientation sessions, none of those carried the reek of thousands of human bodies and open waste trenches and dampened cooking fires and a kind of rotting she couldn't identify. Sophie took a first deep breath and threw up.

She has always had a delicate stomach.

It will be important not to get sick around Hendrik Anderson.

She is unsurprised that after they pass through a solid, dignified door to the left at the end of the entrance hallway, they enter surroundings that are entirely different. Now they are indeed in unpublic space, although by no means private space. They are descending a wide bare staircase, between walls that are drywalled and painted pale green, not panelled and wallpapered. Light bears down clear and bright from the ceiling, not from muted, soft-coloured, up-tilted lamps. And there is a smell. Not a bad one, but slightly acrid and sharp. She would say *medicinal* if this weren't a place where it's far too late for medicines.

There is a corridor in the basement with two wide blank

metal doors leading off it, and at the first one he says, "I'll step ahead for a moment. If you'll wait, please." She obeys, because down here there is something different about Hendrik Anderson, too; something scalpeled or chemicaled or otherwise scientific, expert and remote.

He slips through the door, closing it quickly behind him. Rather than yield to a fresh temptation to bolt, she stares at her hands. They are real and calming, if also alive enough to be trembling.

Not as she can expect Phil's to be.

Hendrik Anderson reappears looking reluctant again as if his doubts, too, have resurrected. "I really don't know about this."

"It's fine," and she puts a hand once more on his arm, looks sincerely again down into his eyes. "Truly. I'm fine. Believe me."

"Well then," he says, and steps back.

Isn't it amazing, that he would do this?

Once through this last door, she finds the real chill of the place. "This isn't where we do our work," he says, close behind her. Embalming and make-up and so forth, he must mean, and it's obvious this can't be where anyone could do any work, their fingers would freeze, they'd be clumsy and make garish mistakes. No, this is a meat locker of sorts: a small, steely, preservative anteroom. No hooks, no dangling corpses, but a single metal gurney bearing a long lump that is Phil, mostly covered by plastic.

Most of that plastic is covered in turn by a black and green plaid blanket; the sort of blanket that might be packed up for a picnic, or to shelter a pair of lovers on a porch, on a beach, in the woods. On a wicker sofa, on a patch of lawn behind a workshop. Here in this spartan space is a blanket so incongruous and discordant Sophie feels tears rising up, clogging her throat, blurring her vision. Because the blanket is so

homey, domestic, warm. Sexual. Because this man Hendrik
Anderson has thought it might camouflage mortality and also
comfort her. A sweet, heartbreaking, erroneous notion.

"Thank you. You're very good." And then, "Could I be
alone now?"

Here come his doubts again, showing up in a quick, distressed frown. She imagines him imagining her falling into
hysteria, howling, screaming, tearing her hair. Or weirder,
that she has in mind chopping off some of Phil's hair, or
scraping skin, or cutting fingernails, gathering ingredients for
a nasty witches' brew, or a huge, disastrous curse. Not that he
would believe in that, but he might believe Sophie does. Or
he might be leery of more luridly personal acts: initials carved
on Phil's dead chest; Phil's deceased penis sliced away.

He must at least assume she has something to hide.

As she does.

It's also possible that he basically thinks, if Phil's own
loved ones don't care what happens to him, why should a
mere mortician? "For a few minutes, then," he says. "But if you
need me, I'll be right outside the door. Just call out if
you start feeling upset or queasy." She hadn't thought of that:
that part of his concern might be for her well-being, not his
own. In that case, what a nice man.

"I'm all right. Don't worry. No harm will come. But thank
you. I won't be long."

She'll be as long as she wants. When he has gone, she turns
her full attention to the gurney, the blanket, to Phil. "So here
we are," she says aloud. "Alone at last." Kind of a joke; Phil
might have smiled. It's stupid, though, and embarrassing to
hear her own lonely voice in this metallic, echoing room.

All that's visible above solid plastic and dense plaid blanket is Phil's rigid, untroubled face. His pores are large. His

forehead is unlined. He needs shaving. She reaches out to his cheek with the back of her hand. What does she expect? Something less like cold porridge than this.

She ought to know better.

But touch, that's the point: to incise into memory his magic tricks, the clever sleight of hand rendering her finally unhorrified by skin; causing her to wonder at the rabbits he could pluck from her with his dextrous fingers, the scarves he knew how to draw from her body's sleeves, the several ways he could cut her in two.

Ah, was it really so good? Never mind, it's what she'll remember; intends to remember.

Warily—bravely—she raises plastic and blanket, and peering downwards sees a Y-shaped railroad track of bright careless stitching heading from naked, broken, newly hairless chest towards the darkness below, perhaps also now broken and newly hairless. Someone else might want to examine those parts. Nora maybe. Some evenings lately, Sophie has watched Nora across the table or across the living room, sitting with elbows propped under her chin, or legs curled beneath her, and thought, *Phil has travelled there, there and there, all over that woman, that Nora, and vice versa.* Sophie was more bemused by this than jealous. In a way it created connections between her and Nora, pulling and pushing ones, attractions and repulsions.

Hard to know if these connections counted if only one of them knew.

It's surprising how unstiff Phil is. The time for rigidity has passed, Sophie knows this, but she is still startled, trying to draw his arm into view without dislodging too much the camouflaging plastic and blanket, to have it come free without resistance. It's very heavy, though. The limbs of other dead people Sophie has touched were often astoundingly light; like picking up baby birds.

She has helped carry dead bodies, she has wrapped them in plastic and cloth, she has helped bury them, without much time and with very few words, even less ceremony than with Phil, this body going up tomorrow in flames.

A purplish-grey fattiness has settled around his upper arms, his forearms, his wrists and, she sees, turning over his hand, on the fleshy part of his palm, and at the base of his fingers. The lines and creases there are filled out by this freshly risen doughy substance under the skin.

But the skin itself—here it is, her impulsive, vital, second-day purpose dreamed up in the night. This skin remains roughened, there are calluses at the tip and base of each finger, nicks and scars from old tool cuts and scrapes. She can stroke the palm and its thrilling abrasiveness.

Here is Phil's heart line, sliding from the side of his palm to the space between middle finger and forefinger: not very long, or very deep. Here is his life line, slicing hard across his palm in a curve from the very base of his thumb to a point between forefinger and thumb. She should tell Beth, who has on idle evenings read all their palms, a typically frivolous entertainment picked up in long hours in hotel rooms and backstage, waiting for her interminable pageants and competitions to start—she should tell Beth it's all nonsense. Otherwise Phil's life line would have to come to a premature end.

Does this make the heart line false, too?

Tinier, intricate, criss-crossing lines speak of ambitions and aptitudes, skills and terms of desire. Phil worked with his hands, used dangerous tools with speed and great skill. His fingers smelled of wood; not like the outdoors kind of woods, not piney underfoot or arching and dark overhead, but of cut, chiselled and carved wood that bled resin into his flesh. These lines, calluses, scars, rough now-discoloured pads at the base of each finger, pregnant with clean raw wood scent, they touched Sophie, caused her skin to rise up and fall back. "You understand," Phil said, "I love Nora, but in a friendly, calm sort of way. Not like this," as he wrapped this large hand under a breast and lifted it up, up to his mouth.

She moves around the gurney to the other hand, the one stroking her face, her round belly, her voluminous thighs. This hand is surprisingly different. Both its heart and life lines are deep and long and slightly meandering. There are smaller lines that do not appear on his other palm, and a few seem to be absent. The callused bumps at the base of each finger are more pronounced. So she has two hands to memorize: either a full depiction of Phil, or two separately incomplete ones.

Nora's the artist, she's the one who takes shapes and ideas and visions and does something with them. Sophie will be the engraver, etching each ridge, hollow and line of Phil's hands, the length and breadth of each finger, each curve and bump, into memory. For what purpose? Maybe to bear in her mind like a keepsake; maybe only, after all, the way other people hold on to significant restaurant menus, birthday cards, movie stubs.

No. More than that.

These moments in this frigid room will have to last her a long time. She has very deliberately made herself not good at remembering detail. She can *perform* detail, she's good at that, but not with the exact shapes, scents, movements and sounds that bring certain recollections to life. They have to creep up on her unexpectedly, or in the dark. Memorizing Phil's hands could dangerously sabotage that trick of forgetfulness.

Martha Nkume's hands were leathered. If her destiny had ever been legible in clear lines of life, love, preferences and ambitions, it no longer was by the time Sophie knew her. In that place only newborns and the youngest of toddlers were soft and unknowing.

It's Martha's hands that went on waking Sophie up in the night; it's Phil's that could for days and nights at a time erase, soothe, smooth away Martha's fingerprints. Now what?

Now she will be able to close her eyes and conjure Phil's hands; with luck even replace one dream with another. She replaces each hand carefully under the plastic, she smooths the plaid blanket. She takes a last look at his face but it is empty and strange and has nothing to say that wouldn't be unfamiliar to her, and probably grim. She is not inclined to lean down and kiss him.

It's hard to turn away, but in another way not. Like before, lifting off after two years on the ground, when she leaned her head against the plane's window and looked for the last time at the troublesome landscape below, its capital-city traffic jams giving way as the plane climbed to dense patches of green and then great swaths of brown emptiness that she knew were not truly empty, and then she was above the clouds and it was over.

Although it was not.

She is surprised, because she has forgotten about him, to find Hendrik Anderson waiting outside the door. That plaid blanket he placed over Phil, that cozy touch, who would think of doing such a thing except a man accustomed to taking details into account, and to considering the hidden, unspoken, undemanded comforts of others? And he trusted her, if not necessarily to behave well, at least not to behave excessively badly. He must have had faith, or anyway a hope, that she would not cause really serious harm, even though he must know at least a little of the serious harm people can do. He has been worried, but gives her the gift of not asking, and that surely signifies large spirit, great heart. They climb wordlessly back up the stairs, his hand under her elbow, and whereas a few months ago she would have flinched sharply, now she does not. At the top they pass into public space finally. She can feel his relief. "Would you care for a coffee?" he asks. "I expect you're chilled right through from that room." And so she is. Chilled right through, as he says.

Nora likes to warn, "Watch out, those people are greedy for anything they can find out about us," although she also says, "Whatever they don't know, they make up," so Nora's unhappy either way. And the alternative is pushing through those tremendously heavy wooden front doors into the daylight, to Nora and Beth. "I'd like that. Thank you."

He surely doesn't invite any random mourner for coffee. Perhaps she looks either far more or much less solid and sane than she feels; or he's drawn to over-sized redheads, or he is lonely, or bored. "I have some forms that need signing," he says.

Oh. "All right. I can do that."

He is leading them to another door, this one tucked to the right and recessed slightly. Of course—he must live here, she hasn't thought of that, but then she has thought little of him at all except how to get her own way. Now she wonders how unnerving it is to sleep so near the permanently at rest, how unappetizing to eat a few rooms distant from vats of whatever it is that replaces cooling blood in dead bodies. In high-school biology classrooms various creatures floated about sightlessly in jars of formaldehyde. "Pickle juice," kids called it, removing its sting. But no doubt the infusions and chemicals used here are more complex and sophisticated.

Not that it matters. "Does my living here make you uneasy?" he asks. How did he know?

It is another different world, though, a real home, on the other side of the door: all light and air, with hardwood wainscotting and floors, pale yellow walls, dark-green-upholstered sofa and wing chairs that Phil, for one, would have admired, not to mention the tall pewtery-blue drying cupboard full of books and CDs. "This is lovely," she says.

"It is, isn't it? It helps to be on the premises when you run a business that doesn't have regular hours, but mainly I'm here because it's just a hell of a gorgeous old building." He is looser here, freer. Well, in these rooms he's a man who belongs in the T-shirt he's wearing. Not to mention that no catastrophe occurred downstairs, and he must feel relieved.

The sofa and chairs in this living room have high backs and wide arms and deep cushions, although the sofa has an unmatching dark-blue crocheted blanket folded over its back, reminding Sophie, although it's quite different, of the plaid one this man spread protectively across Phil's poor ruined body. The drying cupboard is pegged rather than nailed or, far worse, glued. A refinished old bench runs along the base of two back windows, loaded with blooming begonias. "Phil would love this," Sophie hears herself say.

"Why's that, then?"

"He knew good furniture. He built and designed furniture, you know. Did you ever meet him?" She is reminded of grey, stitched Phil below. Obviously that's not the same as meeting him.

"I saw him around town. I've seen you, too, but I guess we've had no occasion to meet." He smiles in boyish fashion. "I tend to go out of town if I want to kick over the traces. If I hung out at bars here getting snapped up every night, it'd be hard to be credible trying to console the bereaved the next day." Is he suggesting he didn't know Phil because Phil was in bars every night getting snapped up? Well, all right, sometimes Phil was. Still, considering she's among the *bereaved*, he sounds a little too casual and lighthearted.

"Make yourself comfortable and I'll get our coffee." He disappears through a doorway to, presumably, the kitchen. Sophie drifts to his rear wall of windows, with its benchload of begonias. He has a large backyard, although not as enormous as Phil and Nora's, draped in maples and sectioned here and there into gardens—shrubs, perennials, low, flowing ground covers. There are two Muskoka chairs and a table, very cozy and companionable. He must have a companion, then?

In another life, she and Phil might have been together like that, sitting outside in Muskoka chairs viewing their gardens. In another life, maybe they will be.

She has no belief whatever in other lives. And Phil appears to have drifted off. When did that happen? Perhaps while she was downstairs scrutinizing his hands. At any rate, he's not overhead, or anywhere else, in this room.

Hendrik returns with a tray, a pot of coffee, two mugs, cream and sugar, setting it on a piecrust table between the wing chairs. Those plump hands of his will, like hers, touch Phil's flesh, turn it, shape it—best not to think about that. "I'm sorry," he says, "the cupboards are bare or I'd offer you something to eat. I meant to go shopping, but things happened and I ran out of time." He stops. "Sorry. I didn't mean how that sounded."

"I guess when somebody dies, there's no telling all the effects." Sophie stops, too. "Sorry. That didn't come out right either." All she meant was, everything from Phil's absence to Hendrik running out of time to shop, from the huge to the infinitesimal, from loss of skin to a shortage of snacks, is entirely fascinating.

"Then let's not apologize any more, let's just agree we won't take offence and blunder on."

Smiling feels peculiar, requiring muscles that haven't been used much the past couple of days. "Okay," she says.

"Are you crying?" he asks, leaning towards her and frowning. Is that how it looks when she imagines she's smiling?

"No. Thanks, I'm fine." She runs through some of the tinier lines of Phil's palm, she examines his fingerprints.

"Would you like to talk about him?" Hendrik's voice turns formal; more as it sounds on the other side of the door.

"No, really, I knew him fairly well, but basically as an employer." St. Peter, St. Sophie—just like Beth she could star in one of Nora's depictions of pronoun-based theology.

"You work for the artist as well, don't you? The widow, I guess." There's no inflection, positive or negative, in his tone, so there's no telling what he thinks of Nora, or her work, or her attitudes, or the fame she briefly but vividly and perhaps permanently brought to this town.

"Yes. I take care of most of the household details and the finances"—has she just suggested Phil is a mere household detail, his send-off from the planet simply one of her fiscal chores?—"so she and Phil, well, Phil up till now, can concentrate on their work."

"Do you like doing that? And living here?"

"It's a job. I don't know, really. Do you?" One way to dodge complicated questions is to turn them around. Also she is interested: what does Hendrik Anderson think, how does he feel, about his work?

He shrugs. "I'm used to it. My family goes back three generations here, which means knowing all the old-timers and everyone's personal histories and family connections. There's a lot to be said for knowing a place in your bones." Funny. That's exactly how Phil put it: that he knew this town, unfathomably and unreasonably but fervently, in his bones. "And I like the idea that sometimes I can make sorrow easier to bear. You can't take grief away from anyone, but sometimes you can lift it a bit. Make it easier or more comprehensible, whatever seems required. And I like being able to acknowledge the people and the lives that I know and the ends of their stories. *Respecting* all the family and community and how it unfolds, in the end."

How gentle he sounds and, yes, respectful. A different way, certainly, of regarding this town. "I don't expect," he says, "that your experiences would give you much affection for people here, though. What some of them did was disgraceful. But," his shoulders rise and fall, "they are what they each are. Sometimes there are reasons. Not excuses, of course."

How remarkably tolerant. Still, he is right: people always have reasons, if not good excuses. He must wonder about her own. "Thank you for letting me downstairs. I'm very grateful. Why did you?"

"I guess because you seemed determined and sure of yourself. And we may not have met, but I know you've been places and seen things that make you different from other people. I mean, that your reactions would be different." Does he mean he takes her for a hard woman capable of striding casually through the dead? Probably not. That's not quite what he said. "And I guess I felt bad. On the phone, discussing the arrangements—any arrangements are fine, they're entirely up to the loved ones, but I was on the verge of bullying you. It's just that ritual can be important to grieving, so I was urging more ceremony instead of recognizing that people tend to know what they need." A dubious proposition, it seems to Sophie, although a kind and responsible one.

If she told him about Martha Nkume and Mary and Matthew, would he have any idea what she was talking about? "It's okay. Nora was sure what she wanted. I was just passing it on. I knew what you were saying."

Who sits in the other chair out in the garden? Why is Hendrik Anderson serving her coffee in his sunny quarters, talking to a woman he's barely met and who is unhappily and intimately connected, today, with his work? How mysterious and surprising and exhausting other people's purposes and intentions can be. "I should go," she says, putting her mug down sharply. At the house phones will be ringing, chores and names must be dealt with and then ticked off her list. Also, she is no longer entirely comfortable here.

And she needs time to remember Phil's hands, carefully trace all those bumps, scars and lines so that she doesn't drift in the practised direction of forgetfulness.

"Then," and Hendrik stands too, "I'll get those forms that need signing." Oh right, her chore. "And please be sure to call if there's anything at all I can do." She is being shepherded from his apartment through the door into the wide carpeted hall of the funeral home proper. That other different world. He dips briefly into what she takes to be his office and returns with papers attached to a clipboard. "Sign here," he says, "and here, and here. And that's it. These are your copies. Or the widow's, rather. Let me know if you think of anything else, I'm happy to do whatever I can." Happy?

Will he return now to his gardening, or is there work to be done even on a body that won't be seen again, and is to be burned?

Maybe he'll take time to go grocery shopping.

At the heavy front door Sophie says, "Thank you. For the coffee. And everything else. Trusting me." Stooping, she touches her lips to his cheek. An odd gesture, perhaps, although who is to say at this point what sort of gesture is odd? He accepts it, at any rate, just as gravely, and out she goes through the door he holds open, into the heat of the day. When she looks back she sees him watching, nodding at her before he closes the door, and unreasonably she feels for a moment as if he has turned her away, shutting her out of a cool, dim, friendly space.

Nine

First Nora rang Lynn's doorbell with no intentions past lunch, then, seeing Lynn's naked husband, ran off with him in lusty, happy, ruthless frame of mind. Now she's about to call Lynn with no idea of what to expect, except that obviously there won't be similarly delicious results.

She was incautious in those days, and cruel. Now she might be less so.

She could almost persuade herself this is a courtesy call, but really it's not so much a plan as just another desire: this time a powerful one to say Philip's name to someone. Nora means not to Sophie or Beth, not even to Max, and certainly not to one of Philip's clients or barroom companions, but to a person who knew Philip in ways that resemble her own; who knew his habits, knew his youth, knew his skin, knew his laughter and anger and appetites.

Knew also his capacity for departures.

It's a long way from twenty-six to forty-three, although at the moment the passage seems swift. Much can happen to a woman—or a man, look at Philip—in that many years. Lynn was taller than Nora in their youth, and also more narrowly built. Nora pictures her bulkier now: rather like Philip, heavier in the trunk, more marked elsewhere. She also imagines Lynn, unkindly, with carefully streaked hair, a little too much make-up, bright, manicured nails, and a brisk outlook that comes of having a life and then, however unwillingly, starting over: finding another husband, bearing and raising children while simultaneously devising her own separate pursuits—all that, Nora expects, takes it out of a woman, although no doubt adds it back also.

She has no picture of what Lynn's second husband would be like. As unlike Philip as possible, probably.

She will call Lynn from the embrace of the living-room sofa, a lumbering legacy from her own childhood. Nora's mother and long-lost father bought it when they married, that's how old it is. It's been reupholstered several times, currently in a worn, heavy maroon that Philip was planning to tackle one day soon when he could grab time from his paid labours. Nora inherited it from her mother, who left all her possessions to her only daughter, her only child, and even Philip judged it a worthy piece, while considering much else Nora inherited junky and ugly and fit only for auction and scrap. Which was true. Nora's mother took up hairdressing, she scraped by, she raised her daughter with a reasonable minimum of forlornness and martyrdom, she had a few relatively more cheerful years on her own after Nora left home, she got breast cancer, then bone cancer, then died.

Not much room in a life story like that for acquiring furnishings that would meet Philip's standards.

Nora isn't dim-witted, she realizes the ways she more resembles her footloose father than her mother; or perhaps most resembles the woman who ran off with her father before Nora was old enough to remember him. It's a choice, which part to play, and who wants to be pitiful? Anyway, those were different times. Nora's mother did not have Lynn's freedom and possibilities, her many advantages when it came to re-creating a life after loss.

For all Nora knows, her father's dead, too. When her mother died, Nora did not even consider trying to locate him. She was unforgiving. If he didn't care they were alive, he had no right to know if they died.

Calling Lynn is different.

"Hello?" says a voice Nora has not heard for years, but which is immediately, surprisingly familiar. Nora's own voice has grown huskier, while Lynn's sounds freakishly youthful. There's that memory of Lynn playing basketball in high school, of watching her loop balls off her fingertips into high-up, distant baskets.

Later memories are of less grace.

"Lynn, it's Nora. I hope this isn't a bad time to call, but I have something to tell you. Are you alone?" She only means that if it's not a bad time for Lynn now, it may be in a moment, and so is there someone around to comfort her, or subdue her, or simply be witness to fresh news from history stepping into her household? Nora intends rectitude, even kindness, she certainly doesn't mean to sound threatening.

She hears Lynn take a deep breath. "Nora," she says. Then, flatly, "What do you want?"

"It's about Philip."

"Yes, well, it would have to be, wouldn't it?" Brisk, yes. Cool, only to be expected. Bitter, still? Could Lynn sustain bitterness all these years, even after she must have gotten everything she could have wanted, excluding Philip, and must now, in middle age, surely be in a mood for counting her blessings? "What about him?"

There's a limited number of ways to put this. "I'm afraid"—and so Nora suddenly is, having finally to say words she has been finding unsayable—"that he's dead. He died in the night."

There's a long pause. "Last night?" as if time might be the point.

"The night before. I found him when I woke up yesterday morning." Is it tactless to remind Lynn that it's Nora who has wakened beside Philip for nearly two decades? Surely not.

"I see," Lynn says finally. Then, "What happened?"

For an instant Nora thinks Lynn is asking what she herself did upon discovering Philip. She almost says, *Well, I screamed, and I jumped out of bed*. That would be stupid. "His heart, I imagine. I'm not sure. They've done an autopsy, but I don't know the results yet, although I'll maybe hear later today." Because it occurs to her that that's probably information Sophie will be bringing back from the funeral home. "Some kind of natural cause, anyway. Otherwise I would have heard. This isn't a friendly town any more."

"So I understand." Of course Lynn will know what's gone on here. The place, and Nora, were in the newspapers, on TV and cheesy radio talk shows—even a dignified, professorial Lynn would have tuned in for the happy thrill of all that. "You mean they've looked into whether you killed him and decided you didn't?"

That's blunt. "More or less."

"So why are you calling?"

Why indeed? "Just because I thought you should know. That you'd want to be told, even though it's been a long time. But maybe you don't. Anyway, I decided to. It's hard to know the right thing to do." That didn't come out well; it sounded pathetic, and too much like a plea.

"Yes, isn't it. At least, I imagine it is. For someone who isn't used to taking the right thing to do into account, I expect it's difficult to know how to begin."

Nora considers hanging up. Honest to God—after seventeen years! "What I meant was, I didn't know if you'd care or not. I'm a little surprised. It sounds as if you still do." She remembers more clearly now that Lynn never grew quiet, or acquiescent, and eventually Philip had to just throw up his hands and walk off. "I guess I thought it might matter to you because there was a time you cared about him." She will not say the word *love*. "Anyway, haven't you had what you wanted? Children, after all, that must be a good result of what happened."

"Well, you know, it's not as if I wouldn't have had children with him as well, although I suppose not these particular children." Lynn has persuaded herself, then, that Philip would have changed his mind, or could have been tricked? "Still, you're right, I have a fine life. In fact, I live just as well as I know how to. But in case you're wondering"—how swiftly a voice acquires long fingernails—"big betrayals do have their effects. In case you don't know, they colour everything. Or shadow everything. You never feel safe again. Naturally I blame him for that. You, too, of course." She sounds as if she's been mulling and refining those words for the entire seventeen years. If so, how impatiently she must have waited for her chance to say them.

At last, Lynn's lucky day.

"I'm sorry you feel that way." Nora would like to be clear, she would like there to be no misunderstanding, it would be too bad to imply what she doesn't mean or believe. "That *sorry* is a regret, you understand. It wouldn't be true to apologize."

"Oh, I know there'd be no apology. If there wasn't one then, there wouldn't be one now, would there? Anyway, as you say, I have a good life so who gives a shit?"

Nora and Philip lay, damp and pleased, in her narrow bed over the sandwich and variety store. One of his arms was around her, the other thrown over his eyes. She was curved into his body, where she fit, she thought, nicely, admiring the stretch of his long, satisfied thigh. "Are we serious?" he asked. "I feel serious."

Nora tensed. "I do, too."

"Then I'll have to tell Lynn." Nora nodded so that he would be able to feel her head moving up and down on his chest: assenting. In this position he could not see, and she did not mention, her flaring up of alarm. There would be repercussions. She was agreeing to something rather larger than pleasure.

"I'm a little scared."

"It's my responsibility. I'll take care of it."

That wasn't quite what she'd meant but those words were good, too: that he cared so much; that he would be responsible; that as he said then, as they said often in those days, "I love you."

"When it's done, we can start over." By which she understood him to mean he had taken a wrong turn, a couple of wrong turns, and now intended to right himself. This would include not only Nora instead of Lynn, but striking out on his own instead of working for a furniture maker who, as he said, "has taught me a lot, but cuts corners. I know how to do better myself now."

She thought of him as a surprising, unlooked-for gift who had presented himself all unwrapped. He admired her, he said, in part because she had courage of a sort he could recognize, which was not the leaping off cliffs or diving into deep waters sort. "You don't give in. You do exactly what you see." He was referring to Nora's work, and was somewhat wrong. She has never done exactly what she sees. Also, he said, "I love making love with you. We go well together. That means something, don't you think?" Yes, she did. Going well together had myriad meanings, bodies among them.

Imagine the miracle of life's sudden perfections! She had a gallery, she was working with concentration towards the particular goal of a show at that gallery, and on top of all that, joy enough on its own, this splendid specimen of a man was willing to change his life utterly, mainly for her. She was entirely triumphant in every respect. She hears now the voice of the woman over whom she once triumphed. What was that for? Something not nice, slightly rancid. "I'm sorry," Nora says again. "He wasn't a bad man. It was love." She shrugs, although realizing Lynn cannot see her. "What do you think people should do about that?" Because that's the question, isn't it?

Not to Lynn. "I think people should dig deeper. They ought to try harder. It's not supposed to be easy. We're not supposed to give up. That's what I think."

How stern, and inhuman, and unnecessary.

"He knew that. He didn't give up. We had years, and it wasn't all easy." Not everything is a matter of pledging love in a narrow bed over a sandwich and variety store. People have to stand up. They must traverse their days. They have to remake their affections over and over. They make large decisions—to move here; to choose Philip to have a vasectomy rather than have Nora undergo actual surgery; to do their work in roughly the same space but apart, so that they would always be together but not. There's the world, too: bankers, for instance—the huge deep breaths it took, buying this place, sleepless nights, frozen days. And buyers and, more irritatingly, critics of art, and questions of who does the shopping, issues of cash flow and the merits and demerits of art, artistry, craft, as well as discussions of limits. In Philip's work, was it still remotely all right to help destroy distant forests by working with teak, for example, or was that more or less as wrong as importing ivory? Or recently, how much, in Nora's work, might be excessive, or negative, or over-whelming, or defensible in content and impact? More gener-ally, how about famine, how about war and human brutality (as seen on TV and in newspapers as well as, in the past few years, from Sophie), and other sorts of current affairs—these were interesting, sometimes crucial, passionate conversations.

Others could be less interesting, although also passionate: did Philip have to play poker *every* Thursday night and go out drinking two or three other evenings, did Nora *need* to have Beth living here to accomplish her purpose—all the business of what Lynn seems to call *digging deeper, trying harder.*

All that, plus neglecting to go fuck often enough in the woods.

"He's dead, you know," Nora says, wondering still at these impossible words. "Nobody's safe. Nothing's secure. It isn't just you." She is suddenly angry again. What is this girlish notion that if not for Philip and Nora, Lynn would have peacefully and uninterruptedly marched and drifted through all these years, safe and secure? *Grow up,* she would like to say. *Life is full of surprises, and often enough they're not safe ones.* "There's all kinds of loyalty after all. And betrayal."

Anger, not really with Lynn, can be the only reason she bothers to say this. At best, she and Lynn were only acquain-tances. When they encountered each other in that coffee

shop down the street from Max and Lily's gallery, Lynn did
not begin to understand Nora's pride and excitement; just as
Nora, to be fair, found Lynn's recitation of her satisfactions
banal. If Lynn doesn't know for herself that betrayal may take
a number of forms, as does loyalty, Nora's words will tell her
nothing, even though over time these matters surely become
delicate and apparent. Say Philip has been disloyal in some
ways—maybe with Sophie if that niggle of doubt amounts to
anything, or with any number of women, all unknown, over
any number of years—yes, that would hurt badly, that would
count big. That could push Nora a considerable distance
towards resentment, aggrievement, some tone of voice not
unlike Lynn's. But it counts also that at the worst moments of
public tumult he said, "Fuck 'em, you do what you want," as
if it could be no other way. He insisted on staying in this
awful town, but he also stood beside her, sat beside her, lay
beside her, held her up, held her close. He not only told
reporters, when asked for his views on events, that his wife
had a perfectly legitimate outlook that she was perfectly free
to express in her work, but also bought them drinks, a jolly-
ing influence. He scrubbed and painted meticulously over
scrawled words on the front fence.

There is very little point in relating these excellent qualities of Philip's to Lynn. Nora recalls, belatedly, that this
woman took scissors to Philip's clothes before tossing them
onto the sidewalk in front of that recently purchased stuc-
coed little rowhouse; that she ruined a pair of tables he was
working on by carving his initials deep into them and then
carving deeper Xs through them; that she made a number of
menacing, hissing, middle-of-the-night phone calls to Nora's
apartment; that once she stood on the street below screaming upwards, "Die, bitch, die," at the top of her lungs.

Pride or love? At any rate, so much drama.

So much grief.

This is probably not a good time to ask Lynn if she, too, found some satisfaction in those outbursts of hers. Because, to tell the truth, Nora did. At the time they seemed to round out and confirm the amazing, true, real emotions floating around her and Philip, adding a spicy ingredient that not every romantic relationship gets to savour or for that matter endure.

It's not impossible that Lynn enjoyed becoming, for a time, a ripper, a hurler, a hisser, a screamer.

They were young. It seemed worth the trouble.

It was.

Die, bitch, die? "That's it," said Philip, and stomped downstairs to confront Lynn. Who went away weeping, don't forget that either.

"I'm sorry," Nora says helplessly and for the third time. "I just wanted to tell you. I thought it was something you ought to know."

"When's the funeral?"

Surely Lynn wouldn't attend, to add yet another layer of unpleasantness to an already unpleasant event. "Tomorrow, I hope. Here, at a place called Anderson and Sons Funeral Home. Why, did you want to come?"

"I can't see why I would. But there's no RSVP required anyway, I imagine?"

"Not at all. Whatever you decide. The more the merrier," Nora says, and puts down the phone.

The more the merrier? What a thing.

"I love you," Philip used to breathe into Nora's hair and into her breasts and belly and thighs, and she believes that he did. But already, she sees, she grows accustomed to the past tense. What if her memory works as selectively and capriciously as Lynn's? What if what she learns is the forgetting of delight? What if she forgets to remember Philip's laughter and whisperings, what if the rawness of his quick rages fades, along with the light touch of his breath, his tongue, on her throat, her shoulders—people must forget all sorts of things in sheer self-defence.

If they forget, how do they account for the resulting gaps in their lives, years during which they were apparently talking to air, embracing space, reaching out to touch vacuums?

Or the other risk, like Lynn's creation of something that didn't exist in place of something that did. As if it wouldn't have been a far larger betrayal if Philip had stayed with her, on and on, *digging deeper, trying harder*. At least be truthful, that's Nora's rule. At very least, be where you want to be.

She hopes that's where Philip was. It's a terrible thing not to know absolutely, and now she can't ask. They've been talking for seventeen years, she supposed they could talk on for ever, she was obliviously counting on time. If he were here now, she could recite to him what she told Lynn, and what Lynn had to say, and how she heard Lynn's voice and its various tones. *The more the merrier*, he would mock, tickled or cross.

On occasion, before first Sophie and then Beth arrived, she and Philip fell together on this ancient sofa and pounded out with their own merry lust the contaminated sorrows of Nora's parents: the false hopes with which it was chosen to furnish the beginnings of that other long-lost, upended marriage. From her corner now, she can see Philip's eyes lighting with mischief, she sees his shoulders, his zippers, his buttons, his thighs, his penis soaring up into interest and view. On the next cushion, right here, is one place all this occurs. The shock of permanent absence, that sharp lightning strike sizzling through tendons and bones, crackles right out through her toes again, making her jerk back, a repeated reflex of rejection. *Never again?*

From her bedroom to this old piece of upholstered furniture, even the insides of the house are turning against her, baring their teeth, inviting grief indoors that was previously barricaded beyond the walls, outside the gate where those horrible villagers lurk. She is trapped between nothing good out there and now nothing good in here either.

What do those villagers—all right, townspeople, some of them—see from their uphill perspective? Blasphemy, evidently. Sacrilege and heresy. A taunting invitation to the lighting of torches. A mob of the berserk; but then, that's what mobs are—a person here, a person there, there and there, whipped into a single-celled, single-minded, dangerous creature.

If there were many residents resistant to mobbery, they were mainly mute, and so not very brave. Which is its own kind of sin. Or perhaps Nora didn't hear them, another sort of sin.

Her mistake was to underestimate the power of image; an especially unfortunate lapse, given her faith in the power of image. Walk into a room, she likes to think, and see a painting, or a sculpture, or even some less-defined piece that's intended as art, and if it's any good, bam!—there's an impression, an emotion, an idea, a frank point of view.

Evidently she failed to take into proper account the fierce power of the negative bam.

Or she just didn't care. That came to be more or less Philip's view, although he was mainly restrained in expressing it, and was more protective than could reasonably be expected. Although she was not particularly reasonable on the subject.

They walked, a couple of years ago, she and Philip, into
the opening of a sculpture show. They were acquaintances
of the sculptor and his work, and were happy to leave the
house in Sophie's good hands while they took a weekend
away in the city. It was a relatively casual event—Nora recalls
wearing black trousers and a loose blue blouse she might have
worn anywhere—but there, in the close-packed, chattering
gallery crowd, was Beth: in long eggshell dress with translu-
cent pale green beadwork at the throat, carrying a glass of red
wine. She looked perfectly vacant. Untouched and untouch-
able, alert but remote. Anyone can be beautiful; there was
some other factor at play that kept Nora manoeuvring to
hold her in view. Pictures came to mind, a set of images, a
meandering stream of notions that had something to do with
Beth's compelling, faint aroma of sorrow; those bones ready
for shifting, skin ripe for translation.

Nora couldn't explain even to Philip why she wanted Beth
here when she'd never needed or used a model similarly
before. He said finally, "I don't know what you see in her, but
I guess if it's what you want, go ahead. What's one more?"
When they already had Sophie, he meant. How hard could he
argue, anyway, when he was himself a beneficiary of Nora's
trust in first glances?

He would have preferred Beth at least to return to a room
or an apartment elsewhere in town at the end of each day,
but that would have been too expensive even if Beth had
agreed to so isolated an existence. Eventually it might not
have even been safe. As it was, it was strange that Beth could
just pack up and move in, as if she had no other life. Maybe
she didn't, she's never said, but how is that possible?

Beth is useful, beautiful, malleable and obedient, and this
is what Nora's hands and Beth's body have together created:

Beth hanging, gangly and tiny-titted, from a metallic cross, fine bubbly blonde hair obscuring her face, tendons straining in her thin arms, blood trickling down her gaunt thighs and calves, dribbling in drops of crimson fabric off the tips of her painted toes.

Beth emerging baffled, and triumphantly nude, from the dark gaping mouth of a cave. She is steadying herself with a hand braced on a perfectly oval grey rock, the other hand trailing white chiffon (real white chiffon, embedded with a hundred, two hundred glittery sequins) that drapes and falls clear out of the frame.

Beth standing at the summit of a great hill, a huge piece, her arms spread outwards, rich bright yellow and red and green gown (strips of real silk) cascading downwards, enveloping the hill and stitched intricately with tiny figures of hopeful people gazing upwards, the word BLESSED embroidered in large, loose, pale yellow stitches in the low right-hand corner, near the flourish of Nora's signature.

Beth at a feast with a row of lipsticked and eyeshadowed and rouged women of various colours wearing variously embroidered gowns (real fabric, real embroidery) leaning into each other at a long table, some laughing, some solemn, some plain and some lovely, with one off to the left in throat-to-ankle black velvet looking away from the rest. On the table, carved on its edges with veiled, leaping dancers, a splendid array of pastas and sauces, green and chickpea and bean salads, light and dark breads, and right in the centre a huge, chocolate-iced cake. Also in the centre the gaunt, remote Beth-figure standing, raising a mirror-sparkling crystal (real mirror, real crystal) glass of red wine. Or blood.

Two men, their long, perfectly sloped, identical, bent backs to the viewer, washing Beth's feet with rags. The backs

are Philip's, each spiny knob and carved muscle detailed from
years of scrutiny and memory. Beth wears one of her own
loose, mid-calf-length dresses, a soft yellow one hiked high on
her thighs. Her legs are spread wide so that one foot rests in
the hand of each man. Her head is thrown back, her eyes are
closed, her lips curve gently upwards in pleasure.

All of this was slow and delicate work. From Beth's perspective, possibly arduous sometimes, perhaps boring. She
was perfectly flexible, at any rate, and perfectly patient.

Only those few pieces to trigger such tumult! Philip said
it at least ought to please Nora that she became famous; or
infamous. So did the town. Perhaps by now they're symbiotic,
like those birds that catch bug-meals and long rides aboard
hippos, hippos that are cleaned and groomed by the birds.

Outrage and offence, another outbreak of words along the
lines of "Die, bitch, die" outside her windows—whatever happened to love and redemption? So old testament, rather than
new; like furious old wife rather than hopeful new one.

Philip said, "They think you're ridiculing what they
believe, and that makes them feel threatened, which makes
them angry, and then they lash out."

So?

"So of course I'm not saying they're right, I'm just saying
even if they're crazy, *we're* not. It shouldn't be as hard for us
to understand them as it is the other way round." Because
they, he and she, were smart and sane, he was suggesting. Nora
did not see it that way. She thought he might want to move
past nostalgia for happy, innocent childhood summers. "It's
not nostalgia," he snapped, sensitive, it appeared, on the point.

Still, he was good about cleaning and repainting the fence
after the "sluts" and "whores" and "blasphemers" and "Jezebels"
began to appear overnight. And he was very good about

saying, "You just do what you do and don't worry. It'll never be really dangerous, nobody would do any real harm while I'm around." Big, gregarious Philip, fellow drinker, old pal, grown child, good guy. Except he's not around any more, is he?

Even if they are short of benevolence, why aren't more people at least curious? Philip was, Nora is: *If this, does that follow?* And *What happens if you look at it this way?*

What happens if it turns out a whole noisy portion of humans doesn't like questions at all, only answers, and doesn't care for alternative views?

Not much that's good, it appears.

Nothing has happened, really, since early spring. The nine-day wonder died down; and anyway, the series is done. Certainly Beth's purpose here is finished, and it's well past time for her to move on. As Philip pointed out several times. "I'll get to it," Nora promised. "It's hard, though. She's no trouble, and I don't know where she'd go." Nora can sound kinder than she is. Does she by any chance actually contain a sliver of new testament–type human trying to get out, the same way fat people are said to have thin ones clamouring for an exit?

"Who cares where she goes?" Philip said. "She has to go somewhere sometime. If you're having trouble, ask her to whip you up a tea that works for evictions."

Yes, the tea thing does get on people's nerves. And Philip could be as soft as a cushion or as hard as the frame of one of his chairs.

In the morning he smelled first of sleep. Then of soap, spicy and sharp. By noon his scent was dusty and wood-grained, fresh in its way as a forest. By nightfall, sweaty. By the time he rolled into bed, all that and often beery and smoky as well, the full range of his day was contained in his skin. Nora doesn't know how to locate a man's scent on canvas. He frowns, he tilts his head back and laughs.

Nora rises up from the enemy sofa.

This time, once upstairs there's no invisible hand keeping her out of her bedroom. She slams the door behind her, although more by mistake than from temper. The force of the slam makes the old windows shift in their frames; the sound rings a bell. She has done this before, and with temper. At Philip, intent on going out, never mind what she wanted or said.

"How can you drink with those people?"

"First of all they're my friends, second of all they're not *those people*, and lastly I don't intend to hide away in this house or change doing what pleases me."

So, slam!

Softer sounds, too. A grunting noise every time—for years, every time!—he buttoned his pants. It wasn't exactly an irritating sound, only noticeable. Also the huge, happy exhalation when at the end of the day he threw himself into bed, glad to be there.

On their shared dresser top, he keeps only a black comb and a hairbrush—look, there's a few of his mostly dark hairs, a few grey, caught in the brush—and a small box containing a jumble of jewellery debris, including cufflinks for those rare occasions when that sort of dressing up was required. "Shit, goddamn things," he said, wrestling till Nora stepped up to fasten them for him; his wrists dusted with tempting male hairs.

Sometimes she helped tie his ties, too.

His ties are slung around a hanger in his side of the closet. He only has half a dozen because what use are they to a man who works with his hands and dislikes feeling restrained?

"Bibs for men" he called them, complaining of strangulation. He hasn't bought a new tie since he and Nora were married. "I have enough to last me a lifetime," he said, and so, it turns out, he did.

She lays them out on the bed. They are multicoloured, and of several widths and fabrics.

He has those two aging dark suits she mentioned to Sophie. They are not interesting, and can be given away. The shirts, though—the white, pale yellow, the blue, the cotton, the linen, the flannels—she'll keep these. She pulls them from their hangers and folds them, too, on the bed. There is a Philip-scent to even the freshly washed ones, of soap and sawdust and something else more elusively his.

She dumps the contents of his bureau drawers in a great pile on the floor, a litter of socks and underwear, folded sweaters, coiled belts, more work shirts of the plaid flannel variety. In their first days together, it didn't occur to him to do his own laundry. "It's not magic, you know," she told him. "Fairy hands don't take it away in the night and return it by morning." They had all sorts of household chores to sort out between them. Not without resistance, not without complaint, they found a system for vacuuming, getting meals, clearing up, doing laundry, doing business. Then they found Sophie. Fairy hands.

Nora can't see putting out only her own laundry for Sophie to do. They're in a new balance now.

What a mess of *stuff*, his possessions all over the floor and the bed. The ties, shirts, sweaters and some of the underwear she gathers up in her arms and staggers off down the hall. In her studio there are many overflowing baskets for potentially useful spare materials, scraps.

Too sudden? Of course. Maybe. Who's to say?

In the studio what is already piled up and scattered—paints, brushes, embroidery threads, needles and glues, beads in jars and beads that have rolled into corners, heaps of displaced and unsorted fabrics, easels here, canvases there—looks chaotic. Disorder easily becomes the normal state of a large room belonging to only one person. This is the one space in the house that is Nora's.

Except, she guesses, the whole house is hers now.

Is there a way to capture vacancy? To depict desolation?

It's not so much the literal content of a sketch or a painting that's important, as intention and style. Anyone can do thunder and lightning, shock, disaster, despair. It's the selection of materials, the relationship of one thing to another, the singular eye, Nora's particular interpretation and touch, not anyone else's, that make all the difference.

So she picks up a sketchpad and pencil, and tosses a few shirts on the floor, and the ties, and begins—because this is all she can think of to do—tracing fast and slowly, carelessly and intently, lightly or with precise, concentrated detail, page after page, for quite a long time, the lines and wrinkles and discarded shapes of his absence.

Ten

The outdoors is a foreign country to Beth. The light seems to her either garish or contrastingly dull and diffuse, and in either case damaging to people like her, with their lives in their skins. The air is unpredictable and unfamiliar as well, causing her to sniff warily, trying to distinguish harmless from hostile like a small, tender animal. What is unknown is unnerving, and Beth has never in her whole life been familiar with the world beyond walls and doors. Even when she was a child, occasions to frolic in the open air did not much arise. So it's not surprising if stepping outside now, all by herself, causes her heart to leap a few times in anxious distress.

It's been fine living here, staying in, letting Nora bend and display her at will, turning her, in a way, into someone else altogether. Beth doesn't need to know if the town is a good or a bad place, and doesn't especially care except for how upset people got, upsetting Nora, and then a few times Beth herself was scared by raised, angry voices. But mostly Sophie takes care of daily necessities, and Nora and Philip have been in charge, and even in the bad times Beth was able to stay— Nora told her to stay—pretty much to herself, out of sight.

This will now end. But—here's another spin on second days—what prospects instead!

At the front gate one turns left to follow the street slightly downhill into town, or one turns right onto what, within steps, becomes a highway into the country. Sophie would have gone left at the front gate, towards the funeral home, carrying the blue gym bag with Philip's clothes. Beth, then, will turn right. She is restless in ways beyond the reaches of teas. Mainly, though, she's stepping out in order to keep speechless; because who knows what would come out of her mouth if she started talking? To Nora, she means.

Besides, the loud slam of Nora's bedroom door made it perfectly clear she prefers being alone. That's all right. Except it means that for once being inside is too weird; really quiet, and lonesome. The thing about living with three other people is that usually a person's only alone if she wants to be, and there's almost always some rustle or step or voice that says at least somebody's around. It's not that Beth misses Philip, not at all, but she does find herself missing the way the house worked inside itself, and sounded, and smelled, up until yesterday morning.

The highway is fairly busy, a two-lane route much used by trucks, so to be safe Beth has to walk as far as possible off it, on gravel or in the long grass between the gravel part and the slope to the ditch alongside. Everything's kind of shrunk in the heat. What were probably bright orange wild lilies a couple of weeks ago are now bald, brittle stalks. The ditch is empty of water. She must take care not to go so far she can't comfortably get back. Thin sandals aren't exactly good walking shoes. Transports roar past, reminding her fleetingly of her father, who repaired such trucks for a living. One, a silvery tanker, announces on its side that its rounded, steely belly holds milk. Another, its separate compartments open to the air, is taking chickens someplace. That's sad, all those birds crammed together, off on a trip, no choice in the matter and no good ending to their journey either.

Cars aren't so bad, but these occasional trucks whip up the flimsy, fly-away skirt of her dress, green today with tiny white dots but in the same style, as are most of her dresses, as yesterday's fluttery calf-length pewtery one. She wishes for a hat: one of those broad-brimmed kinds you see in movies, English movies, ladies strolling or gardening, sheltering their skin. Beth feels exposed and vulnerable to drying up, like the ditch, or the lilies.

If Nora gets pictures in her head, so does Beth. *Impulse control:* such a dry term, as if its very dullness has an effect. And maybe it does. "Take a hundred deep breaths," they used to tell her. "Count and concentrate." There are lots and lots of ways to practise. Counting a hundred breaths is one, because by the time you've done that the urgency of the impulse, if not always the current desire itself, should have vanished. Beth is pleased to have thought up for herself the idea of coming out here, removing herself from temptation altogether. Not to mention escaping that atmosphere that feels darker today, and lower, and sort of airless as well.

Now Beth sees that besides counting breaths for calm and restraint, it's also possible to concentrate on her feet and their surroundings: the grasses and tiny white and yellow sticking-up flowers and little purplish ground-crawling ones. A good number of wild plants—burdock, dandelion, chickweed—are harvestable for teas. They heal or hearten, cure or calm, oh, there are all sorts of ways to use ingredients fresh from the ground, and if Beth had brought her new encyclopedia of useful plants and herbs with her, she could have sat by the roadside and made a study of what's probably right here at hand. She has never done this and now it may be too late. What she knows about the effects and components of teas comes from books, with their descriptions and recipes, their photographs and drawings of particular plants, good for this, useful for that. This is how she has learned that some teas require flowers, some roots, others leaves, and that some ingredients are supposed to be boiled down to essences while others must be hung up to dry.

It's all really complicated, page after page and book after book of variations and consequences. Not easy, learning all that, but she had, as far as she knew then, all the time in the world, and if it turned out she didn't have quite that much, still there were several years with little else to do except listen to sad voices or angry ones, and hear a good deal about *impulse control*, and try to tune everything out with nicer words like *infusion*.

Out here, though, it becomes obvious that even so much study, and all those drawings and instructions, are vastly different from being in the midst of the actual greenery, which is more mixed up and untidier than it is on a page. How did people ever figure out what was safe and what wasn't? Never mind what should be boiled and what must be dried? It had to be trial and error. Error would be terrible, but maybe back in those days individual lives weren't so important and nobody especially cared.

Beth has been thinking recently about asking for some space of her own, maybe a corner of the kitchen or of Nora's glassy studio, to grow some of her own herbs. Just a little garden of pots, nothing grand or wild. She was thinking this should be her next step just because real experts don't do what she does, which is mail-order for ingredients and when they arrive, store them in jars in the fridge and in a row at the back of the kitchen counter. Now any kind of herb garden anyplace is most likely out of the question. A missed opportunity? A matter for regret? Hard to say. Everything's going to be different.

It already is different. Look where she is, walking in the air and light of the countryside, all by herself!

Sophie wouldn't have been nice anyway about Beth using the kitchen to grow stuff, or about her bringing in armloads of things like burdock for cooking or drying. Sophie is sarcastic enough already about the teas Beth makes with the ingredients from her tidy jars. To tell the truth, Nora's not always kind either, but Nora's an artist and gets to have big unpredictable moods. Because whether they're good moods or bad ones, she makes something with them, they don't go to waste; kind of like Beth studying teas: making something out of large events, and fortunately, like Nora, something good. Beth perceives troubles and ailments and honestly does the best she can to alleviate them, if not always cure.

Sophie, on the other hand, has no excuse. She's just a servant, like a hotel maid, and so what if she's seen things other people have not? She'll go on about the homeless and landless and stateless and hungry and brutalized and what they're owed by everyone else as if all that isn't just luck, like getting a good judge or a bad judge at a pageant. Good luck, bad luck. Karma, even, who's to say the homeless and landless and stateless and hungry and brutalized didn't earn their disasters in previous lives? You never know, is what Beth thinks. Sophie seems to believe she's entitled to look down her nose at a lot of people, but especially Beth just because Beth is beautiful, even though Sophie herself most likely isn't a truly good person either. With Philip, for instance. That wasn't good, if it's true.

Beth could shut Sophie up in a sentence if she wanted to. That's a nice, secret kind of power to have, the kind that comes from silence, and not correcting wrong impressions. Sophie doesn't know much about Beth. Neither does anyone else. Could Beth tell even Nora? No, the most wonderful person in the world would have to be inside every minute, each smell, word and sound, to know. Beth can't even properly explain to herself, but she doesn't have to. Doesn't care to. "What's done is done," her mother used to say if Beth failed to come first, second or even third, "We'll do better next time." *What's done is done* is a good motto in some situations.

The mothers always drank tea, plus coffee and wine, depending. The girls mainly drank bottled water, although sometimes unsweetened juices. Mothers could eat what they wanted, but not the girls.

Later, when the time came when plates were full and Beth could eat as much as she felt like, the food was unappealing, and she wasn't hungry. She hasn't been hungry for years, really. So her sense-memories aren't tastes, they're smells and sounds, sweetish and sticky: hairsprays and colognes and perfumes and powders and skin creams, voices rising high with tension, soft and sugary with praise and encouragement. "You were great," girls, Beth included, told each other. And, "I love you in that dress," and, "Oh, I wish I could wear that colour," and so on. Friendships, maybe they were friendships, could be passionately real in their way, if sometimes brief, and girls did a lot of fun things together, like playing Hearts and Crazy Eights and euchre while they waited for this and that, and telling each other's fortunes with Tarot decks and by examining palms. But everyone knew what the point was, which was winning not just tiaras or sashes or even big cheques, but a long, slim, creamy leg up on the future.

Such hopes, such dreams, such possibilities! Others might aim, or say they aimed, to be physicists, teachers, doctors or diplomats. "You," said Beth's mother, "you have your special beauty. More special than anyone's."

A person can look and look into mirrors and see their own individual features, but it's still hard to detect a whole magic effect.

Beth remembers light, too: its sudden and radical shifts. There was the sharp glare of dressing rooms, for fixing or camouflaging last-minute flaws, a loosened strap, hinted zit; then the blackened spaces behind curtains, all anxious whispers and jitterings in the dark; and finally the blinding radiance of the stage, the stroll, the turn, the jut, the easy, brilliant smile. Also, out on the road, the darkness of highways between cities at night, broken by endless white lines and an occasional river of headlights; departures at dawn, sudden sun rearing up into the eyes. Driving into the light, leaving light behind.

Between these extremities, accidental days and weeks of grey: regular life, Beth supposed, for those not like herself. There were weeks when she woke and went to sleep in her own bed in her own little pink-painted room, heading off to school in the mornings. How did the other girls in the pageants and contests find the time and information to come up with desires like *physicist, doctor, diplomat?* But maybe those were as false as Beth's aim to carry music to the world's children. She dropped in and out of school to the tune of more essential demands, inaudible to anyone but herself and her mother. "Beth has a larger destiny," her mother told irritable or maybe worried teachers. "She does her lessons while we're away, doesn't she? Can she read? Can she write? Can she do arithmetic?" Yes, she could. "Then what's the problem?"

If Beth wasn't always in class long enough to study a novel or a play right to the end, she could still finish reading it if she wanted to, or if she needed to turn out some kind of paper for her long-distance homework. If the idea of algebra's unknown X was intriguing, there'd be time when she was old, maybe thirty, to look into its qualities, if she still cared. For the moment, her mother said, "Take advantage of what you have while you have it. I wish I'd realized that."

Beth wouldn't want to be bitter later on, angry about lost opportunities.

Now she hears, *while you have it.* That must have passed her by at the time.

At the time Beth's particular kind of rarefied, upper-atmosphere beauty had high purposes, nothing as commonplace as attracting the attentions of boys, who anyway, when she was at school, steered clear of her and certainly did not call her for dates; as if she scared them. Well, girls, too. It's not that they were friendly or unfriendly, more that they drew apart when she appeared. She walked as if she wore books on her head, or tiaras. She didn't care. She was beyond them. She went places, she won things, she had opportunities and gifts they could not dream of, just as her mother said.

How far has she walked? Gravel pokes into these thin sandal soles. There's so much bright green and bright blue out here. Funny how those colours work together outside, but otherwise not. Like, you wouldn't paint a room in bright green and bright blue, and a dress in exactly these shades would look tacky. "No class," as her mother said sometimes, looking over Beth's competition.

There was her mother: adjusting hems and hair, breathing hope and ambition, back at the wheel, driving them on.

Later smells and sounds were harsh and metallic. That was

in the time of disinfectants and unpampered bodies, and voices that yelled, wept and whimpered; others that comforted, commanded and advised *impulse control*. The point is—the point is, this air out here is starting to smell gentle to Beth, this light begins to feel kind. The sounds aren't so strange, just occasional traffic and birds and invisible rustlings through grass.

Or it could be she's excited. Happily on edge. On the brink of something joyful. Maybe this is how her mother felt, driving home full of prospects and plans, talking about decisions that would need to be made soon.

Everybody's got a story—how obvious, how banal. Beth, too, although she keeps hers to herself, and tucked far back in her mind. It's also true that the elisions and collisions of individual stories create and break love and care, they lead to murder, rape, slaughter and war, as Sophie enjoys pointing out, and also to acts of generosity, kindness. Experiences and trajectories ricochet off each other, they take slow curves and sharp turns, they wreak confusion here, salvation there and—this is the hardest thing—there's no way to predict which detail or tiny decision may grow huge in its consequence.

There is, for instance, a way of seeing what happened with Beth and her mother as an outcome of failed air conditioning in their van on a summer day even hotter and more humid than this one. A mechanic who, for reasons of lassitude or incompetence or pressure in the plot of his own unknown story, fails to spot signs of an exhausted bit of equipment under the hood; which creates an excessive scratchiness of voice and mood in the overheated front seat during a long drive home from a pageant; which leads to—well, leads to catastrophe, really.

Or: in a longer-term view Beth's father's choice of careers repairing highway rigs like those now and then hurtling past her results in insufficient funds for plane fares except for Beth's and her mother's farthest-flung journeys, so that they must mainly travel by road with their mountains of luggage and garment bags.

Or: if at that one particular pageant Beth had lost instead of won, if she'd even come in second rather than first, that might have put a dent in her mother's hot, exhausting enthusiasms. An extra word or absent gesture, who knows what makes a difference? If, if—a multitude of slightly altered circumstances and moments, and that day would have gone entirely differently, and this day would not have arisen, Beth would not be picking her way over gravel along a rural roadside, examining the airy August light and promising weeds. She would be, at this moment, in some other place, maybe even some other country. She would never have caught Nora's eye, would not have wound up living with Nora and Philip and Sophie, shifting her limbs and expressions to Nora's commands.

This is just life, of course, the extraordinary luck of the draw, torrential water under the bridge.

The pageant at which Beth comes up once again the winner is a national one. The prizes are concrete and promising, and include a cheque for ten thousand dollars, and a full-length mink coat. This is big time. Beth bends and sweats under the weight of the coat, but her mother strokes it as if it's a lush, favoured pet. She tries it on, too. "So lovely," she says. "Such luxury."

"You keep it," says Beth. "It looks nice on you," although too tight all the way from her mother's shoulders on down.

This pageant has taken place five hundred and fifty kilometres from their home, via a complicated interplay of highways and roads. Heading home without air conditioning in the van, Beth is light-headed, her mother perspires, heat rises in shimmering rhythms off asphalt. "Oh dear," is her mother's view. "But it's only a few hours."

Beth is seventeen, a weary young winner, as well as spoiled, possibly, in unusual ways. Her mother is—what?—in her early fifties. Her waistline is failing her, she has chunky hips, only the buried bones of their resemblance remain. She has deep lines around her eyes, some of them probably from squinting for so many hours at so many highways. Brackets have formed at the sides of her mouth, and railway-track lines along her top lip. There's something tissuey about her cheeks, her throat is a river of small, choppy whitecaps. Flesh on her upper arms swings at each turn of the wheel. Beth is propped against the passenger door watching her, hearing her voice. She thinks her mother is old. She thinks her mother's very red lipstick and highlighted cheeks are overdone and also the wrong colours for the altered textures and shades of her skin. Beth can't imagine ever being that old, so far gone.

She wishes that instead of home, she was going someplace like a beach. With friends. She doesn't have the kind of friends that drive to beaches for happy days playing in water and sand. Well, she doesn't have any kind of friends, really. There's a commercial, Beth's probably seen it three dozen times in hotel rooms here and there, for some kind of beer or cooler or soft drink or juice. The product doesn't matter, the young men and young women playing volleyball in the sand do. They chase each other through dunes and water, they gather around a beach campfire at nightfall with their drinks, they look so pleased with themselves and each other, they've had a totally excellent day. They look like people who live like this just about every day.

Her mother says, "That coat is just stunning, don't you think? And the money's a good nest egg. I'm thinking, though, that we can't wait any longer, we need to get down to business right now." She means today, she says, or tomorrow. She speaks again of Beth's *gifts*, and of her *accomplishments*. She says, as she has said so often, "You are lucky. I wish I'd had your opportunities when I was your age." Instead, she married Beth's father when she was a year older than Beth, and commenced mourning her multitude of lost choices.

"Here's how I see it," she says. How she sees it is that they must decide, finally and absolutely, between pursuing ever-higher-level pageantry, aiming at scholarships, cars, clothes and jewellery, leading to any beauty-related career from advertising to acting; or diverging immediately towards high-end modelling, with its international glamour and travel, magazine covers, famous acquaintances. "I know your body isn't quite right for that, but it could be. The thing is, you're already nearly too old. Some girls are only fourteen, fifteen. So we really do have to decide right away."

None of this hopeful future, except perhaps its immediacy, comes new from her mother. That's why it must be the heat that helps turn Beth's stomach over. She watches her mother's face glowing with hope as well as humidity, her streaked hair piled carelessly up off her neck, damp wisps stuck to her forehead. Her hands on the steering wheel are scattered with tiny red heat-dots. She keeps picking at her white cotton blouse, pulling it away from the moist skin of her breasts. She hikes her light denim driving skirt higher. The skin above her knees looks crackled, like an old painting. The flesh of her thighs is dimpled and plump.

What is this old woman doing, living Beth's life in her hoarse, on-and-on voice?

Not that Beth has any better ideas.

Even Beth's mother is not indomitable, however, even she gets worn out, worn down. By the time they're pulling into the driveway of home, she is complaining of a violent headache. When she goes upstairs to grab a quick shower and to change her clothes and locate the Aspirin, Beth stays downstairs. "I'll make tea," she says, and it takes a while, but she does.

This is long before Beth makes a study of teas. She is not subtle or delicate in her preparation, but she is certainly blinded by insistent, irresistible, unexplainable, indefensible purpose. Impulse.

At the first sip, her mother's mouth curls radically. "Oh, Beth, this is terrible stuff, it's undrinkable, what on earth is it?"

"I know it doesn't taste good, but if you drink it down in one swallow, it'll fix you right up, I promise." And just like that, just because Beth says to, or because she doesn't think not to, Beth's mother does.

It's like watching a movie; about aliens, maybe. It involves some dissolution of edges and borders, as if her mother collapsing, heaving, to the floor is transformed from human form with all its crumplings and wrinklings and streaked hair and dotted flesh and bright lipstick into some other, unknown and unfamiliar, more wavery creature. All jellyfish and strange colours.

Beth looks away. She tilts her head back, turning her attention upwards.

Are there sounds? There must be. For sure there are smells.

"Oh, dear God," says Beth's father when he gets home from work. Beth hears that.

It doesn't seem to occur to him or to anyone, not even to the men who come in the ambulance, that anything about this is deliberate. Beth herself, they must suppose, is in shock, immobilized as she is in the kitchen, staring hard and determinedly up at the ceiling. They may be right about the shock. They take her arms and lead her outside and drive her to the hospital, too. She makes no resistance. Anyway, she's too slight to resist burly men. At the hospital, her mother goes one way, Beth another. In a very few hours various people arrive in Beth's hospital room wearing strange expressions. They talk and talk, to each other and to her.

Her father comes, too, several times. He is agitated. "Why?" he cries, but Beth cannot say. Also he asks, "What did she do?" as if he might, if it were explained properly, be able to rest blame on Beth's mother.

Beth doesn't have words. She is surprised, too. She'd thought, insofar as she thought at all, that it would be faster. Easier. And then—well, she hadn't supposed consequences, more just poof, a vanishing.

More particularly a silencing.

Who knew the contents of mouse-killer, even vigorously mixed with extra-strong tea, would be so stomach-wrenching, bowel-churning, lip-frothing?

Also, who knew they would be so immediately discernible inside the dead human body, which surely to God she never meant to be dead? Her awful, disastrous mistake. Somebody should have instructed her better about resisting swift unconsidered compulsions, and about consequences and flat, hard results, not just about skin-toning and blush, straight hems and dipping necklines, tiaras and sashes, mink coats and pretty speeches about the importance of music. But it seems nobody ever mentioned cause and effect, action and reaction.

Or if anyone did, she can't have been paying attention.

Once in, there's no out. She is steered here, driven there, finds herself in rooms painted ivory, rooms painted green, rooms painted grey, each with its own shape and formation of heavyweight furniture. People talk and talk, in excited high voices and dark, lower ones. Tones are harsh or wheedling or solicitous, faces are grim, or they smile in familiar, false ways. Sometimes men, sometimes women take her by the elbows, or urge her with hands in the small of her back, to move in this direction or that, stand up or sit down or lie down. Not even her father puts his arms around her.

So many words, all of them wrong.

What would be the right words?

There aren't any. This is why she mainly keeps silent. Let other people make what they will out of that.

In the last place, where there are so many different urgent and unhappy voices, Beth finds quiet in a small brown room of books. It's the pictures first: tendrils of stems, little flowers, fat leaves, pale, bulbous roots. Living things that are useful and silent and still. One thing leads to another, pictures to useful, silent, still words.

She sees what she did wrong, how unfortunately indelicate her blunt recipe was. A product of ignorance. Cruel and destructive.

She will not be so ignorant or cruel or destructive again.

She is, leaning astonishingly over these books, becoming *gifted;* she achieves some *accomplishment.*

There are particular hours when she has to go to other rooms, where people talk on and on about loss and responsibility and the likelihood or unlikelihood of further offence, and the importance of *impulse control* and its practices. They assess her in light of various symptoms of detachment, and urge confession, discussion, getting it *out of your system,* as if her act were a spirit that could be driven out, not truly part of herself.

Beth learns about holding on: to paragraphs and pictures of fat roots and thick leaves and unremarkable flowers.

And one day, having achieved, they say, a *more coherent sense of reality*, she is returned into the world. It's more or less true that she knows what she's done, even if she can't feel it. Or won't. It's not that she doesn't remember, she just doesn't care to. Anyway, her teas really are designed for good purposes. Once out, she gets to try actually making them. She practises and practises, observing each taste and every effect.

She finds work of a sort her mother never dreamed of, posing for artists and students. Naturally she has had to tell lies, there's a big gap of time in her history that must be accounted for. So she has padded her resumé with more pageants, more modelling, further triumphs on one stage and another than ever really occurred. She has even given herself a small role in a small movie, just as if her life had unfolded in a way recognizable from the overheated front seat of a van. "And then," she tends to explain, reaching truth at last as if truth were a far shore, "I met Nora and she had her ideas, and they seemed like something to try for a change."

So different have Nora's ideas been, casting the contorted Beth into earthly and heavenly representative of mythic sacrifice, compassion, redemption, celebration, grief and suffering, and so hidden has Beth been in Nora's household, even dodging, mainly successfully, most of the cameras that haunted them briefly, so absent has she been from that past and so present here, that she is now as remote as a fourth cousin from the girl who years ago walked gracefully and sang sweetly and spoke softly on stages and who carried home tro-

phies, tiaras and sashes and who then, in a radical alteration
of heart, poisoned her mother's most bitter tea.

How far has she come? Not too far, but it's time to head
back. The walk home is more boring than the way out. Once
a person's seen fields and weeds and ditches and trees and the
gravelled side of a highway, there's not much more to it.
Nature is pretty enough, and useful, but this distance down
the road it's mainly uncomfortable. Beth's sandal straps pinch
and rub, their soles give hardly any protection. Still, she can
go slowly, there's no need to hurry.

Careful, careful, patience, patience: precipitous action,
inattention to *impulse control*, that's what gets people in trouble. There are no rules against hope, though, there's nothing
to stop her, as she steps homewards, from constructing and
decorating her most perfect idea, picturing how she will
redeem, at the good and right moment, everything that
Philip's absence, his death, have made so wonderfully and
suddenly and clearly redeemable. She can't wait. She must
wait. She can do that.

Eleven

So that's what happened: a plumply bloated clump of blood decides to go for a middle-of-the-night adventure, setting out with its individual molecules holding as tight to each other as colourfully scarved and snow-suited little school buddies going tobogganing. Once launched from a cautious start, however, this clump, this clot, loses control, gains momentum, helplessly rolling and tumbling faster and faster, barrelling through arteries, still clinging tight together until— *wham!*—an unforgiving collision with the heart of the matter.

The tree at the bottom of the tobogganing hill.

Of course, the form Sophie brings home, a photocopy of one from the hospital, doesn't exactly put it that way.

Nora and Sophie are at the kitchen table again. Beth appears to be out, which is unusual but not interesting. Nora is going through the paperwork Sophie handed over from the funeral home. Places where she's supposed to sign, acknowledging receipt, confirming arrangements, are handily marked by Hendrik Anderson with an X. It's all densely written, a blur of type except for the line on the hospital form: Cause of death.

What a lucky man, Philip Lawrence, leaving aside his relative youthfulness: except possibly for a single breathtaking
instant of pain, just whoosh, thump, you're dead. "It doesn't
sound," Nora says bleakly, "as if he suffered."

"Yes, there's many worse ways to go, that's for sure." Sophie
doesn't intend this the way she ordinarily might: that isn't it
just good northern-hemisphere fortune to go out after a full
meal, a pleasing evening, indulged and contented and, except
for the death part, perfectly safe. She doesn't mean it that way,
but it's how, from the habit of hearing Sophie on these matters, Nora hears her now and thinks how irritating that even in
death no one measures up to Sophie's standards for suffering.

Surely under any circumstances it's cruel enough that
beneath the cover of skin, any sort of assault may be in the
making. A blood clot waits for the right moment to take a fatal
spin through the body. A tiny cluster of badly intentioned cells
gathers adherents, drawing more and more like-minded ones
together until there's enough to defiantly announce themselves as a big, fat, unbeatable tumour.

Any of that. One knows these things, but not properly.

Look at Nora's own compact body, which ordinarily she's
rather fond of—the fact is, anything could be going on in
there. Things that can't be seen are suddenly scary. Even
Philip would have been frightened if he'd known; but then,
he never had to know, did he, except for one brief, shocking,
terrible instant?

Why terrible? Possibly it was glorious.

Nora's mother's tortured effort was painful and slow, and
in that way a relief to everyone, not least herself, when it finished. Uncle Albert's death, though, his was more like
Philip's, also a bolt from the blue and possibly, now that Nora
considers it, his last, best, most spectacular rapture.

Uncle Albert typically comes to mind in bad times. There are reasons for that, mainly that a profoundly negative influence can be as powerful, and as useful, as any positive one. It is possible to suppose that without Uncle Albert Nora might not have experienced that blessed toppling discovery of what she would do, which began, using crayons and long sheets of paper, with translating stories—Uncle Albert's grim stories, to be sure—into pictures. Or that without Uncle Albert she might not have learned the keen-edged, stubborn art of resistance. Or the sharp art of the question. Unintended consequences from Uncle Albert's perspective, of course, but anyone who seeks influence risks being surprised by its results.

Shortly before she came here to live, Sophie underwent a short course of therapy, but all it did, she told Nora and Philip, was make her impatient. She knew the sources of her particular fixation on performing good and preferably arduous acts. What she'd needed, she said, was not a repetitious discourse on history but a way out, some means of modifying history to render it bearable. Nora understood what she meant. She, too, knows sources. Use them, make something of them, don't get agreeably stuck in them—she and Sophie found hard, common ground there.

Still. If Nora had not found crayons and paints and then threads and materials and miraculous new generations of powerful glues—all that lemonade made courtesy of Uncle Albert's pinch-lipped bag of lemons—if she had not, there'd have been no Max and Lily to meet, and therefore no gallery to celebrate, and therefore no encounter with Lynn, and therefore no Philip. Temporary influences and relatively minor events turning into something like blood clots gathering steam, or cancer cells increasing in bulk and capacity.

Only better than those things, of course.

When he turned up each summer of Nora's childhood, she at first mistook Uncle Albert for something like a big, exotically colourful bird flying in overhead and choosing her and her mother, his sister, to alight among briefly: a wonder, a mystery. He called this annual month-long visit a "furlough," as if he were a soldier on leave from the adamant, single-minded army of God. He settled his oversized rump in the living room as if sisterhood made Nora's mother his natural host, albeit also an awful doomed sinner.

There was no obvious resemblance between brother and sister, which made him in Nora's young eyes an even more glamorous guest in their shrunken two-person home. He was also the only man, in Nora's experience, her mother seemed to know well.

The volume of the house rose markedly with his preacher's voice, which he didn't trouble to mute in small spaces. "Take me as I am," he liked to say, "as you take the Lord." At some point that began to sound blasphemous: who exactly did he think he was? But not while Nora was very young.

For four Sundays a year, little Nora and Uncle Albert marched off together to his small and peculiar denomination's small and peculiar services. Much later it dawned on her that her mother allowed her to go with him just because she yearned for a few hours of peace and quiet, and maybe a nap. "I don't suppose it can do you much harm," she said dubiously.

The plain, cement-block building where Uncle Albert worshipped (or for those few weeks a year where he was, perhaps, worshipped) looked from the outside as if it might be a garage, or an appliance repair shop. Nora perched still and obedient on a grey metal folding chair near the back. The services involved a great deal of shouting, or at least loud

voices full of strange, vibrating passions. The best part each
week was when one of the men told a story, because all the
stories were amazing in some way. There was Joseph and his
coat of many colours and his mean, envious brothers;
Abraham actually agreeing to slaughter his own son; most
hugely the apocalypse coming fast, the ultimate war between
evil and good. These were awesome and very cruel pictures.
Nora could see Joseph's brothers envying him his bright coat
and the love of his father—who would not?—but not the
vengeance they chose. She was horrified by Isaac struggling in
Abraham's arms—imagine!—blind with betrayal and shaking
with terror as he learned what his father and God had in
mind. She conjured armies of stallions and men with flashing
swords overhead in a sky dark with rolling clouds, lit by
flashes of lightning during what was called, for some reason,
"the end game," which sounded like no game she knew.

Then, when storytelling time was over, she watched as her
mysterious uncle, that flamboyant, raving bird of paradise,
stepped up to the front. She also watched the congregation,
few in number but large in eye-popping fascination. "Brothers
and sisters," cried Uncle Albert, "salvation is our purpose, it is
our destiny and our fate whatever the costs to wash souls in
the blood of the lamb. However hard it may be, however
lacking in familiar comforts or difficult the journey, we must
consider the lost souls of savages, consider what we must do
to redeem them, consider our duties, consider our heavenly
joys!" There was a confusing push-pull to this, involving guilt,
sacrifice, future reward, although that only became clearer in
retrospect; what Nora knew as a child was that when Uncle
Albert was speaking, she sometimes got muddled.

Not the grown-ups, however. Coins clattered onto collec-
tion trays. Congregants rose to their feet and stood swaying to

the rhythms of Uncle Albert's words. Some people fell, mystifyingly, to the floor. Women, mainly. One moment they were modestly dressed, quiet-spoken, their fervent hands gripping the shoulders of their small wide-eyed children; next moment they were rolling about howling, modest dresses flown upwards, their small upright children very wide-eyed indeed.

"How was church?" asked Nora's mother.

"Okay." Weird and interesting was what it was, but Nora didn't want her mother asking more questions and getting nervous and deciding not to let her go any more.

When Uncle Albert gave her crayons and big sheets of rough paper and told her, "Draw what you heard this morning," he intended instruction, of course, not pleasure, much less ambition, purpose and desire.

Many-coloured coats were easy. Horses were really hard, although setting them to rearing up on dark clouds, with lightning flashing and men falling around them, was fun, challenging, and consumed lots of colours and paper. What sort of knife would Abraham carry? Something very sharp, very silver.

This knife could be improved with a careful glueing of tinfoil rather than plain silver crayon; and so it began, and so it grew, from crayons to coloured pencils and paints, from scary old testament tales to any stories and people at all, and from tinfoil to beads and bits of glass and tag ends of rags—all this took on its own life well beyond Uncle Albert. Nora's mother learned to say, "No drawing," which she also called *fiddling*, "till you finish your homework." A teacher said, "You might want to consider a career that uses this talent you have"—a new notion. Still, there Uncle Albert persistently was: "In the beginning," as he himself might have thundered.

Where was his own beginning? By the time Nora was twelve or thirteen, she was asking questions about him that her mother, it seemed, couldn't answer. "All I know is that he got involved with those people when he was in his early twenties and next thing we knew he was a preacher. We didn't come from that sort of home, and I don't know how he hooked up with them. Or why. And then he went off overseas, and that was that." Wasn't it odd that a sister didn't ask, and a brother didn't say? Perhaps he thought his brand of salvation too basic and obvious to need explanation. Perhaps her mother thought he'd be offended if she asked. Perhaps she was right. He was definitely a man who favoured answers, not questions.

Nora didn't go to hear him preach any more. He said the same things over and over, in the same roaring tones. He was irritating and boring at home, too. He didn't leave room for anyone else. He spoke of being called to leave behind his family and all other "worldly affections" in order to follow his "sacred course"; which meant he'd missed the illnesses and deaths and funerals of both his parents, and the wedding and subsequent abandonment and divorce of his little sister. Nora noted that leaving his family behind did not apply to turning up on their doorstep each summer. "I'm sure that's a good point, dear," said her mother, "but try to be kind. He's still my big brother. He used to make sure nobody picked on me at school and I remember him reading to me and teaching me card games and how to ride a bike. Things like that you don't forget."

"*He's* supposed to forget, isn't he?" Nora no longer imagined him as a beautiful bird; she thought she must have been far too easily dazzled. Now he didn't like to see her drawing or painting, spoke, naturally loudly, of "false gods" and "sinful images." When she was fourteen, fifteen, she used his annual visit to try sketching the man himself, without him noticing. His broad nose wasn't hard, his hairline was straightforward, but his eyes were a trick. She worked and worked at getting the right, fierce light in them. Lines were one thing, lines were easy. Emotions were hard.

Even Nora's mother sighed sometimes. He wanted oatmeal at his place at the table at seven each morning. He pointed out that Nora's mother's troubles must be the consequence of disobedience; hers, not her husband's. "The woman is servant of man, as man is servant of God," he liked to say.

"That's ridiculous," Nora hissed to her mother. "What century is he living in?"

"Just two more weeks, dear. Be patient."

If he was a man out of time in their lives, how much more dangerously out of step was he the other forty-eight weeks of the year? But perhaps, unlike Nora, those lucky far-away people had jungles or deserts they could sneak off to, dense trees and wide rivers or a huge sky to absorb his hectoring voice. Perhaps they had their own lives to save and their own liberations to see to. Maybe they regarded him, if they regarded him at all, as just another pesky but irrelevant fly.

Finally, though, some fed-up overseas soul must have decided he was more malarial mosquito than fly and booted him onto a plane, home for good. Then the fun really started. "My mother isn't your servant and neither am I," Nora told him, full of adolescent and female righteousness. "You should learn to get your own porridge." Breakfast was the least of it. She said, "You don't get to say how I look or where I go." He was presuming a permanent role as household standard-setter, and her mother wasn't standing up to him. She wasn't standing up to Nora either. She seemed tired in general.

He complained endlessly that neither his church nor his country had adequately attempted to save him or his mission. "No one cares," he said bitterly, "for the true word, and all those souls being lost." He now focused on Nora's soul, and maybe her mother's. "You know," he told Nora, "the duty of the child is to honour her elders. Honour means obey, did you know that?"

"No, it doesn't."

One good reason not to have children is the grievous contrariness of adolescence. Nora's mother owed Uncle Albert for drawing fire from Nora that might otherwise have been directed at her. Nora owed him for honing her skills in stubborn refusal. Her weapons were short skirts and tight tops and multiple ear-piercings, as well as more make-up than even she was comfortable with. "If you go about like a harlot, trouble will follow and lead to damnation." He actually talked that way, even at breakfast, even about eyeshadow and lipstick.

"Oh, piss off."

"Nora," her mother said helplessly.

Nora had a boyfriend, what was his name? Ron, Don, one of those. She liked the feelings that rose up with his hands and his mouth, although was aware he was practice and not the real thing. She got home from their wrestlings very late, once in what really was the middle of the night. In the morning she had trouble waking up for school. There was Uncle Albert, upright at the kitchen table, frowning so hard he was trembling. "The Lord," he roared, slamming his fist on the table, "strikes down the likes of you. Change your ways, my girl, or be damned to the fires of hell."

She was tired, she was exhilarated, she was young and triumphant and blooming and strong. "I'm not your girl.

Anyway, how about you? I thought God was supposed to be love, but I don't ever see you being loving or even nice. Aren't you scared"—very bold this, and fed up—"of going to hell yourself for being so hateful?" He rose from his chair faster than such a big man should be able to move. He slapped her hard, *whack!* Nora slapped him back, *smack!* At which point her mother stepped between them, and soon afterwards Uncle Albert packed up and left, although not silently. "I am warning you one last time," he told rude, disobedient Nora as well as her anxious, disobedient mother, "you are damned to hellfire if you do not bend to the will of the Lord."

"Yeah, right," said Nora, watching the red-faced old man— not so old, maybe just fifty—lift all his possessions, in two suitcases, into the trunk of a taxi and drive off without looking back. Unforgiving. In a huff. Hardly Christian.

For a time he lived on a rotating basis with members of his ferocious church, but their numbers dwindled, times changed, the church building was sold to an insurance agency, and Uncle Albert, embarrassingly, took to preaching loudly in the open air. Several times he was arrested for public mischief, breaching the peace, being a general nuisance, and Nora's mother was called to bail him out. Then in a park one spring day, in full, furious oration, mid-sermon, an aneurysm blew out his brain.

Nora's mother wept for the brother who'd protected her and read to her and taught her to ride a bike and play cards. For all Nora knew, she wept also for the brother who harangued and commanded, who slammed his fist and slapped her daughter. Nora herself was just startled: her first real acquaintance with death. That he'd been large and very strange and annoying and *present*, and all of a sudden was nowhere.

Nobody disappears entirely, though. Uncle Albert lives on, in Nora's world specifically, in stories turned, for better and worse, into pictures. Also, from opposing his Cyclopean fervency she was perhaps predisposed to be entranced, ringing Lynn's doorbell, by a naked, glinting, mischievous man.

She has had no pity for Uncle Albert. Now she is surprised to find that she does. Not sympathy exactly, but pity. Because he counted on something, he believed: in his case, that taking his word to the heathen wherever they were, from distant deserts and villages to kitchens and parks, would vault him to his picturesque, angelic, harpish version of heaven—authority over others on earth, gratitude and salvation in eternity, what could be better? No wonder he felt sure of himself. But his world overturned. Arrogant missionaries became unwelcome at gunpoint, young nieces were heedless, the number of women willing or even able to cook oatmeal for breakfast, much less to roll on floors with their muted dresses thrown over their heads, markedly dwindled. Everything he thought he knew flew right out the window, his foundations slid from under his feet, his structures collapsed, his brain exploded.

With the exception of her brain blowing up, that's more or less what's happened to Nora. So in that sense she finally feels if not sympathy, at least some empathy for Uncle Albert, and some pity for his mid-life surprise, a sudden whoosh, thump, much like Philip's.

Uncle Albert's funeral was minuscule, just Nora and her mother and a few hangers-on from his church. Who knew such people were in only temporary decline, that they would rise up once again in myriad fundamentalist forms to take aim, among many more fatal targets, at people like Nora? At Uncle Albert's funeral, held in a tiny, spartan chapel borrowed for the purpose, their voices were few and small and quavered with age rather than rage. But if people marched in the street here and clamoured at the gate shouting, in good approximation of Uncle Albert, "You will burn in hell," it made sense to Nora to lie awake sniffing the air in the night, listening for cracklings.

If asked—and she was asked, just did not answer as well as she should have—she could have said her work was far more fundamentalist than people of any faith who opted for rules, anger and punishment; fundamentally, in her view, missing the point of their faiths. They have dark views of both humans and gods, those people; also, apparently, of their own subterranean impulses. All very well for Philip to suggest they were basically frightened. So what?

What should it matter to Nora if the butcher, the same wretched man who'd taken offence to her early representation of lush bleeding hearts on a tray, was offended again, arriving at their door bearing meat but stopping short in the doorway of the living room, where Nora had just carried the first three Beth-pieces so that Sophie could pack them up to ship off to Max? Why should Nora have to care if this white-aproned Jason Schmidt, a man who resembled one of his own sides of beef, pointed at the pieces and in a tone falling far short of praise thundered, "What are those supposed to be?"

"We'd have been smart," Nora later said to Philip, "to turn vegetarian. No butchers in the house then."

That was when they were still making jokes.

Who knew, too, that the blood-speckled Schmidt was so extroverted, such a leader of his small but dedicated community church, that he was able to bring its members several Sundays in a row from their plain side-street chapel to the gate in front of Nora and Philip's house on the hill, where they set out with shouts and placards to denounce, almost immediately in front of resulting reporters with cameras, tape recorders and notepads, the residents of the house? Well, except for Philip. By definition he could not be a *harlot* or a *Jezebel*. Jezebel? Nora couldn't think what Jezebel had to do with anything, unless they just meant untrustworthy, subversive women in general.

Certainly their objections were pronoun-related. The perversity they perceived involved a crucified woman, they saw blasphemy in the mere presence of tits. That was their sole, voluble point.

The women congregants, those traitors, tended to wear not the muted print dresses of Uncle Albert's day but unbecoming pastel stretch pants and, on bad-weather days, cheap, heavy jackets, unpleasant boots and dark woolly hats. (No, they didn't, not all of them, that's just how Nora prefers picturing them.) Nora bundled up and went to the porch, sketchpad in hand, to stand calmly (but not calmly at all) drawing them. That was her initial public statement on the matter: stubborn work.

Voices were raised. Old menacing hymns were sung. A few small stones were even thrown, although those tended to be tossed by kids darting among the legs of the grown-ups. "It'll blow over," said Philip, but offence spread virus-like. Venomous letters to the editor were written to newspapers well out of the region, rabid-voiced calls were placed to radio phone-ins far away, and there were, Sophie reported, vigorous discussions under way in Internet chatrooms. The media enjoyed this sort of story, reporters and editors entranced by conflict between woman and mob or, alternatively, between fancy-pants artist and faith. "You could not buy this amount of attention for any money on earth," Philip said. Which was true. Not many relatively obscure artists are so abruptly thrust into fame.

By the second Sunday, signs saying, "Death to blasphemers" were being waved to embarrassingly frightening effect and Nora called the cops, who caused the crowd to disperse. But shit continued arriving, plain or paper-bagged, overnight on the doorstep. Hateful words kept appearing on the front fence, so that Philip sighed and headed outside with scrubbing brush or paint. One woman found herself capable of spitting on Sophie's shoe in the bakery. "Heavens," Nora remarked to Philip, "who could have imagined all this?"

He was less flippant by then. "You, maybe," he said quietly. That stung.

Nora ordered a household boycott on the products of the Old Town Bakeshop, on the grounds that Mavis, the owner, had silently accepted not only her spitting customer's discourtesy but its unhygienic result. Philip, while he said to Sophie, "Whoa, spitting, that's nasty," also complained that a boycott was, as he put it, although smiling, to Nora, "cutting off all our noses to spite your face."

"Fuck off," she said.

He missed his cupcakes and cream puffs. Nora suspects that now and then, out on his own, he disloyally sneaked back to Mavis. "It's only a few assholes," he argued, "it has nothing to do with the kind of people I hang out with. Remember them, Nora? The other people who live around here? The ones you've liked well enough for years until now?"

She supposed so. She used to have friendly acquaintants here, did she not? But why, then, was there little in the way of defence? Why did the pathetic clutter of people at the gate grow larger the second week, and still larger the third? "That's your town out there," she told Philip. "Getting to be quite a mob, don't you think?"

"They're not all from here. It's the kind of issue that draws cranks from all over."

Apparently so. Some people gravitate to causes that permit—encourage—the unleashing of rage. They discover passions in themselves they may never have particularly noticed before, and enjoy the permission to behave in a group in ways that are ordinarily well out of bounds. There were squealing tires and footsteps, what might have been footsteps, out in the darkness of night. There were hateful, hissing phone calls reminiscent of Lynn's, both less personal in obvious ways and more personal in their capacity to frighten.

Nora was braver in daylight. "What a bunch of rubes, what a backwoods place this must look to the rest of the country," she told Philip. The disturbances were, briefly, juicy national news, although, unlike Philip, Nora had no clue how to deal with the media. She was not only no hail-fellow-well-met, she preferred her work to speak, or remain silent, for itself. An actual review, for instance, of one of the contentious pieces called it *provocative and compelling*. It went on to say that "What might have been a parody of *The Last Supper* is instead a finely visioned, luxuriously wrought, almost sexual and definitely sensual claiming of the female view of sacred event," and Nora saw no particular need to add to that.

But Philip said that while sketching protesters was provocative (that word again), it was insufficient. "You need to say something for the record yourself," he said on the third Sunday.

What should she say, though? She was no theologian, not even religious. Ideas of goodness and love were interesting— look at Sophie!—and the visual connections were too, but beyond that Nora was curious, not connected.

"Would you say you're a Christian?" was the first question one of the reporters asked after Philip herded a small crowd of them onto the porch, where they could hear her over the racket of the disgruntled rabble left at the gate.

"Those are the stories I'm most familiar with and the ones I've used, but as I understand it, just about every religion has at its heart love and respect for whatever's sacred in every human. Male and female, I would point out. As if any worthwhile god would care about gender." She thought that sounded all right, even if Philip was wincing. "All the great religions have that in common," she went on boldly, "but people distort them for their own purposes. For a sick kind of power mainly, I think."

"So you're saying your paintings are the real truth?"

Had she said that? That would make her insane, as mad as the people out in the street. "No, of course not, but then again, I don't think those people"—gesturing carelessly towards them—"should be claiming truth either." She glanced at the wavering placards. "I guess by and large I would say that if there are blasphemers in this town, I'm not among them."

A cameraperson grinned. A reporter wrote fast. Nora did seem to be making them happy. "Do you think Christ was a woman?" another one asked.

"I can't see what difference it makes. It does interest me, though, how much these people hate women. So much anger and noise about the mere idea and image of female divinity."

"Hate?"

"That's what it looks like, wouldn't you say? All this over a pronoun? Come on."

"Oh, good work," Philip said dryly as they watched the results on the late TV news. "That should calm everything down."

What she should have said was something more like, *Look
at the different kinds of beauty and love in my work. At the
potential beauties of faith, too—shouldn't they include and be
everyone?* Also, *See how humans fall short in practice. Why is
that? Shouldn't we ask?* Instead, she finished up with a bright
smile and another wave of the hand. On TV the smile looked
exceedingly glittery, the wave rather frantic. Oh well.

Philip was right, in a way: in the longer scheme of their
lives here, the uproar didn't last long. Demonstrators' interest
dwindled on the fourth Sunday, when just one camera and
notebook showed up. On the fifth Sunday there was an early-
spring ice storm, which damaged a tree at the front and killed
a couple of shrubs and prevented activity at the gate or anywhere else. And after that, barring occasional bags of shit and
unpleasant phone calls, it was over.

Much got broken in a fairly brief time. Not Nora's will,
certainly not, but some trust, some affection. She wasn't
about to take the inhabitants here on faith, as it were, any
more, that's for sure.

She's not sure about Philip either, and whether something
may have been broken there too. He did his best for her but
honestly, his heart didn't feel totally in it. Now the question
arises: did the strain of straddling the fence, not to mention
painting and repainting it, wind up months later killing him?
Not that alone, of course not. But it was an anxious, strenu-
ous time.

That doesn't, at the moment, bear considering.

How fortunate Nora has been in her important men:
Uncle Albert, who commanded "Draw the story"; Max, who
urges always "See more, look harder"; and Philip, who pulled
her close and said, "Don't worry, you just go ahead and do
what you see," but who also said, "They're frightened. We

ought to be able to understand that, whether they understand what you're doing or not."

What is she going to do without that voice? And the rest of him.

What if she decided to see him after all, one last view, as any normal widow would do? And while she was at it, what if she also ruled out cremation in favour of keeping him perfect and whole? She could still do any of that, there's always at least a couple of days when widows have power, and there must be better farewells than a leap out of bed and a scream.

But already he is not perfect and whole, and already she has seen him, that last encounter when she turned to him in their bed. Better to concentrate on his head thrown back with laughter, pushed forward with anger, all his range of expressions and postures, the tilt of his shoulders in one mood, the slant of his hips in another. Long ago she did quite a few portraits of him: a focus on musculature from the waist up, barrel chest, taut forearm tendons, straining neck, that sort of thing; and from the waist down, those marvellous hip-slopes some men have, like arrows, and those long thighs, those planted feet. Somewhere out in the world, Max may know where, there are also renditions of his face, done back when she was practising the hard discipline of the portrait. "Let me see, let me see," Philip would demand, and when she did he would say, "My God, aren't I gorgeous," and they would laugh.

Now she lays her head on the table. Right in front of Sophie, as if they are friends and have no secrets, Nora puts her head down. She feels Sophie's hand on her forearm. The gesture is kind. It's a moment. It is, in fact, a surprisingly comforting, almost tender one.

They hear the front door open and close, and light steps in the hall. Nora raises her head, Sophie leaves her hand where it is. Here is Beth in the kitchen doorway; but what an unfamiliar Beth, with her fluff of angel hair plastered with sweat and darkened by dust, her floaty dress dirty and limp, her feet and legs grimy. Grubby once-white sandals dangle from her fingertips. "Heavens, what's happened to you?" Sophie asks.

"I went for a walk. Out along the highway. What are you doing?" Beth's eyes are on Sophie's hand, on Nora's arm.

"Looking at the paperwork from the funeral home. Come join us if you like." And strangely, instead of going upstairs to get cleaned up, Beth does sit down at the table. There's a hot outdoorsy, musky sort of smell to her, and dust puffs out of her skirt. "Why were you walking?" Nora asks.

"I got restless." Does she mean bored, could she be bored by a death in the house? Ah well, doesn't matter, it's Beth.

"Do you think," Nora returns her attention to Sophie, "many people will show up for the service?"

"Quite a few said they hope to, but it's hard for a lot of them on short notice. Did you get hold of what's-her-name? His first wife?"

Nora laughs. "I certainly did. I can't say she's warmed to me over the years. But at least she knows, so that's done."

"Do you want to talk about some of the details? There are some questions about music we'd like played, and Hendrik—the funeral home guy—says he'll do his best to find whatever we want, or we could take music with us tomorrow. He has a minister he uses, too, somebody sort of non-denominational, is that okay?"

"I suppose so."

"He wanted to know if anybody else would be speaking. He says I can phone him later about that sort of thing if we want. Then I guess we'll have a few days afterwards to pick out the, uh, the urn, and decide what we want done with it."

Nora notices another slippage: that Sophie speaks of *we*, not of *you*. As with sorting through Philip's possessions, Nora will have to decide at some point which incidents and expressions and moments to carry with her for the next twenty, thirty, forty years. This may require an enquiry into at least a few facts, just so she doesn't go forward wrong-headed. Only, not yet.

"Hendrik says relatives or friends often say a few personal words. Will you want to, do you think?"

"Me? Heavens, no." The thought of having to be coherent about Philip, for one thing; but also, what business is it of anyone's how Nora feels about him, and what sort of man she saw him to be? "Would you?"

"No," Sophie says sadly, "me neither."

They do not ask Beth. And yet of the three of them, she might be the most eloquent. For sure, she's the most experienced when it comes to speaking in public. Also, it'd be easiest for her because she was unattached to Philip, and might bring some joy to the proceedings by pointing out the way to the future, the happy side of events.

"Max might, I suppose," Nora says. "He was fond of Philip, I think." One more thing to be unexpectedly uncertain about. This is exhausting. "Oh, God, I'm so tired. I can't think. Why can't I wake up?"

"I'll make tea, shall I?" Beth asks brightly, and the other two roll their eyes, but nod, and then bend, heads together, over the forms, and start talking about music of all things.

"Tom Waits," Nora suggests.

"Tom Petty," Sophie counters. Mysteriously this causes them to giggle again over "some Tom, anyway," and who laughs about funerals? Not Beth, who is very seriously trying to come up with some combination, quite tricky, to promote energy and tranquillity and letting go of history and being awake to new prospects—all that in one teapot?

This comradely moment is broken, Beth's concentration is disrupted, they all jump, at the unlikely sound of the door-bell. Opening the door has sometimes been an unpleasant business, but here's something they've forgotten about the place: kindness and old customs. That there are some good people, generous or courteous ones.

When Sophie answers, with Nora hovering behind in the hallway, there's a boy on the doorstep, maybe ten or eleven years old, dark-haired and chunky, holding a cake box which he thrusts into Sophie's hands. "This is for you. My mum says to tell you she's sorry." His mother must be the woman out on the sidewalk—bravely or cravenly offering up her plump son, however watchfully, to dubious appetites.

"Why, thank you," Sophie says, and, "What's your name?" but the boy is already off the porch, down the walk, out the gate. "Thank you," Sophie calls more loudly, waving to the woman, who waves back in a *You're welcome* gesture.

Back in the kitchen they open the box to find a carrot cake, it looks like, or banana, iced in white. "I'll be damned," Nora says. "Who was that?"

"I don't know. I've seen the mother around, but I don't know who she is." They are as astonished as if this were the miracle of the loaves and fishes. The story of yet another, very recent painting, as it happens, a late addition to the series, not yet seen by anyone beyond the house, not even Max. In this one, Beth-bones are stripped nearly bare on a platter, her fishhead-eyes glassy, tattered baguette clenched in her fish-jaws, multicoloured thin fabric fingers reaching ravenously in from the edges. A grim piece, although it didn't start, and wasn't actually intended, that way.

More miracles. Sophie answers the second time the doorbell rings too. Nora still hangs back, wary, and Beth has at last gone upstairs to shower away the effects of her lengthy, unlikely walk. Her tea was fine, they've certainly tasted far worse, but Nora and Sophie have now opened a bottle of wine.

This time it's a casserole, its bearer Joy Geffen, who runs the only fabric store for miles. Both Nora and Sophie are familiar with her, and Nora moves to the door beside Sophie. "I'm so sorry for your loss," Joy says. "And I'm sorry about being so late to bring something over. I didn't hear till this morning, and this is the first moment I've had. I hope you like macaroni and tuna?" Comfort food. This is like the old days, when Nora and Philip moved in and people showed up bearing whatever—cakes, casseroles, advice, information—they thought might be useful to newcomers.

No advice now, though, just food. "Thank you, Joy, this is kind of you." So it is. Nora is remarkably touched, she's afraid she suddenly has tears in her eyes, how excessive.

"It's nothing, really. I'm sorry, that's all. I just made extra of what we're having for dinner. I hope you like it, we always do."

"We'll get the dish back to you as soon as we can."

"No hurry, no hurry," and like the boy and his mother, Joy is gone, and Nora promptly loses some, although not all, of her gratitude. Because the question remains: where was Joy Geffen when she was needed? Where was her voice, and all the other voices, of the appalled, the offended, the upstanding citizens who would tell those self-righteous thugs and lunatics to go home and mind their own philistine business? Who would say, *This is not us, and does not represent our community or our views or our behaviour or, for that matter, our faith.* Nora does not recall Joy Geffen doing anything beyond continuing to sell her the fabrics and needles and threads she continued to order.

The third person to appear is the wife of one of Philip's poker pals. Susannah and Dave Hamilton are a few years older than Nora and Philip, early fifties, both lawyers although with separate practices. "We have enough trouble figuring out who does what at home," Dave said back when the four of them had occasional dinners. "We'd be a disaster if we tried working together."

Philip said if he were ever charged with a crime—what crime did he have in mind?—he'd hire Dave to defend him; whereas if he and Nora were ever talking divorce, his aim would be to get to Susannah's office before Nora could. Another joke, of sorts. Philip said, "He's sharp, she's cutthroat, that's a good range of talent."

Susannah phoned Nora several times during the mess. "I feel so bad, let me know if there's some way I can help." Philip reported that Dave offered to be "right on top of it" in the event of actionable libel or slander. Was it unreasonable to wish, again, for defenders at the actual gate, to feel anything less was inadequate to the cause?

"Dave and I," says this woman on the doorstep with the grave, round face, mop of curly grey hair, small angular body, "we are just devastated. Dave's running late in court today or he'd be here to say so as well, but we'll be at the service. Tomorrow afternoon, isn't it? But I didn't want to wait till then to tell you how upset and sorry we are, and I figured yesterday was too soon to bother you. Anyway, there's nothing sensible to do, is there? I couldn't think of anything but food, so I picked up pasta salad, and here's a box of cookies. Also bought, I'm afraid."

The box says the cookies come from Mavis's Old Town

Bakeshop. Oh dear. But there are no more rules, all bets must be off. "Thank you, Susannah. It's all very strange."

Susannah nods. "It must be. So sudden, and he always looked the picture of health and vitality. His heart?"

"Yes." In a way.

"Is there anything I can do? Call anyone, organize anything, get something you need?"

"No, we're fine, thanks. Sophie's taken care of the arrangements."

"Well, you call if you think of something. I have to go back to the office for two or three hours, and then I'll be home, so either place, just phone. And otherwise we'll see you tomorrow, okay?" Nora nods. Susannah and Dave seem to be good at offering help as long as somebody specifies what form help should take. Left to themselves they come up with vague offers of legal advice, pasta salad and cookies.

She is too harsh. People offer what's within their characters and definitions to offer, and that's that. "Thank you," Nora repeats, and smiles at Susannah because she has, actually, located a morsel of gratitude. "If I think of anything, I'll be in touch." She won't, but there's something to be said for ordinary customs and courtesies, she can see that.

When they close the door Sophie says, "Isn't that great? Now we don't have to worry about having food in the house. Is anybody else hungry yet?" Sophie has her own customs, all of which, in response to either happy situations or sad ones, evidently involve eating. Nora rather admires Sophie's frank appetites, although would prefer to suppose they apply only to food, which they may or may not.

At dinner even Beth nibbles at the casserole and the pasta salad, then has a sliver of cake and two—two!—giant chocolate chip cookies. She is oddly jumpy, gives off an impression of something thrumming under her skin, but maybe that's just the sugary effects of dessert.

In a way, although not in a literal way, this feels like their last supper. It's not that Philip is here among them, but by dinner-time tomorrow he will be entirely, heartbreakingly, thoroughly gone. A handful of dust. "Oh," Nora says into the middle of silence. Sophie is gazing out the kitchen window into the backyard, remote and presumably absorbed in her own thoughts. Beth wriggles like a child in her chair. Whatever is the matter with her? Philip never liked her. "I have no time for women who *drift*," was one way he put it.

He wouldn't like Nora much at the moment, then, would he?

They've made a minor mess, the three of them, with crumbs and casserole debris, bits of icing and cake that tumbled from the server en route to their plates. All from the offerings of townspeople bold enough to come to the door with their kindness and old customs. Goodness, generosity, thoughtfulness, courtesy, maybe affection for Philip, maybe respect. Maybe shame, maybe guilt—too bad it's too late to know, and really too late to care.

Twelve

*A*nd so winds down the long second day of Philip Lawrence's remarkable absence; an absence now recognizably final, no more imagining he's just out for a few hours or gone for a couple of days, no more sensing his presence either dispersed through the universe or overhead and observing.

Second days tend to be given over to practical arrangements—funeral plans, flower orders, ministerial consultations—and the less diverting but onerous burdens of coming to grips. Absorbing new information. In another sort of household, survivors might turn to each other, hold each other up, join in mutual grief and consolation. In this household, not so. On the second day they have turned away from each other instead, into their own notions, memories, and even some hopes.

Tonight Nora is back in her own bed. Well, for one thing she is disinclined to ask any more favours of Beth, whose fervency about granting those favours has made Nora, perhaps for no good reason, uneasy. Anyway, she has to learn sometime to be alone in this room. A couple of nights ago she made the mistake of sleeping with her back turned to Philip. Now, too late, she lies facing the flattened space he formerly occupied. If she stares long enough, will flatness come to seem normal, or will she always be conjuring Philip's bulky shape in the night, and would that be comforting or go on being a hard, heavy, constant lump of sorrow? She faces, too, a bewildering kind of solitariness that contains no breathing except her own after so many years of mutual inhalings, exhalings.

This is crushingly, silently, lonely.

Still, is it shameful that while shocked and unconsoled, she is no longer quite surprised? At some point today the empty spaces—Philip's chair at the table, his place on the sofa, silences rather than voice, laughter, footsteps—have grown less startling. It does seem to be the case that the quality of Nora's disbelief has become smoother, rounder, less knife-like.

On her second day of widowhood she has had a frenzy of sorting Philip's possessions and drawing sketch after sketch of them. She has been reminded, yes, that there are a few people outside these walls who perform right, or at least appropriate, acts, and as a result she, Sophie and Beth have some decent food in the house. After dinner, Beth made a pot of tea, naturally, and Nora and Sophie killed another bottle of wine. Nora heard more about the funeral home as Sophie saw it today, and the fellow who runs it, whom Sophie seems charmed by, given that in a low-key, low-voiced way it must be his job to be charming. Sophie remarked that the funeral home is not unlike this house, in that it is large and high-ceilinged and old, and that she thought Philip would have liked Hendrik Anderson's own living quarters within it; but whatever was she doing in the man's apartment?

All this has occurred in its unfolding way, but if Nora were going to illustrate and summarize the day with colour and texture, the resulting canvas would be wholly flat black. No shiny glimmers, no glossy hint of a way to see through or lighten it, just a huge, blank, bleak, wall-sized painting, neither absorbing energy nor casting it.

This is unbearable, but there's no way around bearing it anyway.

Beth is just down the hall, back in her own bed. She should be sleepy after that long walk and, by her standards, an unusually full meal, but instead she is wide awake and alert. Her skin, well creamed, smells like flowers. It also seems to her that there's some hint of Nora remaining on the pillowcase, in the air of the room.

Yesterday's orgy of toast, tonight's casserole and cake and those enormous chocolate chip cookies—they went down like butter. Maybe that's why Sophie eats—because of things bubbling up that need tamping down, drowning under the weight of pastas, cookies and cakes. Beth runs her hands up her body and feels her hipbones protruding, her collarbones jutting like the wings of a plane. She is still beautiful. In a way it's Philip who makes her prospects possible, although he wouldn't have intended to do her this favour. Do unintended outcomes count? Not a good question.

Amazingly, she is hungry again. After the others are asleep, she can creep back downstairs to the kitchen and quietly forage through the leftovers. And then there's tomorrow. Is this anything like how Nora feels all the time, seeing pictures, building them up, decorating them and filling them in? Won't Nora be surprised! This is almost intolerably exciting. Maybe that's what's making Beth hungry.

Patience, patience. Even if Nora's just down the hall, it's

best to wait for the happy, right time, when it comes. Beth will know when that is. Possibly tomorrow, when surely it will be time for everybody to perk up and start to look to the future.

And Sophie?

What about her? She doesn't matter, she'll be out of the picture, just *poof*.

Sophie's bed, where Phil rarely was and never slept, is soft in the centre, her body having made its deeper and deeper cocooning impression over four years. Except in deepest winter, when cold winds can whistle through walls and window-frames that aren't nearly as solid as they appear, Sophie sleeps naked because it's enough to be sunk into this mattress without pyjamas or nightgown touching off more painful sparks on her electrical skin. A condition soothed by that human salve, Phil.

Hard to say exactly when today Phil's attention wandered off. Maybe while she was talking to Hendrik Anderson—Phil might have found theoretical discussions of death tedious when he was in the midst of the thing itself. He might have wanted to pipe up to change the arrangements, or correct misapprehensions about eternity, and drifted off frustrated and bored when he could not do any of that. So where is he now? Still out there somewhere, maybe saying, *Oh, no,* and *Are they forgetting?* and putting his hands over his eyes? Does he have hands, does he have eyes?

These are not answerable questions.

In Sophie's mind, he has hands. This is her accomplishment on the second day of his absence: if she closes her eyes she can see each line, ridge and callus. If she concentrates hard she can feel each one, too. A certain light of anticipation has recently kept her aloft. Now what will she do? Still, she may be soft, collapsed at last in the embrace of her bed, but there's also a hardness that builds up around death; like Phil's calluses, the frictions of repeated mortality create a padding of toughness, given time.

Has there been enough time?

Thoughts are often exaggerated and dark in the night. Spirits sink hard. That's why people all over the world—even Phil—are most vulnerable to death in these hours. Even in the refugee camp this was true. Tomorrow's going to be a long, hard, strange day, and Sophie ought to be getting some sleep, but there are risks to that, too.

What does Sophie dream of when she dreams badly? What causes her to rear up, waking the household, sending her to the wicker sofa on the front porch a couple of months ago with a glass of sedative wine, to be joined by a man she'd wakened, with a sedative six-pack of beer?

The nightmare part is sharp and precise: the sudden, unshakeable grip of narrow bones on her wrist. But around that moment there is, like smoke or ill-will, a surrounding story that is so known and smelled, seen and felt that it scarcely needs telling, and therefore, in the nightmare, is scarcely told.

It was, as Nick promised (and what has happened to Nick, has he by any chance had his heart broken, his purposes defeated, his aims injured as well? Given all that can happen to a person in a relatively short time, it's entirely possible that by now he's a dark-haired, wiry, keen-eyed stockbroker; an unrevolutionary insurance agent concerned with risk-avoidance rather than risk; a dutiful suburban father of two), anyway, it was as he said it would be, a two-year package of time. A package Sophie tries to keep unexamined and wrapped, except for the habit of pointing out, irritatingly as she is well aware but can't help herself, the gentle and beneficent sway of this place and time compared with the vicious, unearned cruelties of other places and times.

Because people don't know how lucky they are. Careless, lackadaisical Nora, for instance, who not only no longer bothers to clean up her own kitchen or answer her own telephone or for that matter arrange her own husband's funeral, but also couldn't be bothered weighing her whims against the angry sensitivities of real humans. Fine for her, becoming famous, not so nice for Sophie, having her shoe spat on in the bakery, stepping out in the morning to shit on the doorstep, rude words on the fence—"We'll keep an eye," the cops said. "But it's just minor vandalism, no real harm intended, just kids." So it most likely was, but kids don't come out of nowhere, they have adult permission, spoken or silent, backing them up. They should see how other kids have to live. They should have to bear down on their own survival, not be free to make mean, grotesque mischief.

As should Nora.

Or look at Beth, surrounded by plenty and able to survive on the back of her own beauty, without a notion of real deprivation, and what does she do but deliberately, unnecessarily shrivel herself. Sophie has seen elsewhere this business of thinned, scant flesh dribbling off a jutting framework— of course Beth makes the perfect Christ on a cross, of course she's a good martyred saviour at a last upchucked or uneaten supper, no question her eyes convey the right remote and redemptive expression to offer salvation. The woman is starved—and how must she feel tonight, with a normal amount of food in her belly for once?

When people are starving, they have to be introduced to nourishment slowly and cautiously, one tiny morsel at a time. Otherwise they get sick and may even—oh, the irony—die.

With the exception of details like smell, dirt, fear, corruption, courage, despair, music, death—those small aspects of life in the camp—Nick's description of the work they would do, which Sophie actually did, was fairly accurate. Unskilled mainly, but necessary to freeing up those more vital, doctors and nurses and even administrators who knew best how to bargain and cajole and threaten and pull strings and make do and save. What Sophie could do was dole out portions of water and food; help dig toilet pits; clean minor wounds; distribute, under supervision, minor medicines; hold children while mothers' wounds and illnesses were being treated, embrace mothers whose children were injured; watch for the endangered, and watch out for the dangerous; help wrap bodies, and help bury them.

Healing or blistered stumps hung where legs or arms used to be. For these she offered crutches and creams. All this was best seen with slitted eyes, blurred, not too close, which she imagined worked more or less both ways: that to residents of the camp, she and the others were mainly ghosts drifting past, stopping here and there, doing this and that, while their own real lives hovered close to the ground. Because she didn't expect to be particularly noticed, it startled her to catch a youth, a woman, an old man regarding her briefly but certainly with the purest raw hatred.

Who could hate Sophie, who was doing her best?

Anyone might hate Sophie, who was lucky, and had had insanely irrelevant thoughts of doing good deeds, and who had chosen to be there, but could choose to leave.

In the nights, sometimes people sang. When there was laughter, she wondered where in people's hearts songs and laughter came from.

She was also surprised by the people she worked with.

They'd arrived from all over the place, but mainly European countries and North America. Some were volunteers, like her, others were professionals: the doctors, nurses, administrators, full-time employees of one aid agency or another. Nobody was actually old, or very young, but otherwise there was a range of ages from twenties to fifties. What was surprising was that by no means everyone was there for the reasons that in the beginning seemed most obvious and essential to Sophie. They might be brisk and efficient, or frustrated and angry, but they sang, too, in the evenings, and there was laughter in their quarters also. When, early on, Sophie blithely spoke of doing good in the world, they grew wary. The word *good* made them nervous. They were there for reasons of needs they perceived and brutalities they were shocked by, but they shied back from *good* as if it were bad.

Even Sophie became too busy to be conscious of virtue for long. There was far too much real life, and real death, to deal with moment to moment. And moment to moment was the only way to respond. Seasons changed, wet to dry and back to wet. Many of the people had been farmers until driven by various marauders with various vicious purposes out of their homes. They were unaccustomed to charity, and to the unvaried, unfresh diets of charity. They were as shocked as anyone could be at the overturnings that had occurred in their lives. Acts of grace and generosity among them were not as common as might have been hoped. Sophie tried to stay focused on only one wound, one spoonful, one life at a time. Two years go slowly that way, but more manageably, too. "Don't get too involved," was one theme of staff meetings, "or we can't work effectively."

But what was *too involved*, exactly? Was it *too involved* to tell a story or two to restless children, or to teach and be taught a few songs, or to lift a howling child from the ground, or applaud a teenager taking his first one-legged steps on crutches?

It was definitely insufficiently involved—although what was one miserably sunbaked or mudcaked, not-very-skilled volunteer to do about it?—to allow what looked like perfectly healthy boys and young men, and some older ones, too, with muscles and all limbs accounted for, to shoulder entire bags of food from a truck and simply walk off. The camp's second-in-command, Doug Smithfield, who'd been around, just shrugged and told her, "There's an underground economy. There always is." And who were these men? "Some are criminals, obviously." War criminals? Responsible for others' visible wounds? "That can happen. It's impossible to know everyone's history. And if we're suspicious of some people, at least they're here and not roaming around where nobody's keeping an eye on what they get up to." She supposed that was reasonable, if also useless and limp. Wet season turned to dry and back to wet and what became visible, though, was the mutuality of these transactions. That a few of her colleagues, not many, just a few, were selling food to some of those muscular, multi-limbed men. And other things, too: cigarettes, liquor, they used those currencies also. *Too involved?* So it seemed.

But of course the already-strong were corrupt and probably dangerous, what possible surprise could there be about that? Silly Sophie. Anyway, theft and greed could at least look comprehensibly human. She would never have nightmares about stolen food and black markets.

It's Martha Nkume, out of hundreds and thousands of people each with a particular story of sorrow or triumph or sheer stubborn survival, who came home with Sophie, bony grip firm on her dreams.

They might easily not have met. Women regularly tended sons and daughters lying on cots in the medical tents. Martha was one of those, an infant in her arms, someone older, a girl, on a cot. Martha was so gaunt, her infant so paltry that either of them might have been the one lying down, being treated. Or in this instance not being treated exactly. The girl's eyes were closed. She lay under a light sheet flecked with blood. The pulse barely perceptible at her throat was all that distinguished her from a corpse. Sophie paused. She had no idea why she was kneeling beside this woman among many, and putting a hand lightly, cautious of breakage, on her arm. Maybe just because Sophie had a moment to spare; or maybe to draw the woman back from whatever far place she was staring at.

She turned towards Sophie. She examined Sophie's face with unusual, personal attentiveness. "Daughter," she said at last, pointing to the girl on the cot. Then, gravely and slowly, "Bad men. Bad men."

Sophie nodded. There was no shortage of women and girls injured, at home or in flight, by very bad men. "Sophie," she said, indicating herself.

"Martha. Matthew," looking down at the infant. "Mary," nodding towards the girl. Even after many months, Sophie didn't have the hang of gauging ages. She thought the unconscious girl might be ten, or maybe fifteen. Martha, her mother, had the bleak, dogged look of any number of mothers.

"Can I get you something? Can I help?" Perhaps water, or a cleaner sheet, or she could hold the baby for a few minutes and give this woman a rest from what looked to be a dangerously slight burden.

Martha's eyes narrowed. Even seated, it was clear she was quite tall for a woman, rather like Sophie that way, although much thinner, of course. She didn't have very much hair. Matthew's belly was bloated, his hair rusted red, the shape and shade of profound deprivation. He would almost certainly die. Sophie wondered if Martha knew that. "Get bad men," Martha said.

Well, that was a large and hopeless request, wasn't it?

Or not.

It's one thing to have learned to communicate through several broken languages. It's another to comprehend the facts of serious crime through semaphore and basic verbs, nouns and adjectives in two unrelated tongues. Sophie and Martha went back and forth, back and forth quite a few times before Martha nodded at Sophie's finally convinced, stricken face.

A simple, brief, brutal event. Mary was one of Martha's several daughters and sons. She was twelve. The night before, while three men held back a frantic Martha, three others dragged Mary away. When they returned, they held Martha while the other three left, and when they were finished, they tossed the girl back to her mother and went away. Early this morning Martha and another woman carried her to this medical tent.

Those muscled, fully limbed men, Sophie thought at first, used to making off with whatever they wanted. What took her so long to understand was that three of the six men were aid workers. Colleagues. Martha recognized their faces from food lines, from daily staff patrols, from this very medical tent. "Our people?" Sophie asked, pointing to her own chest.

"Yes. Bad men."

So it sounded. "Show me who." Although, Jesus, what could she do?

Martha again regarded Sophie carefully, and then rose. She looked down at Mary. "She die, I think." Sophie thought so as well. Who could commit such an atrocity, much less commit it on this helplessly frail bag of child-bones? Someone Sophie had sat beside at breakfast, someone who told stories and showed photos of family and home around night-fires, someone who bandaged wounds every day in this tent— what sort of corruption was this, that didn't show up in expression, voice or benevolent task? Had this sort of thing happened before, only Sophie had happened to pass by, not pausing, asking no questions? It must have. She felt blind, she felt stupid.

She felt rage. "Show me the men," she repeated, relieved that Martha seemed to understand that the alien fury in her voice was Martha's friend, not her enemy.

They walked like any two people strolling, one carrying a small child and with Sophie's hand under Martha's elbow, up one row of tents, down another, around the administration and staff quarters, through the loading and unloading areas. "Him," Martha pointed finally. Then again, "Him." Both men drove back and forth to the capital city, bringing freshly landed supplies and now and then freshly landed staff. One of them, in fact, had driven Sophie here many months back. They worked hard. Their road trips could be very dangerous. How could they work so hard, and so bravely, and then turn around and do this? Sophie shook her head; Martha seemed to realize this did not mean disbelief.

Back at the medical tent they found the third man, just starting his shift. His name was Stan Dowling. Sophie and he sometimes worked side by side, applying fresh dressings, doling out Aspirins. Not a doctor, not a nurse, only another helper, like her, but a few years older, and a veteran of several camps. Stan was good at jobs that took strength, such as lifting people straight off the ground and setting them, gently enough as far as she'd ever seen, on fresh cots. Sophie wondered what he would have thought, reaching Mary, if he'd gotten that far, looking down at what he'd done? Maybe here, in a different place and in daylight, he wouldn't even recognize her.

How could he?

Not for a minute did Sophie disbelieve Martha. Perhaps that was strange.

Not for a minute did she hesitate, either. Leaving Martha behind, she hauled Stan out of the tent with a hard grip on his arm. He was too surprised to resist. "What?" he asked. "What the hell is the matter with you?"

"You know." How large she was, menacing and unbeatable.

Ah, but not really. Another hard lesson.

The men were questioned, so was Martha, so was Sophie. Then the men were put on planes and sent home. Sophie protested, of course she protested, over and over, and bitterly. How could this be? Almost as great a crime as rape itself, the condoning of rape.

Doug Smithfield was assigned to calm her down, help her to see what were considered the larger ramifications. "Of course we can't have these bad apples, everybody understands that," he said. He was being avuncular, the older, wise, worldly man. "But imagine what would happen if we made a big fuss, had them charged, put on trial, and the information got out. What would happen to all the people here if we lost donor support because of it? Which we would. We have to keep focused on the big picture, Sophie." She was asked to weigh short term against long term.

"But what about those men? They're not even punished."

"Yes, but they're gone, they can't hurt anyone any more."

This did not strike Sophie as true.

Mary was also gone by then, whether from injuries or hopelessness or history didn't much matter. Then Matthew slipped away also, one moment breathing in his mother's arms, the next moment not.

Martha's gaunt hand gripped Sophie's arm hard. "Say my children be care," she said. She meant her other children, the ones Sophie had no way of finding. They were not in the camp. They could be anywhere, doing anything, they might have been kidnapped or killed, they might be in hiding, they might have taken up any side in any of the several conflicts occurring, they might be killing or raping or being raped, or for that matter they might be thriving and safe, who could know?

Martha died with her long bony fingers gripped around Sophie's wrist.

There is no reconciling to heartlessness. Land mines blow off little legs, boys bear weapons larger than themselves and grow up to be men grown hard in the process. Rape flourishes, yes, along with other hatreds and vengeances. Threats of violence and results of violence seep deep into the psychic soil. Sophie's, too. She, who had never hated before, hated those men and that camp. How glad she was—no, not glad; breathtakingly relieved, and guilty for her relief—to fly off at last.

Home, her worried parents asked, "Isn't it enough to know you did your best? Nobody can save everyone from everything, and even justice doesn't always work out very well." They might have emphasized *that* more, mightn't they, around the dinner tables of her childhood?

She moved into her bedroom upstairs in their home. She decided she wouldn't go out, then found that she couldn't; that she was paralyzed by the prospect of witnessing tragedy, or just something bad in somebody's life which, having witnessed it, she would have to do something about, and would fall short. She was frozen in this state of immobilized terror for months, until her worried parents sent her to a therapist, who wanted her to talk about them, and about dinner tables and, of course, about her notions of virtue. Janet, as she urged Sophie to call her, asked her to consider whether she'd become so "obsessed" that she could not accept anything that unfolded in unsatisfactory or unfortunate ways. She asked Sophie to consider why, when and how ideas of virtue and sacrifice might have gotten so tangled together. *I don't care*, Sophie thought. *Just make it stop.*

Then in the nick or the fullness of time, she was discovered by Nora and Philip, who whisked her here to do one simple chore after another. She has learned, except sometimes at night, how to flatten that whole two-year package of time and most of its contents into something Phil would be able to carry out to the recycling box under one arm.

A couple of years ago she read in the newspapers of an international investigation whose final report documented a terrible flourishing of crimes by aid workers such as those against Mary. Did anything come of that report, did very much change once people had expressed their surprise and alarm and pledged better intentions?

Probably not. That's how Sophie's own heart has hardened.

Her head is light, though, she is rising and floating, tipping and turning this way and that into regions where hot, faint, phantom figures begin to creep and slither around the edge of her vision. Oh no! Sophie nearly cries out at the sound of a door opening and closing in muffled fashion, light footsteps out in the hall, slipping past her door, down the stairs. Do they belong to someone who lives here, or are they the first of a new, or old, battalion of ghosts?

Here is Phil's life line, here's his heart, there are his aptitudes and desires—one line at a time and, please, only his hand, and no dreams. Surely that's not a whole lot for a reasonably good woman to ask, is it, even if she is not exactly the reasonably good woman she once was?

THE THIRD DAY

Thirteen

max is here, Max is here, oh, hurray! There's the distinctive clattery sound of his ancient yellow Fiat out front, the distinctive clattery shudder that follows the ignition being turned off, and Nora is pelting downstairs, almost colliding with Sophie at the front door. Here is Max, unfolding himself from a low car that these days fits him snug as an outgrown sweater, stretching his long, arthritic body and turning, his old arms opening. Nora flies off the porch and they fold around her. Max's big belly presses like a hot-water bottle. She is in good hands.

Until this moment the day has been an odd combination of fast and slow: a matter of bracing for the funeral and waiting for it. For a mere instant when Nora woke and glanced over at Philip's pillow, she thought, *Oh, he's already up.* The lightning-strike fact of the matter sent her leaping again—is she going to jump from bed every morning from now on?—although quietly this time. She has pulled herself more sensibly together since then, and was just now upstairs trying to locate dark stockings that do not have runs.

For her part Sophie has mainly been occupied, between

cups of coffee to keep her alert after a restless, unhappy, but blessedly unnightmarish night, handling phone calls. Word keeps spreading, and people from further and further afield want to know what happened and when the service will be. "Today?" some cry. "Oh no. I can't possibly get there today." They speak accusingly, as if this is Sophie's fault.

"Yes, I know it's difficult, but if you can't get here, I'm sure there'll be other chances to pay your respects later on." Not that Sophie could say what those might be. Anything beyond this afternoon is a blank. What happens then, do they all come back here, and hope for more food to turn up at the door, and pass another evening, and go to bed, and get up for another morning, carrying on as usual, with the notable exception of Phil?

Surely not.

Besides the future, the day's mysteries include a shortage of leftovers. "I can't think what happened," Sophie told Nora a couple of hours ago, peering into the fridge, lifting lids.

"Really? I didn't have anything after dinner, did you?"

"Strangely enough, no, not a bite. Could it possibly have been Beth? I thought I heard footsteps heading downstairs in the night."

"Well, I don't suppose it matters, except it's strange if she's suddenly taken to eating. I wonder where she is, she's usually long up by now."

Sophie shrugged. "Sleeping it off maybe."

Neither of them has been especially interested in checking Beth's whereabouts. The point is only that Sophie has had to open a tin of salmon to make sandwiches for their before-funeral lunch. Hendrik is providing food for the reception, or whatever it's called, afterwards. Hearing Max's car, Sophie has hurried to the front door as well, and watches from the porch as Max rocks Nora, then draws back to hold her at arm's length.

"My dear," he says. "Such a shock. You're very pale, have you eaten? Whatever happens you must eat, it's the first rule of life." It's his first rule anyway. Like Sophie, he appears to view food, and a fully fleshed body, as a barrier against sorrow and trouble. If Nora and Philip had made it to the city for their lunch with him, it would have been a very good meal.

In that parallel universe, unimaginably remote now in both distance and time.

If Nora looks pale, Max looks old. He *is* old. He is, in fact, almost exactly the age, seventy-six, that Nora's Uncle Albert would have been had that aneurysm not blown up in his head. Max must wonder what, precisely, is waiting for him. He must be fairly constantly alert to fatal outcomes; as Philip ought to have been, as obviously everyone ought to be. Arthritis is only one of Max's several ailments, most serious the skin cancer which he may, or may not, have fought off a few years ago. It is altogether surprising and even unfair that Philip is dead and Max is not.

What a nasty thought. "I'm so glad you're here, Max."

At first meeting, back when Nora was young, Max struck her as wary and dubious and forbidding. It seemed to her he only accepted her and her work at Lily's behest, not from his own judgment, and it's true that Lily's was the more obviously benevolent voice. "I like very much," she told Nora, "how *unyielding* your work is. Bold in technique and powerful in content, and with no sentiment to fall back on to make it too easy." Some artists she and Max represented found Lily the tough and demanding one, Max a pussycat. So there was that variability, too.

Max, though, turns out to be not only dealer but loyal supporter, defender, protector. Nora likes how he gnaws at her about determination and possibilities; beauty as well. "I can sell, that's not the issue," he tells her as he no doubt tells others. "The issue is to do what you see, and then to see further. Never let up. We won't worry about whether or not I can sell it, we'll just keep in mind," and he smiles, although it isn't a joke, "whether I'll choose to." The Uproar Series, as they call it between them, made him uneasy, and not entirely for the obvious reasons. "They are probably your most skilful work so far, Nora, and they are extraordinarily beautiful, so perhaps it is too much to ask that they also be pure." Pure? What did he mean? "I see in them some of your anger, but perhaps this gives them more power, we shall see over time."

She suspected he would be in less doubt if she'd never told him about Uncle Albert. Even Max is not immune to reading too much into histories.

He's not immune to windfalls either, and recently sold the entire series, in a single great whacking deal, to a small organization of wealthy rogue Anglicans. "I'm not sure I like that," Nora said. "I realized they wouldn't be hanging in the town hall, but I'm not happy if they're being used for purposes that might not be mine."

"My dear," said Max in a tone rather chillier than today's *my dear*, "that is hardly relevant, is it? Of course they have their own purposes, but who is touched, who interprets and uses your work—all I can say is that if you wish to be safe, then hide what you do in a cupboard under the stairs. But I know you do not want to do that." She supposed not. Well, she was sure—what would be the point of work nobody saw and didn't care about one way or another?

Max's explanation for what happened here was not unlike Philip's. "Wherever people place their hope is a place they will bleed. So for revenge, or from pain, they try to make you bleed also. It is only what happens. It is human. Mad sometimes, but human."

Sometimes love—or beauty, which may be much the same thing in Max's lexicon—can arise out of anger. Sometimes rage is recovery from love, and vice versa. In some complicated, confused way, in Nora's mind today this has something to do with Philip as well.

Max, unlike some in his world, uses words like *beauty* and even *love* easily. Beauty, he says, is not a gauche, hopeless notion, although he adds the obvious proviso that "beauty is large, and should not be confused with a taste for landscapes, or pictures of horses and flowers." He has learned to appreciate, for instance, Nora's use of various materials and stitcheries, possibly guided by Lily, who caught on right away.

Lily died a decade ago, one hard, baffled year after a stroke, and Max is old. What does Nora want from him now?

She wants to be pulled and pushed right up and over this mountain of sorrow, that's what. She wants what she hoped for from their lost lunch: "New visions," as Max put it when they were making the date, although ordinarily he avoids words like *visions*. And she wants assurance and guidance and comfort from a veteran of radical shiftings who with Lily uprooted himself and moved from country to country to country before finally settling in this one, and who lost Lily, his companion on all their journeys, and who must therefore know a great deal about change after change and loss after loss.

Is it fair to want so much? She has known him as long as she knew Philip, and look what happened to him. "You're right," she says as they reach the porch and Max lifts his free hand to rest on Sophie's shoulder, "we should eat. It's too bad you've missed the casseroles and desserts that came to the door yesterday, but there's not much left of those. You can imagine how surprised I was at food being dropped off. It seems there are a few kind people here after all."

"Of course there are. You know that."

Max, who is Jewish insofar as he is anything, was unsurprised by the ferocity of attacks on Nora and her work. He suffered some collateral damage himself—a broken window, some spray-painted anti-Semitic slurs on his gallery door. "You are right to worry," he told her. "One never knows." But at the same time, again like Philip, he urged a moderate outlook. "Don't forget all those who defend what you're doing."

Yes. But not enough, and not loudly enough.

"I wish," Sophie says, "a few more friendly types would turn up so I didn't have to make sandwiches. Would you like something to drink, Max?"

"Please. A Chardonnay if you have it, even though it is not yet noon. And in return, Sophie, I make quite a good mayonnaise, if you would like that for the salmon." He hasn't exactly cut back or trimmed down or sacrificed any major desires, never mind age, cancer, arthritis, big belly. He is wearing his funeral suit, vest and all, despite the heat outside, but now carefully removes the jacket and unbuttons the vest. "Ah, that's better," he says.

Nora and Sophie haven't showered yet, nor are they dressed for the occasion ahead. There's still a little time to sit at the kitchen table, though, the three of them and their wine. "To Philip," and Max raises his glass. "To Philip," Nora and Sophie reply, surprised by tears springing up unexpectedly at so simple a gesture.

"I was trying on the way here to remember the first time I met him. Would it have been at that first show you had with Lily and me, Nora?" Yes, it would. By then she and Philip were a pair, although Lynn was an unhappy figure still being moved out of the picture. "I think he was enjoying himself. I seem to recall some amusement as well as impatience." That's putting it kindly. Philip was merrily rude to several people who, for all he knew, were important to Nora's career.

"Pompous," he whispered loudly, leaning down to her ear. "Assholes," he added.

"He could be pretty brisk with anybody who was trying to sound important about things he thought were stupid," Nora says. "There was one guy that night with his nose practically on a canvas, going on and on about individual brushstrokes. Not my work, somebody else's. And there was Philip bent over his shoulder saying he'd have to remember all this horseshit about pure verticality next time he was staining a sideboard."

"Why?" asks Sophie, who doesn't like the sound of an unnecessary meanness that didn't even take the trouble to rise to the level of cruelty; although Nora makes it sound like a cherished memory.

"Why did he say that? At the time, I thought he was just being mischievous. Now I think he still felt out of his element in those days, and that was his way of holding his own. He got more confident and adept later on."

"Although," Max says, "he was always snobbish about being a craftsman, wasn't he?"

"Oh, God, yes. I remember once, a couple of particularly obnoxious people drove up here to order some piece of furniture, and it was clear they knew nothing about him, just heard he was the new big thing, and arrived obviously expecting to deal with a hick out in the boonies. Philip came into the house and asked me to go hold the fort with them for a few minutes, and when he went out again he was duded up in overalls and an old flannel shirt, talking in an aw shucks sort of way—really, all he was missing was a straw between his teeth. I don't think they even noticed, since that's what they were expecting, but he was totally enjoying himself. He let them swan around for quite a while before he told them he wouldn't dream of letting any honest piece of his end up with a pair of superficial provincials like them. I'm not sure they were embarrassed the way he meant them to be, but they sure were indignant. And bewildered. He enjoyed that, too. What did you think of him once you got to know him, Max?"

"He amused me. I saw him being mischievous, but in a serious way. And, of course, as long as he caused you no harm—I mean in the sense of sabotaging your work and success—I was quite prepared to enjoy him."

"And did you?"

"More and more. He did fine work and took it seriously. He developed, I think, a good sense of perspectives and balances, and only mocked what he took to be false."

"A little too many perspectives and balances sometimes."

"And so?" Max shrugs. "He knew you were responsible for yourself. And agreement of temperament is not necessary, only balance of temperament. As with me and Lily, you see. I recall him saying on TV that you did not make suggestions about the shape and design of his work because you respected his knowledge and eye, and he could not imagine making recommendations about your work because he had an equal respect for yours."

"That wasn't exactly the same as saying I was doing the right thing, though, was it?"

"But you had that assurance yourself. I would not suggest he disagreed with you, but I would say Lily and I had many disagreements over the years, but what was important was that we respected each other's separate judgments and skills."

"That's why you took me on, isn't it? Because Lily pushed."

Max waves his hand slightly. "Probably. At the time. Not because I disliked your work, but because Lily understood it best and first. That's what I mean: we looked to each other, and so did you and Philip, although in different ways." He glances at his watch, and at Sophie. "But now perhaps we could make those sandwiches you were speaking of. Nora, you might start getting ready." For the funeral. In less than two hours. He sounds the way Nora imagines a father would sound: keeping track of time, getting them organized.

"Okay. I won't be long. Then your turn, Sophie."

Left on her own with Max, Sophie is tense. He is Nora's ally, not hers—as if it's a war, or a game? But it's not, it's only a series of duties to perform and endure. She will make lunch. Then get ready. Then comes the funeral. It'll be nice to see Hendrik Anderson's calm, solid face. That and Phil's hands should hold her together if by any chance she starts falling apart.

Max is poking around in the refrigerator, finding eggs for his mayonnaise. "The young woman, Beth," he says, now reaching for a bowl in the cupboard overhead, "she is here?"

"Yes. Mind you, I haven't seen her yet today, but somebody did a good job of going through the fridge overnight. Although ordinarily she hardly eats anything. Usually she's just kind of around, being useless."

"You dislike her?"

"Not especially, I just think she's not very bright. Well, look what she does—she lives off her body, and what use is that?" Oh, Sophie, Sophie. She shakes her head at her own unkindnesses.

Max shakes his, too, but he's smiling. "You are speaking to the wrong person about that, since I have also lived somewhat off her body. As has Nora. So I would have to say it does have its purposes, although perhaps more for others than for herself, and so yes, I suppose that is a little bit sad."

They are side by side at the counter, Sophie buttering bread, Max stirring his mayonnaise into the salmon. "I imagine," he says, "it has been a strange couple of days here. Not least for you, Sophie. Philip's death makes a great difference, doesn't it? It feels quiet, and there are spaces where there should not be."

Be careful. "Yes, everything's off balance. Like somebody jumped off a see-saw and sent us all flying."

Max nods. "Everything goes flying, very true. Have you thought what you will do? When everything comes down, how you will land?"

"Not yet. I don't think there's been time for anyone to think ahead, and I've had a lot to do. Making the calls, taking the calls, dealing with the funeral home."

"You did all that?"

"I guess it's my job. But Nora's ideas. I mean, not having any visitation, just a service in double-quick time and straight to cremation." Sophie shivers. "The funeral home guy thought it was awfully fast too. Unceremonious. So it looks like, I don't know, wiping Phil off a blackboard. Just erasing him." She hears her voice rising. "And Max, it *does* feel that way. I don't know why Nora is in such a rush."

"Well, you know, Sophie, in my religion, among others, we have services the next day after death, or even the same day. My Lily's was the day after, and I mourned her with all my heart. A longer time or a shorter time, it can be a matter of custom, not grief. In any event, perhaps we revere custom more than we should, especially if altering it causes people to think more closely about the one who is lost."

Lost. Sophie has lost skin, tenderness, touch, hands, purpose, even a minor kind of salvation. "Maybe. But Phil had his own friends, and there's people upset because they can't get here and probably some people still don't even know yet, and isn't it all supposed to be about him? Shouldn't it be what *he* would have wanted?"

"No. No, the departed have departed, and I don't believe they bother themselves with worldly concerns." All worldly concerns? Including Sophie? Including Nora? Including everything in Phil's entire life—just uninterested, just like that? Can that be how Max thought about Lily—forty years and suddenly he would be of no interest to her? Sophie has never considered Max a hard man before. But, "It's our attachments that matter. Lily is always alive to me, and Philip will be, too, for those who cared for him. But they themselves have moved away, and we cannot imagine where that is, or if it is anywhere at all. Which is only the great, last mystery, beyond solving. The ceremonies acknowledge our attachments and the mystery, and so are only for us, I think." He pauses, then asks quietly, "Will you miss him a great deal, Sophie?"

"I feel strongly about all death," she answers, quick as she can. "I've seen too much of it." She immediately regrets that; it's cheap, using real suffering to account for her present distress. "But yes, of course it's a huge shock. I've lived here for so long he was family in a way." She stumbles over the word *family*. Oh, she cannot keep talking, she just can't.

"Sophie?" Max sets down the mixing bowl and turns to face her.

"Yes?" She keeps her head down.

"We all have different affections and loyalties, and you know mine are particularly for Nora, but I would like to tell you while we're alone that I believe you are carrying a special burden with considerable compassion and grace. Do you understand me?"

He knows. Does he, how could he? A stab in the dark, then? "Thank you," she ventures. "We're all doing our best."

"No, Sophie. It is hard, what you are managing to do, and you should accept my admiration. And perhaps, on Nora's behalf, although as we both know she would not agree, my gratitude. You are earning it, and you should accept it. Only between us."

It is dangerous, it is even a breach of Phil's trust, but, "Thank you," she says again, in shakier tone. It's a relief. It's not so lonely if somebody knows. Goodness, good behaviour, they can take many forms, and if some are more ambiguous than others, well, that's the tricky, complicated world of grown-ups, isn't it? The ambiguity of Max's particular virtue is, it seems, that he is not inclined to betray Sophie or Nora or Phil. Quite an accomplishment.

Now that her armoured but very real grief is acknowledged, though, Sophie sags where she stands. Max puts an arm around her. He's a nice man. No wonder Nora holds him in such high regard. "How did you know?" she whispers.

"I watch. I listen to tones. I can sometimes feel things."

When? Max spent a rare day here some weeks ago—a short holiday in the country, much time on the porch, everyone with their feet up talking about work and nothing else very important except, now and then, world events—what could he have seen? Nora's a watcher, too. Nora calls watching a requirement of her job, and makes a little joke about the fortuitousness of that, given that observing is also her inclination and nature. Does Nora see less acutely than Max, or is she just more careful about what she will see?

"I've been watching you for a long time," Phil said to begin with, and without will or warning, just like throwing up, Sophie is weeping into Max's shoulder, his arms folded around her, one of his big hands stroking her hair, the other tight on her back, an old man maybe, but firm as a tree. She is gulping for air, she is crying so hard she makes deepthroated, gasping, hiccuping sounds. She would throw her head back and howl inside these arms except even now she is aware of Nora upstairs, and how could she explain the depth and volume of her anguish if, curious and alarmed, Nora came down?

Finally she is able to step back and allow Max to dry her cheeks with his thumbs. "I'm sorry," she says.

"Ah Sophie, we do our best for many reasons, do we not? I know you have done yours. In his way, Philip did his best as well. Life is complicated, and then suddenly it is much too simple. Strange, isn't it?"

Yes, it is.

Max has brought air into the house. An outside voice, and moreover a deep one. Those missing bass tones. He also bears an external eye, private solace, a larger outlook on Phil. Sophie takes a deep, ragged breath. Finally, there is such a thing as taking a deep breath in this house. She takes another, and another, and is herself again. Or at least the self that functions and copes. "I'll pile the sandwiches on a big plate, and then people can eat whenever they're ready." Max nods, he gives her a last pat on the shoulder, and takes his place—actually Phil's place—at the table. That looks strange; but somebody would have to sit there some time.

It would be nice if some similarly warm and consoling event were occurring upstairs, but it's not.

All morning, from behind the closed door of her room, Beth has been listening to the sounds of the household: the other two getting up, going downstairs, voices rising to her room from below, more trips up and down stairs and then Nora pounding down, Max's voice joining Nora's and Sophie's, and then Nora returning upstairs, Nora going into the bathroom, the shower being turned on.

And nobody this whole long time has tapped on Beth's door or called out to ask if she's okay.

She is not okay.

Look what she's done to her stomach, filling it with poisonous overnight foods—what was she thinking, heating scoops of casserole, cramming herself with cookies and cake? She could feel food dulling history and impulse, but until she was full to bursting with sugar and starch and disgust, she had no idea how heavy food gets; in every way an anchor. She dragged herself back upstairs to bed thoroughly weighted, and then pains in her stomach kept her awake. She did finally sleep, but woke up queasy this morning. Inert, too, even though food is supposed to bring energy, isn't it?

And nobody cares. They're probably more interested in what happened to the food than what's happened to her. Nora, too, not just Sophie. But Nora has a lot on her mind. It doesn't mean she doesn't care, only that other things have grabbed her attention.

So Beth must grab it back.

It's in her power to transform the day.

There now, there's the surge food is supposed to provide, like a furnace clicking on—just so, Beth finally rolls out of bed and onto her feet, and immediately, once she's standing, feels far less pinned and weighed down. She meant to wait, but no, she can't. Yesterday would have been wrong, but this is the time, this is the day. Nora, now out of the shower, now leaving the bathroom, needs a future, and once Beth reveals it, they can proceed through the rest of the day with their eyes and hearts skipping over the moment, cast forward instead. That sounds right, doesn't it? Of course it does, and without hesitation Beth aims herself directly from her room to Nora's. Nora is standing, plump and pensive in mid-calf-length black skirt, black stockings, flat black shoes and navy-blue bra, taking from a closet hanger a black top, long and gold-flecked— an outfit normally worn to openings and other city events. "Nora. Listen."

Beth's intention is to raise Nora instantly from misery or weariness or inattention into the thinner, finer, happier atmosphere Beth inhabits simply by standing up, getting moving. "Beth!" Nora clutches the black and gold top to her chest. "You startled me." Not exactly welcoming, but, "Can I help you with something?"

She can, yes; but more the other way around.

"I've been thinking." Beth is interested to hear how she's going to put her ideas, what's going to come out of her mouth. "About plans. What we do next. Wait till you hear."

It's only natural that Nora looks confused. "Can it wait? Max is here, you know, and we'll have to leave soon. I want to get back downstairs."

"No, please, just a couple of minutes, okay? It'll make all the difference. Listen. It's about what to do when we leave here." Beth hurtles on so that open-mouthed Nora will have no more space for words. Beth can see her perfect vision so clearly right now, and she knows it can save, and she just has to say it.

"See, we go back to the city. I mean, nobody wants to stay here, right? We find a house, or one of those half-houses, what do you call them? Brick, anyway, with a little yard with a fence and vines growing up it, and flowers, and I'll have a herb garden. You need lots of light, so there'll be big windows in the room where you work, and it should be on a side street because you don't want too much noise when you're working, but it has to be sort of downtown. And high ceilings, and white walls so we can hang your art right, and we'll have all new furniture for starting out fresh, we'll have such a good time shopping for exactly what we want, just for us. I can do modelling, or maybe get other kinds of jobs when we need money, and I'll do the cleaning, and I can learn to cook, too, so all you'll have to do is your work. Just the two of us, can you imagine?" She is breathless. Perhaps she has spoken too fast. So much, and it's only taken a moment to say. Maybe it spilled out so full tilt that Nora can't take it all in at once, and that's why she's standing just staring at Beth.

Or she's overcome by the splendour of the picture Beth has sketched right in front of her eyes. Oh, there's lots more details: a fireplace in the living room, white-painted brick flanked by white-painted built-in shelves, flowers always blooming in pottery vases and crystal ones on mantels and tables, and candles as well, tall and short, scented and not, lit every cozy, intimate evening. Soft music, and Nora's latest, most dazzling works—whatever they'll be next, they are certain to dazzle—lighting the walls. "Isn't it perfect, Nora, isn't it beautiful?" Beth finds a use for slightly pouched bellies: she rests her clasped hands on hers.

Nora stares harder. Nora frowns. Finally, watchfully, in a way Beth can't interpret, Nora says, "That's quite an idea, Beth. I can see you've given it a lot of thought. But you know,

I haven't even begun to think about futures. I can't, it's far too soon. There's Philip, you know."

Didn't she get it? Does she not grasp altered circumstances? "But that's just it, you won't have to think about him, you can do what *you* want, isn't that just amazing?" Beth sees Nora stepping lightly into this conjured cottage and being . . . content. Happy and content. *Finally*, Nora would say then, as if she had crossed a long desert to her reward, her true oasis in a warm, fruitful space.

Honest to God, Beth can *see* that, true as true.

Nora takes a deep breath. "Beth, please. Think. Try to imagine being with somebody you care for, day in and day out for nearly twenty years, and suddenly you don't have them any more."

Yes. And so? "That's what I mean, how amazing that is. I *love* you, isn't that amazing too? I don't mean sex, not at all, don't think that, I mean *love*. And you're free. We can do anything. You have your whole life in your very own hands."

Now something bad happens. Nora throws up those hands, violently, so that Beth takes a step back. "Beth. I do not have time for this." There's a sound in Nora's voice Beth has never heard before, not even when she was raging about the people in town. She is low-voiced and harsh, a stranger saying, "I don't know what the hell you're talking about, and I don't think you do either, but I'm not listening to any more of it. You have no idea. There's something the matter with you, but I can't deal with it now," and shrugging herself into the black gold-flecked top she whisks past Beth and is out the door and into the hallway and gone.

Oh.

Beth sinks onto Nora's bed. Such a big bed. So much space.

How come the largest possible events can take almost no time?

How come when something's so true, it doesn't just naturally *come* true? Beth *saw* Nora and herself in their brick city cottage. She smelled the herbs, she heard muffled traffic, she listened to her voice and Nora's in low evening communion. She felt Nora brushing a hand over her hair, passing by, the way, but different, Nora sometimes brushed Philip's shoulder, or he touched her arm. Just little, enormous moments.

This is the second time a desire has simply flowed through Beth uninterrupted in the direction of fate. Bricks collapse, white walls darken. Nobody cares. People who've made a living off her, how ungrateful they are, and blind, and unworthy.

Beth turns on her side on Nora's bed. She's so heavy. Why does no one take care of her? Admiration is different. Lights and tiaras and sashes were never the same thing as care. Even her hours spent bending to Nora's visions didn't add up to true attentiveness, much less respect or affection, it seems. All her pictures turn out to be wrong, and acting on them turns out so badly. She only wants to be safe; for someone, one single human to care. Is there really no one? Was there ever someone? Could there have been? How do other people decide things, weigh them up, pick one choice or the other so that they're loved? Is that what regular people do? How do they learn that?

Maybe by not being so particularly admired. Maybe they learn in the absence of extravagant beauty. Without so many mirrors and glass, light and darkness.

How desolate, how bereft, how swamped with grief Beth's crushed, collapsed little heart is.

Also, how busy her mind.

Nora's, too. Once escaped from her room, and it feels

exactly like that, an escape, she could go left, down the stairs, back to the safety of the kitchen and Sophie and Max, as she told Beth she was eager to do. Instead, she finds herself turning right, along the hall to her studio, to stand in its light. That was shocking. Just shocking. Who knew? Should she have known? It takes a minute or two to catch her breath and stop shaking, a few moments to absorb that awful, pathetic encounter.

Who on earth has been living here in this house?

Here on these tables are lined up Nora's own paints and brushes, threads, needles and glues, around the walls are piled her own fabrics and canvases. Off to the right are her own easels, one medium-sized and one, especially Philip-built for her, magnificently enormous—how restful, and how luxuriously mournful it would be, to stay here alone, in this room all her own, for the rest of the day.

She can't stay, of course. She has Sophie and Max waiting, a glass of wine to finish, sandwiches to eat, a funeral to survive—and then? Nothing as peculiar as what Beth proposed, that's for sure, at least Nora will have saner prospects than that after she has performed her first duties in her new role as widow. There is Philip, care for and love of Philip, grief for Philip, all sorts of aspects of Philip to acknowledge today. She can worry and think about the rest of it later, but this is his day; so okay then, deep breath, and a firmer one, and another—that's better, that's manageable, and so here she must go, here she goes. Now.

Fourteen

Two women in black, plus one in pale yellow, march out the front door, cross the porch side by side, descend the steps, and make their way to the street and the limousine Hendrik Anderson has sent. Sophie walks in the middle, separating Nora from Beth so that a view of the group weights and tilts towards the two in black, leaving the one in yellow looking light and liable to fly upwards.

Max follows behind, joining them last in the car.

Does anyone enjoy going to funerals? Surely only those very remotely attached to the deceased, with their amiable curiosity, or sociability. Oh, and enemies, too, if only to assure themselves this truly is the final appearance of someone triumphantly outlived.

Philip didn't have enemies. Well, maybe Lynn.

Or unquantifiable, indefinable Beth, who knows? They are all, especially Nora, surprised, even Beth is surprised, that she is among them, but here she is in her pale yellow dress and flat ballerina-style, twinkle-toed shoes and her brushed-out angel-hair, silently making known her intention to be a part of all this. What part, no one has enquired, but Nora has taken care to place Sophie between Beth and herself on their way to the car, and inside it.

As buffer, Sophie is on the alert. Nora told her and Max only the skeleton of Beth's proposition, but even so little sounded quite fantastic and mad. When Sophie stood from the kitchen table to go upstairs to shower and dress, Nora asked her to check on Beth. "I left her in my room. God knows what she's doing. Do you mind?"

Sophie frowned. She thought she did mind. "I'll see."

"That's different," Nora said when Sophie was gone.

"That Sophie is not so much your employee, or that Beth shows herself to have larger desires than to be your material?"

Both, maybe. And both unpleasant, and somewhat critical, as if it's Nora who comes up short here—this from Max? "Shit, I don't know. Obviously I'm not very good at deciphering people."

"Mysteries. People are bound to be unknown to each other in small or large part and therefore naturally surprising, don't you think? Now. Tell me about Philip. And you. How you are doing."

Nora began with the moment she turned in bed, the leap up, and the scream. "I keep thinking of me sleeping and him all alone. Struggling. I don't know." She waited for her voice to get strong again before telling of the others running into the bedroom, Beth in her nightie, Sophie with her flying robe and with all her red hair aflame. Max's eyes sharpened, but he made no comment. "Thank you for being here, Max. You and Philip, you're the two who always make sense of things, but not," her breath caught again, "any more."

"You may be surprised. I still hear Lily's voice. Sometimes she comforts me, sometimes she makes me brave, sometimes she is just present, alongside me. Being Lily, she gives me advice and good counsel." Nora, although mourning Philip's living voice, wasn't sure she would want to hear him on and on for years into the future. "Let yourself grieve. This is not a time to be proud. Pay attention to Philip and who he was in your life, and later what you remember will be the joy of knowing you have experienced genuine sorrow."

A convoluted sort of notion. And joy—such a deep, hearty word, when was the last time Nora felt anything like it? Nor could she imagine it in any sort of foreseeable future. If joylessness was what Max meant by genuine sorrow, that's what she had. That and rust; she felt rusted nearly away the past couple of days by disbelief, and by desperation to undo events that could not be undone.

Proud? No, but she could at least carry herself proudly. "All I want to do is get safely through this day." *Safely?* What could be safe? "On top of everything else, there'll be people I don't want to see. Who don't deserve to be there."

"And you are still a little angry that Philip wasn't as angry with them as you."

"Oh, Max, I'm angry about so much right now, it's hard to tell."

"Philip especially."

"Yes! Off and on. How did you know?"

He shrugged again. "Lily. I was furious. Forty years, and then she left me, and I felt betrayed. That was wrong, but these things don't have to be true to be real. Then in time I came to think Lily would be pleased that I cared so much I was furious." A point of view, no doubt; yet when Lily died Max turned mirrors to walls and sat shiva, and at the end said, "I've done my best for her. I can rest." It now sounded as if his rest wasn't totally peaceful. If Lily still spoke.

"Yes," said Nora, "I see." Although she didn't, really. Too much confusion today; as if the house itself had decided to go clattering and banging about, raising layers of distress and dislocation like dust.

"It would be foolish to tell you that you will recover, because in very many ways there is no recovery, only change. But there can be good surprises in good farewells, so you may feel as I did with Lily that something is completed by the end of this day. My only advice is, you should be attentive to your heart as it shifts."

Whatever. "Thanks, Max." She leaned across in her chair to let her head rest on his shoulder, and his arm reached around her again. She liked his voice, and his presence, and perhaps what he was saying would come clearer later, when she might have a larger perspective and context; for the moment it was nice enough, resting her head.

Upstairs Sophie did, in fact, poke her head into Nora's room, out of obedient habit plus a wish on this of all days to do whatever she had to do as well as she could. Max had helped; a thorough weep had as well. She found Beth lying across the bed staring up at the ceiling, hands crossed over her belly. Melodramatic as ever. Shockingly full of shit. Sophie's resolve grew very weak very quickly. "Get up, Beth, this isn't your room. And get a grip. Phil's dead, for heaven's sake, people have other things than you on their minds."

Beth was off the bed and onto her feet in such a singular swift motion that Sophie stepped back. The look! And the voice. "You're not my mother," Beth warned in a low, hard, scary tone. "Don't tell me what to do. Don't ever do that."

Whoa. As Phil would say. Sophie turned right around—let Nora deal with the drawn-draped battiness inside her bedroom.

Although Nora hasn't dealt with it, and now here they
all are in a long black car being driven to, of all astonishing,
outrageous events, Philip's funeral. Time in the past couple
of days has become more and more tangled, stretching and
spiralling, twisting with far greater complexity than the
dailiness of regular life suggests could be possible. Also, it
exists on a pinpoint: only now. Nora looks out at the tidy
lawns and contained, thriving gardens and blank doorways
floating by as if she has not seen any of this before and
knows nothing about it; as if it holds promise, and she is
young and does too. But it is this moment, not that one. The
car turns into a wide driveway, then under a portico where
a plump man in a dark suit is waiting to open her door. Nora
wishes these were times when veils still shrouded faces. She
would like, not to hide exactly, but to keep herself private.
The man's hand reaches for hers as he helps her from the
car, bowing slightly. "How do you do. I'm Hendrik
Anderson. I am very sorry for your loss." His voice is lighter
than his body. "If there are ways I can be of service . . ." and
he lets the sentence trail away. His next word, in brighter
tone, is "Sophie."

Sophie is awkward gaining the pavement, having been sitting in the centre, and being not exactly petite. By the time
she's on her feet, Hendrik steadying her, she is flushed. "It's
good to see you again," he tells her. "May I say, if you don't
mind, you look splendid." So she does. The dramatic effect of
black suit, black stockings, brilliant springy red hair suits her
remarkably. The snug fit of the suit doesn't hurt either.
Getting ready, she considered her appearance a sort of last
gift, both spartan and lavish, to Phil. *There you go, then. You
did more for me than you could have imagined, and now this is
all I can do in return.*

Something like that. Hendrik Anderson's admiration is quite nice as well.

His guiding hand moves on to Beth, who emerges swaying and bending, graceful and hardy as a forsythia branch. No ungainly exit for her.

Whose eyes meet whose here? Not Nora's and Beth's; or Nora's and Sophie's either, Nora perhaps recognizing a posthumous, brilliantly red-haired, black-wrapped gift when she sees one. Beth's and Sophie's eyes do meet, in one brief hard look; Sophie's and Hendrik's in a warmer one that comes with an acknowledging nod. Max has made his own way from the car and takes Nora's elbow. Hendrik fits himself between Sophie and Beth. In this formation they leave the side shelter and under bright hot August sunshine make their way around the corner of the funeral home towards its formal front entrance. One woman is red-haired, one is blonde, one is dark. None of them is very old, or very young. One has gratefully relaxed her fierce grip on virtue, one is becoming less beautiful, one is lost for visions but watchful. Hendrik, speaking up to include the full group, says, "There's already quite a number of people here. I don't know if any will want to speak—normally we would know details like that—but it should be a pleasant service."

Pleasant service. Nora's eyes narrow, but since she's walking ahead with Max, Hendrik Anderson doesn't see this. Sophie admires how he's trying to keep people soothed and benign. It's not his fault the arrangements are haphazard, or the people on edge. Mourners must generally be on edge, but this is different. The three of them are not exactly like members of a real family bringing to a loved one's funeral their disparate but predictable modes and levels of grief, their varying interests and very long memories.

Beth isn't listening. She is watching Nora and Max walking ahead. Her eyes are, specifically, on Nora's straight, stubborn, unloving spine.

"I've brought some music," Sophie tells Hendrik, passing him a CD from her purse. "I've marked the song we'd like played at the end of the service. Is that okay?"

"That's just fine. Thank you." He doesn't even look to see what it is. How calm he is when so much is uncertain and, for all he knows, tasteless.

More uncertainty: on the front steps stand a couple of strangers, the woman smoking, the man with his hands in the pockets of a dark suit. He is balding and blue-eyed and thin-lipped, and looks more irritable than mournful. She is wearing white sandals with bare legs and a pale blue cotton dress, belted with a narrow white leather strip that causes her hips to appear broader than they probably are. Her fingernails are painted bright red, with toenails to match. Her hair is chin-length and, yes, streaked honey-blonde. "Lynn," says Nora too loudly, and holds Max's arm harder.

Well, well.

Sophie looks curiously at this woman, this *Lynn*, as their small brigade moves up the walk, up the steps. Here is someone else Phil must have loved, however unsatisfactorily. A man of wide and various tastes, it seems; many compartments, or several stages. She is struck, regarding their tableau, this visual evidence of Phil's experience, by what a small space she herself could have occupied. She had four years in the household, a couple of months in his hands, no time at all in his bed. Whereas with this woman for a few years, and then with Nora for many more, he accumulated hundreds, thousands, millions of words, touches, views, moods, adventures, every variety of embrace they desired in any time and any place that they chose. With them he even had time and leisure for silence. Whatever he and Sophie knew of each other was comparatively an eyeblink. There are photographs tucked in envelopes in the sideboard back at the house of Phil as a ruddy, glinting kid with one cheerful parent or other; as a sullen, spotted adolescent standing off on his own, hands jammed in pockets; a few from those swift moments when a boy's body shoots up, fills out, shoulders and features reshaping themselves into a different, grown creature, not finished, but with the mould clarified and beginning to set.

Soon after those photographs were taken, he would have met this smoking Lynn, and a few years after that, Nora.

The woman takes a deep drag and, after looking about briefly, tosses her cigarette into Hendrik's shrubbery. "Lynn," Nora says. "I didn't know you smoked. You didn't used to, did you?" A peculiar greeting to the woman whose husband she made off with nearly two decades ago, but Nora hasn't thought of Lynn, that wounded bride, that righteous figure in their brief domestic melodrama, as someone with weaknesses. "Die bitch, die," this woman screamed, not remotely weakly, from the street below Nora's apartment.

"Nora," Lynn says, not screaming now, nothing so hot, or even warm. She indicates the thin-lipped man. "This is my good second husband, Bill. Bill, this is, let's see, my considerably less good first husband's second wife." He nods. No one shakes hands and, evidently a man of few words, or a grumpy one, or uncomfortable or timid, he doesn't speak.

Lynn surely rehearsed that. Now it's Nora's more extemporaneous turn. "This is our friend Max, and this is Sophie, Philip's and my assistant. And Beth, who has modelled for some of my work. Everyone," and her voice also is level, but sharp, "this is Lynn, my good first husband's first wife, and her second, no doubt also excellent, husband Bill."

There is this to be said for so comedically brittle a scene: it's a diversion. It exposes a whole welter of prickly emotions that are, even cumulatively, much smaller than grief. Some of the people who formed a mob at the gate wore buttons that read, "What would Jesus do?" which Nora thought, as a matter of fact, was a question they might well be asking themselves. At the moment she is wondering, What would Philip do?

Philip would throw a big arm around this Bill's shoulders. He would say, "Come on, let's get out of here, go get us a beer. Do you play pool? Are you interested in poker?" But Philip isn't available to play merry host, he isn't here to look from Nora to Lynn to Bill and remark, "I bet we have some things we could talk about, right?" and let loose one of his head-back belly-laughs. Nora says quietly, "Actually, it's nice you're here. Philip would have been pleased."

"Do you think so? Would *pleased* be the word?"

"Maybe not. Maybe impressed, though. Or touched."

"Or gratified."

Okay. Nora turns abruptly to Max. "We may as well go in, shall we?" Philip, who never opposed non-lethal tensions as long as they entertained him, would be enjoying this. He might even, as Lynn suggests, be gratified, not only by all the attention but also its jittery qualities. That same jitteriness, however, does make it difficult to concentrate on happy moments with him, on characteristics and memories and pleasing pictures. He wouldn't like that so much.

Sometimes he feels likeable, other times not. Sometimes his appealing qualities have their opposing aspects; which is ordinary enough, and rather like love, in that qualities which at some point attract may well come, down the road, to repel.

Hendrik Anderson was right, there's a good turnout; a surprising number, really. There are Philip's poker pals, some fellows he drank with, or fished with, and wives. Ted Marlowe, that's nice, it's probably not all that common for a doctor to attend the funeral of one of his patients. Dave Hamilton and Susannah, too, they must have juggled court schedules and appointments to be here. At a glance there's no sign of Joy Geffen, who perhaps feels an offering of food was enough and the loss of an afternoon's business too much. There are also familiar faces besides Lynn's that don't come from around here, but from other parts of his life: clients, suppliers, people like that, who turned into friends, and who could shift gears quickly enough, or were idle enough, to get here in time. It appears some people have ignored the no-flowers rule. There are several stiff, unappealing arrangements, the local florist rising ineptly but profitably to the occasion. Still, people have tried. In this town, never mind elsewhere, Philip had a life, lives, with little connection to the women now moving to the front row of seats: Nora first, followed by Sophie, then Beth. Somewhere behind them come Lynn and her Bill; but it is Max, Nora, Sophie and Beth who take the places for family, which is a stretch, all things considered.

Nora's eyes are locked on the plain casket, a sight that nearly knocks her to the floor. Philip is inside, right there. This is real. This is so staggeringly real that she falls into her seat as if stabbed, every surface and organ in sharp, shooting pain. It all hurts, all over again. She can feel Max looking at her, alarmed. Did Philip feel pain anything like this, alone in the night?

Look at that box—has she made some bad, irreversible mistakes here? If he'd been in charge of arrangements, Philip would have paid better attention to shadings and grains in the wood, whatever it is, of the casket. It wouldn't have looked so *utilitarian* in his hands, although he might have liked its simplicity. He used to say, "Too many people think style is decoration. I think it's paring back until only what's essential is left." Gingerbread, curlicues, wooden or brass folderol made his lip curl. "Camouflage," he called it. "And worse, cheap sentiment." He told customers attempting rebellion, "You want to make a statement, not fiddle around with extra bits. Let a piece be honest and say what it needs to. Leave it alone." This less-than-imposing box may fulfil his requirements for honesty. It definitely makes its own simple statement. But something much more complicated is inside, and should that not be reflected?

Something may be inside, but it is not Philip. Remember that. Hold in mind, along with much else, Philip the young, grinning, forthright, promising, naked man in a doorway.

This straightens her up, this makes her smile.

Sophie closes her eyes so that she can not only see Phil's hands, but can feel one resting comfortingly on her shoulder, moving tenderly to her throat. In this way he is still taking care, being careful, which is good, and causes her lips to curve upwards.

It must say only good things about him that he leaves women smiling.

Except Beth. Beth, dressed in pale yellow, presenting herself calmly and firmly, feels quite vividly the quivers around her of unease and antipathy and, as she knew there would be, acquiescence, although she's also perfectly aware of Nora making sure Sophie stays between them. She watched that tense, mean little scene out on the front steps with a mildly interested eye on Philip's first wife, assessing his tastes, which must have been wide to include both that woman and Nora, never mind Sophie, who Beth believes must be included. Beth has walked past those people on the chairs back there as if she were strolling a runway, fully conscious of movement and beauty and an exaggerated, professional grace that once was water to her and air, and having done all that, heard all that, felt all that with the acuteness and inevitability of a dream, she now cannot take her eyes off the casket.

She has never seen one before; has never even been to a funeral home. How plain and sharp-cornered it is. Signifying plain, sharp-cornered death, not abstractly or remotely but raw and up close. If she stood and took just a couple of steps, she could touch death. Imagine! She has a great desire to do that very thing, but—*impulse control!* She trembles, her fingers tap on her knees, her toes and heels click up and down. Sophie, sitting quietly beside her, doesn't like her, and Nora, two spaces down, is avoiding her. Who loves her? Who should love her?

Grief rattles right through her and into her bones.

She smells the perfume in the humidity of that last, long drive home. She can hear her mother's hoarse voice speaking of Beth's promise, her several glittering futures. Here's the weariness of her complaint of a terrible headache. To cure and end all of which, Beth prepared tea. And the words: "I know it's bitter. Best to just drink it right down."

She did that. To her mother, yes, but her mother also existed apart, an unhappy, hopeful woman who had been beautiful, and who mourned lost opportunities; who sat for long hours on hard chairs and drove many miles in search of those lost opportunities; who was even a child herself at one time, with playmates and parents and adventures Beth has no way of knowing about. A woman who later had conversations, maybe even tender ones, with Beth's father.

Who then writhed her way out of experience and a whole long known and unknown history, right out of life. At Beth's hands. She looks at the plain wooden box, she looks at her hands. "Oh, Mum." She hears that from inside her head. She didn't truly know; now she nearly does. She never called her mother anything as cozy as *Mum*, but that's the word, glass in her skin, that comes to her now.

How could this be?

A sharp elbow slams into her side, a sharp voice whispers, "Beth. What the hell's the matter with you? Stop it. Sit still."

Daddy, too, whom she hardly called *Daddy*.

There would have been a service for her mother, there would have been people attending who knew her mother in ways Beth has no notion of. Horror would have accompanied them to that funeral, along with their sorrow. Beth might even have been more on their minds than her mother. Her story, what she did, would have wrapped itself around both her parents, crushing the life out of them. She hears her father's tragic voice asking why. She smells the blood and feathers of dead birds he brings home. She sees her mother's wide brilliant mouth, hears that husky voice speaking of *accomplishments, prospects*. She hears "Kentucky Woman" and recalls white dresses and edged, drawling accents and the scents of mascara and powdery blushes. There are hotel rooms with landscapes over the beds and television sets hidden behind cabinet doors, bolted down. She sees miles and miles of fields and expressways, roadside lilies and daisies speeding by, city towers and lights appearing ahead, fading behind. She speaks about the importance to the world's children of song. She takes a turn down a promenade. She finds that point on the kitchen ceiling, a circular flaw, a water stain maybe, to watch.

She has *accomplishments*, she has *prospects*. See her smile invitingly, innocently, madly at all the judges in the world. She wins some, loses some, is rescued and saved again and again, perhaps due to beauty, by lawyers and doctors and others, until she is finally free, and then she is rescued and saved one more time, by Nora, who no longer needs her. Who does not want her. How can someone who has touched, bent and shaped her, who knows every inch of her and has used every pore, not want her; not care? Beth's mother touched, bent and shaped her. And used her. And cared.

What does Nora know? What does she see?

Beth's mother said, "If you're not feeling well, or you're unhappy, or someone's said or done something that's mean or unfair, don't let it show when you're up there. Do your best. Always hold on to that smile. Don't cry till you win." All right, she can do that.

Now there are three women smiling.

A blond-bearded, wispy-haired fellow in clerical collar bends to introduce himself to Nora. "I'm very sorry for your loss. I'll do my best to say what needs saying. I hope you won't find the service impersonal. It's more difficult, not having known him."

Nora nods. "I'm sure you'll do fine." Although she realizes immediately that he was not seeking reassurance, simply speaking a fact.

He begins the service with the 23rd Psalm. Just about everyone knows it and can recite along. It has a calming effect. Good for him. There is something to be said for ceremony; although after all she was probably more right than wrong in her choices, and anyway it's too late to change them.

He speaks the little he knows about Philip Lawrence, gleaned from common town knowledge and from details

passed by Sophie to Hendrik Anderson: that he was young for
a visit from death; that he was a well-known designer and
maker of high-quality furniture; that he had many friends in
this town, where he not only lived for the past fifteen years
but spent happy summers in childhood with grandparents
whose names are old and familiar here. That's about it. Like
a wedding, that other life-altering ritual, it seems the words
of a funeral don't take very long.

But wait, there's more: the impersonal part, vague but
pretty words to do with death itself, and faith, transitions
from one aspect of life to another, by which he presumably
means the eternal sort, and evolutions of grief from shock to
serene or respectful or affectionate memory. "What each person leaves behind when life ends," is how he puts this. He
looks relieved when he comes to an ending himself. "I would
now," he says finally, "invite anyone who wishes to say a few
words about the life of Philip Lawrence to do so."

Oh dear. There's one of those awkward, shuffling silences
before someone does rise, there are footsteps and here's Dave
Hamilton standing with a hand hovering over the coffin,
glancing briefly down at it. He begins speaking in the anxious
tones of a lawyer summarizing, without notes, the case on
behalf of a guilty defendant. "I saw Philip at least once a
week, and was always grateful that a person didn't have to
own his work to be his friend, because I sure couldn't afford
anything he made." Can that be true? He's a lawyer after all,
and lawyers have money, so maybe, in fact, he didn't really
like Philip's work. "We played poker just about every
Thursday for years, but he wasn't very good and he never got
any better. If he had great cards, he couldn't help smiling, and
if he had bad ones, he was too obviously downcast." Here and
there, people chuckle—who knew comic relief, however mar-

ginal, would be welcome? Clever Dave. His voice relaxes, he smiles.

"He was bad at bluffing, that was his trouble. But what he brought to our games, besides the money the rest of us won"—more laughter—"was his good nature. He liked a good time, as everyone does, but he also knew how to create a good time, as everyone doesn't. He was intelligent and knowledgeable about current events—well, as we all know, there've been times when he was part of current events, and he even managed to enjoy some aspects of that difficult period. All in all he took pleasure in his life, and gave others pleasure, so it's especially unfair that he's gone so early. His chair at our games is going to be hard to fill. We'll miss his energy and enjoyment. And . . ." Dave looks down, gives the coffin a smile ". . . his money, of course." As if this is just another lost game. Also as if Philip was not actually quite artful about bluffing.

That looks to be it for Dave Hamilton, who heads back to his seat. Now Max is rising and taking his place. He looks at Nora, looks at Sophie, looks around at the rest of the room. "I am here," he begins, "as friend and admirer, and as someone with great respect for Philip's attention and care for his work. He created comfort, he understood how important that is, and he also gave comfort to those around him." This makes better sense. It not only sounds more or less true, but takes Philip seriously, as a serious person. "He understood that the design of his work should be simple and beautiful, but also comfortable, because life is often complicated and not comfortable. This is not a peaceful understanding, but it is a wise one. Those fortunate enough to possess his work should appreciate it in that spirit, as those of us fortunate enough to know him appreciate the fullness and generosity of his presence. He was no more perfect than anyone else, nor in death does he become so, but those who mourn him most profoundly will be sustained by the memory of a man who lived as fully and lovingly as he could, which is a great deal for anyone to leave behind in the world."

When Max takes his seat, Nora takes his hand. "That was nice. Just right. Did you prepare it?"

"No. I only thought that although those were fine words from that other fellow, we shouldn't leave it like that."

Quite right. Time to wrap things up, though—except the minister, evidently insensitive to conclusions and pushing his luck, beams through what he must take to be just another awkward, shuffling pause and asks, "Would anyone else care to add a few words—a friend, a member of his intimate or extended family?" By *intimate* he must mean Nora; she's all Philip had. By *extended*, who knows? Sophie perhaps, or even Beth, if he only means household. Apparently Lynn thinks he means her because here she is, striding as if by personal, heartfelt invitation up to the front, with her bare legs and honey-blonde hair and wide hips and flashing red nails. Nora's grip on Max tightens. The minister looks pleased, Hendrik Anderson alert, if not alarmed.

"Most of you don't know me," she begins, "but in the midst of all this admiration I feel I have a few things to add. In case you don't know, I was Philip Lawrence's first wife, briefly but unforgettably, before he ran into his current wife." His no-name wife. Nora leans forward. "Obviously we haven't been close for a long time, and I don't know what sort of man he was at the end—a better one than before, one might hope, although I doubt it—but when we were young I learned a great deal from him." Lynn's eyes narrow on Nora before skipping off, her expression as hard as her eyes. "As I've already told his last wife, it was instructive to care at a young age for a man of low principles and high desires. Given to whims but incapable of self-discipline. Although I'm surprised to hear he wasn't better at poker, since he was a very good liar back in my day.

"Some of you will think these aren't nice things to say about the dead, but I don't believe you should leave with only one or two points of view. That hardly seems fair to the whole man, such as he was. Philip was more than you saw, and I think you should know that, contrary to some opinions," and she gives the casket a glance, "there isn't much in the way of proper love or fidelity in there. Not much of anything, I guess, in the end." She stops, she regards Nora again. Her lips and hands are trembling as she considers the entire front row of women, and Max, and off she goes, sandals clip-clopping past everyone, right out the door.

Well. That was a moment. There's a long silence, then shuffling and a man's voice saying, "Excuse me," and another departure. Good husband Bill, it must be. Will it have come as news to him how bitterly attached Lynn has been to Philip all these years? How passionately, it turns out, she still cares? That her attachment and passion are negative hardly matters. Bill will be wondering—oh, Bill will be wondering quite a few things. Meanwhile, Lynn's performance has pretty much sucked the air from the room. Who will restore it?

Step up, Nora.

She had no intention of doing this, but she's the only person in the room who can, wife-wise, widow-wise, trump Lynn. And Philip stood up for her and she has that favour to return. And although it keeps shape-shifting, and so is hard to keep adapting to and stay on top of, this is Philip's day. For all these reasons, Nora finds herself standing at the front, her turn beside the casket, wearing a small, crooked grin. What a lot of faces!

What a lot of very interested faces.

"That's a tough act to follow," she begins. "But I must say, it occurred to me while Lynn was speaking how much Philip would have enjoyed this. Obviously I disagree with her about one or two matters, not least that beyond what Dave and Max have already said, Philip was in fact a very good husband; for me, if not necessarily," she lets a smile drift over Sophie, "for anyone else. We had a good time for a lot of years, although nowhere near enough years, and one of the many ways I'm going to miss him is that later today we'd have had some great laughs talking about this. He'd have liked knowing how much people cared about him one way or another, and he'd be pleased to have stirred things up right to the end. Nothing could be more perfectly Philip."

This is, generally speaking, not entirely true. Perhaps that's what Max meant by pride? "I'm grateful you're all here to say goodbye to our friend. My friend." Her voice crackles. "My dear Philip." She can't say any more; she casts a glazed, lost glance around the room. Max rises and takes her hand and leads her back to her seat.

Hendrik Anderson clears his throat, fending off further disastrous ministerial invitations to speak. "Yes, thank you everyone. Let me bring this service to a close now with an invitation to silent prayer and farewell as we wish Philip Lawrence godspeed. There is a book of acknowledgements in the front vestibule for anyone to sign who hasn't already done so, and there are refreshments in the main room off the vestibule. We hope you'll be able to stay and visit with each other and share more of your memories."

The music Nora and Sophie finally chose yesterday is no

Tom after all, but a Leonard—a Cohen song they agreed would suit all of them, Nora and Sophie and Philip. "It's very long," Sophie said, "but beautiful."

"Yes."

"It's not exactly funeral music."

"No."

Now, after a service in which music must constitute only the most minor shock and surprise, the opening bars of "Dance Me to the End of Love" commence their grim lilt. Hendrik comes to lead them out, and when they stand, there is the strangest, most intimate moment: these two women Nora and Sophie would, if they could, float in each other's arms around Philip Lawrence in his plain box, they would dance light-footed up the aisle past all the staring people and out the doors and down the street to the words of "Dance me very tenderly and dance me very long" for Nora, "Dance me through the panic till I'm gathered safely in" for Sophie, "Dance me to your beauty with a burning violin" for Philip, Phil.

They do not do this. They proceed sedately up the aisle past all the people, followed by Beth and by Max, and when they reach the large foyer, the song still surrounding them, Nora whispers, "I could leave now and feel we did the right thing and it's finished."

"Yes," Sophie says. She notes a new, generous aspect to Nora's *we*.

There's no leaving yet, though. Hendrik is drawing them into the waiting reception room with its urns of coffee and tea, its tiny cream-cheese and egg salad and ham sandwiches and half-slices of banana bread. People drift in, although a few are making good their escape, following the example set by Lynn and Bill, who must have sped out of the funeral home and right out of town. Dave Hamilton approaches

Nora. "I hope I wasn't too jokey. I just wanted to say what a good guy he was."

"Yes, he was. What you said was just fine."

Dave turns to Max. "I'd have liked to say what you did."

"Thank you." Max nods gravely. "I'm glad he had people here who gave him pleasure. Such a troublesome place."

"Yeah, I guess." Dave Hamilton glances uneasily at Nora. "But he took things in his stride." Nora did not, is what she takes him to mean. Whatever Philip needed to take in his stride here, she was at the root of it, she caused it, maybe it killed him.

Well, that's excessive, isn't it? But this town has a gift for rubbing her raw. At least her opponents have convictions, however demented or dimwitted or shrill. She finds it hard to forgive this nice, sorrowful friend of Philip's; but, then, she is not required to forgive, and no doubt Dave Hamilton is unaware of needing forgiveness, so that's all right, isn't it?

There is something to what Lynn said: that Philip, for all his support, his easy shoulders and comforting arms, was inclined to take easy routes to his desires, and could be unfortunately relaxed in his principles.

At least Nora is getting her tenses right. Next thing she knows, she'll be referring to herself, without a blink, as a widow.

She is also an amputee, missing a large, vital, balancing limb—what will she do without him, dancing to the end of love all alone?

She doesn't suppose deciding a future is a job she can just hand over to Sophie. "Here, you take care of it," she could say. "You look after my life, I'm tired and my feet hurt and you're good with details and plans." Anyway, Sophie is busy with Hendrik Anderson, chatting and nodding, smiling even, for all the world as if they're exchanging courtesies after a perfectly normal social event.

While Beth appears to be going quietly, publicly nuts.

Will this day never end?

Beth's pale yellow dress drifts around her as she picks up a plate of tiny sandwiches and begins whirling about the room with a smile of such wolfish intensity that people shift at her approach and smile back very uneasily. Only the bravest person would refuse one of the sandwiches. Now she is back at the table, pouring tea, picking up cups and saucers and handing them about with the same ferocity, only now, along with the unnerving smile, tears are pouring down her face, and she doesn't wipe them away, doesn't even seem aware of them. Her nose runs, too, as weeping people's noses do—an unpleasant prospect, accepting tea from her hands. Although people do. Although they immediately look around for places to set down their cups, and then begin to head for the door.

Beth is clearing the room, she is wrapping things up. Nora ought to be grateful. Max steps forward. He puts a hand on Beth's arm—puts a hand entirely around her thin arm—gives her a little shake and starts to draw her out of the room. She pulls back, but he frowns, and a frowning Max is formidable. Sophie heads in Nora's direction, while Hendrik Anderson and the minister move out to the hall where they can shake hands with people as they leave, which is probably where Nora is supposed to be too. Max and Beth sail out swiftly, Max so determined and Beth so light it looks as if her feet don't touch the floor.

"What a shambles," Nora says.

"Although you were right, Phil might not have thought so."

There remains that, it's true. And the music. Not entirely hopeless, not a total disgrace.

Hardly anybody got to the desserts. There's still an untouched plate of banana-bread slices, another of small chocolate macaroons. They look home-made. After Hendrik Anderson finishes his work in the basement, does he hurry upstairs to bake?

Nora reaches out for a macaroon at the same time Sophie does, so they bump knuckles. "Still, I'm a bit speechless," Sophie adds. Which about wraps it up.

When, with everyone else gone from the room, they turn to leave, they find themselves moving arm in arm, slowly. Hendrik Anderson and the minister, who looks to be suffering a little from shock, are shaking hands at the front door. "Thank you," Nora says to Hendrik Anderson. "I'm sorry if the service went oddly, but I'm grateful you tried to keep it on track. And no one can say it wasn't entertaining."

"You're quite welcome. I expect when you can look back from a certain distance, you'll decide it was fine, in the sense of being appropriate. It sounds to me as if what you said was right, that he would have enjoyed it himself, and you know, that's not always the case. Some funerals don't suit the person at all."

"Well, this one sure covered the bases."

"I'll be in touch in a couple of days, shall I?"

"With the bill?"

"No. Well, yes, but I meant about the remains. Whether you'll want to keep them yourself, or if we should arrange a cemetery burial, and then there are different types of containers to choose from. But there's no need to discuss all that now. I'll contact you when it's more appropriate."

When Philip is a few handfuls of ash. How much does a big man amount to, reduced? What is his colour then, what is his texture?

What possible forms does he take?

"We won't need to discuss it," Nora says. "If you could send the ashes along in a box with your bill, that would be fine. I don't want things dragging out."

He bows slightly, as he did when he helped her out of the car—only an hour ago? Time twisting again. "As you wish." For a few minutes it felt as if he almost liked Nora; now it seems he doesn't again. As they separate, it's Sophie whose arm he holds, walking back to the car. They can see Max and Beth, both in the front seat this time with Beth wedged between him and the driver. Hendrik holds back, letting Nora move ahead on her own. "This may be inappropriate," and he turns his human, kitchen-and-living-room, non-funereal face up towards Sophie, "but I wondered, would you mind if I called you?" Well. Yes. It is inappropriate. Particularly for an undertaker, his timing is shockingly bad. Although, of course, from his perspective it's not as if he's asking the widow. And it's not as if he would suppose anything's out of bounds after that funeral.

"I'd like that."

Now two women in black, one in pale yellow, travel in a large black car homewards from Philip Lawrence's funeral. For Beth there's no whirl graceful enough, no tea powerful enough, no winner's smile brilliant enough to undo what she did. Who is she to be now? Sophie is restless, vividly conscious of moments that divide, like being in a plane, shifting rapidly overhead from one landscape to another. Now what?

Nora's inattentive gaze is turned inwards rather than out at the tidy houses and streets of this town. She is preoccupied with various notions. If Max is right about the beloved dead speaking up, Philip will have something to say, which she can hope will be something sympathetic and clever and amusing and useful, but she'll do what she does anyway, if only because now there are no reasons not to, no brakes whatever. She'll have to be careful, though. Directions will need to be clear before she begins. Visions, like Beth's teas, have to steep; and like Beth's teas, they may turn out pale, dark or crimson, it all depends not just on shapes and materials, colours and textures but also, of course, on the main thing: intentions.

Fifteen

*A*nd so winds down the third day since Philip Lawrence died presumably, possibly, in his fortunate sleep. "Now comes the harder part," says Max as the black car glides to a stop in front of the house.

How different the place looked the first time Nora saw it. Ramshackle and begging for work, for one thing. Full of hope and rampant possibility, a home for fresh starts for another. Now it could be a house she has never been in and knows nothing about; a shelter for strangers.

Sophie stood on the sidewalk contemplating what was intended as a haven of untortured, unimportant, unambiguous, life-saving tasks. The house didn't immediately strike her as one that would end nightmares; it actually looked more the sort of looming place that could actively promote bad dreams. She opened the gate anyway, and there she was. Now, nearly four years on, here she is.

Philip was a few minutes late picking Beth up at the bus depot. She'd never been on a bus before and hadn't found it very nice: crowded and smelly and not her kind of people. Waiting for Philip, she noticed nobody particularly noticing her, which was unsatisfactory and reassuring, both. Once out-side here, seeing the size of the place, she imagined many small, safe, closed rooms behind brick. Philip was polite but remote, apparently considering her Nora's project, not his own.

As he did till his dying day.

Night.

The harder part? Yes, no doubt. Starting now.

Beth is first inside, flying up the steps as soon as Max has hauled himself out of the car and released her. She is across the porch and through the door ahead of them all, and by the time they're in the front hall, they can hear her already upstairs. Shortly there's the sound of the shower. Well, she can't stay there for ever, can she?

If Philip were here, this would be the time for a few stiff drinks and a grim-and-gleeful blow-by-blow account of the funeral's mishaps and very odd moments. Bluffing, betrayal, fresh alliances and affections of various sorts. Lynn, of course; Lynn most of all—oh, what fun! In his absence Sophie silently pours wine, then joins Nora on the living-room sofa. Max is in Sophie's usual chair, upright in deference to his arthritis and whatever else may ail him these days—a certain grey cast of skin at the moment. "I will just have this one glass," he says, "and then if you don't mind I'll lie down for a few moments before going back."

He is old, he is old, what will Nora do when he is gone too? "Why don't you stay overnight? It would be lovely to have you, and you shouldn't drive both ways in one day. You could have my room and get a good rest. And it would be nice for us."

"No, thank you, that's kind, but I will be fine and I prefer my own bed. You must come to town soon, though. I still owe you lunch and a conversation whenever you're ready."

About futures. What comes next. "Yes, all right, I will. Thanks for hauling Beth out of there, Max. What the hell was her problem? Do you know, Sophie?"

"Not a clue. Not grief, I'm sure, so maybe it was just Beth being Beth—trying to grab the spotlight, even from Phil." Phil. All right. What people are called means something. *Sophie* is a hearty sort of name, whereas *Soph*, say, would be someone more marginal, less significant in a room. And no one would call Beth *Elizabeth*, or *Betty*. *Elizabeth* is too rigorous, *Betty* too plain, but *Beth* is perfectly drifty.

Although Beth has not been exactly drifty today. Her mood swings have been unexpected and dire, her frantic hopes are unendurable—everything connected with her has been fraught and embarrassing. "What will you do about her?" Max asks; which is the question, isn't it?

"Send her on her way as soon as I figure out how to, I guess. Only I don't want to cause any more harm." More harm? What harm has Nora done Beth? All she has done is transform her from a merely beautiful, fortunately boned, blessedly fine-skinned young woman into something approaching an icon. That's a rare kind of gift; not that Beth has ever said thank you. "If I do it wrong, it feels as if it'll bring more bad luck, that's all."

"Your view of the rules of the universe?" Max's eyebrows rise in amusement. He does not, Nora knows, believe the universe has particular rules when it comes to moral balancing acts.

"Nothing," she replies dryly, "seems out of the question right now."

"That is true, nothing human is ever out of the question. You know, I meant what I said about the hard part coming next. The duty is only to be strong enough to endure it."

Duty? Perhaps. He sets down his glass. "On the subject of being strong and enduring, however, I believe that short nap now will restore me."

"All right, but remember you're more than welcome to stay over if you change your mind. Use my room. The drapes are closed. If Beth is racketing around, shoo her downstairs, okay?"

Beth is not racketing around, Beth is in her room working quietly and just as fast as she can. Again no one is calling up to her, no one is tapping on her door, not even Max, whose slow, heavy footsteps she hears on the stairs and then entering Nora's room and closing the door. No one here cares for her. No one here even feels they *should* care for her. She learns things too late.

How narrow she has become in two years in this house! After her shower she puts on the same plain blue linen pants she arrived in, with the same tucked-in plain yellow blouse, the sort of bus-passenger outfit she's hardly worn since she came here and took to the romantic camouflages of those floaty dresses. It's obvious in the mirror how loosely the pants hang at the waist, how her collarbones jut under the fall of the blouse. No wonder she was so hungry last night! A person could starve to death in this house.

She has pinned back her wet hair rather than brushing it out. She doesn't bother with make-up. Her eyes look smaller, the left one wonkier. There are things that have come undone inside her today. Of course she is beautiful anyway.

Her heart's beating too fast, it feels as if it could batter its way through its thin skin-and-bone walls.

People go on and on about love like it's the most important as well as the most common thing in the world. But maybe it's not either one. Maybe that's sad, or maybe not.

Hearts downstairs beat more slowly. "I think," Nora is saying as Sophie tops up their glasses and takes back her usual place in the chair Max has vacated, "I think I'd like to spend the rest of the day getting pissed."

"Sounds like a plan." Sophie raises her glass. "Tell me about his first wife. Lynn? Was she always so awful?"

"I don't know much about her, except I really thought she was nicely settled into a better life than she ever would have had with Philip. I mean, if it hadn't been me, there'd have been somebody else, he always said that even though they were fond of each other, it was a mistake to get married. Of course she was upset when he left, but making that scene was really something, after so long."

"The drive home with her husband will be interesting."

"Yeah, I bet." They grin at each other. How strange that they each think, *This is nice.* Just for the moment, *This is nice.*

"Phil?" Nora queries after a silence.

Sophie considers the levels and layers of her possible answers. "Phil," she says finally.

There. Let the chips fall.

"I see. Oh well."

Not exactly predictable, Nora. Or predictable only in her unpredictability. Or are they both just getting drunk extra-fast? In some unpredictable moods, that happens to people. Altered energy levels, Sophie imagines. Quicker into the bloodstream and up to the brain. She touches her head. She does enjoy the wiriness of her hair. Phil said he did, too. Nora's, while shiny, has nothing in particular to recommend it. "Beth," Sophie says aloud, "really thought the two of you could move away and live happily ever after together?"

"Yes, and very wound up she was. Happy Philip's gone, and of the opinion I should be as well. No sex, she was clear on that score, that it wasn't about sex at all, just some weird kind of love. At least she called it love. I'd say it was an insane few minutes. You were right, there *is* something wrong with her."

"I wouldn't have imagined that, though. Should I be offended she picked you and not me? Do you think it's my size or my personality that put her off?"

Wine and brief laughter—that's a pretty good deal for the third day. "Still," Nora says finally, "I ought to go do something with her. Not that I have a clue how, but at least I've had enough to drink that I don't care as much. Although I guess it'd be good to come up with suggestions for what she might do once I've gotten her out."

"Pass on the burden?"

"The responsibility anyway. Same thing maybe. Pour me a little more, would you, Sophie? Then I'd better stagger upstairs and give it a shot."

In the event, Beth pre-empts her. They hear her thumping, unusually gracelessly, down the stairs, followed by the heavier, slower, clump-clump of Max. When she appears in the living-room doorway she is dressed in plain blue pants and yellow tucked-in blouse, with her hair pinned back and no make-up, so that she looks surprisingly pinched, fan-shapes of tiny lines visible at her mouth, a patchwork of dry skin formed up at her hairline—once these things start they travel fast in thin skin. "I'm packed," she announces. "I'm leaving."

What?

From behind Beth, Max signals, palms up towards Nora and Sophie. "Yes, Beth has asked to come with me, and she is welcome. She will be company on my drive back. We should go now, I think. It will be getting dark, and I would like to be on the highway."

"But what about all your things, Beth? And where will you go?"

"I have what I want. Max can drop me at the subway." For all they know, she's going to throw herself under a train. Or sleep on the streets. She has lived with them for nearly two years, day in and day out, but is suddenly capable of springing one surprise after another. Then again, strays are bound to be affected by their scrappy, mysterious histories. They flinch from an extended hand, or wrap themselves ingratiatingly around ankles, or bite for no earthly reason. And sometimes they just wander off.

Like Philip.

Now that Beth's going—isn't this often the way?—Nora feels a twinge of concern and even affection for the waif she was, until moments ago, gearing up to be rid of. Two years, all that work, those many hours spent in the studio scrutinizing and shifting Beth's skin and posed bones, not much conversation because Nora was concentrating and anyway Beth never had much to say for herself, but still, there they were—and now it's perfectly possible she'll never see Beth again. That strikes Nora as sad, another loss; although probably only because this has already been such a big, bad week for abrupt and irreversible absences. It's not as if she's going to ask Beth to change her mind and stay on. "If you're sure. But take good care, okay?" A stupid thing to say; at least Beth must think so, since she doesn't reply.

Sophie frowns. Beth is so thin, if not necessarily frail, and appears to be wobblier in her emotions than anyone has supposed. What happens to someone so unprotected and apparently prone to misjudgment when she goes into the world? But fortunately this is not Sophie's house, and she cannot invite Beth to stay. Guilt and relief trip over each other, not for the

first time. "Yes," she says, "you take care. Call if you need anything. Let me know where you are and I can send on anything
you've forgotten." Beth doesn't dignify that remark either.

From the porch, Nora and Sophie watch her sling two fat
suitcases into the small storage space of Max's car. Max opens
the passenger door for her, a courteous gesture, before stepping back up the walk. "You will be all right here, you two?"

"Sure, don't worry. But you be careful, Max. On the drive
back." Nora doesn't just mean highway hazards and traffic.

"I shall be very careful, but I am happy to take her. As to
where, that will be up to her. She is an unusual young
woman, but I believe competent enough. Perhaps we will talk
on the way and I'll learn her intentions. The important thing
is that she leaves by her own choice. That saves you difficulties, I think."

"I think so, too. Thanks, Max. For everything. We'll talk."
Nora leans forward, kisses his cheek. As he turns, he and
Sophie touch hands, exchange glances. That's new. Nora
and Sophie wave as Max's car grinds and clatters away. He
waves, too, but Beth does not even look back.

Her absence, considering she's such a slight person, feels
like a great weight lifted. Out of sight, out of mind? That's
awfully cold. Still, there it is. Sophie says, "Thank God that's
over," and they turn back to the house, two women still wearing black and due to a good deal of wine, not entirely steady
on their feet.

A very few nights ago four people lived in this house. Now
there are two. The living room feels enormous, the sofa and
chairs and tables all outsized. Nora resumes her corner of the
sofa where Philip should be close enough to touch with her
toes; or he could reach out to her shoulder. Sophie is back in
her wing chair observatory. It's hard to absorb all the sway

and tilt of the past couple of days. Nora's voice is mellow and slurred when she says finally, "Philip's ashes."

"What about them?"

"There ought to be something fantastic to do with them, don't you think?"

"You mean put them someplace he liked? That's a good idea. How about the river? Except that's probably against the law. Under a tree, then? In his shop somehow?" Or across a significant patch of yard behind his shop, that would mean something, too.

"No, no, I don't mean scattering them or burying them, I mean *using* them."

What the hell is she talking about?

"Listen." A great bubble of fresh grief rises up into Nora's throat; followed by a familiar bubble of something more comforting. "How about *Portrait in Ash*, don't you think Philip would like that? Or just *Husband*. Isn't that an odd word? *Husband*. So old-fashioned, like *shepherd*, something there's no real call for any more. A profession whose time has come and gone." Sophie is gaping. "Don't look like that. For heaven's sake, how long have you lived here?"

As if Sophie, with her hand over her mouth, is the offending one. "Not so long you can't still surprise me, that's for sure. You're talking about using him in your work?"

"Exactly. I'll have to be careful, though. I wonder where I could find out about working with ash? Especially that kind of ash. Because if I screwed up, I couldn't exactly run out for more, could I?"

"Is this a joke?" Nora's version of all that *You're kidding* Sophie has already had to put up with?

"Not at all. It'd be like a tribute, sort of. A monument. Why, don't you think Philip would approve?"

Sophie has, come to think of it, no idea. He might be affronted, enraged, he might be amused, he might, for all she knows, be honoured and touched. He grows less tangible. His image wavers. Sophie keeps a good grip on his hands, although even if they're nothing like cheap department store sculptures of hands raised in prayer, cast in fake plaster or bronze, they're banal enough compared with what Nora's suggesting.

And there is Nora, yes, growing shiny with purpose, intention, drunkenness. How lucky she is, seeing no need, apparently, to be even a *nice* person, much less a good one. As if she's entitled to these antagonistic, angry, frivolous, enthusiastic, freakish outbursts. Put her in a refugee camp and only the figures and shapes might appeal. The lumps and bumps of impromptu graveyards would form tapestries, and reaching arms would be slips of fabric, wonderfully embroidered. How chilly, eerie and enviable.

No wonder she gets into trouble.

"I can see you don't approve, Sophie, but most people only have headstones. Don't you think Philip would like the idea of a different sort of memorial? Something unique? I can't think he'd appreciate sitting in a closet or up on a mantel, or for that matter being buried. He liked being the centre of attention."

So he did. But Nora seems to think there is a good use for what remains of a human. Whereas there is not. There may have to be ends, but there are no good uses. Well, except for organ transplants, but that's different.

Nora straightens, as best she can. "I guess it sounds strange, but everyone who cared is bereft in their own way, and this would be mine." Sophie likes the sound of *bereft*, even from Nora, who may or may not know how deep and hard a word it can be. It's better than *bereaved*, anyway. That's a sort of collective, a group: *The Bereaved*. Not personal, not individual.

"Have you made plans yet, Sophie? Have you thought what you might want to do?" If Beth hadn't got a jump on events, this is how Nora might have approached her: easing into the subject while inexorably easing her out of the house. It's more than a hint that Sophie had better get a move on. She has more life to pack up than Beth did, and even if she'd thought of it, wouldn't have been able just to toss a couple of suitcases into the back of a car. Obviously time's up, but Sophie wishes her head were clearer—Nora's a hard one to keep up with, she's just full of surprises.

"I don't know. I'll leave as fast as I can, but I haven't had time to think where I'll go. Can you give me a couple of days?"

Nora's eyebrows go up, her mouth down. "Sophie! I didn't mean you should leave, I was just wondering if you have anything in particular you want to do. Because if you don't, I have a suggestion. There's lots of reasons you might hate the idea, but let me pull a Beth and spring it on you anyway."

Was Nora's mind not the first to leap ahead of the others' two mornings ago, when she woke up to find Philip dead beside her? Even drunk, and as she says *bereft*, she is light-footed as she vaults across chasms of dread and sorrow and loss. So Sophie imagines. "What idea?"

"That you'd stay on. If I'm going to do this, it seems to me I'll have to stay where he always said he belonged in his bones. Which does not, let me say, cheer me up one little bit. But there it is. And I don't want to be here on my own. So if you don't have immediate plans, what would you think about staying, too?"

Sophie has two economics degrees. She used to have huge, world-saving ambitions, massive, hopeless desires. She is more fit than she once was, thanks to Phil and, to be honest, Nora as well, but the question remains, fit for what?

She also thinks Nora sounds oddly pleading. Well, Sophie can see why she wouldn't want to stay here alone. "If you're sure. Maybe. For a while. You're right, otherwise there's a lot to think through all at once." She remembers to add, "Thank you." But how will they co-exist, even with plenty of extra room in this newly spacious house, when Sophie has only half her previous duties and an awful shortage of recognizable joys, while Nora's busy playing about with Phil's ashes?

Oh—is that how Sophie sees what Nora does? As *playing*? Frolicking with this outrageous notion and that one as if it's a game, like rope-skipping or hopscotch?

"Good. Eventually I'll be selling the house and we'll both need to make plans, but meanwhile," Nora takes a deep, obvious breath, "it feels right for the people who cared most for Philip to go on taking care of him."

If that's Nora's idea of taking care of him.

But how long has she known? Right from the start, or has she just worked it out?

Nora uncoils from the sofa and for an instant Sophie presses back in her chair. How stupid—Nora's not about to attack her, she is saying, "I'm absolutely starving all of a sudden. Are you?"

They fry eggs, they make toast, they're having breakfast, evidently, at nightfall. Nora looks at her watch. "Max and Beth will be nearly back by now. I wonder where she'll go? I hope she's okay." Easy to be benevolent, even pitying, from a distance.

"Maybe she has relatives."

"I'm not sure. All the time I spent with her, and I only know she wasn't in touch with anyone. I didn't actually get the impression she had any family, but if I ever asked, she wouldn't talk about anything except all those damned beauty pageants. Nothing about actual relatives. Or friends, for that matter." Even so, it really is bad not to know. Because the truth is, Nora wasn't much interested, beyond Beth's various postures and uses—what a good thing there's no particular connection between an artist's virtues and her work's values.

Just as there's not necessarily a connection between visions, hopes and desires, and what actually comes of them. This is the best time, when pictures are still so unformed they're also still perfect. The moment work begins, when it starts taking on real shape and shading and purpose, that's the moment it will begin losing perfection.

For the time being it's companionable to be sitting at the kitchen table, eating a night-time breakfast with Sophie.

The more the merrier?

"Bear with me," Nora says. "Honestly, I don't have bad intentions."

Do Nora and Sophie sleep on this third night? Oh yes; not like the dead, but near enough. And do they dream? Yes again, but tonight's dreams are not sweet or bad or useful or even especially sad. Neither of them dreams of Philip Lawrence, three nights dead now. Sophie dreams of adding by hand reams of household sums for no identified purpose; Nora of cleaning paintbrushes over and over, an infinity of the things, an endless task. These are tedious ways to spend the night, but easy ones. *The harder part* must pick up in the morning, and the morning, again, after that. There is no way to absorb fatal information, and no denying it either, which is precisely the shocking dilemma of grief: that things happen—bang!—out of any day and out of the night, and there's nothing to be done about it, and that's almost all there is to it.

THEOPENING

Sixteen

For all the density of black in this large, high-ceilinged room, the atmosphere is the reverse of funereal. There's not a syllable of muted reverence in the swell of soaring, multiple voices, nor is the style of so much blackness remotely sombre. Nora, for instance, is tanned to the visible navel in a slim-lined, one-shouldered, short black number slit to the thighs. Very glamorous, very fit for her coming-out party, a deliberate, bold, fleshy statement: *I'm back.*

Although not back as she once was. Adapt or perish, what doesn't kill you makes you stronger—that's the sort of difference being spoken by her spare body, scant dress.

Sophie, by contrast, is even larger than she used to be, and is also one of the few who've opted for flamboyance, with a gloriously red, massively ballooning-out dress. In colour and size she takes up more than her fair share of space, like a deep, old-fashioned sofa in a room otherwise occupied by the expensively spindly. She's here partly for a change-of-pace treat, partly as an effort of loyalty; loyalty having taken several turns in the past year or so.

Nora and Sophie have both learned, it seems, what Beth

used to know: that style and colour have their own language, they have something to say, truth or lies.

Speaking of Beth, what on earth is she doing here, what was Max thinking? There she is, just coming through the door and already taking up more space than she's due as well; not because she's bigger than she used to be, although she is, or because she's excessively colourful, which she isn't in a knee-length straight black dress that leaves her arms bare but is high-collared in a fashion that would not be out of place on a nun, but because of her unwieldy accessory: the wheelchair in which she's rolling a not-awfully-old man.

Sugar daddy? Nora and Sophie catch each other's eyes through the crowd, and raise eyebrows.

Despite Max's cranked-high air conditioning, it's growing uncomfortably warm with too much humanity on a hot city night. Look at these sleek people sipping their wine, listen to the cumulative roar and mosquito-whine of their social voices. See also a few of them exchanging lowered words, deliberating, frowning, nodding—it's the discreet who need watching, they're the thumbs-up, thumbs-down people, the ones doing business. It's not quite ten o'clock, too early to know for sure, but the room feels promising, there's a good, high hum to it.

Max's gallery, expanded since Nora's first visit, now has four sizeable rooms. The smallest, which after the loss of Lily contains a single big cherrywood desk rather than two, always has one or two favoured works hanging, but it's mainly an office. Tonight it will be opened only for business purposes, the private discussion of prices, and with luck the writing of cheques. "My first errand of the day after an opening," Max likes to say, "is the bank. We do not approve of sober second thoughts." His little joke, but he is also serious when he pats his belly and says, "If I worked only for love, I could never have this. With love only, no one eats."

Max is among those in black. He is shrinking, and his belly is not what it was. Several months ago he had a few tiny strokes, cerebral accidents as they're called, that have slowed and altered his judgment in ways he is still discovering. He has sold his beloved yellow Fiat. "I take taxis," he shrugs. "This is life." One of these days he'll be gone, too. Tonight it's possible to locate his progress by watching people shifting and swaying, making way for a happy elderly man moving through the crowd like a child through a cornfield.

Almost no one has left yet, and some, like Beth, are still arriving. They show their invitations to the hired doorman and once inside are offered white wine or red by more hired staff. This front gallery is the largest, but people are also spilling into a smaller one, where there's food. The two servers there are busy trying to keep the tables along two of the walls from chaos. How hungry, or greedy, people show themselves to be in their table-side jostlings, even though they are not exactly among the deprived of the earth, and the food, from tiny hot quiches and samosas to chocolate-dipped fruits, isn't especially interesting. "We feed them," says Max, "but not well."

The third, most intimate gallery is closed and locked.

In his invitations and advertisements, Max has named the show "Philip etc." in fat, black, eye-catching, romantically cursive script. All the work does involve Philip, it's true, although not always in obvious ways. He appears here in a fierce orangey blotch reflecting fury and flames, there in a glued cufflink—*PL*—on a muscled forearm, the tracing of a hand, carefully callused, holding the chopped-off remains of a red-patterned silk tie. There is the upholstery-fabric blue-grey of his eyes and of grief in one work; in another the shape of his mouth attached to a brilliantly yellow background, in the form of two close-set rows of outsized, clownish, shiny red buttons.

That he was closed-mouthed in an open-mouthed way: not uncommon to camouflage secrets behind bold appearance, but who, besides Nora and Sophie, will see Philip in this? The piece is already sold, the buyer, according to Max, a woman who likes the notion of a swoop of unusually wrought, vibrant red lips over one of her sofas.

There are in these pieces not codes exactly, but distillations and private commentaries, but they'll be hard for outsiders to decipher. No one here will know, for instance, that the big, curiously old-fashioned, particularly joyous-looking portrayal of round and merry, colourfully snowsuited children setting off down a tobogganing hill is not joyous at all. That the subtly angled tree at the bottom will prove fatal.

Max may have named the show "Philip etc.," but Philip cannot possibly be himself, a separate figure, a man on his own from his own point of view. It's Nora's memory and eye that see not only those cheery youngsters headed for doom but the tendons and veins of Philip's calves, and how they became especially prominent at his ankles; it's her perspective that views the way the flesh of his thigh shaped itself as it hung from the bone when he was lying in bed with one leg propped up; it's her senses, not his, that know the precise warmth of the flesh of his shoulder, the little dip where it encountered his neck, the rippling up and down of his spine. Oh, the attention she has paid to the details of Philip—far more in his absence, as a sad matter of fact, than when he was present.

That's too bad. Still, a person can stagger back from rude shock all she wants, but she does finally have to stagger forward again, the only choice the manner of staggering. This is Nora's way, all this tonight on these walls.

What do other people do with sorrow and loss, with anger and error, with recollected delight for that matter, if they have no gift for transforming? Nora has come to see Philip through many different materials and manifestations in the past year. She has also come in several not-quite-identifiable ways to love him, she thinks, sufficiently, and somewhat differently. That's here, too. She misses his presence moment to moment (including this moment when he ought to be at her shoulder), that loose loyalty of his backing her up, but in the face of impossibility she has done what she could, and if the two of them can no longer be connected in lying-down, getting-up ways, they are at least strung and beaded, glued, painted and stitched together on these walls, in these pictures.

Most of which she is entirely prepared to release into the world of blank walls over strange women's sofas.

What do other new widows do? They weep, they flail, they collapse. Or some take cruises, or lovers. Nora, too, wept and flailed and even fell into excessive sleep for a day or two, a week or two, but there's still the business of blood flowing, heart beating; the certain, and on the worst days dismaying, absence of death that means a person has no choice but to stand up. Nora was in no mood for cruises, or even for lovers (not yet), but that blood insists on flowing in quickening surges, the heart beats faster, there are luring ideas, pictures, notions, impulses, desires. Who knew *Life goes on* would turn out to be more than three glossy words? Life does go on, in whatever off-kilter, mutated form.

So Nora got down to work.

Not even in her sandwich-and-variety-store days had she worked so fiercely and done so much in such a short time.

Once standing, once started, she went for ten hours a day, twelve, a ferocious outpouring. She rummaged through old photographs stored in the sideboard, and through the designs and woods and fabrics and files left behind in the workshop. She considered the many ways Philip was at home in his body, confident that it would do what he wished, move as he desired it to, even only striding over the lawn—that it would not fail him. Misplaced confidence it might have been, but real enough to him, and how to catch that presumptuous grace with elliptical references of colour, shape and material?

Sometimes she worked so close to memory that she sat down and wept. There he was, in her eyes and her hands, but never quite there.

At night she mainly slept, as she once would have thought, like the dead; except for occasional dreams of Philip dropping by with, it seemed, the sole intention to seduce and enrapture, so that she woke vibrating and thrilled from better sex in his absence than they'd recently mustered energy for in his presence. Was that ironic? Pathetic, anyway. One of the paintings here tonight is a big, shiny, acrylic depiction of an all-day lollipop—they don't, she believes, exist any more— swirly and round, a temptation so large and daunting it should last for ever, but under determined application of tongue is destined to vanish.

Something like that.

Now what?

Now, despite the edgily festive spirit of an opening, its buzz and hum, tonight is almost as thorough an ending as the morning she woke and leaped up and cried out.

Now, right this minute, there are greetings, air kisses, wine, samosas; there are people saying, "Nora! You look wonderful! It's great to see you again! This work is fabulous!"

All those exclamations!

Of course she looks good. With the aid of an hour and a half of weights, yoga and fast-walking at the start of each day, and with the clear intention not to end up like Philip any time soon, Nora is pleased to be pared-down, muscular, pliable. If Philip could be stitched and painted and glued, she could now be stringently sculpted. Tomorrow she is to be interviewed and photographed for a national newspaper. The *hook* the writer seeks, his sad-sack, inspirational angle, has to do with a year of widowhood spent examining a beloved deceased; although even that might be of inadequate public interest if Nora hadn't already made that big sacrilegious name for herself. Philip was right: the town did wonders for her. Now that she's left it, she, too, can make that sort of joke. There's still not much joking about Philip himself. The distancing that occurs when a private passion enters the public world is well under way, and she feels quite able to discuss her work and Philip in professional, articulate fashion, but there'll be no spilling of secrets, or even privacies, and it's most unlikely there'll be any great comedy either.

Speaking of privacies—three of tonight's works are of Sophie in one lush form and another. Sophie turns out to be a surprisingly frank and adjustable subject, but more difficult to explain than Philip in relation to the show's dead-husband theme. Nora would not, for the sake of Sophie as well as herself, never mind Philip, dream of telling an interviewer, "This was our assistant for a time, and briefly my husband's lover. You can see her appeal." In the end, Nora thinks less of Philip for the affair, and in one or two depictions of him, although not of Sophie, this is reflected; but those are the risks a man takes, yielding to whims, breaking promises, dying.

Ah, it appears she can still be angry. Now and then.

In all three portraits Sophie is naked, depicted with unusual realism in various postures and degrees of voluptuousness. Although nowhere near as voluptuous as she is now, chugging through the crowd with Hendrik Anderson following agreeably in her billowy red wake.

Sharing the house after its population was so suddenly halved was easier than either of them could have expected. For one thing, unlike Philip, Sophie had the advantage of being alive, and of having made Nora no promises. For another, Nora discerned no particular desire in herself—indeed a reluctance—to interrogate Sophie on the how, the why, the when or most of all exactly the what of the thing. What would be the point? In what, when Philip could no longer speak for himself, lay anyone's interest in asking? Maybe the answers, anyway, are in these portraits of Sophie: all that wide-open flesh, all that looseness and unclothed capacity.

Nora did ask, "How long?" and when Sophie said warily, or at least softly, "Only a couple of months, just this summer, hardly at all, honestly," Nora rewound the weeks to try to pinpoint a trigger that could have ricocheted him into the space between Sophie's thighs, but—what a clever, masked man—even hindsight provided no specific, particular moment. If he were alive, she'd have grilled him and then for all she knows killed him. As it is, there's a sketch here of him black-masked like the Lone Ranger, standing flat-footed, legs apart, with a gun in each hand. Herself and Sophie camouflaged as Philip's twin pistols: another private commentary, and a cartoonish joke.

That a person can apparently be wounded and unspeakably furious, but remain attached by some kind of love, is a revelation of sorts. Then again, love is a simpler matter when its object is static. All in all, Philip may be pretty lucky he's dead.

In his wake and absence, Nora and Sophie fell into routines: drinks before dinner, a catch-up on the day, the to-and-fro of running a household—rather like marriage, that easygoing, and almost as familiar. Occasionally they also fell into memory: "Remember the look on his face the first time we found words on the fence and had to repaint it?" Or, "Remember that combination of sawdust and oils, or whatever it was? I miss that smell around the house, do you?" There was even something about knowing Sophie and Philip had been together that became, eventually, strangely attaching. That in a way they were both his remains; his relics.

Were widows not once upon a time referred to as *relics?* Nora could ask Sophie, who was always better at Scrabble.

Sophie's not a bad person. She generally means well, give or take the odd husband: one of Nora's, now one of her own.

Hendrik must know about Sophie and Philip, and clearly he does not care. Poor Philip: not lightly or easily abandoned, but here are Nora hanging him tidily on various walls, Sophie blooming, and Hendrik one happy man.

How did this come about?

If not slowly, at least quietly. Nora was busy for so many hours each day, and Sophie's chores were so few—of course she found other activities, and more and more often was out of the house; seeing, she confessed finally, evidently embarrassed, or shy, Hendrik Anderson when he was free from his duties. She was hanging out at the funeral home. Or more accurately, in his quarters at the funeral home. "It's a nice place," she insisted. "He's a nice man."

"I'm sure he is. Under the right circumstances."

When they finally invited Nora to dinner, and she saw how easy Sophie was in his kitchen and at his table, and how they regarded each other across that table, there was a moment when she could barely breathe for the congestion of fresh sorrow; envy, too. A dollop of bitterness. She also saw what Sophie meant when she said Philip would have liked Hendrik's place. And she thought, *Sophie would never have been so comfortable and happy otherwise.* By which she meant, without Philip.

Two months ago, on the first day of summer and shortly before Nora left town, she stood up with Sophie when she and Hendrik got married in Nora's backyard, the funeral home having been deemed either inappropriate or too likely to be otherwise occupied. Sophie was awash in very pale green, fabric and skin, for the occasion. "Imagine at my age," she laughed, "getting accidentally knocked up." Obviously she was doing much more than running a household and posing for Nora and having pre-dinner drinks and long conversations with Hendrik or Nora or both. How would she have met the undertaker of her dreams had Philip not required his serv-ices? More unintended consequences. They pile up.

The townspeople will be counting the months on their fingers. Not that this will harm Hendrik's business, these things happen and are hardly scandalous any more, and even if they were, there's never a shortage of dead to be dealt with. Anyway, Nora has to get out of her head that vision of vil-lagers with pitchforks and torches. Now they will just have lurid recollections to tell themselves of blasphemy and death in the house on the hill.

Of merry widows.

Of egotistical widows who appear to imagine the towns-people will think of them at all; whereas out of sight, out of mind is more like it. Back there, Nora and her household will become just a remote recollection of a few bright, sharp, inju-rious moments. People are only the stars of their own films, not anyone else's. In the long scheme of things that means that even the lunatic butcher will be reduced to a mere walk-on in Nora's own flick.

It's lonely, though, having to carry the whole movie herself after years with Philip as co-star. Being a third at dinner, no longer part of an even number, is the least of it really.

Philip would be happy, Nora thinks, he would be genuinely pleased for Sophie and Hendrik. He would wish Sophie well, in an easy-come, easy-go way, and if he were here now might say to Nora, "Isn't it great how things have worked out for her?" and would mean it, and would reveal nothing to Nora at all. He went to his grave with that secret; although *grave*, in this instance, is metaphorical. Philip doesn't have one of those. She hopes he likes where he is.

Finally Nora and Sophie and Hendrik make their way through the crush to fetch up together. "My God, Nora, it's crowded," Sophie says. "Are you pleased? You must be."

"Yes, Max does these things right, doesn't he? I'm so glad you could make it. You're well?" Because in the earliest months, Sophie threw up a lot.

"Perfectly fine now." As pregnant women sometimes do, Sophie rubs her belly reflexively, comforting and being comforted is how it looks, as well as somewhat smug. "I was wondering how I'd feel watching people check out those portraits of me, but there's so many people I don't see how anybody can see anything."

"I've never been to something like this." Hendrik's round face beams, newly balding spot likewise. "I need to talk to Max about buying one of the pictures of Sophie. Or maybe all three."

"They're awfully, um, lively, aren't they? Where would you hang them?"

Hendrik operates at a higher pitch than Philip's bass, but his laughter is just about as satisfactory. "Maybe in the foyer right at the entrance, what do you think? That'd take people's minds off their troubles the minute they walk in the door. Plus give them something more gorgeous to talk about than flower arrangements and bodies."

Lucky Sophie. Nora grins. "Yes, I can see that. The perfect spot. Very uplifting. How long are you two in town?"

"Till tomorrow night. Soph and I have a major hotel room and we want our money's worth."

"What if somebody dies?"

"Then they'll just have to wait, won't they?" Sophie says Hendrik's work not only doesn't trouble her, it's among his appeals. Nora almost understands what she means.

Sophie leans slightly, nods leftwards. "You see who's here?"

"Beth, yes. Max must have tracked her down, I wonder how he did that? And why. Do you know who the guy is in the wheelchair?"

"No, but I bet she's not his nurse." Nora and Hendrik laugh. Sophie is gratified by this recent ability of hers to amuse. It seems to have something to do with heeding Hendrik's instruction—advice—to "lighten up on yourself now and then, okay?" Okay. She was well on her way to doing that anyway, under Phil's tutelage, but Hendrik puts these matters in broader perspective. A man whose profession is death learns to take a longer, lighter view of anything less, Sophie supposes. If he's smart. Which he is.

What a surprise, this monstrous, easy affection Sophie has come to feel towards Hendrik, this man whose plump hands are adept with the chemistries of transforming corpses into recognizable loved ones, deft with the tiny stitcheries that hold features and expressions in place. They treat every body,

dead or alive, with the tenderness it is due. He elides the
awful distance between life and death, makes it run through
his fingers like a single bright ribbon.

All that.

It wouldn't be fair to compare him and Phil, whose concerns, at least until the last moment, were entirely weighted
towards life, but it is fair to say Hendrik is a very different
man to be with. Phil was enveloping, not to mention distinctly encouraging, whereas Hendrik feels simply solid. Phil
cultivated carefreeness, which is different from care.

It seems she does compare them. Fair or not, dead man
must lose.

Hendrik didn't exactly court Sophie but he did, with cautious invitations to his home and gentle questions about her
history, her nightmares, her pleasures—her life—demonstrate
a real interest. Sometimes, naturally, he was busy. Later,
although he said "I wouldn't tell anyone else these things,
only you," he recounted funereal tales. As to the business
itself, "I'm one of the few independents left, but I won't sell
out to a chain till my dad's gone, and maybe not even then.
It's important to him that I'm the third generation." That was
good, that sounded loyal. A decent man.

It's interesting that a substantially older, plumper, balding
man may have his own brand of attractions, even if they don't
much resemble Phil's, or even Nick's. On a winter evening as
they sat on his sofa watching rising snowbanks out his window, Hendrik said quietly and politely, as if offering coffee, "I
wonder, would you care to go to bed?"

Why, yes, as a matter of fact.

An actual bed makes a difference. So does the privacy to
thrash about and make noises. So does the leisure to rest,
even to stay overnight. The thrill of danger is absent, but

what luxury in its place, not least time for long conversations under quilted cover of dark.

There's not so much space for Martha Nkume's hands to get a bony grip either, when Hendrik's body is nudged into Sophie's.

With Nick, she'd taken birth control pills. Phil had long since had a vasectomy. Stupidly, Sophie supposes, the question of birth control, or even safety, didn't arise between her and Hendrik. What were they thinking, how could it be that she was actually surprised to be pregnant? "I have something to tell you," she said to him hesitantly, fearful that interest and delight would not carry them through.

"Oh," said Hendrik. And, "Oh." Tears came to his eyes. He rested his head on her shoulder.

Hendrik, one of her increasing burden of miracles, also had his whole life flipped sideways by the morning the women woke up and Phil failed to.

Sophie's image of Phil's hands, so gravely and deliberately etched into memory, is now almost entirely commemorative. It's a long time since she's felt them—so long they might as well be hanging on a wall now, like Nora's paintings. Hendrik has said, "From the sound of it, I'm sure I can only be grateful to him," which is probably true. Sophie remains grateful herself. She can still see Hendrik hurtling out of his office just off the entranceway of the funeral home as she stood there holding the blue carry-all containing Phil's clothes.

What would Phil say of all this, if Phil had a voice?

But he does not.

Sophie and Hendrik speak of death, naturally—it's his work after all. "Death," he said once, "is the one certain gift every parent gives to their child. Us, too," and at first this was shocking. Not a nice thought at all, the sort of remark Nora might make on one of her more brutal days.

"You mean we've condemned our own child to die?"

They know they're having a daughter. A daughter! Imagine!

"*Condemned*, that's not the right word. At least I hope it's not. All I mean is, once a person's born, death is absolutely the outcome, and it's wise to bear that in mind if only to stay alert and make every day count. But really, for as long as it lasts, it's life that we're giving—oh Sophie, I didn't believe this was going to happen to me. I'm so happy." Her, too. It takes some getting used to, though, happiness, and his way of thinking.

Hendrik *glows* when he puts his hand on her belly. She catches him regarding her sometimes with an unnerving rapture. If Phil in his way saved her, it occasionally feels as if in a not dissimilar way she's saving Hendrik. "I've had girl-friends," he says, "womanfriends, I mean, but not everyone likes the business I'm in, or they can't cope with the uncertainty, that it's hard to make plans, or it's just hard having death in your face all the time. Whatever."

So it seems he was lonely. Or resigned. There was no one in particular sitting in that second Muskoka chair in his yard after all. "But there was something about you, Soph"—no one else calls her *Soph*, but that's okay, too—"when you came through the door that day with the clothes. The way you knew what you wanted, and were determined to get it. And of course," and he smiled, glinting upwards at her, "you're beautiful, too. Quite a package, all in all. I thought, *I'd better grab this one*."

To be considered beautiful and brave and determined—that's a bit over the top. Day-to-day, night-to-night co-existence shades and modifies their impressions, though, and incipient parenthood is a challenge in itself—how often has Hendrik listened to Sophie throw up? "I'm sorry you're suffering," he said. "I wish I could help."

"That's all right, you've done your part. Save your strength for walking the floor with her at three in the morning."

"It's a deal."

What Sophie likes, besides Hendrik himself, is that living right inside a house of death, maybe like skydiving or tightrope walking for someone fearful of heights, puts terror where it belongs: right in the familiar, habitual heart of the matter.

"From what I've seen," he says, "death itself is easy enough, it's the dying that's hard." So in that way lucky Phil, slipping off in the night with one quick, easy step. Other people endure long, awful journeys to the same destination. At visitations and services, Hendrik hears all the stories of death either begged for or fended off beyond reason. "There are people," he says, "who just refuse to recognize that that's what's going to happen, no matter what. That can look brave, but it tends to be sad." The best deaths are also the rarest: "People who understand it will happen and set out to meet it by gathering up their own grace." No, Hendrik says, he can't put it better than that. Some people, given the opportunity, die well; many don't. He makes it sound a shame to miss the chance to try. Someone like Phil, for instance, would never find out what, approaching the end, he was made of.

Truly, and in a funny way these conversations have become ordinary and interesting to Sophie, not morbid at all. "Sometimes I think humans are simply *arrogant*," Hendrik says. "So much resistance and struggling, as if our own non-existence is the worst thing that could possibly happen—don't you think that's just insane self-importance?"

Sophie has heard the word *arrogant* before. From Nick, long ago, and from Janet, too, during Sophie's brief, untherapeutic therapy. And perhaps she was arrogant. That compulsion to sacrifice, much less save, must at least have reeked of self-importance and pride. Quite possibly her real problem was less an obsession with virtue and more a wilful blind spot when it came to appreciating the gratification involved. A failure to realize that no good act is without its rewards. Being human.

Being human is a broken-hearted business. She was wrong (if human) to set herself to forgetting as much as she could of what she'd learned about heartlessness. That deliberate amnesia, it now seems to her, came close to making her heartless herself, or at least hardened. She did try after all, she did something. She bears permanent witness. There will always be nightmares, the sights and the pungent smells, the remembered sounds, joyous and grief-stricken, will always appear on TV from one terrible place and another. Sophie will send money, and she will write, passionately and repeatedly, to politicians and governments and aid agencies, conducting the business of witnessing as best she can: both the most and the least she can do. Unlike Martha Nkume, she is just lucky. Unlike Martha's wizened little Matthew, or wretched, wrecked Mary, Sophie and Hendrik's daughter will also be lucky, arriving in a world intent on providing whatever she needs and, moreover, able to do so. A cosmic crapshoot has landed them in this time and this place, rather than that one. A tragically lopsided crapshoot, as a matter of fact.

Hendrik says, "You're not a better or worse human being. You did a good thing, and now you're doing a new, different, surprising good thing. Isn't that great, Sophie? So many good chances?"

It's great all right.

She likes it that Hendrik can talk about complicated mysteries in ways that are simple, but not stupid. "I have no more idea than anyone else what follows death," he says with a shrug, "although myself, I'd bet it's nothing at all. More arrogance, that we can believe in anything but our own disappearance. And putting faith in a system of fair punishments and rewards afterwards, that's part of it, too." It's true there are at least six men in the world Sophie wouldn't mind seeing in hell. She is less interested herself in reward, as it happens, than in punishment. On some scores she has no forgiveness whatever.

"My suspicion," Hendrik says, "is that all we have is the space between the hour we're born and the one when we die, so what's to be done but our best?"

An awfully benign outlook. And possibly a little *too* simple. Sophie is still thinking it out for herself.

Still, happily, *our best* isn't necessarily severe or particularly attached to mortality. Happily, it also includes driving here in the big black car previously ridden in by Sophie, Nora, Beth and Max to Phil's funeral, and splurging on a hotel suite where, as Hendrik says, "we can play in the Jacuzzi and call up for anything that strikes our fancy from room service and walk around naked and watch movies in bed."

Sophie intends to enjoy Nora's party, and the hotel, and then tomorrow, as well, wandering the city with Hendrik as best she can in this lumbering state. She is not comfortable being this pregnant, but is persistently astonished by how *cozy* she feels. Like a large, self-contained package of warmth.

Which is probably basically how she appears, too, to anyone looking at Nora's portraits of her. When Nora broached the subject of posing, Sophie didn't expect the results to be so literal and recognizable. It also took considerable getting used to, disrobing in Nora's glassy, airy studio, letting Nora drape one naked leg over the arm of a chair while Sophie's other foot rested on the floor, with obvious results. She wasn't sure why it mattered whether her hair was pulled up, back or loose, but it seemed to to Nora. So much actual touching involved in all this—had Nora touched Beth so intimately and often as well? If so, it wouldn't be totally surprising if Beth were misled into imagining something more personal. It was personal enough to Sophie, aware that the hands adjusting her flesh had been intimately familiar with Phil's flesh, too. She couldn't tell, being regarded by Nora's cool eyes, if those eyes were mainly an artist's or a wife's. Whether Nora was pondering shape and colour, or speculating about what pleasures Phil might have found there.

What would Phil have thought, looking on? *Uh-oh*, he might suppose.

Of course, what would he also think seeing his lavish Sophie spending herself so quickly and remorselessly on his mortician? *Frivolous*, he might say of her. *Hard*.

Or he'd be glad for her. She has no idea, actually, what he would think. Honestly, her heart's been so busy with change she doesn't even think about him all that often, except for grateful reminders of what he made possible. But tonight's different. He's all around, scarcely avoidable.

When it came time, rather hurriedly, for the wedding, there was no one better than Nora to stand up beside Sophie, and no place except that significant backyard, where once upon a time she lay down with Phil. Although truthfully, in the event he scarcely crossed her mind.

Sophie chose a long, loose, pale green gown which went brilliantly with her hair, although less brilliantly, on the day, with her skin, since she was slightly ill with nerves and pregnancy. Mavis from the Old Town Bakeshop, not redeemed or forgiven but useful, spread her wings to produce canapés and crudités, as well as a three-tiered cake that was a one-tiered leftover by the end of the day. Sophie's parents were there, and Hendrik fetched his father from the nursing home for a few hours. He also, having spent his whole life in the town, had several old, close friends in attendance. And there was Nora. The sun shone. The words of the service, so familiar, were new and astonishing when applied to them in particular. Everyone hugged and laughed and Sophie's mother said, "I'm so glad for you, dear, he seems a nice, clever man—well, he must be clever and nice, mustn't he, since he loves you?" Her father said, "Way to go, kid. You toughed it out and came through." For the very first time, Sophie looked at them properly, a handsome pair in their sixties, still dealing with the fragile or duplicitous or brave of the world, and saw them as a couple, a team, a pair of elegant Percherons doing their work and companionably respecting each other with—this was the point—not much to do with her, really. They had their own lives; a good thing to realize before her own child arrived to become yet another loved but separate person with her own life.

Sophie and Hendrik spent the first night of their honeymoon where they were accustomed to being, in Hendrik's—their—bed in the funeral home. Nora immediately put the house up for sale.

Sophie tries to believe—although how could it be?—that in its way, this show and celebration tonight must be about as important to Nora as that day was to Sophie. People have different moments that glitter, and for Nora tonight must be huge. That's why Sophie's here: tit for tat. Anyway, it's not every day she and Hendrik get invited to swish art show openings, is it? And if not for Nora, Sophie would not be the subject of any paintings. Now all those hours in Nora's studio have landed up here, under the eyes of total strangers. One part of Sophie is shy, another part has an urge to lounge casually by the portraits of her in preening *Yes, that's me* fashion.

Beth must always have felt like this: an object of eyes and attention, of admiration for nothing beyond her features and shape. It's okay for an evening, but for a whole life? No wonder Beth was vague and self-absorbed and annoying. Being looked at but never acquiring the habit of looking is bound to create a few distortions of view. "Max found her?" Sophie asks. "And you didn't know? I wonder why he did that."

The night of Phil's funeral, Max said, Beth asked to be dropped at a busy intersection downtown near his gallery, and a wave was the last he saw of her. "She said she would be fine," he reported, "she seemed to have plans," although he claimed not to know what they were. "She did not speak much in the car, not at all about her intentions," he said, which may or may not be true. Max is an ethical confidant, which of course is a good thing, but it can be frustrating, too. The woman lived with them for two years, for heaven's sake. Still, since she's here tonight they were right not to be overly fretful— whatever she's been up to, it didn't involve anything drastic like throwing herself under a train.

Beth's vanishing, unlike Phil's, had no power. She wasn't especially missed; why would she be? In her absence Sophie and Nora drank a lot more wine and coffee than tea, but that was a minor change, as Beth had been, really, a minor presence. Nora did say she regretted not reacting more sensibly when Beth sprang her surprise. "A crush isn't such a big deal. Her timing couldn't have been worse, and the fantasy was unnerving, but I feel sort of bad. Maybe I should have known. And I could have been kinder."

The story of Nora and Beth's first encounter is, as Sophie heard it, nearly romantic: Beth a vision spotted from across the room at an event much like this one, and pursued by Nora for purposes of her own inspired creation.

Or, like a gazelle, or a giraffe, some elongated wild creature, Beth was hunted down at a party by a wilful, powerful predator, and hauled off to have her bones gnawed on and chewed over. That's another, bloodier way of hearing the story.

Beth doesn't look too much like prey from this angle tonight. She doesn't look too much like inspiration either. She looks attractive enough, but hardly spectacular. Just an ordinary art-loving opening-goer, except for the older man in the wheelchair she wears like a flash piece of jewellery.

"Max said he wanted tonight to go back to its sources, or be circular or complete—something like that," Nora says, "but I wasn't really paying attention, and I didn't know he meant Beth. I'm afraid he can be off centre sometimes these days. She looks different, doesn't she? It's not just that she's put on some weight—that should make you happy, Sophie. Maybe it's the hair, all pulled back like that."

"Bear in mind I never did see what you saw. I just thought she was kind of irritating and empty-headed. Like a pet, only she wasn't affectionate, and she didn't shed on the furniture."

Again, Nora and Hendrik laugh and laugh. How delightful, what fun.

Beth is leaning over the man in the wheelchair. He looks unhappy and anxious. They may already be discussing departure, so soon after arriving. "Maybe we should go rescue them. She looks out of place, although shouldn't she feel at home at something like this?" Sophie sets out again through the crowd, followed by Nora, followed by Hendrik. He tells Nora, "These days it's easiest if Sophie goes first. It's like driving behind a transport—if you can get into the slipstream, you save a whole lot of energy." Sophie snorts.

Beth sees them coming and straightens as if they're a firing squad aiming her way. She perceives dismay in their expressions; or puzzlement; or curiosity—it's interesting, anyway, that with or without beauty, and despite her intentions, she can fascinate, she still has whatever it is that draws attention just by standing around. She nods slightly. "Sophie. Nora. Hello."

"Hendrik Anderson," says the man who steps around Sophie. "We've met, but you may not remember me. I run the funeral home." Beth flushes, she looks down—what does she recall of the funeral? Oh, everything, in awful detail. That great horrible avalanching of knowledge. Full-tilt, full-bore recognition. What she'd done. And the dismal, desperate fact that she was not loved by anybody on earth.

That equally she didn't love anyone. Not even Nora.

"This is my father, Daniel. Dad, these are some people I've told you about. Nora's an artist who used to paint me—this is her show. And Sophie, I've mentioned her, and Hendrik Anderson."

Hendrik reaches down to shake Beth's father's hand. "Or you can just call me Sophie's husband."

Beth's father. Why did they assume she either had no close relatives or had nothing to do with them? Because she said so, or suggested it; because she called no one and no one called her in two years; because she told Nora, more or less, they were *gone*. "I hope you're enjoying this," Nora says, also reaching to shake the man's hand, which is trembly, feels frail. "I'm pleased so many people are here, but it makes it difficult to see anything."

"Your work," Beth says.

"Yes. What I've been doing for most of the past year." Beth and Nora lock gazes. Each is surprised. Neither is as remembered. The room does not, of course, fall silent, just seems to for a tense second.

"Are you pleased with it?"

"I'm . . . content enough. It was the best I could do."

"Where did you live?"

"In the house. Sophie stayed, too. With," and Nora smiles, "equally obvious results."

"I thought you hated it there."

"Yes, well, that's true, but this seemed like work that had to be done there. Then I bolted as quick as I could. Although not," Nora goes on—carefully or carelessly?—"as fast as you did."

"There wasn't anything to stay for. So I went home." On the word *home* Beth looks down, touches her father's shoulder. "I live with Dad. He has Alzheimer's. I take care of him."

So that accounts for his speechlessness. And maybe for the wild rearing look in his eyes and the anxious head-tossing. "Is a crowd upsetting for him?" Nora asks.

"In a way, but I figure colours, lights and sounds are good for him, too. It's wonderful how many things people can do in wheelchairs these days. We can go practically everywhere, can't we, Dad?" His head falls back and his eyes roll some more. "If he was really old we couldn't do so much, but it's the early-onset kind, and his body's still strong. He used to be a transport truck mechanic, didn't you, Dad? So it's fine to go out and about, not that he's been to an art gallery before, but one thing's as good as another, isn't it?" How bright Beth's eyes have become, and how very chatty she suddenly is, words tumbling out as if they've been stored up for quite a long time.

Also how muscled her arms are, now they see them up close. Her father's a fair-sized man, so managing him must take strength. "Actually, he can still walk, sort of, but when we go anyplace the wheelchair's easier because he can't wander away and get lost." Oh. Yes. They can see a seat belt and shoulder harness attaching him firmly. That's unpleasant. But who are they to say, they're not responsible for a man with Alzheimer's, are they? For all they know, Beth is a saint, in her way. A perfect daughter.

She certainly looks as a saint might. She is plain enough now.

"Are you," Sophie asks gingerly, impossible to know which subjects are tender or difficult, "doing any modelling these days?"

"No, looking after my dad's full-time work."

"And where are you living?"

"In his house. The one I grew up in. We've had to change things around—like Dad has a hospital bed in what used to be the living room because it's too hard to get him upstairs. Some people think it's like being a kid again, going back home, but it's different being in charge. There's a lot of responsibility, like making sure all the doors are bolted so he can't take off, and keeping him out of the kitchen, things to do with safety like that."

This is not a Beth they're familiar with. Although when Philip died she became a Beth they weren't familiar with either. How many Beths are there, and under what circumstances does each one arise? Of course much the same applies to each of them: new Noras and fresh Sophies have also made themselves known without a great deal of warning.

"A lot of changes," Nora says, her voice taking on the false, jolly tones some people use with strange children. "But I bet you're still brewing up those teas of yours, aren't you? I bet that isn't different." She is only making desperate conversation. Where is Max? A heads-up would have been helpful. Pity, if that's what triggered his hunt for Beth, is not unambiguous. It can be cruel, as well as patronizing, as well as kind. Max must know that. Is getting Beth here another result of those little strokes? He does occasionally have odd whims. He also forgets things, and to compensate has become tidier and more precise about details. He takes care to write everything down, and forges on regardless. What could Beth have to do with any of that?

Beth's father is now flapping his arms. He looks panicky. Beth pats his shoulders. "No, I don't have time for teas and that sort of thing. Anyway, I didn't take into account before that there's so much pollution in the air and ground and most likely the water, nothing can be totally useful and pure. It's interesting, though, if you know what you're doing."

"Yes. I guess." They've all given things up. Or been given up on. "Do you not get out on your own at all, then?"

"No." This is said proudly, and with a toss of Beth's skinned-back ponytailed hair—it has grown out, and not attractively. She already has a row of tiny hinted lines along her upper lip, and deeper ones alongside her mouth, exactly what Sophie always predicted would be the fate of thin women. Her make-up, too, is less than deft, seen under hard gallery lights. "No, I can't. I didn't know how ill he was till I phoned—that was the night Max drove me back—but when I realized he was sick and all on his own, I knew I had to take care of him. It's fine, it's worked out best for both of us, hasn't it, Dad?"

Dad makes a few garbled sounds; hard to know if he agrees. This looks hellish. Sophie in particular shivers. Not only are she and Hendrik about to have a child for whom they'll be entirely responsible, they are about—here's a new thought—to have a child who may someday be entirely responsible for them. Who could bind them down and wheel them willy-nilly through the world, ignore their desires, hover over them doing good in what looks like no good way at all.

Who knows what sort of father this man has been, though? Sophie and Hendrik intend to be excellent parents. Loving, naturally, but they've also discussed discipline (no physical, many possible variations otherwise) and indulgence (not too many possessions, lest their child become spoiled) and hopes and ambitions (they intend to support and encourage any particular talents and gifts, but not force or push). These are splendid, hours-spinning conversations. Mutual dreams. A vast layer of cement between them.

They are bound to stumble and make mistakes. They intend to forgive their own imperfections, hoping their child does as well but—what if she doesn't? What if she grows up and turns on them and takes over their lives and they can do nothing but mutter and flail?

That's far-fetched. Soon a child's voice will ring out in the rooms of the dead. Kiddy cars and train sets will race up and down that dusky, massive front hall. Adorable little outfits will drive out whatever lingers of shrouds. It's just this proximity to Beth and her trussed father that gives Sophie the unpleasant sensation of hair rising on the back of her neck.

Nora, watching Beth's hands on her father's shoulders, wonders how closely this scene resembles what Beth had in mind for Nora herself: to be Beth's prisoner.

Her new house is, in fact, eerily similar to the one Beth described for the two of them on the unfortunate day of

Philip's funeral. It is semi-detached and nearly downtown, actually a mere ten-minute cab ride from this gallery. It has a bright, separate room for Nora to work in, it is on a side street not overburdened with traffic, it is brick, it has a fireplace, it even has a low brick wall fronting the sidewalk and a little patch of garden and lawn. Unlike Beth's vision, the furniture is not new, but Philip-built and familiar: the bed, of course, but also end tables, coffee table, a mantel, as well as two deep blue-green slip-covered sofas with extra-wide arms that were designed but unstarted when he died. Sophie, who took a matching chair for herself, explained to the customer who'd ordered them why Philip was no longer capable of fulfilling their contract. She got the name of a craftsman, no Philip but a careful man able to follow Philip's design, from Hendrik, who knows people accustomed to doing fine work with wood.

After just a few weeks Nora can already move confidently through her new home in darkness without turning on lights: one measure of feeling at home. The place contains Philip's comforts, but no history and no ghosts. She can no longer be halted by hearing a door opening and closing downstairs, causing her accidentally to think, *Philip.* Nor can she be startled by a half-empty closet or the bare place inside a back door where his boots used to be. She is relearning solitude and the pleasures of doing whatever she wants, even—especially—when what she wants is to do nothing at all.

She has, for better or worse, exactly what Beth predicted: her freedom. Now it looks as if freedom would not have been Beth's intention. Not that Nora would be helpless and ill, like this poor man; and probably he's very lucky to be in the hands of so attentive a daughter. Still, there is a whiff of captivity here. Is it possible art bleeds into those it portrays? It

would be insane if the time Beth spent impersonating a saviour mutated into a fancy she was one.

Beth would not disagree that previously, she had some
strange and terrible moments. *Impulses,* including a tragic and
regrettable one. There's no undoing history, though. Never
mind the paintings she once posed for, she has no gift for res-
urrection. Apparently not only is she someone no one will
love, she herself also does not love. It turns out she cannot
even properly care. She is, however, able to care *for,* which is
far more straightforward. And who knows, repetition of caring for might possibly lead to actual caring, which might
eventually translate into love of one kind or another.
Meanwhile, though, she is just fine. Really. Long ago people
congratulated and then released her because they decided
she'd achieved a *more coherent sense of reality.* Now she actually feels that.

Of course, in the process of all this, she has had to undo
her own beauty. Beauty is too easy, for one thing. For another,
it draws the wrong kind of attention, the kind that isn't interested in anything else. Mostly, it has led her into error and
miscalculation. So now she courts plainness, and not just
because of raw drudgery and the perpetual shortage of time.
Plain people suffer from duty, as they deserve to. They can be
invisible, too, they can disappear for as long as they need.

Her father is disappearing as well. Does he imagine his
method is better than hers, or her mother's? Does he imagine
anything at all? Beth is still imperfectly dutiful, and there are
times she could knock him sharply on his head to try to dis-
lodge knowledge and memory, things he could tell her about
herself or himself or her mother, his wife. He must have had
his own views of Beth, perhaps as a stranger-child floating
through the house, out the door, returning laden with tiaras

and sashes and trophies. Was he proud of her? Bemused? Resentful or disinterested? Pleased at all to see himself reflected in her left eye?

Hard to say what goes on in that dazed, greying head, but striking it wouldn't accomplish a thing, not any more. On this score, she has developed excellent *impulse control*.

Patience, too. No ailing father is more closely looked after than hers. He can forget her name and his own, although he can still blurt out "Beryl," which was her mother's name. He can shit himself three times a day. He can make his muddled attempts to get away. He can do all that and much, much more, and Beth will be permanently, persistently present. Other people would buckle. Other people *do* buckle. But even if she can't make him thrive, she can pay him the same close attention that once went into posture and make-up and voice; with the same discipline that kept her bent at painful angles for hours beneath Nora's gaze, and never mind that her father, *Dad* as she calls him in public, really has no idea. Sometimes there are flickerings, sometimes a light in his eyes, sometimes a sad sort of struggle, like tonight, doomed to fail, but basically he has no notion of what she is doing for him.

Which in a way makes her efforts even more noble.

He is hers. "Aren't you, Dad?" she asks aloud, forgetting for the moment just where she is. She often talks to him when they're alone. She can untether words and tell him anything, a pleasing relief to be free to confide her own life, with its pageants, other girls, long journeys on highways of darkness and light, the faint, mysterious enticements of algebra, the various levels and meanings of beauty. Last impulsive, terrible moments. Nora. Men like Philip. Life, such as it was, in the big old house on the hill.

She was startled, driving back to the city with Max, to see how far the city had continued to extend in her absence; how unaccustomed she'd become in, really, such a short time to wide streets and bright lights and, most of all, so many people. People everywhere. It was alarming how easy it would be to be lost here; to disappear.

That was before she realized the value and challenge of invisibility.

She also hadn't realized, setting out with Max, that at the other end of their trip, having given destinations no precise thought, she would have no place to go. But, "You can let me out here," she told him at one random downtown corner, because why not? One purposeless place was as good as another.

"Are you sure? Where will you go?"

She was still beautiful then. She could smile enigmatically and say, "I'll be fine, thanks for the ride," and be off with a wave.

The night grew darker, and still the streets were busy. She wandered for a while, waiting for something to make itself known, her two suitcases, even on wheels, an impediment. Maybe, she thought, a temptation as well. She grew furtive, moving close to storefronts to keep at least one side protected. People even slept on these streets. Where could be safe in a city where ill fortune might lead to sleeping on sidewalks?

When she phoned her father, she had no idea if the number still worked, if he would still be living in that house, if he would speak to her or hang up. In the event he answered, but seemed unclear who he was talking to. "It's Beth," she repeated. It made sense he might not know her voice because it was a long time since he'd heard it, but obviously he ought to recognize her name.

"Yes," he said. "Hello." She was surprised he stopped there, when he should be saying, "Where are you?" or "Are you out?" or "What have you been doing?" or even "Why are you calling me?" and "How dare you?" For that matter, "It's good to hear your voice. Come home, Bethy, all is forgiven." Any of that. Not, "Yes. Hello."

"Daddy." She sounded like the toddler who actually did call him *Daddy*. "Can I come home?"

"Home. Yes." Still in that vague tone; she couldn't tell if he was giving her permission or not. He didn't sound wildly welcoming, but he wasn't refusing her either.

In those days he still knew who she was. When she arrived, he opened the door cautiously. He said, "Beth." He didn't prevent her from walking past him. The house looked foreign, but also familiarly similar, except messy. There was the same floral wallpaper in the dining room, the same beige sofa and easy chair in the living room, even the same sun-faded gold drapes. Maybe that's what was strange. She would have thought, if she'd thought, that he'd have redecorated, bought new furniture, rearranged the rooms. If it gave her a jolt to see the kitchen floor, how could he have borne walking across it, living with it, all this awful time?

There were no photographs in the living room or anywhere else. That was different. Missing were all manner and sizes of framed family photographs—the three of them blowing out birthday cake candles, sitting before Christmas trees, those festivities when families are together, however remote they are in day-to-day life. Neither were there signs of Beth's triumphs. The shrines to her successes were gone, replaced by jumble, bric-à-brac, junk.

Signs of a man on his own. Throughout the house, things were just set down and not picked up: ancient *Reader's*

Digests, silted coffee cups, a pair of pliers. She would clean and tidy, first thing. He would feel better and look better if his household was neat. He seemed to her smaller and greyer-skinned than she remembered. He was watching her. She said, "Shall I get us some tea?" and his eyes widened. Well, she'd forgotten; or hadn't thought. "It's okay, I just thought we might like something to drink. How about," seeing his further alarm, "coffee, if you'd rather? Or a beer?"

They've both had adjustments to make. He wasn't used to being so constantly cared for. She wasn't yet accustomed to caring for him. They didn't have much of a background together either, not much in the way of old habits, easy references and jokes to fall into, just the two of them. She thought at first that might be a good thing; although perhaps not. At any rate there she was with a man she wasn't very familiar with, whose life she didn't know at all clearly, even in bare outline. What did he think, how did he feel, marrying a beautiful woman who so soon began fretting over her lost opportunities? What were his feelings when Beth was born? Did he actually like hunting ducks? Did he enjoy his work or was it only a job? Did he have friends where he worked, buddies he joked with, the rough humour of men on their own? Did he like salads, did he prefer beef over fish or vice versa? She had no clue. It appeared he didn't either. She didn't realize right away that even if they'd had days, weeks and years worth of moments, just the two of them, he might well not recall them.

She wouldn't say she hasn't been tested right to the limits. It is very, very hard to hold to high purposes, to renunciation really, when their object moves further and further away into some mysterious, distant landscape of his own. It's only in those occasional head-knocking moments that she minds that he no longer knows her name. She does mind that he watches her constantly and, it seems, warily. There is someone in there behind those dark eyes, but there's no telling who.

Cleaning up his messes is disgusting. Wiping him, dressing him, stripping him down, washing—even seeing—his skin in the shower, is more distressing than she could have imagined. It's the wrong way round, caring for a full-grown older man, a father, especially in those ways. Making sure he doesn't wander takes a lot of foresight and energy. Before she understood what was happening to him, he got away a few times, out the door, down the street, around corners until he was thoroughly lost and upset, weeping when he was found and the police brought him home. A few times, too, he has struck at her, launching out with his fists, still powerful and now dangerous.

All that alertness and worry and drudgery, in addition to keeping an orderly house—he's not old, and Alzheimer's, his doctor says, doesn't kill by itself. "You need to take breaks, nobody can do this all on their own, there are resources to get you some help. Frankly, it's a mistake for anyone to give up their own life in these cases."

He is not many years older than Beth, he is not the family doctor she used to know, he has no history with them. He doesn't realize this isn't a matter of *cases*. He imagines intense daughterly duty, but has no notion of its qualities and components. "I know," Beth tells him. "I won't. I'm all right for now."

It's amazing what she's found herself capable of, but the doctor's right about one thing, it does get exhausting. She can tell her father over and over where they're going and what they'll be doing—for a walk around the block, to the supermarket, to the opening of a show of her former patron Nora's new work—and he retains none of it. He is always anxious about destinations, permanently uncertain, frequently angry. She hopes he'll behave himself here, but even if he makes a scene, she's glad that they came. She looks at self-satisfied Nora, at flagrant Sophie, at that plain older fellow, the undertaker who is Sophie's new husband, and feels pretty much what she hoped to: a sort of comparative shininess, a relative purity. A tiara sort of triumph.

Because none of them knows what she knows: the grandeur of dogged, hard, invisible sacrifice. Not even Sophie, taking this easy way out after a couple of years of trying half-heartedly and mainly failing to help distant strangers, now caving in to marriage, motherhood, life in, of all places, a funeral home—what a defeat, what a waste. And certainly not Nora, with her scratching of paint and scraps of materials, glued-on bits of this and that mistaken for meaning. Nora looks like a different woman from the one Beth recalls saying she loved, however mistakenly. Now Nora looks just like most of the other smooth people in this big room: more attractive in a worldly sort of way but toughened and, for this evening at least, thoroughly masked.

Imagine her talking to Beth as if Beth were an idiot child! "Do you still make those teas?" in that phony voice—as if Beth and her interests and passions were negligible, merely quirks. Beth may have changed focus, but the study and practice of teas not only saved the raggedy bits of her soul for a time, they prepared and strengthened her for the vital project in which she is now engaged.

She rests her hands on her father's shoulders, leaning into them only slightly. He gets especially upset if he feels forced. Some people would probably think it's strange that her father's is the only flesh Beth has ever been intimate with. She must be missing something—as with love, or care— that's built right into other people. Desire, she supposes. Even her desire for Nora had nothing to do with flesh. That wasn't, as she tried to make clear to Nora, what she was talk- ing about. She was talking about protection and purpose at a passionate level. Anyway, even if disinterest is highly unusual, that's nobody's business, is it? Just as her history, her great, capacious, disastrous, tragic, blundering impulse, is nobody's business.

Her father's doctor says—warns—"He might well live for years," but he doesn't know that's all right. Beth still has a lot to do, drilling the severe practices of care right into her bones.

And then? Well, the world suffers no shortage of helpless people, does it?

People who need help, she probably means.

Now look, here comes Max, making his way through the crowd towards them. Prying Max, who drove Beth back to her destiny, trying every way he could to find out what she thought she would do, as if she'd be fooled into confiding even if she had known. She is strong in so many ways, which people like Nora and Sophie, and certainly not Philip or Max, ever bothered to notice.

Still, she was pleased to hear Max's voice last week, invit- ing her here. Her father's phone doesn't ring very often. "Do come. It would feel right, I think, to have everyone together again, even for only an evening." Beth didn't know what he could possibly mean by *feel right*, but yes, it sounded like something to do.

Then again, if he found her, did that mean he first had to hunt down her history? If so, did he tell Nora and Sophie? They don't look as if they've learned something bad. They look uneasy, but not horrified. People hide things, though. Certainly Beth does.

Max looks different—shrunken and a little unsteady. His accent has thickened. He looks quite old now. Who looks after him?

"There," he is saying, "this is what I wanted, all of you here together for a few moments."

Really? Why?

Max, who observed Sophie and Phil's secret and kept it; Max, who has been Nora's supporter, cheerleader, butt-kicker; Max, who took the trouble, and it must have been considerable, to track Beth down; and Max, who has had little strokes that very occasionally manifest themselves in unaccountable consequences, says, "I hope you all agree this is fitting to the occasion?"

Who knows? "Sure," Nora says dubiously. "It's nice to see everybody again."

"Ah, all right, you indulge me. Put it down to my weakness for circles, and this completes one. Nora. Sophie. Beth. You look splendid. You gentlemen also, of course." He stands back, smiling—what does he see? Really, what did he ever see, what does he want?

His view of their former household must have included elements—of family or just a version of benign collegiality—that none of them dreamed of, or thought to enquire about. With these results. Which are minor, really, not at all catastrophic. As it is, they are an intent knot within a larger, noisier, more festive group; two women in black, one in red, with the men in their lives. A year ago, two of these men were not part of their lives. Another, not among them tonight, was vital, but being vital, it seems, does not count. Vital is unexpectedly and haphazardly destructible.

This is not exactly a circle of happy nostalgia, if that's what Max had in mind. Still, they smile back at him, except for Beth's father, whose smiling capacities may be among those many things lost to him. They look posed for a group photograph, like graduates of some difficult course of study. "Very nice," Max says. "Very nice, how you all look together."

Yes, perhaps; but it soon becomes awkward, since all together they have little to say. Well, Beth always was something of a conversation-stopper; and now she's this hot-eyed unglamorous person making them jumpy, unsure.

So this clumsy moment is her fault? That's hardly fair.

"Now," Max continues at last, presumably having seen what he aimed to, or his fill. "Now I have something just for you people. Soon I will open the third room to everyone, but first a preview only for you of the other work of Nora's we are showing. If," he offers his arm to Nora, "you will indulge me a little more? Shall we?"

All right. If it's important to him. For sure it won't mean anything special to any party-goers except them. Some of them. The women.

This time Nora and Max lead the way through the crowd, which continues to bend for him. Beth pushes her father's wheelchair. Sophie and Hendrik follow behind. Max takes a key from his trouser pocket, turns to others pressed near. "In a few moments," he tells them. "For now, however, if you don't mind, the artist and her group only." Once unlocked, the double doors slide apart from each other on tracks. Max keeps them open just wide enough for first Nora, then the wheelchair and Beth, then Sophie and finally Hendrik to enter. The room is high and bright and smaller than the two outer galleries, and, when Max pulls the doors back together and relocks them, the noise suddenly diminishes so radically it seems almost like silence.

Sweet Jesus, thinks Sophie. *Heavens*, thinks Beth. She leans forward into the wheelchair. Sophie leans back into Hendrik.

Nora turned in bed, she leaped up, she screamed. Beth arrived from one direction, her nightgown awry, and Sophie ran, grappling with her robe but otherwise buck naked, to find fortunate and unfortunate Philip, lucky and unlucky Phil, cooling in his bed. Now here he is again. There's no end to the man.

A little white card says the piece is untitled and NFS— not for sale. Max feels, and Nora agrees, there's no need to say more.

Is it art? Reviewers and critics will no doubt generously, or gratuitously, render their judgments, but meanwhile Sophie, Hendrik, Beth and for sure Beth's father don't have any idea. They're not experts. They do know it's not something any of them would hang over a sofa or fireplace. Nora, the only one besides Max who has seen it before, believes that, whatever else it is, the piece is beautiful, and if it is complicated and even ambiguous, well, so are affections and fates; not least her own. When the show is over, it will hang on the largest unbroken wall of her studio where, by and large, she thinks she will be able to live with it, although admittedly would not care for it in her living room.

This is how love bends and modifies and reshapes itself over time and new circumstance. This is how it ends up:

Philip hangs in a frame two-plus metres high and a metre and a half wide. Not everything is contained within the frame, which itself is roughly cobbled together from strips of walnut left behind in his workshop. There are actually three Philips, which some may judge a mistake, unnecessarily confusing. That would most likely be Philip's impression, as a matter of fact, as a passionate advocate of simplification in his own work.

Oh well.

Touching the outer edges of the frame is his middle-aged, final figure, hands on thickened hips, spare flesh on his torso, stocky legs leading to feet set firmly on the base of the frame. A tiny navy-blue-ink inscription on his left hip says, "Climb aboard, matey."

He is evidently naked, but his full-canvas depiction is blocked by a smaller Philip, this one sunny and pink and holding a glued-on photograph of himself raising a fish, toasting the camera with it. In the photograph he is grinning. The painted figure wears the same grin, and its other hand holds a length of narrow glued-on wood with fishing line running off it and out of the frame, a green whirligig lure knotted on to its end. From the lure dangles a tiny, lacquered newspaper headshot of Nora herself. This might leave an impression that she regards herself as having been cruelly and possibly unfairly caught, but that is not her intention. Her intention is to suggest the taut line between them. The fishing line and lure come from his tackle box. The figure itself falls between youth and middle age. It, too, is presumably naked, with a defined waist and muscled thighs, and feet that slip into the feet of its older counterpart as if they were slippers. It is the form of a man finding his feet. Also it is still the man to whom Nora could say, "Want to go fuck in the woods?" and he would drop tools and off they would go, although by then more often to soft bed than adventurous forest.

It is the centre, third, smallest Philip, though, on whom the eye is intended to begin, and also end up. This is Philip as Nora first saw him: slim and young, empty-handed and naked, staring out boldly, his eyes a real challenge. Within those eyes, darkening them deeper than they were in life, is a mixture of ash.

Ash also streaks across his limbs and shades his jawline and cheeks. İt tints his uptilting, rosy, wavering penis.

Ash hints that in the perfection of this moment, its radiant randomness and several glorious outcomes, there are other, shadowing factors to consider as well. These suggestions also darken the background.

Ash adds a predictably gritty texture, tempering but not too much toning down the bold, hopeful goldenness of his youth.

Nora's youth, too.

It wasn't as awkward to work with as she'd feared, finer and different but really not much more challenging than sand, which she has used in the past. It was not sand, though. She couldn't say it was exactly Philip either, but it was unsettling, at best, to sprinkle portions of it into paint, mixing it in until the desired shade and density and consistency were created, then drawing her brushes through it, applying it. That Philip could disappear, then reappear in this diminished, foreign form—that took some getting used to. Some moments of real revulsion, to be honest, at the beginning.

There were worse finds, harsher materials. A few bone shards that didn't entirely burn. Two darkened, unincinerated teeth. In the painting a blue stream, a real blue ribbon, flows across a corner, with tiny burnished blocks of wood samples along its shores. The two teeth are tucked among them, not very noticeable. The bone shards stick like rocks out of the stream.

You'd think he did nothing but fish, so much presence has she given this watery theme.

In the end, there was a morsel of ash left. She considered tossing it, as Sophie once suggested, into the actual river where he fished, or around his workshop, something like that. Instead she has kept it: a skiff of leftover Philip dusting the bottom of a very small ring box. She may yet give it to Sophie; what better place than a funeral home?

Even Sophie has not seen this piece before. She was in and out of the studio at Nora's invitation throughout many of the pieces that are hanging in the outer galleries now, and of course she spent many hours posing herself, but when Nora finally said, "I think I've got the ash project more or less figured out," Sophie drew the line there. She understood there were things she was never going to understand about Nora. She wasn't even disgusted any more by the idea of Nora using Phil's ashes. She just didn't want to see it.

She also suspected not much good would come of it, and her first view supports that. "Those are remarkable likenesses, Nora," she says. "Lively, like Phil. Nice and bold." She does not like the piece, however. Even though it's large enough to contain multitudes, it looks cluttered, neither one thing or another, not even one Phil or another, and none of the three Phils is Sophie's. Not one pays special attention to his clever hands, for example. Also, not one shows him from the perspective of lying beneath him. Also, the eyes are too dark, and do not shine with anything like sympathy, or tenderness.

This is Nora's version of him, not Sophie's.

She looks more closely. Oh, dear God, what's that by the stream of blue ribbon? Could those two pebbles be teeth? It's months since Sophie's been sick, but this could do it. She puts a hand over her mouth. The other returns to her belly, a shield. She leans back harder into Hendrik, whose hands are firm on her shoulders. Does he imagine her overcome by these views of her naked dead lover? Does he fear that, confronted by the perfections and splendours of Phil's vanished flesh, she regrets the loss, and that in comparison to this bedecked, painted man, he himself comes up short? She takes her hand from her mouth and reaches it up to his, intending to let him know that beyond nauseating teeth and ash, bad enough, these depictions are only distressing for being all history and no hope.

Hendrik is mute, but then he didn't know Philip. Beth says, "Wow. That's really something. It's big. It's sure got a lot in it, hasn't it?" So it does. Trust Beth for the obvious.

Look at her father, though—he is growing more agitated, making loud garbled sounds, now gibbering, now nearly howling, "Nononono," and shaking his head violently, flinging his arms wildly. He may not know the person in the painting, and certainly he can't know what it's about or what it contains, but something is causing grief in his poor addled head, his poor distressed heart.

He is giving, unmistakably, a stingingly negative review.

It doesn't help that Beth starts pat-patting his shoulders, then pushing down on them, her mouth tightening. If Philip hadn't died so early, he might have grown into somebody demanding and feeble, he might have become a burden as well. Beth presses more firmly. She'd like to smack her father. *Shut up and sit still*, she is inclined to cry, as she has heard mothers cry to their children in stores. Mothers don't get to smack their children in public without somebody interfering, though; much less can a daughter slap a distraught and disabled father.

This painting of Philip, it's like he's a god or something. Which he was not. Which diminishes Nora further, doesn't it? Beth glances sideways at her. What caused her to think Nora was worthy of the life Beth was offering? Such devotion should have had an object that would hold up over time. The

fact something didn't unfold as foreseen doesn't make it not
real. Nora does that tonight, she makes it not real, with her
ordinary self and with these portrayals of a corrupt and
unworthy man. For once, even though he's maddening, her
noisy, frantic father makes sense. This room is too bright, the
visions of Philip are disruptive and false, and the actual people turn out to be shadowy. It's good to have come, just to
know this, although it makes her a little angry, too. It's not
nice to find out you've wasted hopes on things that don't
measure up.

How fine it would be to be whisked right out of here and
be instantly home, tucked up in the big bedroom, in the high,
wide bed her parents occupied through their marriage, the
lights out, her father restrained in his own bed downstairs,
their sordid night-time rituals all taken care of. Except this is
not a magic world. Beth takes a deep breath. "It's interesting,
Nora," she says, "interesting work, the whole show," as if she
has properly scrutinized the whole show, "not just this. A lot
of work. I think my dad's had enough excitement, though.
I'm sorry, but I think we should leave."

Sometimes he comes in quite handy.

"That's too bad," Nora says. Although it is not. "But I'm
glad you were able to come." Which is not very true either.
"Will you come back, do you think, when it's not so crowded
and loud?" Not even Max, Nora expects, wishes for that.

"I'd like to, but I doubt it. It's not so hard getting around
our own neighbourhood, but it's complicated, coming downtown. Maybe since you're living here now, you could visit us
someday at my house? You and Max both? And you two, if
you're ever in town," Beth adds, turning to Sophie and
Hendrik. She is not unaware of forms of politeness, and her
circle of acquaintances is very limited. Mostly, though, if

there's one thing she knows nearly for sure it's that you never know what can arise more or less out of the blue. "I still remember how to make a good tea. We don't get many guests. It would be nice."

"We'll see, shall we? We'll be in touch." Although Nora cannot foresee a circumstance in which she would suddenly crave a jaunt to the suburbs to see Beth. What an awkward, mute occasion that would be! So these words are just standard courtesies. They don't mean a thing; even though there is, in fact, something in Beth's father's desperate limbs, the strain of his face that cries out for transformation.

"Nononono," he is crying, his eyes jumping from the painting of Philip to the faces of Nora and Max. As if it's their fault he's upset. Which maybe it is. It must be terrible to live in such constrained, baffled fashion. Max leans to place his older-man's hand on Beth's father's arm. "I am sorry," Max tells him. "You are going home now, do not be worried. Perhaps I shall see you again on some better day."

Max's voice does settle him down somewhat. His eyes keep darting anxiously, but his voice falls to an unhappy murmur. Although this may be only a matter of Beth turning the wheelchair away from the people and the painting towards the doors, which Max is quick to unlock and open. No one has protested, nobody has said, "Don't go yet, Beth, please stay a while longer." Well, they wouldn't, would they? Nobody cares, nobody has ever asked her to stay.

"See you," she says. "Nora. Sophie. Thanks for inviting us, Max," and off they wheel, Beth and her fortunate, unfortunate father, his wheelchair something of a battering ram against the current of people. At the front door Beth pauses, she turns, she looks coolly back, one last, long, measuring scrutiny of each left-behind face.

Now, with the doors to this gallery opened, other people begin to drift in. "Well," Nora says finally. "That was pretty weird, wasn't it?"

"Of course it was," Sophie agrees. "It was Beth. I'm surprised, though. I wouldn't have thought of her as somebody who'd dedicate herself to anyone but herself. Well, except," she grins, "maybe you. But isn't it odd that she's taken this on when she never mentioned him before and we even assumed he was dead."

"It is a kind of death," Hendrik suggests. "Very hard. It can take a long time."

"Still, we know she's alive and well, in her way," Nora says. "She looks healthy enough, and she's certainly not vain any more. Rather the opposite, by the looks of it. At least she has a home and a family of sorts, I suppose."

Sophie shivers—all the things *family* can be.

On some later day they can settle in, just like old friends, to deconstruct the evening, and Beth and her father, and families, and Max, and even this portrait of Phil—conducting what Hendrik calls, perhaps because of his profession, an *autopsy* of the night. Sophie couldn't do what Nora does, she wouldn't want to be Nora, and she sure couldn't have that painting hanging anywhere near her—ashes! Teeth! Beth isn't the only unenviable one. Sophie thinks it would be terrible, worse, to be Nora, saddled with such capacities, but there it is, and for one unlikely reason and another they seem to have turned shared flesh into something else, so Sophie's objections are really neither here nor there, are they? Hendrik puts one arm around her, one around Nora. "Would you mind if we left, too? It's getting late and Sophie's been on her feet quite a while."

It's true Sophie does look excessively flushed even against the flames of her dress and her hair. "She has a touch of high blood pressure we're keeping an eye on," he explains to Max. "But we'll be back tomorrow for a better look-round. And you know I'm interested in those portraits of Sophie, right? Should I write you a cheque now?"

"No need, but if you are sure, I will mark them as sold. It can be useful to boost people's sense of demand with a reminder of diminished supply."

"I'm pleased you'll have them," Nora says. "I like knowing they've found a good home."

Sophie has been looking forward to the hotel suite, its Jacuzzi and room service and movies in bed, but now, abruptly swamped, she longs to climb into that long, black car of theirs and drive straight home through the night. To where she and Hendrik belong, where they could get right back to the business of creating their own shifting pictures, which do not hang on walls but are real and include a whole world: the eyes and bony hands of Martha Nkume and the flat, hard knowledge of heartlessness, yes; but dreams of good hearts as well.

She could drift and dream all the way home; except Hendrik would be disappointed, he has been looking forward to this get-away, excited by his own plans, and Sophie is happy enough not to be entirely free, so of course they'll go to the hotel. "Yes," she tells Nora and Max, "I'm sorry, but I am tired. It's the crowd. I'm not used to so many people. I'll be fine once I can put my feet up."

"Will we see you again?" Hendrik asks Nora. "Will you be here when we come back tomorrow?"

"Could be. There's a newspaper interview that's being done here. I'm really glad you came tonight, though. And it was . . . interesting to see Beth, although I still don't quite understand what you meant by wanting things to come full circle, Max." As he used to know and maybe still does, circles are only tidy in theory. Outside geometry, they don't necessarily close.

"An old man's foolishness, I expect," he says. "It was only for me, to make things come to a better end than they began. I had not anticipated Beth as she is. I thought she would be remote and lovely, like porcelain, as I remembered her. But that is all right, too. I am glad you came, Sophie and Hendrik, the picture would have been incomplete and wrong without you. Thank you."

"It's been a pleasure," Hendrik says.

"We wouldn't have missed it," says Sophie. "Do you expect to see Beth again, now that she's asked you?"

"Perhaps," says Max. "I feel for her, but more for her father. I have so much more than he. So far."

"Well," says Sophie, "you don't have Beth. Hard to say if she's a blessing or not. Will you see her, Nora?"

"I'd go to keep Max company, I guess. Probably not for myself, although I do feel bad now for abandoning her, even if she abandoned us first. But really, you know," and Nora laughs, "I'm far too selfish to go around visiting random sick people. It's not really in my nature."

"Good," Hendrik speaks up unexpectedly. "Don't, either of you." Why not? Hendrik isn't usually a man who butts into other people's lives with advice.

"Anyway," Sophie says finally, "aside from Beth, are you happy with how tonight's gone, Nora?"

"Oh, *happy*—you know, that never seems real or possible to me. Kind of like Beth, actually, those speeches beauty queens like to make about wanting to make the world *happy*, as if that made any sense. But a happy person wouldn't do all this," and Nora waves her arms to indicate everything on the walls, "so I'm not unhappy about not being happy, if you see what I mean. But as I told Beth, I might be just about content at the moment. I know that sounds small, but honestly, it's really fairly immense."

She has followed all this way, this whole long distance: from Philip in flesh to Philip in bone, paint and ash. That's about as loyal as anybody can get, well beyond any *Till death do us part*. Nora expects Philip would like that; or he'd laugh.

"Then good," Sophie says. So it is.

"You be well," Nora tells her. "You take care."

"You, too. See you soon. Maybe tomorrow."

Max was wrong about Philip's voice going on and on in Nora's head, giving advice or solace, but if Nora doesn't actually hear him, she can picture him saying now, "Bye, Sophie. Good girl. Way to go." At the front door Sophie and Hendrik wave, unlike Beth, wearing the smiles of people leaving something not unpleasant but still a relief to escape. Then they're gone, back to their little two-person world, still a small astonishment to Nora, who could not begin to be someone like Sophie.

But then, she doesn't have to be someone like Sophie, does she? "If I pay you your percentage, Max, is it okay with you if I make one of those portraits of Sophie a gift to them?"

"Yes, of course. You do realize, though, that would be a substantial gift. They are not inexpensive."

"I know. That's all right." For the time being Nora is comfortably off, if not flush. Philip, of all people, turned out to have a healthy life insurance policy—who knew? Also, the house sold for a surprisingly high price that covered the cost of her much smaller new home, thanks to the tentacles of the city spreading in the direction of town—the upside of urban sprawl. And this show seems to be doing all right, and there'll be postcards and prints, Max's usual endeavours. Surely she can afford to be generous with one lavish nude. Not all three, her future's not as certain as that, and not at all as certain as Sophie's and Hendrik's, who are sitting on something better than gold, since there's no bottom to mining the dead.

She can call the portrait a baby gift. "Look," she can point out to the child later on. "Look, that's your big naked mummy up there."

That would naturally require Nora to visit Sophie and Hendrik in that godawful town, which she supposes she'll do. She could always turn the town into something else: rocky landscapes, gingerbread houses, little flames flickering orange here and there, stick figures and tiny torches.

Oh, for heaven's sake, let it go. There was a moment on her last day in the old house when she stood in the bedroom doorway looking into a room empty of furniture, of Philip, of herself, of touch and turmoil and pleasure and laughter and rage, not to mention empty of death, when she almost, almost, believed herself unable to leave it behind after all. But once out on the porch she also remembered rude words on the fence, shit on the doorstep, placards and cameras, anger and injury, and decided nostalgia must be for a time, which cannot be replaced, and not for a setting, which can be.

She drove off, unlike Lot's wife not only not looking back but untempted.

If Philip were here he might turn now to his multiple portrait, head cocked, hands on hips, and say, "You know you're the only one keen on it, don't you?" Yes, that's fairly obvious. "But you know, I like not going to waste. I like the colours and textures and odd bits and pieces. It's busier than I'd have chosen, but I like you remembering me this way. And I especially like not being sold. I'd draw the line there."

Something like that.

Max, having gone off to fix little red-dot *sold* stickers to not only the Sophie portraits but several of the other works in the two larger galleries, including the acrylic lollipop and the tobogganing kiddies, returns to say, "More people are beginning to leave, Nora. Will you come to the front door with me?" Because, of course, it's proper to shake hands and embrace and kiss cheeks and say "Glad you could come," and "Pleased you enjoyed it," and "Thank you," and "Goodnight." Nora is, naturally, glad that people have come, and pleased they've enjoyed and in some instances bought. "We have done well," Max whispers.

She should be safe financially for quite a while, then. As to other kinds of safety—well, apparently there's no counting on those. Apparently grit, the determined ability to navigate and survive any unexpected day that crops up, is a more necessary quality than she would previously have imagined. Even Beth looks as if she's learned something about that. It's a courage that's different from stubbornness, anyway. Look at Max, he is bendable—he's had to be—but more than that, he is brave.

It'll be a while before she has a new round of ideas, much less enough work in hand for a show. It's entirely possible this is her last opening party with him. "How about you, Max, have you had a good night?"

"I have indeed. Your work is very fine, and the night has gone well, and although you perhaps think it foolish, and perhaps you are right, your little group all attended." Maybe what pleases him most is still having the power to make something he wants come to pass. Nora hasn't looked at him this way before: that absent other methods, he finds his own ways to make circles and other shapes that satisfy him.

Only a dozen or so people remain. The night's catching up. "Would it be awful if I left now, too, Max?"

"Not at all. Best for you not to be last on the scene, and I can always tell people you became overwhelmed."

"Overwhelmed by what, grief?" When Max nods, she slaps his arm. "You old devil."

Although she is nearly overwhelmed, not by grief, exactly, but by a kind of awe. From here in the doorway she can look back past what remains of the crowd, through the wide-open doors of the smaller gallery, and see Philip, triple Philips, looking back. A person has one life and then, as in fire, flood or war, is thrust willing or not, ready or not, into another. Like Sophie's refugees, in hiding, on the run, searching for places to be safe, although often enough suffering and dying instead; while survivors barter and scrounge, they make things where nothing existed before.

Nora, too. She is lucky so far.

This is a different kind of luck from Philip's good and bad fortune, slipping quietly out of life in the night.

She slips quietly into the night herself, arm upraised for a taxi. Years ago she stepped out this same door on to this street, although in daylight, and in a mood for celebration. In a diner just down the block she ran into a woman she once knew in high school. Tonight she'll go home, hang this one-shouldered, slashed-to-the-navel black number back in the closet, and lie alone in her enormous Philip-built bed where, on an August night a year ago, in another place, they fell asleep together and she woke up alone.

She won't knock again in her life on a door that's opened by a grinning, lithe, naked man.

She takes the next taxi that stops, gives the driver the address she's still getting used to, and waves to Max, who waves back although he is already turning away, his attention moving on as attention does when people are alive and attending to the next thing, which is always something right up until the very moment it's not. Which makes the exhilarating, terrifying, luxurious, thrilling, glad-to-be-alive, diving-into-darkness question, as Nora leans back while the taxi makes its way through the city's wide streets of neon and light, what it always is. Again, and again, and again, it has to be, *Now what?*

JOAN BARFOOT is the award-winning author of nine previous novels, including most recently, *Critical Injuries*, which was longlisted for the 2002 Man Booker Prize. Her work has been compared internationally with that of Anne Tyler, Carol Shields, Margaret Drabble, Fay Weldon and Margaret Atwood. She lives in London, Ontario.

A Note on the Type

The Berling typeface was designed by Karl-Erik Forsberg for the Berlingska Stilgjuteriet in Lund, Sweden, in 1951. It belongs to the modern text typefaces and like most of these, markedly shows the influence of the Neorenaissance.